I Accidentally Summoned A Demon

Jaide Harley

Exquisitely Chaotic Publishing

Scripture quotations are from the Holy Bible, New International Version®, NIV® Copyright © 1973, 1978, 1984, 2011 by Biblica, Inc.™

I Accidentally Summoned A Demon

www.jaideharley.com

Edited by Voss Editing

Proofread by On The Same Page Editing

Cover Design by Jaqueline Kropmanns

ISBN 979-8-9869360-0-0 (ebook)

ISBN 979-8-9869360-1-7 (paperback)

ISBN 979-8-9869360-2-4 (hardback)

For all my patrons who inspired and supported me to follow through on my publishing dream.

Soundtrack

1. You Are So Beautiful— Tommee Profitt, brooke

2. I Feel Like I'm Drowning— Two Feet

3. Even If It Hurts— Sam Tinnesz

4. Can't Help Falling In Love- Dark— Tommee Profitt, brooke

5. Wicked Game— Ursine Vulpine, Annaca

6. Man or a Monster— Sam Tinnesz, Zayde Wolf

7. Creep— Scott Bradlee's Postmodern Jukebox, Haley Reinhart

8. Devil's Backbone— The Civil Wars

9. Work Song— Hozier

10. Carry You— Ruelle, Fleurie

11. Heaven— Julia Michaels

12. I Walk The Line— Halsey

If you prefer to go in blind, carry on and don't read below. If you are in need of content warnings, find them below and in more detail here: https://www.jaideharley.com/content-warning-for-iasad/

DISCLAIMER:

This book contains a school shooting that may be triggering. There is discussion of characters' opinions and references to the Bible, religion, angels, demons, heaven, and hell. The content of the book is not a reflection of my personal beliefs, or intended to be taken seriously as an interpretation or statement of the Bible's depiction of any of these themes; rather, this is a work of fiction with no ill intent meant toward any religious organization, implied or mentioned.

Contents

Chapter 1

Unexpected Guest

K atherine clutched the script to her chest, covering it with her cream-colored cardigan as she rushed through the rain. Racing down the uneven sidewalk, she avoided puddles and sprays from cars driving through overflowing gutters. The sun hovered above the horizon, but stormy clouds gave the illusion of night.

By the time she got home, rain soaked her cardigan, wetting several script pages. She grimaced and set the papers on the kitchen table before removing the cardigan and hanging it on the back of a chair. She kicked out of her boots and peeled off her socks, dropping them with a *slop*.

Auburn hair stuck to her freckled skin as she pulled the strands out of her face. After grabbing the wet papers, she spread them on the wooden floor. A circle made the most sense; she could sit in the middle and read while the pages dried, never having to get up. Pages laid out, she went to her bedroom.

Water made everything stick. It complicated getting undressed, especially when wearing leggings. Clothes off, Katherine was tempted to leave them in a pile on the bathroom floor. She scrunched up her face, knowing she'd be mad at herself later if she left them.

She hung the wet clothes and got in the shower, shivering. Though the hot water took away the edge, echoes of the chill remained. Closing her eyes, she tried to rid herself of the annoyances from the day. Running home in the rain was the least bothersome thing that happened.

Acting was something she'd always wanted to do, but she was shy. She longed for the confidence to go on stage and had worked up the nerve to audition for something last semester. She only had a small part in the play, but it was enough to encourage her to try for something bigger. Auditions were the next day, and while others got together for practice, her awkwardness left her out of the group running lines and going for pizza. In fact, Ashley made a point to say Katherine wasn't invited.

As if that wasn't bad enough, her year-and-a-half crush on Jason Macker was going strong, and now Ashley had her eye on him. Katherine felt invisible most of the time, more so when Ashley entered the room.

There was also the minor fact Ashley was going for the same part as Katherine.

Katherine let the heat from the shower calm her nerves, desperate to do well tomorrow. She'd worked hard and wouldn't give up because of a bad day. A portion of the play included songs, and while she loved to sing, doing so alone was intimidating. That meant the rest of her audition had to shine enough it didn't matter.

Once showered, she applied vanilla and pear leave-in conditioner to tame her curls before putting on dry leggings, an oversized cable-knit sweater, and wool socks. The chill lingered, so she stayed bundled and decided to make a hot drink.

The old floor creaked as she passed the circle of papers to the kitchen. Aside from the bedrooms and bathrooms, the house had an open floor plan. She started the tea kettle and grabbed her favorite oversized mug with the Oscar Wilde quote, "With freedom, books, flowers and the moon, who could not be happy?"

She opened the cupboard, fully aware she should have herbal tea to help her relax and sleep before auditions, but there was also hot chocolate. Sugar would probably keep her awake.

But, chocolate . . .

Self-control could wait a day. She snatched a pack of hot chocolate, made the drink, piled on tiny marshmallows, and sat in the middle of her script circle. Leaning forward, she skimmed the first page and sipped her cocoa. Halfway down the page, thunder cracked so loud the house shook.

Then the power went out.

It seemed perfectly quiet before, but as everything shut off in waves, the background hum she'd filtered out was gone. Now it was truly quiet. Almost unsettlingly so. Was the universe telling her to give up on this ridiculous idea of becoming a stage actress?

After a few moments of dwelling on the existential crisis, she maneuvered toward a kitchen drawer where she kept matches and flashlights, stubbing her toe on the way. Whimpering, she hopped on one foot, almost falling before sucking it up and lowering her foot.

She bit her lip and ignored the pain as she hobbled to the drawer, fumbling around until she found the flashlight. Turning it on, she found the matches and the bag she brought home from choir. The bag contained white, scentless candles used during a Harvest Festival celebration at church. No one else wanted them. If for nothing else, she could use them for crafts.

She lined the candles around the outside of the script circle, but that didn't illuminate it enough, so she added ones along the inside as well. Once they were lit, she could read the script again. She sat in the circle, but her tummy rumbled.

"I just sat down," she muttered. Frowning, she rubbed her stomach, glanced to the kitchen, and did a mental recap of the contents.

Today was Friday, payday, but she was busy and didn't get groceries before the rain. Leaving when she was all warm and bundled sounded terrible. Saturdays were always hectic at the stores, but she'd have to brave one. She checked the date on her phone—the thirteenth. Tomorrow was the day she'd prepared for over the last several weeks.

"You'd think my stomach would be too full of nerves to be hungry." Kat stepped over her circle and shuffled to the kitchen cupboards. Tea and baking ingredients—nothing easy to fix.

Except a microwavable brownie. The power was out, but the brownie only called for hot water, and the kettle was still hot. She snatched it, along with a spoon, and poured the powder into a mug. Returning to her circle, she waited for the brownie to thicken while she read the script.

If she got the part, she couldn't tell anyone from church. The play was a dark comedy about a woman who discovers her husband cheating, so she summons a demon to kill him. She summons the wrong kind, and hilarity ensues. Kat was going after the part of the betrayed wife, Constance, who follows the demon around and tries to discover how to send it back to hell.

Kat skimmed lines that weren't hers and enunciated her own aloud. As she read the scene where the demon is summoned, the room grew brighter. Outside, the full moon shone through a break in the clouds, into her living room window, right on her. She smiled and took a bite of brownie, taking it as a sign to keep practicing. The pages were almost dry but brittle. She read the Latin words used to summon Constance's demon in her head before speaking them. Pronunciation was her focus. Ashley's pronunciation was off, so Kat hoped getting it right would impress the director.

"*Fasciculus hic*—ow!"

Running her finger down the edge of the paper caused a paper cut. Blood pooled and dripped onto one of the candles while she examined the wound. Kat stuck her finger in her mouth and waited until the bleeding slowed before she tried again.

"*Fasciculus hic nugarum vage et male translatus est, sed scire non debes.*" She was supposed to yell it. She considered moving on, but it was important to get it right, so she said it again louder. Thunder crackled toward the end of the phrase, and she shuddered. She shook her head at allowing the sound to scare her. *It's only thunder.* She repeated the phrase a third time. "*Fasciculus hic nugarum vage et male translatus est, sed scire non debes!*"

The thunder boomed. The reverberation wobbled her shelves, causing books and pictures to fall off. A gust sent papers flying, blowing out the candles. Moon now covered with clouds, she was left in darkness.

Kat shivered, glancing around. "That was weird." She looked for the open window that sent everything flying. The chill she'd almost gotten rid of returned with a vengeance when she saw a figure by the window. Inside her house.

She clambered away and knocked into the blown-out candles, spilling wax on the floor. "Who are you?" She fumbled for the flashlight.

The figure moved from the window with abrupt, inhuman movements. *The dark's playing tricks on me.* She looked around, but it wasn't light enough to see much. Creaking from the left made her attention snap that way.

"Stay away!" She found the flashlight and shone it toward the person. They moved, leaving a trail of dark mist. "Who are you?" She backed away, searching for the stranger.

"I am that which you called for. The spirit you summoned with your blood." He appeared in several places at once, leaving Kat jolting the flashlight. "Death-bringer, shadow of violence, blood fiend, slayer, and torturer of souls. The name you call me does not matter. The only question I have for you is . . . " He paused in front of her, finally in the light.

He had pale skin, teeth that were a little too sharp, eyes red as blood, hair so black it blended into the shadows. His clothes were from another time—a doublet colored black and red. Kat froze as he leaned in close.

"Who is it you want killed?"

She stared, wide-eyed. He waited for an answer. Reaching behind her, Kat grabbed the first thing she found.

Then she hit him on the head with a polka-dot umbrella.

Chapter 2

An Accident

K at slammed the umbrella on the intruder's head, but all it did was shock him. He didn't move, just narrowed his unnatural eyes at her.

"Get out!" She shoved him back and smacked him with the umbrella again. "Out! This is a seriously messed-up Friday the thirteenth prank! What's wrong with you? Who is your mother?" Her frantic tone increased in pitch with every blow she landed. "You have five seconds to get out of my house before I call the police!"

The stranger moved back more out of confusion than anything. He regarded her with a raised eyebrow. Tiring of the hits, he snatched the umbrella. The candles relit, and Kat gasped. He was more terrifying in the light. She hesitated, then lunged for the umbrella. The intruder scowled, and the umbrella crumbled to ashes in his hands.

"What are you doing?" he asked, catching her hand when she swung to hit him.

"What are *you* doing? How did you break my umbrella? Get out of my house!"

She tried to hit him with her other hand, but he caught that as well, pinning both behind her back. The action pressed their bodies together.

"That's enough." He glared, stilling her. "I'm here because you summoned me, human. Now, tell me who you want killed so I can leave this pathetic realm."

"Killed? I don't want anyone killed. This prank has gone too far. Get out!"

He was about to growl, but her knee smashed between his legs, leaving him wheezing and cupping himself. Kat slapped him across the face, ran to her room, and locked the door. She dialed 911 and leaned against the door, listening for movement.

"Nine one one, what's your emergency?"

"Someone broke into my house," Kat answered with a quivering voice. "A man. A man broke into my house, and he won't leave, and he's talking about killing people."

It was quiet on the other side of the door. The house was old and creaky; if he headed her way, she'd hear it. She gave the authorities her address and was about to answer another question, but the stranger appeared in front of her, eyes glowing red.

He snatched the phone and crushed it in his hand. Spinning her around, he pinned her wrists behind her back. "That wasn't nice." He pressed her into the door with his body. "What's your problem, human? You're the one who summoned me. You think I wanted to be torn away from my hounds for this shit? Stop playing games, and tell me who you want dead."

Kat squirmed under his hold. "How—how did you get in here?"

"I'm a demon. A locked door doesn't mean shit to me. What the fuck is your deal? I haven't been summoned in decades, and this is the shit I get," he muttered.

"Please, leave me alone." Tears filled her eyes while she struggled to break free. "I don't know who you are, but please don't hurt me. Take whatever you want, but let me go."

Balls still aching, he was ready for her next attack. When she braced on the door, he let her push back. Instead of slamming into him, he moved, and she flailed back towards the floor. She expected pain, but he caught her before she hit the ground, then pushed her against it, straddling her and constricting her hands above her head.

"I'm not here to hurt you." His brows furrowed. "*You* called *me*. Not the other way around. Why are you crying?"

"Because you're scaring me. Let me go!"

"So you can smack me with whatever other stupid human contraption you have and knee me in the balls? I don't think so. Tell me who you want dead, and we'll never have to see each other again."

"I don't want anyone dead. Are you crazy? Get off me!"

The demon huffed. "Why the fuck did you summon me if you don't want anyone dead?"

"I didn't summon anything."

Each wiggle tightened his hold until she couldn't move. Sirens bellowed and grew closer.

"You're in for it now." She lifted her chin. "I'm definitely pressing charges, you psychopath."

"You called the authorities on me, and you think they're going to do something?" he asked, amused. "They won't be able to see me."

"You're a person." Kat grunted as she tried to get leverage to push him off. "Of course they'll be able to see you."

"I'm not human." He seethed. "I'm a demon *you* summoned. My only way back is to accomplish what I've been summoned for, so for the love of all that's unholy, give me a fucking name."

"You're not a demon. You're insane. I don't want anyone dead. Let me go!"

A knock echoed from the front door, and Kat screamed to get the police inside. Moving off her, the demon covered his ears and cursed.

"Foolish human," he spat. "Go ahead. Answer the door, and show me to them." He opened her bedroom door and waved her ahead.

She hesitated, worried it was a trap. He waved her through again, and she darted past him. Two officers entered, and she turned to the stranger triumphantly, but her victory diminished when the officers ran past him. He crossed his arms and raised an eyebrow, smirking.

"He's . . ." She frowned.

"He must've left," the younger officer said as he stood beside the demon. "Where did you last see him?"

The demon tilted his head to the side. "Where indeed?"

"He's right . . ." She pointed next to the officer.

The officer followed her finger, looking right where the demon was, then past him. "The bedroom?" The officer headed that way and walked *through* the demon.

Kat opened her mouth. No words came out, just a squeak. The demon stalked toward her, and she backed into the wall, making the older officer peer over.

"I told you," the demon said, leaning against the wall. "They can't see me unless I let them. I'd make up something about me disappearing in the backyard unless you want them to believe you're insane." He nodded to the officers who whispered amongst each other and cast doubtful glances her way.

Kat shook her head and closed her eyes, forcing herself to breathe. When she opened her eyes, the demon was still there, staring.

"Well?" He gestured to the officers. "Isn't it against some law for you to make a fake emergency call? Don't make me break you out of jail. You've pissed me off enough for one night."

More than once, the officers glanced over and didn't see the stranger. What happened when he appeared? The candles, the words . . .

Her eyes widened, and she sank to the floor, unable to catch her breath.

"Human." The demon crouched next to her. "What's wrong now? Send them away so we can move on."

"You . . . it . . . not . . . possible." She spoke too quietly for the officers to hear.

The older officer approached. "Are you all right, miss?"

"For fuck's sake," the demon muttered. "Get ahold of yourself. Breathe. Everything's, uh," he patted her back, "fine."

"Maybe we should call someone," the officer said.

Call someone? They probably thought Kat was insane. She evened out her breathing and shook her head. "No. I'm just scared. The last I saw him was by the back door. I kicked him and ran into my bedroom."

"The sirens might've scared him off." The older one rubbed his chin. "Was it someone you knew?"

Kat stood on wobbly knees. "No."

"Did he hurt you?"

She clutched her chest. "No, he s-scared me."

"It's Friday the thirteenth," the other officer pointed out. "All the crazies are out. Why don't we secure the house and leave an officer outside tonight?"

Kat sat at the kitchen table while the cops searched the rest of the house. The demon sat beside her with his feet propped on the table. Normally she'd yell at him, but she didn't want to seem crazy. Part of her wondered if she *was* crazy.

The power came back on while they searched, revealing a mess. The cocoa had spilled, the candles were knocked over, and hot wax had hardened on her floor.

Once the officers left, the demon dropped his feet and sat up straighter, smoothing out his doublet.

"Now that the unnecessary drama is out of the way," he glared at her, "give me a name."

Kat narrowed her eyes. "I don't want anyone dead."

"Then why the fuck did you summon me?"

"It was an accident. I was preparing for a play." She got up and gathered the papers scattered across the kitchen. She found the one with the words and held it up. "See? I wasn't trying to summon you. I was rehearsing."

The demon snatched the paper, scanning the script. Reaching the end, he scoffed, crumpled the paper into a ball, and threw it. "This is ridiculous. The words aren't enough. You need fire, blood, and the light of a full moon." He held up three fingers. "How into the scene did you get? You also have to repeat the phrase three times, and I only saw it once."

"I . . ." Kat paused, remembering the incident. "The power was out. I had candles, and then the moonlight came in," *fire and the light of a full moon,* "and I gave myself a paper cut," *blood,* "and I said it three times to get the pronunciation right."

"This is a cruel joke." The demon sneered. "There's no fucking way you *accidentally* performed a ritual and summoned me! Do you have any idea who I am?"

Kat bit her lip. "I don't."

Black surrounded his eyes and spread like veins. He growled, wings and horns appearing before he vanished in a cloud of smoke.

Chapter 3

Kitten

After staring too long at the spot the demon vanished from, Kat cleaned up the mess. The wax scraped off the floor all right but left a stain.

Eventually, she made it to bed. Still on edge, every little sound set her off. Not until sunlight peeked through her curtains did she fall asleep. At that point, she only had two hours to rest before the alarm went off for auditions.

She'd showered the night before, but her body was so tense she took another. She tied her curls in a messy bun and rubbed her eyes. In the shower, she let the heat hit her shoulders, hoping to ease some of the tension.

Once finished, she wrapped herself in a towel and wiped steam off the mirror. Staring at her makeup bag, she pondered how easily she'd be able to cover her tired eyes. Lifting her gaze to the mirror, she spotted the demon reflected behind her.

She screamed and spun around, clutching the towel. "What are you doing?"

The demon's gaze raked up and down her body, then returned to her eyes. He was calmer than last night. "I want to go home. And you're my ticket there. We need to work with each other."

"Are you insane? I'm practically naked. Get out of my bathroom!"

"I noticed." He raised an eyebrow. "If you didn't wear clothes like last night, you might not live alone." His gaze darted up and down her body again. "Actually seems not bad under there."

"Oh my God!" She pushed him to the door. "Get out!"

"Fine, but I expect cooperation when you're dressed. And please don't refer to that tyrant in my presence," he added bitterly, letting her shove him out.

Kat slammed the door and rested her forehead against it. Insane. All of it was insane, and she didn't know what to do, but she didn't want to miss the audition. She'd worked too hard and wasn't going to let some paranormal being get in her way.

Oh, God, I am going crazy.

There was no time for craziness. She dressed and left her hair down but used detangler to get it more presentable.

When she came out, the demon was lounging on her bed, holding a picture frame she kept on the nightstand. She pointedly ignored him, going into her closet for boots and a jacket.

"Right." He sat up. "A name. Go ahead."

"I'm not giving you a name to kill someone."

"Don't be ridiculous. Of course you are." The demon tossed the picture onto the bed. "Everyone hates someone. Pick anyone. It could be some terrible leader in this country or another. A neighbor you hate. Some pervert you heard about on the news. Pick someone, so I can go home."

"I won't be an accomplice to murder." Kat slipped her boots on. "I don't have time for this. I have an audition I've been preparing for, and I'm not going to let you ruin it."

"The audition for that stupid play that gave you the words to summon a demon?" He scoffed. "Aren't you worried you'll summon another?"

"Now I know what to avoid, it shouldn't be a problem." Kat stood and pulled her jacket on. "I have to go. Leave me alone. This is important to me."

Kat walked out of her room, but the demon appeared in front of her, stopping her advance.

"It's all good and fine that this stupid play is important to you, but you know what's important to me? *Getting home.*" He threw his arms up. "My hounds are probably wandering the underworld thinking I've abandoned them!"

Kat tilted her head to the side. "You have dogs?"

"Yes, human. I have dogs. Dogs I feed and take care of that are now wandering aimlessly about. Do you have any idea how dangerous it is in the underworld? Give me a name so I can go home."

"I'm sorry about your dogs, but I can't do this with you. I need to focus. Sit tight until we figure something out, and stop calling me human. It sounds like an insult the way you say it." She brushed past him and went out the front door, only making it a few blocks before he appeared beside her, hands stuffed in his pockets.

"We got off on the wrong foot." He gave her a side glance. "My name's Nex. What's yours?"

"Your name is Next?"

"*Nex.* What's yours?"

She wrapped her arms around herself. "Katherine."

"Katherine." Nex laughed and threw his head back.

"Why are you laughing at my name?" She turned a corner, and the bus stop came into view.

"Because that higher power you were calling to must have done this to fuck with me, that's why. Now, what about this audition? Is there competition?"

"What do you mean by that? About my name?" Kat stepped onto the bus.

"Katherine. It means pure. About as far from anything that I am. You do seem rather pure." He wrinkled his nose. "You reek of virginity."

Kat's pale skin reddened. She turned away and wrung her hands together.

"What's wrong? Did I offend you by stating the truth? How old are you? Don't most humans lose their virginity while in forced schooling?"

"Shut up."

Several people frowned. *Right, no one can see him.* She pressed her fingers to her temples, holding onto a bar as the bus moved.

"If you're embarrassed, why not do something about it? Honestly, virginity only means something to those who want to sacrifice you for rituals or people who get weird pleasure out of having a woman for the first time. It's safer for you to get it over with."

Kat wanted to reply but bit her tongue. People would think she was insane.

Nex grabbed her and turned her toward him, reaching into her pocket. He pulled out her headphones and placed an earbud in her ear.

"There. They'll think you're on the phone." He crossed his arms, never losing balance as the bus stopped abruptly and shifted everyone else.

"I don't want to talk to you." Kat gripped the bar tighter. "You're rude and creepy and," she glanced around and lowered her voice, "invisible! Leave me alone, and let me focus."

She faced away, and he groaned but otherwise remained silent. At the next stop, Nex followed her off and into the theater where auditions were being held. Kat checked in and waited in the back for her turn. Nex had disappeared while she checked in and hadn't shown up again. She hoped he'd stay away until the audition was over.

"Hey, Kat." Jason leaned against the wall next to her with a grin.

"Hi—hi." She tucked her hair behind her ears.

He inclined his head to the stage. "You nervous?"

"A little."

"You shouldn't be," he said, nudging her shoulder with his. "You're going to do awesome." He winked and headed toward the stage when his name was called. "You look cute today, by the way."

Flushing, Kat gave a nervous giggle. Jason offered her one last smile and went out onto the stage.

"Kat?" Nex appeared beside her and made her jump.

She smacked his arm. "Don't do that."

"You said your name is Katherine."

"Kat's a nickname."

"Is it? No, it doesn't suit you. Cats are vicious and attack with claws. Kitten is more suitable. A kitten bats at you and tries to get somewhere, but in the end is easy to pick up and push around—all talk and no real action. Kitten is much more you."

"Ugh. Do *not* call me that. That's such a gross nickname." Kat shuddered. "And I'm not weak. If you were a person with normal strength, I would've fended you off."

"Sure you would've. Sorry, kitten. I'm afraid it suits you too well not to use," he said, smirking. "If you give me a name, I'll help you seduce Mr. . . . ." He glanced at Jason and made a face. "Preppy, clean-cut, blondie, douchey. That's your type?" Grimacing, he clicked his tongue in disapproval. "How dreadfully boring."

Kat opened her mouth to speak but stopped when Ashley approached. She was in a tight dress that plunged low, emphasizing her cleavage. Kat pursed her lips and braced herself for the taunting.

"Aw, Katherine, look at you like a little schoolgirl excited to be noticed by her crush. And trying so hard to audition for a role we both know you won't get." Ashley tossed back her blonde hair. "It's adorable you think you can play with the big kids."

"Who's this bitch?" Nex glared at Ashley.

Kat ignored him and stared blankly at Ashley. "If you're so confident, why do you need to try to frazzle me?"

"I don't need to." Ashley laughed. "It's fun to get in your head. You make it easy. Who dressed you this morning? Nuns? How do you pull off looking innocent when you pine after Jason every day and probably think about him when you're alone, touching yourself? Because God knows nobody else wants to touch you."

"This is the one." Nex growled, balling his fists. "Give me the go-ahead, and I'll kill her where she stands."

"Go away, Ashley," Kat said. "Practice your lines."

"Already did." Ashley picked at her fingernails. "I practiced with Jason last night. Well, *practiced* is a loose term. Though, it did start some fun roleplaying." She winked and walked away with more swing in her hips than necessary. "Good luck, sweetie. You'll need it."

An annoyed sigh escaped Kat. She tugged at her clothes and chewed her lip while Ashley went through her audition.

"Seriously. Give me the order, and she's dead," Nex repeated.

"No."

"Why? She's a cunt. She's rude to you. Let me kill her."

"No."

"Please?"

"No!"

Nex scowled. "For fuck's sake."

"Katherine Milton?" the director called. "You're up."

Chapter 4

Loopholes

K at rushed down the street, arms wrapped around herself. *Don't cry.*

Nex was right behind her, and she wanted nothing more than to punch him. She didn't get the part. The last thing she needed was him pestering her.

"Kitten." Nex walked alongside her and caught her arm to make her stop. "That audition was bullshit. Let me kill Ashley." He gestured back in the general direction of the theater. "She's a cock-sucking bitch. No one will miss her. Except the director and whoever else's cock she sucks to get what she wants."

"Ew! Oh my God!" Kat covered her ears. "What's wrong with you?" Yanking out of his grip, she continued down the street.

"You know that's all it is, don't you?" Nex caught up. "She practically flashed her tits at him, and I could smell him on her. She didn't fuck that preppy boy you have eyes for. She fucked the director."

"Do you have to talk like that?" Kat wrinkled her nose. "Geeze."

"Don't tell me you're offended by the word *tits*. You have some." He gestured to her breasts. "How can that be offensive?"

"Seriously." Kat stopped and poked his chest. "Shut up. I can't take it. You're so annoying and abrasive. Go away, and let me have a few minutes to be sad. Is that too much to ask?"

"You want to be left alone. I want to go home. The simple solution is to let me kill Ashley."

"I hate you." Kat stormed away.

"I don't care that you hate me, kitten. I care that you give me a fucking name."

Kat ignored him and entered a grocery store, surprised he didn't speak again. As she glanced around, she found he wasn't following her anymore. Sighing, she grabbed a basket. In moments like these, she wished she could buy alcohol. *Two more years.*

Instead, she stared at the wine her mom used to get, moved on, and grabbed a frozen pizza. Normally she wouldn't buy it, but she was too sad not to have carbs. Overcome with guilt, she chose one with cauliflower crust.

The truth was, even if Ashley slept with the director to get the part, Kat had messed up. She froze and stuttered. Every practice she'd done went smoothly, but Ashley's taunting smile distracted her.

After shopping, Kat made it to her porch without seeing Nex. Her suspicion grew. She opened the door and peered inside. Silence. Moving through the house, she found it empty.

Grocery bags set down, she ran into her bedroom to find pajamas and change before he appeared again. She slipped on leggings and another sweater. Once she was done, her shoulders relaxed. Still no Nex.

Returning to the kitchen, Kat turned on the oven and put the groceries away. She slid the pizza into the oven and reached for her mug, but a hand locked around her wrist.

"Based on how uptight you are with everything else, I doubt you'll want to use a mug to drink wine." Nex pressed against her back, his arm over hers, hand clamped on her wrist. She stopped breathing and focused on restarting her heart.

"Can't you leave me alone for one night?" She scowled. "And I don't have any wine."

"I know." He squeezed her wrist until she let the mug go. "Your longing stare at the wine showed me what kind you wanted." He brought his other arm around her side, holding a bottle of wine in front of her and trapping her between his arms. "What's wrong? Are you so young you can't buy alcohol and too good a girl to find a way around the law to buy it anyway?"

"You weren't in the store." She turned to push him.

He didn't budge. "I was in the store. I was giving you your moment of peace."

"Which ended too soon." Kat huffed, shoving against him. "Back off, Nex."

"Why? Do I make you nervous, kitten?"

Kat swallowed hard and noticed his eyes weren't bloodred anymore. They were more amber. Not only that, jeans and a T-shirt replaced his fancy clothes.

"Um, what happened to you?"

"I took a physical form. This is taking longer than I hoped." Nex reached past her for a wine glass. His arms came around her to pour the bottle.

Kat tried to push him back again. "You don't need to be this close to me."

"No." He glowered and held up the glass of wine. "However, it annoys you, and I think I've earned a bit of annoying you since you refuse to send me home. Even though it's *your* fault I'm here."

"Can't you find another way home?" She snatched the glass and moved to the couch. Plopping down, she tucked her feet in and draped a blanket from the back of the couch over herself.

"I tried." Nex crossed his arms. "All the sources I have say it has to be you since I'm bonded with your blood."

"What do you need me for? Go kill some rando, and leave me out of it," she grumbled, sipping her wine.

"I *can't,* kitten. It won't count unless you order it."

"Stop calling me kitten."

"Start cooperating so I can go home."

"So, I control you?"

His jaw clenched. "I wouldn't put it that way."

Kat stifled a laugh. "I do, don't I? You can't hurt anyone unless I tell you to."

Nex clenched and unclenched his fists, nostrils flaring. "It isn't funny, Katherine. I'd proceed with caution if I were you."

"Why? You can't hurt me." Kat shrugged, taking another sip of wine. "That would mess you up."

Nex moved so fast Kat couldn't comprehend how the glass of wine was no longer in her hand or the blanket over her. Those were less concerning than the fact she was lying on the couch, and Nex was on top of her.

"Don't piss me off, kitten. There are other ways to hurt you, and I'm very creative." With darkened eyes, Nex slid his hands down and gripped her hips.

"You wouldn't." Kat breathed, her voice shaky as he settled between her legs. "You can't. That has to count as hurting me."

"Not if you want it." Nex's upturned lips hinted at a dark seduction Kat couldn't believe she was intrigued by. "And believe me, kitten, I know *all* the ways to seduce someone. Even someone as uptight as you. Even a virgin. You think I haven't noticed how you respond to me? I could have you begging for it in a few minutes, and I wonder how you'd feel after giving your virginity to a demon." He skimmed his nose along her neck. "So watch it."

As fast as he was on her, he was off, standing next to the TV with his lip curled back.

"You're a jerk." Kat sat up and grabbed the blanket with unsteady hands.

"Call me what you want. I just want to go home." He tapped his fingers against his bicep. "I'll make it easy. We'll find out where they do capital punishment, and you can pick someone who's going to die anyway. Easy. No blood on your hands."

"But it would be blood on my hands," Kat argued. "Me telling you to kill anyone would put blood on my hands."

"They're going to die anyway!"

"I don't believe in capital punishment." Kat reached for the remote.

"You don't . . ." Nex growled and paced. "Of all the fucking humans, I get this little *angel*," he spat. "Most of the population of this despicable realm would have more than one name to give, and you can't come up with *one*?"

Kat turned on the TV. "I don't like using violence to solve things."

"Get used to it." Nex balled his fists. "Using violence as power is part of this world. Plenty of people use violence as power."

"And I'd be as bad as the rest of them if I did this. Change has to happen with yourself first, then the world."

"You're fucking unbelievable." He stomped back and forth. "Humans are violent by nature! Where's your violence?"

"I don't have any." Kat shrugged. "Look, I work at a bookstore, and we have a lot of older books. Tomorrow afternoon on my shift, I'll find some books and see if I can find a way to undo this and get you home to your puppies."

"They're not puppie—" Nex gritted his teeth. "I've already looked for ways. This is the only way. You have to let me kill someone."

"No. I refuse to go to that extreme. There's always a loophole. We just have to find it."

Nex's eyes bugged as he stood there, fuming. He unplugged the TV before storming out the door.

Kat flinched when the door slammed shut. He scared her, but knowing he couldn't hurt her or anyone else put her mind at ease enough she relaxed with her wine.

Chapter 5

Church

K at's alarm blared, and she groaned in protest, burying her face in a pillow. She reached blindly to shut it off, but a crash made her head snap up.

Her alarm was crushed, and a hand slowly moved away from it. Not her hand. With wide eyes, she squeaked, jumped back, and fell out of bed. She landed on her butt, dragging the blankets with her.

Nex grumbled and extended his hand to find a blanket, but they were all on the floor with Kat. He glared over the edge of the bed. "What the hell, kitten? Don't be a blanket hog."

Kat leapt up, clutching the blankets. She'd changed into a tank top and shorts before bed because wine made her too hot to sleep in layers. Not only that, but Nex was also barely dressed, only wearing boxers. He was sculpted, his body all hard lines and ridges that led her eyes lower. Now was not the time to notice.

She blinked, then scowled. "What are you doing in my bed?"

"Until you send me home, this is *our* bed." Nex propped himself up on his elbow. "I don't have anywhere else to go. So, you better come up with a name, or you'll be sleeping with me every night. I'll warn you right now, I sometimes get affectionate in my sleep." A mischievous smile spread over his face. "Drop the blankets, kitten. It's not as if you're naked, and I already saw you when I snuck in."

"You're horrible!" Kat kept the blankets around her as she stomped to her closet.

"Not sure why that's a surprise. I am a demon. Why are you up so early anyway?" Nex tucked his hands behind his head and lounged back on the bed. "Don't humans sleep in on weekends?"

"None of your business." Kat grabbed a dress from the closet before going to her dresser and carefully pulling out underwear so he wouldn't see.

"Don't bother hiding the underwear. I already went through it, and there's nothing impressive in there. You should consider getting some lingerie. You have a nice body."

"You're disgusting." Kat whirled around to glare at him. "Don't go through my things!"

"I had to." Nex shrugged and sat up. "I had to find space to move in my clothes since I don't know how long I'll be stuck here, thanks to you."

He was trying to get a rise out of her, frustrate her enough to give in. Refusing to give him the benefit, she went into the bathroom without another word.

As she undressed, she considered he might come in while she showered to fluster her. She bit her lip, skipped the shower, and got ready quickly. There was nothing to do about the mess that was her hair, so she put it in a bun.

When she came out, he was going through her closet. She glowered and tried not to touch him as she found flats to wear with her dress.

"This wardrobe looks like it belongs to a forty-year-old woman with too many cats whose husband is a minister. If she even has a husband because she dresses like *this*." Nex's nose crinkled. "How do you plan to get Blondie's attention wearing clothes like these?"

Ignoring him, Kat slipped her shoes on and snatched a jacket. She went to the kitchen, started the kettle, and opened the fridge for yogurt but frowned at the contents. There was a case of beer, a bottle of whiskey, a bottle of vodka, and sodas. She opened the freezer, finding stacks of frozen pizzas, egg rolls, taquitos, and other junk food. On the counter were boxes of Pop-Tarts, bags of candy, and chips.

Kat slammed the freezer shut and spoke through gritted teeth. "Nex."

Somehow, he was on the other side of the fridge. "You called, roomie?" Nex smirked, leaning against the fridge.

"What's all this?" She gestured to the counter.

"Food. You hardly had any." Nex plucked a Pop-Tart from the box. "Everything you have is so . . . healthy. Don't you enjoy life?"

"I enjoy life." Kat opened the fridge again and moved his garbage aside to get to her yogurt. "There's nothing wrong with being healthy."

"There is if you never have fun." Nex took a bite of the Pop-Tart, then offered it to her. "Come on. It tastes much better than the living bacteria you're about to consume."

"Go away." Kat picked up a spoon and opened her yogurt, turning away from him to eat.

He materialized in front of her and stole the spoon as she brought it to her lips, placing it in his mouth and dragging it down with a frown. He grunted. "Eh, not as good as a Pop-Tart."

Kat snatched the spoon and rinsed it.

Nex rolled his eyes. "What's wrong? Afraid I have cooties?"

"Stop talking."

Kettle whistling, she left the spoon in her mouth while she dropped a tea bag in the mug. Steam rose as she poured in hot water, carrying a jasmine aroma with it.

"Wouldn't a microwave be faster?"

"Stop analyzing my habits," Kat snapped, eating her yogurt angrily.

Nex whistled, crossing his arms over his exposed chest. "Someone's grumpy. What's wrong, kitten? Wasn't it nice to not wake up alone? Or is the reason you're upset because I didn't do anything to ease your tension? If that's the case, head back to bed, open those pretty legs, and I'll eat you for breakfast."

The comment froze her. A heated sensation zapped through her, and she took a deep breath, not indulging him with another word. Disregarding his nonstop comments, she finished her yogurt and sipped her tea. Once she was done, she washed her dishes and went out the door.

Outside in the crisp, cold air, Nex came alongside her, dressed like a normal person again. "Where are we going? I suggest somewhere downtown where drug addicts run rampant. How about a dealer who sells to children? Surely you can't find something wrong with killing someone like that."

Kat continued on while Nex listed potential people to kill. She turned down another street, and Nex grabbed her elbow, making her face him as he glared down at her.

"This is fucking ridiculous. Don't make me take this too far," he said, running his finger down her cheek. "Because I don't want to, but I will." He pulled her against him, making her gasp. "If you force me to, I'll take it too far to get my freedom back."

She stiffened in his arms at the sensation of his hand sliding up her dress, along her thigh. His nose skimmed her neck, and it left tingles behind. Hand ascending higher, he nearly grazed her butt.

"A name, kitten," he murmured. "Or you'll beg me to fuck you, and when I'm gone, you'll hate yourself for letting me take you after saving yourself so long."

"You're unbelievable." Kat found her resolve and pulled away. "What's wrong with you? How could you threaten me with something like that? You're disgusting." She wrapped her arms around herself and continued toward her destination.

Nex muttered several curses before following. "I'm sorry, kitten. Can't you understand I'm desperate to get home? Can't you—" He stumbled back.

Kat glanced over her shoulder with furrowed brows.

Nex frowned, then gazed up. "You've got to be fucking kidding me." He glared at the steeple and stained-glass windows. "You're going to *church*?"

"So?"

"Are you doing this to spite me, or is this legitimately who you are?"

"You're really self-centered, you know that? Of course I'm not doing it to spite you. I come every week."

"But church is so . . ." He scrunched his nose. "You can't believe the shit they teach. You're annoying, but you're not stupid."

"I summoned a demon, Nex." Kat arched a brow. "I need to go now more than ever."

"I'm not going to hurt you! We've already established I'm incapable. Come on." He inclined his head to the street. "Let's work something out."

"You threatened me for the second time."

"It wasn't a legitimate threat, for fuck's sake." Nex ran his hand through his hair. "We're bonded. My powers won't work on you. I can't force you to do anything."

"Still wrong of you to say." Kat held her ground. "You're trying to hurt me with words since you can't with actions. You think that's better?"

Expression strained, Nex paced. "Come on, kitten. Let's talk this out. Let's get something to eat."

"If you're going to be nice, we can talk after church while I'm at work." Kat headed to the stone walkway leading toward the church. Silence made her look back, but he was in the same place.

Nex held his arms out in surrender. "Katherine, come on, please?"

He seemed surprisingly vulnerable, pacing across the gate. She tilted her head to the side and looked up at the church, then back at him. He stood just outside the church's property line.

She stifled a laugh, covering her mouth. "Oh my God. You can't come in, can you?"

Nex balled his fists. "Don't do this. Get something to eat with me, and we can talk it out. I promise I'll behave."

Kat set her hands on her hips. "Come get me, and I will." His nostrils flared. In another instance, Kat wondered if his looks could kill. Watching him made her laugh more. "Good to know I have some way to escape you." Kat skipped toward the church's entrance.

"Katherine." Nex growled. "Get back here. Right now."

She continued as if he never spoke.

"Goddammit, Katherine. Get your ass over here."

"Language, Nex." Kat spun back to face him, hand on her chest. "We're about to go into church. It's disrespectful. Oh, wait." She giggled. "*I'm* going into church. *You* can't. Have a blessed Sunday!" She waved and passed through the double doors, leaving Nex outside, sending curses to the heavens.

Chapter 6

Boyfriend

K at rested her forearms on the glossy wooden counter near the cash register of the bookstore. Reading about demon summoning and how to undo it, she made a face at the suggestions. How could she know which points to skip and which to take seriously? She did summon a demon, which previously seemed impossible, so anything was fair game.

Nex closed the book. "You won't find shit in there."

"I thought I got rid of you," Kat grumbled, opening the book to find her page. She'd been a little nervous he'd be angry when she got out of church, but he was nowhere to be found. Even when she went home to get lunch before work, he wasn't there. He always appeared out of nowhere.

"You can't get rid of me until you give me a name." He slammed her book shut again. "We've been over this."

With stiff posture, Kat picked up the book, set it behind the counter, and opened it again. Nex leaned over and moved to shut it, but she was ready and left her hand on the page.

He sipped from a straw stuck in a take-out cup. "It won't do any good."

"I'll find a loophole."

"You won't." Nex circled the counter. "You're wasting both our time."

"You can't be back here." Kat shooed him. "My boss will get mad if she sees you."

"She won't." Nex plopped on the plush chair behind the counter. "No one can see me right now except you. Everyone thinks you're talking to yourself, by the way." He inclined his head to the few people in the store.

Kat's gaze darted to a couple who stared at her with creased foreheads. "Sorry." She laughed nervously. "I'm practicing lines for a play."

Smiling, they nodded and returned to browsing, turning a corner.

Kat swatted Nex with her book. "Why do you have to be so mean? I'm trying to help you!"

"If you were trying to help me, you'd give a name."

Kat sighed and read on, taking notes on anything that might be useful. She got through the book and ignored Nex's obnoxious slurping as he reached the end of his drink. Putting the book aside, she reached for another but paused. Her Bible hung out of her purse. *Duh.*

Nex's lip curled as she opened the Bible. He rose from the chair and peered over her shoulder. "How was *church*?"

"Don't say it like that." Kat searched the pages.

"Like it's a stupid notion where you're taught stupid things? I thought you'd appreciate honesty."

Kat skimmed the glossary of the Bible for the word "demon" and noted the pages listed.

"Honestly, why do you go? You believe all that? You're a woman. Aren't you offended by the teachings?"

Kat squared her jaw. "Not every church is oppressive to women."

"Really? Do enlighten me, kitten. Because it seems as though your church has taught you enough to dress like this." He tugged the hem of her dress. "I mean, who can make a dress look *boring*?"

Kat ground her teeth. "Stop it. I dress like this because I want to, not because someone tells me to."

"Bullshit." Nex scoffed. "No one *wants* to dress like this. Which part of the teaching is your favorite? When they tell you to keep yourself covered so you don't make men sin? Or the part where they tell you to obey everything a man says? Gotta say, kitten, I think you're missing the point because you've blatantly disobeyed me several times."

"Shut up, Nex." Kat wrote more notes and moved to the next page.

"Wait, I have a better one. Do you also agree that you have no free will?"

Kat shook her head and stayed silent, trying to keep her temper in check.

"You know, you're being disobedient and disrespectful working on Sunday. What would your pastor say?"

"Seriously, cut it out." Kat nearly tore the pages as she turned them.

"Come on, kitten. What do you think is so good about church?" Nex leaned one elbow on the counter. "Oh, maybe you enjoy going because you like being told what to do. You are rather spineless at times. Is that what it is? Easier to have someone else decide for you? Do you like letting others control your life? You'd make a wonderful submissive if that's the case."

Kat slammed the book shut and rounded on Nex, chest heaving. "Maybe I go not because I agree with everything but because I like being around the people, okay? Maybe they're all I have left of my dead parents. Maybe they're the closest thing I have to a family. Maybe it's nice to be part of something since I spend the rest of my time by myself. Maybe it's nice to have people check on me if I don't show up for a service or choir. Maybe it's nice to be part of a community that *cares* about me." Fighting back tears, she opened the Bible to a random page. "Maybe it's nice to have somewhere to go on holidays, so I'm not alone."

"Katherine—" Nex set his hands on her shoulders.

"Stop talking for five seconds!" Kat shoved away his hands. "Is that so hard? Do you have so much self-importance you need to fill every empty second? You know, my church is different, not that I need to explain myself to you. They teach that men and women are equal, they welcome *everyone,* and they don't think you have no free will. So shut up. You don't understand, and I don't expect you to. Be quiet, so I can figure this out." She huffed and leaned over the book.

Nex opened his mouth, then shut it. Kat tried to focus, but the words blurred in a haze of frustration. She slammed the Bible shut and braced her hands on the counter, glaring at it as if it was the counter's fault she was in this mess.

Books pushed aside, she left the counter and reorganized the book display at the front. When she got back, he was gone. How he did so much unseen and unheard was a mystery, but she banished all thoughts of him so she could get through work.

Reading books on demon summoning creeped her out, so she gave it a rest by the end of the day and left with several new strategies. Almost home, she found a familiar, faded red sedan parked in front of her house. Frida's car. *Oh no, not with Nex here!* She picked up the pace, hoping Nex hadn't answered the door.

Frida was a successful blogger and Kat's cousin on her dad's side. The family lived on the other side of the country, but Frida's job was to travel all over and find unknown stores and good food to write about online. She stopped in whenever she passed close by but never stayed for more than a day.

Inside, Kat considered turning around. Sitting on the couch were Frida and Nex. And Frida was showing him baby pictures of Kat.

"Kitty Kat!" Frida hung over the back of the couch and grinned. "You didn't tell me you have a hot boyfriend. What the hell? Who keeps someone this fine a secret?"

Kat frowned. "Boyfriend . . ."

Nex stifled a laugh. He sidled up to Kat, pulling her into a hug and kissing her cheek. "Welcome home, Kitty Kat."

"You," she hissed, keeping her arms tight to her sides so she wouldn't strangle him.

"Don't I get a hug?" Frida asked. "I know you've got him, but I'm family."

Kat disentangled from Nex, sending him a dirty look before approaching Frida. They hugged, and Frida whispered in her ear, "He's so hot. Good for you. He filled me in about you guys. It's so cute!"

Nex's smirk told Kat he heard what Frida said. She glared at him over

Frida's shoulder, and he blew her a kiss.

"I didn't know you were coming into town." Kat pulled out of the hug, fighting to maintain a smile.

"I wanted to surprise you. But I'm the one who was surprised when that fine specimen opened the door in nothing but a towel." She winked at Kat and fanned herself.

Kat buried her face in her hands. "Oh, God."

"Why didn't you tell me you finally have a boyfriend? And one who *lives* with you!"

"I . . ." Kat rubbed the crease in her forehead. There was no way around this. He'd laid the groundwork, and she had no explanation for his presence, his clothes in her drawers, or the food in her fridge. "I was trying to keep it quiet?"

"Of course you were." Frida rolled her eyes. "It doesn't matter. Now I know, and Nex said he'd buy us dinner and make margaritas! What a sweetie." Frida bumped her hip against Kat's.

"Oh, the sweetest," Kat said flatly, her pinky twitching at how pleased Nex was with himself.

"Shall we get the party started?" Nex rubbed his hands together like the evil genius he was. "Frida tells me she can get you drunk better than anyone. I'm *very* interested to see that, kitten."

"Aw, kitten," Frida cooed. "So cute."

"It's no—" Kat gave a strained smile to Frida. "I want to get a little more comfortable. You know, not wear a dress all night."

"Go for it." Frida typed into her phone. "I left a bag with new pajamas in your room."

"Oh." Kat's eyebrows raised. "Thanks. I'll be fast." She gripped Nex's arm on the way to the bedroom.

"Am I coming to help you get undressed?" Nex asked, winking at Frida. "Frisky, this one."

Frida giggled, and Kat reconsidered her position on not using violence as she dragged Nex into her bedroom. She shut the door and shoved him against it.

"Oh." Nex's lips curved up. "That was hot. I'll let you be the dom this time because I didn't think you had it in you, and I'm curious, but for the record, *I'm* the one in control, kitten. After this, you submit, and I make the rules."

"I'm going to kill you."

"Me? That's a twist." Nex's eyes darted around. "Technically, that would release me of my attachment to you, but," he tapped his chin, "if I kill myself, would I return, or would I have to start over stripped of my ranks like I would if another being killed me?" Nex lifted his hands in an uncertain gesture. "I don't know about that one. I'll have to research and get back to you."

Kat whimpered, dropping her head in her hands. "Nex."

"Already with the whimpering? Kitten, I haven't even touched you yet."

"Stop it!" Kat balled her fists at her sides. "Why did you do that? Frida's going to tell everyone."

"I figured. She seems like the gossiping type."

"Then why do it?"

"To fuck with you." He picked at his fingernails. "You're keeping me from going home. This is your fault. I don't know why you didn't expect retaliation. Now, if you'd like, I'll go tell her it was all a great joke, and I'm exclusively into men. All you have to do is give me a name."

Kat threw her arms up. "You can't manipulate me into killing someone!"

"Death isn't a big deal. People die every day." Nex waved his hand dismissively. "Trust me, I know. I practically run the end that gets most of their pathetic souls."

"To some people, death *is* a big deal." She expected another sarcastic remark, but his expression softened.

Instead, he brought his hand to her face. "Katherine," his finger brushed her cheek, softer than she thought he could be, "I'm sorry for being insensitive earlier. I didn't know about your parents. If I'm honest, the other reason I said that to Frida was because I was afraid you wouldn't look at me all night, and this way, you have no choice. I'd rather you be angry with me than hurt because of me."

Kat stared at him, mouth agape. "I'm not hurt. I was frustrated, but I wasn't hurt. I can understand how it looks from the outside, but you shouldn't assume, Nex. You never know what someone's life is like or their motivation behind things. We all have secrets and reasons for acting the way we do."

Nex pulled his hand back. "You're not mad?"

"Oh, no, I'm *livid* with you now. The other thing is forgiven. Not this, though." She poked his chest. "How could you do that to me? What am I supposed to do?"

His brows furrowed. Most humans held grudges forever, especially considering the sensitive topic, but she seemed over it already. She wasn't like the humans he was used to. She stared at him expectantly, and he finally smirked.

"I told you, kitten. Play along, or pick a name. I can make this problem go away with a little cooperation on your part."

"Not happening."

Nex shrugged. "Very well." Kat didn't register movement until she was against the wall, pinned by Nex's body, his nose grazing hers. "Then prepare for a fun night because I've spent a great deal of time telling Frida how incredibly affectionate I am. Didn't you know I was touch-starved as a child? Quite tragic. Now I need it more, or I get nervous and feel unloved. Thankfully, I have the sweetest girlfriend who's so understanding and always gives me the attention I need." The corner of his lips curled into a half-smile. "That means I'll be touching you *all* night. I hope you can handle that. We don't want to raise suspicion with Frida." He nuzzled her nose. "Do we?"

Chapter 7

Letting Loose

Frida bounced and cheered at Kat donning the matching pajamas Frida bought on her trip to Hawaii. An inside joke, it started when they were fifteen and sixteen, and their parents made them get matching pajamas, swimsuits, and shirts on a trip to Disney World. Both sets of parents were shocked when the girls said they were too old for such things. Unfortunately, they wore them anyway, and Frida had pictures.

Margarita in hand, Kat stood in the kitchen, wearing shorts way too short to wear in front of Nex, while Frida showed him the photos.

"Kitten," Nex cooed as Frida went through the gallery on her phone. "You're so adorable."

Kat bristled and sipped her margarita.

"You have some too." Frida looked up from her screen. "Where's your phone?"

Kat leveled a glare at Nex. "Broken."

Nex offered a guilty smile and continued scrolling. Kat downed her margarita, then filled her glass and shuffled away from the pair.

A *ring* announced someone at the door. Kat went for her purse, but Nex strode past, gliding his hand along her back. "I told you I'm getting dinner."

"With what money?" Kat whispered, following him with her wallet.

"Money's a nonissue."

He opened the door, handed over cash, and accepted the pizza and wings. Door kicked shut, he strode to the kitchen table, Kat on his heels.

Glancing back at Frida, she kept her voice low. "How is money a nonissue?"

"Human currency means nothing. Especially in this country." Nex snapped his fingers, and hundred-dollar bills appeared in his hand. "It's paper. I can make it myself."

"You can't make money." Kat yanked his hand down before Frida saw. "That's illegal."

"I'm a demon, kitten. Laws don't apply to me. Here, take it." He offered the bills. "I don't know how you can afford a house while working at a bookstore."

"I don't want it." Kat swatted his hand. "I don't have to pay for the house. It was my parent—" Kat took a deep breath and sat at the table. "My parents owned it. I only pay utilities and stuff. No mortgage."

Eyebrows drawn together, Nex didn't respond, just kissed the top of her head and called Frida over. Kat's confusion at the affection was forgotten when he sat next to her and pulled her chair against his, draping her legs over his lap.

Frida giggled and sat across from them. "You guys are cute."

"It's easy to be cute with this one." Nex set one hand on Kat's bare leg and reached for pizza with the other. "One or two slices?"

"I can get my ow—" Kat stopped at Frida's confused expression. "One is good."

"Of course." Nex gave Kat a side-glance. "Always need to be healthy, right?"

"Dude, you have no idea." Frida grabbed a piece of pizza. "She does have a weakness for wings, though."

Nex's lips turned up. "Do you?"

Kat reached for the box of wings, put several on her plate, and pointedly ignored Nex's stare.

As they ate, Kat tried to subtly remove her legs from Nex's lap, but he held her in place. She stopped when she realized each attempt had him sliding his hand farther up her leg, almost going under her shorts. The longer his hand stayed on her thigh, higher than anyone had touched, the squirmier Kat became. More because she didn't hate the feeling, and she should. Warmth spread through her, and the sensation made her antsy.

Feeling the heat radiating off her, Nex took advantage, rubbing circles in her leg until that heat spread through her body. He took it a step further when she finished her wings and was licking her fingers. He grabbed her wrists and licked the sauce off himself, sucking each finger into his mouth while maintaining eye contact. She stared at him with wide eyes as his tongue swirled around each individual finger. By the end, Kat was completely red and throbbing between her legs.

Holding her gaze, Nex kept his grip on her hands. He knew the effect he had on her.

"That was hot." Frida glanced between them. "Shit, do you guys want me to leave so you can, you know, be alone?"

"No." Kat jerked her hands away and succeeded in getting her legs off his lap. "You're spending the night, aren't you? We can sleep in my bed together, like usual."

"If you're going to kick me out of bed," Nex dropped his arm over Kat's shoulders and nuzzled her ear, "then I'll take that alone time."

Frida grinned. "Bed's all yours. I'm good on the couch. I don't want to know what you've done in it if this is how you act publicly. Damn, Kitty Kat, I don't disapprove, but I am surprised."

Kat swallowed when Nex's fingers brushed her neck. She stood and collected her and Frida's empty glasses. "I'm going to get refills."

"I'm full." Frida patted her stomach. "Of food. Not alcohol. I want more alcohol. I'm going out for a cigarette, though." She stood and winked at Nex. "I'll take my time."

Nex's gaze stayed on Kat. "Please do."

While Frida went outside, Kat refilled their glasses. Nex came up behind her and gripped her hips, leaning in until she was flush against him.

"What are you doing?" Kat nearly spilled the pitcher. "Frida's not in here to pretend for."

"I'm afraid I have a burning question, kitten. It's going to bother me until I get an answer." He traced one hand along the waistband of her shorts. "I know you're a virgin, but . . . have you never been touched like this?" He slid his other hand down her leg, past her shorts, playing with the hem and slowly inching it higher.

Kat set the pitcher down and braced on the counter. "What makes you say that?"

"You react like someone who's never felt another's touch. Maybe not even your own." Nex's thumb caressed under the band of her shorts, dangerously close to where a certain part of her warmed. "So, have you not?"

Kat opened her mouth but made no sound when his hand slid from her leg, up her stomach, and stopped below her breast.

His fingers brushed higher and higher until they were dangerously close to her bra. "Not even here, kitten?" He followed the curve of her breast with one finger, not touching, staying below as he dragged it back and forth. "What about here?" His hand traveled down her ribs to the bottom of her shorts, then around to her butt, fingers nearly grazing it. "I can say with certainty, never here." He lowered his other hand under her waistband, touching the top of her underwear. Kat shuddered. "No, you've definitely never felt this before. I can hear your heart racing, feel your breathing, smell your body responding like it's never experienced these sensations." He slid a finger beneath her underwear's band. "Should I answer its call?"

Kat hesitated, trying to control her thoughts. His finger lowered farther into her underwear. She snapped out of it and shoved him away.

"What's wrong with you?" Overwhelmed by the spreading warmth, she wrapped her arms around herself. "Just when I thought you couldn't get worse."

Storming past him was the intention, but he tugged her against him, cupping her face. "Don't get mad at me, Katherine." He rubbed his thumb over her lower lip. "Don't get mad at me for this mutual attraction. I didn't know there'd be one, but I like these pajamas." His hand slid low on her back as he whispered in her ear, "I'd like them better off you. Want me to show you what you've been missing?" He placed a hot kiss against her skin. "The things I would do to you, kitten . . ." He nipped her neck. "You'd be a mess before I got anywhere. Like you are now. Wet and ready for me to feel every untouched part of you."

Kat fisted his shirt, eyes sliding shut. Awareness and excitement pricked all over her skin while his fingers dipped into her shorts.

"Whoa, need another minute?" Frida asked.

"No." Kat pushed away from Nex, but his hands stayed on her hips, only letting her go far enough he could still touch her. Trying to ignore the wetness pooled between her legs, Kat peeled off Nex's hands and hurried toward Frida. "Let's do something fun. All of us together."

Frida entered the kitchen and clapped her hands. "Let's do shots!" Kat followed, avoiding Nex's gaze. Frida poured shots and nodded to Nex. "You doing shots?"

Nex snaked his arms around Kat, pulling her back against him. "What the hell? We should all let loose sometimes." He accepted the shot glass and dipped his head next to Kat's ear. "Shouldn't we, kitten?"

Chapter 8

Confusing Feelings

K at woke with a headache. She groaned, snuggling into the bed and refusing to open her eyes. The mattress was warmer. Harder. Kat ran her hands over ridges and frowned. She blinked her eyes open to find she wasn't on a bed, but a person. A half-naked person. She jumped, but Nex gripped her hips, holding her in the straddling position.

"Stay. I liked where your hands were going." A smug smile formed. "Why are you so jumpy? You could've fallen off the bed and hurt your ass again."

"Let me go!" Kat squirmed, making Nex groan.

"Stop squirming, kitten, or I'll have to do something about it."

Something hard pressed between Kat's legs, separated only by Nex's boxers and her flimsy pajamas. Her cheeks heated. She pried his hands away, then clambered off him. "What happened?" Kat asked. Flustered by him last night, she'd taken way too many shots and didn't remember coming to bed.

"Nothing." Nex sat up, running his hand through his hair. "Give me some credit. I wouldn't fuck a drunk person. I'm a demon, but I'm not completely evil."

Kat assessed the room as if it could provide a hint about last night. "Well, how did I end up . . ."

"Asleep on top of me?" Nex finished, quite amused. "I carried you because you were too drunk to walk. When we got in bed, you asked me to kiss you on the neck again."

"I did not!" Kat hid her face in her hands.

"Of the two of us, I'm the one who remembers what happened." Nex pressed his lips together in a failed attempt at hiding a smile. "Don't be embarrassed. In any other circumstance, I would've kissed more than your neck. By the way, I didn't know you could sing so well."

"Oh no." Kat winced. "Karaoke?"

"A lot of karaoke. Why didn't you sing for your audition? If they heard your voice, the stuttering wouldn't have mattered."

"I don't like singing in front of people unless it's in a group. You haven't answered how I ended up on top of you."

Nex snorted. "That's silly. You have an incredible voice. Anyway, you wanted to try kissing my neck after I kissed yours, so you climbed on top of me. It didn't last long. You passed out."

"Oh my God." Kat pulled on her hair.

"Relax, kitten." Nex removed her hands from her hair. "I'm not complaining. Want to try again now that you're sober?" He brushed his hand against her thigh. "I'll kiss more than your neck. I'll kiss where that ache keeps building."

The sensation of his fingers on her thigh sent excitement right between her legs. Kat stiffened. Never had she struggled with self-control. It was terrifying.

"No!" Kat pulled away and climbed out of bed. The headache grew with the movement, and she pressed her fingers to her temples.

In the living room, she found Frida passed out on the couch. Kat returned to her room and grabbed clothes, temporarily letting go of her throbbing head to glare at Nex. "I'm taking a shower, and you're *not* going to appear in there."

"Very well. I understand. Don't want to have your first time in the shower."

"I hate you." Kat stormed to the bathroom.

The door closed, and she was alone, but Nex's voice echoed in her head.

You don't hate me. You hate that you want me.

Kat's eyes widened, and she glanced around to ensure he wasn't in the room. "What?"

Another trick I possess. I have many very fun tricks. You'll see.

Kat's body thrummed with an awareness that she attempted to wash away in a quick shower. Trusting Nex to keep his word was unwise. A sigh escaped when she walked out fully dressed without him showing up, but she was surprised to find him in the kitchen. Cooking.

Kat sat next to Frida, reminding herself that in Frida's eyes, this was supposed to be normal. Nex hadn't put on a shirt, and Kat forced her gaze to the table.

"Seriously, he's hot, *and* he cooks?" Frida pretend-swooned. "You won the lottery with this one."

Kat opened her mouth, but Nex was suddenly beside her, setting down a smoothie. "A cure for your hangover, kitten." He placed a kiss on her head. "Don't worry. It has your yogurt in it."

Frida mouthed *Oh my God* and made dreamy eyes at Nex while Kat glared at the smoothie. As he cooked, Nex entertained Frida with small talk and jokes. Kat stabbed at her eggs, but Frida was too distracted to notice.

Once they were finished, Frida had to leave for her next destination. They walked outside with her, Nex still not bothering to put on a shirt. His bare torso attracted attention from the neighbors. Kat flushed and avoided looking at him. Instead, she gave Frida a long hug. Frida also embraced a stiff Nex before leaving, waving as she drove away.

Kat's elderly, conservative neighbor looked over. A neighbor who went to Kat's church. A neighbor who peered at Nex in his boxers questioningly.

Kat grabbed his arm, dragged him inside, and slammed the door. "Dude, what the heck? Put on a shirt, for goodness' sake. My whole church is going to think you live with me."

Nex laughed, wiping nonexistent tears. "Oh no, kitten, whatever will they do? Come and pray over you? I hope there's enough power in their prayers to save your soul because living with a demon isn't earning you points with anyone upstairs." He pointed up. "Although, your incredible lack of curse words might. 'What the heck?' Are you that afraid of hell?"

"That's it." Kat ground her teeth. "You're not staying with me anymore. You can make money, so find somewhere else to live."

"I'm not going anywhere." Nex invaded her space. "You've trapped me in this awful realm, and you're going to help me get out, or I'll keep doing this and many other things to make your life hard. Cooperate with me, and I'll cooperate with you. It's that simple."

"You have a physical form now. I can call the police, and they'll be able to see you."

He tilted his head to the side. "With what phone?"

Kat dropped her hands to her sides and lifted her chin. "I don't need a phone. The police station isn't far." She opened the front door, but it slammed shut.

Nex pinned her wrists behind her back, pushing her chest into the door. Her breath caught when he pressed his body against hers. Kat tried to pull her wrists out of his hold, but he squeezed tighter. A jolt of excitement went through her, and she reminded herself that was a bad thing.

"I don't think so, kitten." Nex nuzzled her hair. "Remember, I can disappear. How bad would it look if they came here again, and you had nothing to show for it?"

"You've made your point." Kat breathed, trying to ignore the warmth rippling through her body. "Let me go."

His hold on her wrists constricted. "Why? Because you like this too much?"

"I have class," Kat said weakly.

Nex chuckled and nipped her ear before releasing her, stepping far enough back that Kat could turn but not without bumping into him. "What a convenient excuse."

Kat pushed away, gathered her things, and bolted out the door. Half expecting him to follow, she repeatedly checked behind her but didn't see him.

Focusing in class was difficult. The throbbing between her legs ached unlike anything she'd ever experienced. A couple of guys had caught her interest over the years, but she was too shy to do anything about it. And while her church was different, sex was still a weird subject, so she never explored that part of herself. Although, she'd be lying if she said she hadn't thought about it. Nex was right when he said she'd never felt her own touch. For the first time, she considered investigating it.

She pressed her thighs together and shut out those thoughts. She gave him too much control, and he enjoyed it too much. *Be stronger. Don't let him affect you.* Having thoughts like that for a demon concerned her. Maybe she needed therapy.

Class ended, and Kat had barely listened to a word. She needed to find something to get rid of Nex. After gathering her things, she rushed outside and turned for the library.

"Kat," Jason called from behind.

She spun and tried not to blush. Nex brought out a lot of new feelings, but she still had a crush on Jason. "Hi." She clutched her notebook to her chest.

"Hey, I meant to catch you yesterday after auditions, but you bailed pretty fast." He stuffed his hands in his pockets. "Sorry you didn't get the part you wanted."

"It's okay." Kat shrugged, darting her eyes away.

"For the record, I think you would've made a much better Constance."

Kat's eyes snapped back to him, and a smile crept across her face. "Thanks."

"So, listen, I was wondering . . . Do you wanna have dinner with me?"

Kat blinked, not sure she heard correctly. He waited for an answer, and she reminded herself she needed to speak. "Dinner with you? Like a . . ."

"A date? Yeah, that's what I was hoping."

Kat tucked a curl behind her ear and tried not to smile too wide. "I'd like that."

"Great." Jason beamed. "Can I get your number, and we'll make a plan?"

Kat hesitated. How could she explain that Nex had shattered her phone? "I'm out of a phone right now. It broke, but I'm on social media. You can message me there. I'm on my computer a lot."

"I can do that."

"My last name's—"

"I know your last name, Kat." Jason smiled. "I may have looked at your profile a few times."

Kat pretended to have an itch on her face to hide the growing smile. "Oh."

"Couldn't help it. You're too gorgeous." He winked. "Let's make a plan now. What about Friday night at seven? I can pick you up?"

"Okay."

"Great." Jason pulled out his phone. "I'll send you a friend request, and you send me your address, yeah?"

Kat nodded, rocking on her heels to keep from bouncing.

Jason grinned, touching her arm as he moved past her. "See you Friday."

Once Kat was confident he wouldn't hear or see, she squealed and jumped up and down. She was so distracted that she didn't notice Nex leaning against the wall with eyes too red to pass as normal.

Chapter 9

No More Playing Nice

When Kat arrived home, Nex appeared in front of her. She screamed, setting her hand on her chest. "Stop doing that! You're going to put me in an early grave." She dropped her bag on her way to the kitchen.

Nex followed close behind. "How was class?"

"Fine." Kat poured some water, glancing back at him. *Why the sudden interest in my life?*

"Fine? Nothing noteworthy?"

"I did go to the library. Found some stuff." Kat sipped her water. "It all sounds insane, but so does accidentally summoning a demon."

"That's it? Nothing else you want to say to me?"

Brows knit together, Kat tapped against her glass with her thumb. "No . . . Oh! Actually, yes." She put her water down and placed her hands on her hips. "I have to go out again because, thanks to you, I have no phone and no alarm clock. Besides not popping up in my face out of nowhere, can you maybe also not break my things? As you pointed out, I work at a bookstore. I'm not made of money."

"I replaced your alarm clock and bought you a new phone." He pulled a phone from his pocket. "It's better than the last."

Kat arched her eyebrows, cautiously accepting the phone. "Thanks."

"No more then? Your day was average and normal?"

The phone reminded Kat of her date on Friday. It wasn't that she forgot;

she was distracted by finding ways to undo summoning Nex. She fiddled with her phone. They shared some weird moments, but he did say it was to mess with her, and it wasn't as if she'd be able to avoid telling him when Jason showed up. Unable to contain the smile, Kat's voice raised a couple of octaves. "Jason asked me out."

"Did he?" Nex inched closer. "And what did you say?"

"Yes, obviously. I've wanted to go out with him for over a year."

Nex's eyes grew redder. "Don't you think it'll put a damper on things when he finds out you sleep with another man?"

Kat cocked her head. "Are you mad?"

"Why would I be mad?" Nex scoffed. "You're nothing to me. I just don't understand why you'd date someone who obviously only wants to fuck you. Not very virginal of you."

"Why are you being mean?" She tugged on her sleeves. "That's not why he asked me. He's not like you. He's sweet."

Nex laughed. "Bullshit. You're so fucking naïve it's painful. He's a douchebag who wants to get in your pants, and when he does, that'll be it. You know everyone wants to fuck a ginger to see what it's like, right?"

"Stop it." Kat backed away. "Stop being so mean. I don't see how it's your business anyway. I'm hopefully getting you out of here like you wanted."

"Your stupid research and loopholes are a waste of time." Nex glowered. "Maybe this is for the best. When he does fuck you and leave you, you can give me his name to kill, and I can go home."

"I don't know why you're mad. Are you jealous? You told me everything you've done is to mess with me. You can't be jealous if you're messing with me."

"I'm not jealous. If I wanted you, I could get you." He gripped her hips and hauled her against him. "Your buttons are so easy to push, I could have you spreading your legs for me within the hour. It's a miracle you're still a virgin with how I have you aching for me."

A lump formed in her throat, but she wouldn't give him the benefit. She pushed him away and opened the fridge.

"The silent treatment." Nex sighed dramatically. "Nothing has ever hurt so much."

Kat took a deep breath and removed her spinach from the fridge. Nex meant to speak again, but there was a *scratch* at the back door. The noise pulled a smile out of Kat, and she grabbed dog treats off the top of the fridge. Opening the back door, she found two German shepherds.

"You have dogs?" Nex asked.

"No." Kat gave them each a treat. "They escape my neighbor's yard. He'll be here in a couple of hours to get them. He knows they always come to me." She scratched the smaller one, Billie's, ears. "I missed you, puppies."

Nex snorted, and Kat looked back at him questioningly. He continued laughing an exasperated sort of laugh, shaking his head.

Kat stood. "What's so funny?"

"Your life. I mean, you don't even have your own dogs. You borrow someone else's. It's incredibly pathetic. You do realize how pathetic it is, don't you?"

Kat inhaled sharply, her eyes stinging.

"Your life is pitiful. You live alone, have no friends, go to church to fight off loneliness, leap at the chance to date a douchebag, let the first person who touches you leave you a needy mess and drunkenly asking for more, *and* you have treats for someone else's pets." He cackled. "Fucking wretched, kitten. I'd be horribly depressed if I lived like you."

Never one for violence—unless in self-defense—or cursing, Kat's smack across his face was uncharacteristic. "You *asshole*."

The slap snapped Nex out of it, and he finally noticed her wet eyes.

"That's it." She stalked out the front door.

Nex shook off the sting of her slap. *Idiot.* Outside, he caught up, but she didn't look at him. "I'm sorry, kitten. I didn't mean that. I had a shitty day, and I took it out on you. I'm sorry."

The only evidence Kat had noticed his presence was that she walked faster, feet stomping on the sidewalk.

Several people on the street cast glances their way while Nex tried again. "Come on. Let me make it up to you. I'll cook a great dinner." He matched her pace. "A great, *healthy* dinner."

Silent, she rounded a corner.

"Katherine, come on." Nex moved in front of her, but it was as if she didn't see him. "I'm sorry. I am. Let me fix it." Unable to take her ignoring him, he grabbed her arm, but she jerked free.

After wiping tears, she turned to face him with a glare that made him step back. "I've tried to be nice about this because you're right. By some freakish accident, it's my fault you're here. I'm trying to help the nice way, but it's abundantly clear the nice way isn't going to work because you're a demon, and you're *cruel*. I'm not playing nice anymore. You crossed the line."

"I don't know what that means, but whatever makes you stop crying." Nex reached for her cheek, where more tears streamed.

Kat smacked his hand away and stepped back.

He followed, but it was as if he stepped into a wall. He frowned and tried again, then realized where they were. "Fuck," he spat, sneering at the church. "Don't hide. You can't stay in there forever. Work this out with me, kitten. I promise I'll be better."

Kat shook her head. "I'm getting you out of my life once and for all." She turned and marched toward the church.

He muttered increasingly creative curses the closer she got to the entrance. "I don't know what you're planning, but I doubt it'll work," he called. "Come home with me, Katherine. I'll be nice."

The church's heavy wooden doors closed behind her with a *thud*.

Nex scowled and tried again to get through the invisible shield, but it didn't work. "Fucking holy ground."

All attempts to find a way around the barrier failed, so he returned to

Kat's, pacing in the kitchen. Hoping she wouldn't be as angry when she returned, he tried to make himself useful by cleaning. However, she was so neat there wasn't anything to clean. Making dinner was his next idea.

He was turning on the stove when Lucian appeared out of thin air.

Lucian's nearly white hair hung past his shoulders, his eyes a pale pink, and his posture rigid. "You're still here." Lucian's gaze swept over the house. "The human won't budge?"

Lucian was a demon who frequently moved between realms like Nex used to. If it weren't for Kat summoning Nex and catching him in a blood bond, he'd be able to leave easily, but now he couldn't until his purpose was served.

"No. She's still trying to find ways around it."

"Have you thought any more about my suggestion?"

Nex stilled. Lucian's words the first day Nex arrived floated around Nex's mind. *The easy way out is to let me kill her. Then you have no purpose to serve, and you'll be sent back.* Nex considered it at first. Then he looked into her past and couldn't find a single thing wrong with her. He hoped spending time with her would ease his conscience, but the more time he was around her, the more he discovered she was genuinely, annoyingly good.

"I won't do that. There must be another way." He slammed his hands on the counter. "Have you talked to anyone else?"

"Everyone says the same thing. The only way out is through death. Hers, her choice's, or yours. But killing you would mean you'd have to start from the bottom again. Lilith likes you but not enough to give your rankings back after something like this. She'd consider your unwillingness to kill the girl a weakness."

"Keep asking." Nex gripped his head. "Someone must have succeeded another way. There's always another way. In the meantime, I'll keep trying to get her to agree."

"Very well." Lucian bowed his head. "You know where to find me." As quickly as he'd arrived, Lucian disappeared.

Nex went back to work. It wasn't until he was putting the finishing touches on dinner that he smelled Kat again. Except she wasn't alone. He faced the door as she walked in. Gone was the sweet girl he'd grown used to. In her place was a pissed-off woman who wasn't taking any shit.

She stood in the doorway with folded arms. "If I were you, I'd do that disappearing thing you do."

"What are you talk—" He hissed. The other presence's familiar aura hit him, and he clenched his fists as a man with gray hair and long robes stepped into the house. "You brought in an *exorcist*?"

Kat maintained eye contact. "I tried to play nice." With no hint of apology, she addressed the exorcist. "Shall we get started?"

Chapter 10

Dressed by a Demon

"Kitten, please," Nex pleaded. "Can't we work this out? I said I was sorry."

It was Thursday, and every day since Monday, Kat had brought in at least one new religious leader from an untried religion. Nex had narrowly dodged holy water, and although they all said the wrong things to get rid of him, their strange auras uneased him.

"This one's basically the enemy of your religion." Nex gestured to the priest. "You realize your denomination name, *Protestant*, comes from the fact your denomination *protested against* the Catholic church, right?"

Kat shrugged when the priest wasn't looking and leaned against the wall with her arms crossed. Nex's arms dropped to his sides as the priest roamed with his rosary and vial of holy water.

"Ah." The priest closed his eyes. "I feel it."

Kat pushed off the wall. "You do?"

"Don't act so excited," Nex snapped.

The priest turned away from Nex. "It's here." He waved at nothing, Nex behind him. "I can feel it. It's angry."

"Really?" Nex threw his arms up. "He's not even looking the right way, and you still trust him?"

Kat muttered a quiet, "He's right about the angry part."

"That's their go-to," Nex gritted out. "They always say we're angry. It doesn't mean shit. What can I do? Tell me what to do to make it better."

Kat focused on the priest, who lit incense and chanted.

He waved the crucifix and drew a cross over his chest. "Be gone, demon!" He sprinkled water away from Nex.

"I'd love to be," Nex said flatly. "How long is this going to continue? He's not even speaking the right language!"

"There's a right language?" Her eyes lit up. "Of course. Latin."

"What?" the priest asked.

"Nothing." She typed furiously into her phone. "Thinking out loud."

Frustrated, Nex flexed his hands and inhaled deeply before approaching Kat. He set his hands over hers. Instead of letting her jerk away like he'd done all week, he held her hands. "Katherine, from the deepest part of myself, I am sorry for what I said." He rubbed his thumb over her knuckles. "I was angry and frustrated, but that's no excuse. I'm sorry." He lifted his hand to her cheek. "Are you going to hate me forever? I'll do anything you ask. Having you this cross with me is worse than not being able to go home."

For the first time in days, Kat's expression softened, but she tore her eyes away. She watched the priest, then whispered, "Why do you want it to stop? If we find the right person, you could go home, couldn't you?"

"Not the way I want to. If I'm killed or exorcised by a priest, I'll be sent back to the underworld shamed, stripped of my titles and everything I've worked for. Back to cleaning up blood and torturing instead of having a real job. I don't want that. I want to go back to my house with my hounds. All that goes away if I'm sent back like this. Status is everything there, and if I'm shown to be weak by being sent back by a fucking priest, that's the lowest blow I can get. I'll be lucky if they let me through without a proper lashing."

"Lashing?" Kat's eyes widened, then an irritated frown formed. "Is that true, or are you lying to me because I'm so *pathetically naïve* you know I'll believe you?"

"I don't think that, Katherine. I don't. It was a moment of anger, and

I'm sorry." Nex stroked her cheek. "I'm not lying. You know I want to go home more than anything. If I wasn't concerned about the conditions in which I'd return, why would I fight you on this? Why wouldn't I help you find the right person?"

Kat chewed her lip, eyes darting back to the priest who chanted and scattered holy water. A moment later, she pressed her lips together and squared her shoulders. "Fine. But you have to respect my space from now on. No messing with me, no sneaking up on me and scaring me, no breaking my stuff, and absolutely no being cruel because you're in a bad mood. And if you sleep in the bed, you have to stay on your side."

Nex's lips twitched into a smile. "You'll let me sleep in the bed?"

"It doesn't mean anything. I'm just incapable of not feeling guilty that you're in this situation, and that couch is like a million years old."

"I'll take it, kitten." Nex kissed her forehead. "Thank you."

"Whatever," Kat grumbled. "How's it going?" she said louder, catching the priest's attention.

The priest raised his arms. "The spirit's gone."

Nex gave her a look.

She ignored it, offering the priest a smile. "Thank you so much."

"You come to me if you have any more problems." The priest took one of her hands with both of his and gestured a cross between them. "I'll pray for your safety."

"Thank you."

Kat let him out, and Nex peered out the window until the priest was down the street. "Right." He rubbed his hands together. "Let's talk about the new people I came up with to kill that you can't possibly have an argument against."

"No." Kat held her hand up. "I don't have time for your murder plans. I have to go to the mall."

Nex clicked his tongue. "What for?"

She glanced at him hesitantly as she slipped on a jacket. "An outfit."

His face scrunched. "Oh. For the date?"

"You're not allowed to be mean."

"I'm not. I just think he's a tool."

Kat grabbed her purse. "You saw him once for like ten seconds."

"He's such an incredible tool that it took less than that to identify him as such."

"Whatever." Kat waved dismissively and left the house.

Nex appeared beside her on the street, making her jump. He smiled sheepishly. "Sorry, force of habit. What do you see in him?"

"How is this any of your business?" Kat strolled on the sidewalk toward the bus stop. White and gray clouds blocked the sun, making the already cold air chillier. She focused on that to distract her from the cars racing by.

"Because I want to go home, and instead of dedicating your time to helping me, you're distracted by some random fool who isn't good enough for you."

"You're being ridiculous." She eyed him and fought a smile. "Are you protective over me now?"

"You're my ticket home, so yes, kitten, I'm a little protective."

"That's strangely sweet and unlike you." Kat got on the bus, and he followed.

"It's not sweet. It's out of obligation."

"You don't like to be complimented, do you?" The bus moved, and Kat gripped the bar.

"I love to be complimented. Preferably regarding sex or death."

Kat rubbed her temples and stared out the window while Nex ignored her request not to bring up more people to kill. The suggestions earned strange looks from other passengers, leaving Kat with no choice but to hide her face in embarrassment.

The bus finally stopped at the mall, and Kat couldn't get off fast enough. She sprinted out, sending Nex dirty looks. "What's wrong with you? You can't casually discuss killing people."

"Why not?" Nex strode beside her, his nose wrinkling at the number of people wandering the parking lot and loitering outside the mall. "It makes everyone uncomfortable. It's entertaining. Why do you take the bus? Does the car in your garage not function?"

"It functions fine," she mumbled.

"Then why don't you drive?"

"I don't like driving, okay?" Her suddenly rushed footsteps brought her to the mall entrance quicker. "Drop it."

Surprised at her sharp tone, Nex paused. He considered pressing but decided against it since she'd started speaking to him again. Instead, he followed her inside and stayed silent as she browsed clothes.

At least, he remained quiet as long as he could. Each of her choices made him shake his head. "I can't take it anymore." He snatched outfits from her arms and rehung them.

Kat stuck out her lower lip. "Hey."

"I can't with this." He gestured to the clothes and clutched her hand. "Come on. We're not shopping in the old lady section. You're still young. How old are you?"

"Nineteen, and I doubt I'll like anything you pick. I like to be modest." Kat wriggled, trying to escape his grip.

"Nineteen? Shit, you're basically a baby."

"I'm not a baby." Kat scowled. "How old are you?"

Nex's jaw flexed. "Doesn't matter."

"How old are you?"

He stopped in front of a rack, released her hand, and flipped through clothes.

"Nex." Kat tugged his sleeve. "How old are you?"

"Drop it, kitten." Nex pulled out a dress and handed it over. "Put that on."

"I'm not putting anything on until you answer me."

"Does it matter?"

"Not really, but you're being so weird about it now I want to know."

Nex smirked. "Curiosity killed the cat, kitten."

"That was original." Kat rolled her eyes.

"Put it on." Nex dragged her to the dressing rooms. "I'm doing you a favor."

"Tell me how old you are."

They reached the dressing rooms, and Nex nudged her inside one, tossing the dress on the bench. He braced on the doorway with a look that silenced Kat. "Put it on yourself, or I'll help you put it on." He stepped out and closed the door.

"Where's your sense of compromise?" Kat whined, lifting the dress.

"Two hundred and twenty-seven."

Kat's eyes bulged. She couldn't think of an appropriate response.

Nex grunted. "That's why I didn't want to tell you."

"It doesn't matter." Kat ran her fingers along the soft fabric of the dress. "I don't care. I'm just surprised."

"Sure, kitten. How long does it take to put on a dress?"

Kat shimmied out of her clothes and changed into the dress. Staring in the mirror, she raised her eyebrows and turned side to side. The sweater dress's dark red fabric went down to her knees and loosely hugged her figure. She opened the door, and Nex's eyes darted up and down her body, making her blush.

He raised an eyebrow. "Well?"

"I like it."

"See? You can trust me." Nex leaned against the wall and crossed one leg over the other. "You can still wear the leggings you're so attached to, and you should definitely wear those tall boots."

"How do you know I have tall boots?"

"I had to move them to make space for my clothes."

"Oh." Kat fiddled with the sleeves of the dress, her face heating. "Do you—Do you like it?"

His gaze swept over her. "Very much. You look lovely."

"Thanks." Kat hurried inside the dressing room. She slumped against the door and released a breath that had caught the moment Nex complimented her. Her heart raced a little too fast, and she flattened her palm against her chest. *Remember who you're going on a date with tomorrow and who you're not.*

Chapter 11

Never Been Kissed

L ip stain applied, Kat assessed herself in the mirror. She pulled at her hair, wishing it was tamer. At least the frizziness was low today.

Once she left the bathroom, she put on boots and walked into the living room, where Nex watched TV. While things were better between them, he still drove her crazy with his habits, including always being half-naked. He currently had gray sweatpants on, no shirt, and was eating ice cream from the carton.

Kat set her hand on her hip. "How do you stay in shape when you eat like that all the time?"

"Rules are different for me, kitten. This isn't my realm." He glanced at her, pupils dilating as he took her in. "Fuck, you look sexy."

Kat froze, lips parting while she restarted her brain. "Geeze." She pulled at the neckline of her dress. "Don't be subtle or anything."

"Why should I? You look sexy." He shrugged, looking back at the TV. "He doesn't deserve how sexy you look."

Kat forced her mouth to close while he ate ice cream and watched the screen. She smoothed her dress and sat on the couch away from Nex. Unable to keep her hands still, she repeatedly adjusted her skirt and removed nonexistent lint.

"What happened?" Nex asked, holding a picture of Kat and her parents at her eighteenth birthday party. The last party she had with them.

"Car accident." Kat kept her gaze on her lap and fought the urge to pick at her nails. "Drunk driver." She took a deep breath and followed a seam down her dress with her finger. "I was driving. Not drunk, just . . . driving. The truck hit the passenger side. They were both on that side."

Nex's hand covered Kat's fidgeting one, and he shifted closer. His gentle expression surprised her since he was usually angry or sarcastic.

"I'm sorry, Katherine. When?"

"It'll be a year on Christmas Eve." Kat let his fingers weave through hers, though part of her screamed *bad idea*. Any second, she'd be on a date with someone else.

He squeezed her hand. "I would like to assume you know it wasn't your fault, but I have a feeling you've somehow managed to convince yourself otherwise."

"Not exactly." Kat swallowed the lump forming in her throat. "I don't—I don't really think it was my fault. The drunk driver was in the wrong. I just . . . I wish I would've, I don't know, paid more attention. Had faster reflexes. Something."

"Don't put that on yourself." Nex brought her hand up and brushed his lips against her knuckles. "Loss is difficult enough without blaming yourself."

"Easier said than done."

Nex let go of her hand and picked up the picture again, waving it. "What was the occasion? You look rather happy."

Kat smiled at the photo. "My eighteenth birthday. I wanted to go to Las Vegas."

"You? In Vegas?"

"For the shows," she said, tucking her hair back. "And I always wanted to see the Strip at night. I've heard the lights are amazing." Her smile grew as memories flooded her mind. "Vegas is a ways away, and we couldn't afford it, so my mom and dad turned the house into a casino. The kitchen table was the poker station." She gestured to the table. "The kitchen was the bar. Then Mom brought up slot machine games on our computers and put them inside cardboard boxes she decorated, so they looked like slot machines." She laughed. "Outside was a fancy steak house with candles and white tablecloths and everything. It was a better birthday than if I'd gone to Vegas."

"Sounds like they loved you a lot."

"They were the best parents anyone could ask for." She almost asked about his parents, but she didn't know how that worked. "Did you have parents?"

Nex broke eye contact. "I assume so."

"You don't know?"

"I was told I died at twenty-two, and that's why I stopped aging at twenty-two. All I know is I was born again in the underworld, though I don't know why, and I have no memory of any life before, so it's difficult to say what the truth is. If it is the truth, then yes, at some point, I had parents, but I don't recall it. Nor do I recall what I did to deserve the underworld."

"That's terrible." Kat's expression fell. "I'm sorry."

"We all have our demons." Nex's mouth quirked into a smile. "I hardly remember that part of my life—growing up. It was a long time ago and only difficult when I was young. Before I found my place. It's not so fresh, not like it is for you." He took her hand. "The pain does ease, kitten. Time helps. It never goes away, but it becomes bearable."

Nervous at his proximity and affection, Kat nodded stiffly. He had more of an effect on her than she liked to admit, especially after learning his history. She didn't trust herself with him, so she walked to the window and checked the time on her phone.

"It's early. Relax."

"I can't help it." She tugged on one of her curls.

"It's not like this is your first date ever. Sit down and breathe."

Kat chewed her lip and avoided his gaze.

Nex's eyes narrowed at her hands wringing together. "Wait. *Is* it your first date?"

Kat hid her face. "Don't be mean."

"How's that possible?"

"You're supposed to be nice."

"I don't mean it in a mean way." Nex leaned forward and clasped his hands together. "You're beautiful. Hasn't anyone ever asked you out?"

Kat shrugged, still hiding her face for her original reasons but also to hide the blush from his compliment.

Nex shook his head. "People in this realm are fucking idiots. Don't be embarrassed. I'm not going to mock you. I understand your nervousness now. Come here."

"Why?" Kat dropped her hands to her sides.

Nex beckoned her. "Come here."

Kat sighed and approached.

Nex offered a bite of ice cream, and Kat shook her head. "Come on. It's for the nerves."

"I can't use the same spoon you used."

"Oh, for fuck's sake." He held the spoon out. "Stop being so uptight."

Kat hesitated but gave in. She placed the spoon in her mouth and flushed as Nex watched her. "What?" She slid the spoon out of her mouth and focused on the bookshelf in the corner.

"Have you kissed anyone before?"

The heat in Kat's face and chest intensified, which was answer enough. She turned to leave, but Nex grabbed her hand and pulled her down on his lap, straddling him. Her dress slid partway up her thighs, leaving her leggings and his sweats the only cover between them.

Kat squeaked, setting her hands on his chest for balance. His bare chest. "What are you doing?" The contact had her licking her lips.

"What if he tries to kiss you?"

"I don't know. I don't know how."

Nex smiled lightly and brought his hand behind her head, leaning so close their noses touched.

Kat's breath hitched. "What are you doing?"

"I can teach you before he gets here." Nex's other hand slid to her lower back and dragged her against him. "You want your first kiss with him to go well, don't you?"

"Yes." Her body tingled when Nex's hand drifted up and down her spine.

"Then pay attention." Nex grabbed her wrists, placed her hands behind his head, and pulled her into a kiss.

Kat tensed, but his lips were surprisingly warm and gentle. The motion had her eyes fluttering shut. He moved slowly, threading his fingers through her hair to hold her in the kiss. Kat responded, mimicking his movement. It wasn't long, but when they broke apart, Kat was breathless.

"Um." Kat opened her eyes, and her fingers curled against his skin. "Thanks. That wasn't as hard as I thought it would be. Was I bad?"

"No." Nex watched her tongue escape and wet her lips. "But you should definitely practice more." He cupped her face and kissed her again.

This one was firmer, his lips more deliberate against hers as he slid one hand down her back and brought her closer. An involuntary sound left Kat's throat, and Nex groaned, sliding his tongue along her lips.

"Lesson two is French kissing," he said against her mouth. His tongue slipped between her lips, caressing her tongue.

Her fingers knotted in his hair, and she melted against him, following his tongue with hers. Her heart fluttered as her body came alight, new desires springing up that included more skin contact. The desire spiked both her excitement and nervousness. Nex's hand wrapped around her waist, and he sat up straighter, bringing her down firmer on his lap. They broke out of the kiss when Kat gasped at the contact with Nex growing under her. He moved his lips down her neck, and the doorbell rang.

Kat's eyes snapped open, and she pulled away, nearly tripping as she got off his lap. She touched her fingertips to her lips and tried to catch her breath. Their eyes met, and Nex started to stand. The doorbell rang again.

"I have to go." Kat dashed past him and grabbed her purse and jacket before rushing out the door. She practically ran into Jason getting out of the house.

"Whoa." Jason held his hands up.

"Sorry." She smiled meekly. "Hi."

"Hi." He chuckled. "Everything okay?"

"Yep." Kat nodded, clutching her purse to her chest.

"All right." Jason offered his arm. "Let's go."

Kat took his arm, and he led her to his car where he opened the passenger door for her.

As they drove off, Nex stood by the window. He glared long after the car was gone, eventually going to the kitchen, where he grabbed a bottle of whiskey.

Chapter 12

First Date

Sitting in the car with Jason, Kat reminded herself to breathe. It should've been because she was on her first date. Or because she had her first kiss, and it elicited all kinds of feelings she wasn't ready for. However, her apprehension wasn't for either reason.

This was the first time in a long time she'd been in a car.

The moment Jason parked in front of the restaurant, Kat jumped out. He looked at her curiously but smiled, offering an arm. Kat laced her arm through his as they walked into the Italian restaurant, a small but romantic place with white tablecloths, candles, and a single rose at every table.

The hostess led them to a table in the corner, and Jason pulled out Kat's chair, sliding it in as she sat. He took the chair across from her, and they thanked the hostess when she set menus in front of them.

"Have you been here?" Jason asked. Kat shook her head, and he grinned. "Me either. It's always fun trying new things. I saw you got the part of Elizabeth. Are you excited?"

"Yeah." Kat lifted a menu. "I mean, it's a small part."

"You'll shine. You'll get the bigger part next time."

"If I can manage to get through it without stuttering." Kat laughed, running her finger along the edge of the menu.

"I'm sure you can." He reached over and set his hand on hers. "Hey, everyone gets stage fright. Don't be embarrassed. I've stammered my way through plenty of auditions. You can't expect to get the big part your first time, right?"

"I guess so." Her heart fluttered as his fingers grazed her knuckles before he took his hand back. "You get stage fright?"

"Oh, yeah." Jason chuckled, opening his menu. "I don't know anyone who doesn't. Ash does, too." Kat nodded and dropped her gaze to the white tablecloth. Jason frowned. "Sorry. I know you guys aren't friends. I didn't mean . . ." He ran his hand through his blond hair. "Sorry. What a great way to start a date, huh?"

"It's fine. You and Ashley are close?"

"Uh, close?" He made a face. "I don't know that *close* is the right word. We've known each other a long time. I know she can be rude, but she's not always like that. It's this whole thing with her dad." He rolled his eyes. "So, I try to be patient with her even when she's being rude or making stuff up because, trust me, Ash likes to make stuff up if she thinks it'll make someone nervous. Kinda like she did to you at auditions. Sorry about that, by the way. I told her to stop doing that."

"Why does she do it?"

"It's her dad." He unfolded and refolded his cloth napkin. "She comes from a family of performers. Theater, musical theater, indie movies. That kind of thing. Her dad's a big player in the musical theater world. He puts a lot of pressure on her to always be the best and get the biggest parts. Ash is good enough to do it without messing with other people, but she doesn't think so. Instead of focusing on trying her best, she often tries to ensure victory by messing up other people. Like I said, I know she's not a great person a lot of the time, but I also know how she grew up, so I try to be patient. I'm sorry she's been awful to you, though." He frowned. "After auditions, I told her she needs to cut it out, or she and I can't hang out anymore. Especially because you and I are dating. She said she'd back off. Let me know if she doesn't, and I'll take care of it."

Even though Kat didn't like Ashley, she could understand how hard it was to be put under pressure, how it made people desperate to measure up.

It didn't excuse her behavior, but it made more sense.

"Look, I'm sorry." Jason rubbed the back of his neck. "I shouldn't have brought her up. You make me so nervous I started babbling. I don't want to talk about anyone but you and me right now. Can we pretend I didn't say something stupid and start over?"

Kat's mouth fell open. "I make you nervous?"

"Yeah. Are you kidding? I've been trying to work up the nerve to ask you out for months."

Kat fiddled with the edge of the tablecloth. How could someone like him be nervous to ask anyone out? "Why were you nervous?"

"Well, I approached you once, like two weeks after school started last year. You were so wrapped up in a book you didn't notice me." He laughed.

"What?" She did get wrapped up in books, but she didn't think she was capable of not noticing Jason. She'd had a crush on him from the first moment they spoke.

"It's true. You were reading Oscar Wilde. Well, you're almost always reading Oscar Wilde," he added. "You kept coming to school with different books and were so quiet I didn't know how to approach you. I planned to after Christmas break, but you seemed different after that. You missed a lot of classes. Did something happen?"

Kat stiffened. Him knowing her parents were gone was inevitable. Him knowing there was an accident where she was the lone survivor was inevitable. Still, it was the last thing she wanted to talk about. "I had some family stuff going on," she said. "Was I that bad?"

"Bad? Not at all. You seemed sad, and I didn't know how to help. I tried to be nice, but you didn't seem interested, so I backed off."

Those first few months after the accident were a blur. She spent so much time angry, hurt, and lost. She didn't put it past herself to have shut him out while she was shutting everyone else out.

"I'm batting zero tonight, aren't I?"

Kat glanced up, realizing she'd been lost in thought for a while. "No, sorry." She smoothed her napkin over her lap. "I zoned out a little. What made you try again?"

"Honestly?" Jason leaned back in his chair. "You auditioning for the main part in this play. You were uninterested in being around anyone, but it changed when you went after that part. You really put yourself into it, came to more gatherings while we prepared. It showed me maybe you didn't want to be as alone as it looked on the outside. That, and I have a fresh take on this semester."

"A fresh take?"

"My last couple of semesters, I didn't push myself to go after anything." He rubbed his chin. "I didn't know what I wanted, or I thought I didn't. Turned out I did know what I wanted, but I was too chicken to admit it to my dad. The last thing anyone's father wants to hear is that their son is going into theater." He clasped his hands together on the table and leaned forward, his fingers stretching toward her. "But you inspired me. I decided this semester I wouldn't be afraid to admit what I want. So, I finally got the nerve to tell my dad I was in theater and asked the prettiest girl in school on a date."

Kat blushed, her lips pulling up. "Thank you." She lowered her gaze to her lap, then brought it back to him. "What do you mean I inspired you?"

"Remember that assignment we had at the beginning of the semester? It was something like overcoming fears. Everyone had to think of ways to overcome stage fright, but you had a creative take. Like you always do." He gave her a half-grin that had her heart fluttering. "You said people say to not be afraid, but that advice is no good. It's not that we shouldn't be afraid; it's that we shouldn't let fear control us. Fear is healthy as long as it doesn't consume us. Fear keeps you safe, keeps you alert, tells you when you need to get out of a situation. Or, in the case of theater, it keeps you on your toes, ready to take on a crappy audience, or someone messing up their lines. I can't remember exactly how you said it, but it was something like, 'Fear is a sense we've been given for a reason. It's okay to be afraid, as long as you control that fear and use it to help you like it was intended.'"

"I can't believe you remember." That paper took hard work. She used things she'd learned in counseling and added her own spin. The exercise was therapeutic, but she didn't think anyone listened when she gave her presentation.

"It was so profound it was easy to remember. So, I took your advice. I figured since I was afraid to ask you out, it meant you were worth the risk. And I'm glad I did. Otherwise, I always would've wondered if you would've said yes." He leaned over the table more, and she could smell mint on his breath.

"I'm glad you did too." A smile grew so big it made her self-conscious. She sat back, hiding behind her menu and earning a chuckle from Jason.

After the awkward beginning, the date went better. Jason liked a lot of the classic books Kat did, so finding something to talk about wasn't hard. Time slipped past until the hostess reminded them the restaurant closed at nine o'clock.

Jason drove Kat home. Distracted by being in a car, she had no time to be nervous about her first kiss with him or the fact it was no longer her first kiss. Instead, she counted the stitches on the seat to combat the increasing tightness in her chest.

Outside Kat's house, Jason walked her to the door, and she turned to him, beaming. "I had a good time. Thank you for dinner. You didn't have to pay."

"If I invite you out, I should pay. I had a good time too." He laced his fingers with hers. "Was it good enough to earn another date?" Kat nodded, getting another heart-stopping grin from Jason. "Great, what about next Friday? Same time?"

"That works."

"Awesome. Goodnight, Kat." He stepped forward and kissed her forehead. Lips still there, he brought his hand under her chin, tilted her face toward his, and kissed her.

Kat's breath hitched as his mouth moved against hers. *You're supposed to kiss him back.* She moved her lips, and her eyes slid shut, his gentleness making her giddy.

He pulled back and rested his forehead on hers. "I'll see you at school."

Kat reached for the doorknob and fought the urge to cheer. "At school."

"Goodnight, Kat." He backed up, throwing his hand up in a wave. "Sweet dreams."

"Goodnight." Kat slipped inside and shut the door. Briefly closing her eyes, she touched her lips and beamed. Her eyes snapped open at a bottle clattering. Nex lounged on the couch, two empty bottles of whiskey lying on the ground next to him and a new one in his hands.

Glazed eyes drifted over Kat, narrowing the longer he stared at her. "Was it all you hoped for?"

"It was nice." Kat frowned as Nex tried to sit up but fell back. "Do you need help to bed?"

"Unless you're going to send me back to *my* bed in *my* home with *my* hounds, then I don't want anything from you." He turned on his side. "I want to go home." His eyes slid shut, the bottle in his hands slipping from his grasp.

Kat rushed over and caught the bottle before it hit the ground. His breathing slowed, eyes not opening. Passed out. She grabbed the blanket off the back of the couch, draped it over him, then stepped back, unable to stop staring down at him.

Although she tried not to think about it, their kiss was fresh in her mind. She busied herself with throwing the empty bottles in the garbage, then hung her coat and purse on the coat rack near the front door. She flicked off the lights, went to her bedroom, and fell back against the door to close it.

I want to go home.

Guilt formed a knot in her stomach. She was trying to find a way to send him home, looking through books, reading anything she could get her hands on. Nothing worked.

Kat considered her attempts and where to look next as she got ready for bed and climbed into it. She curled under the blankets, guilt eating away at her until it consumed more than her stomach. She didn't want to be the reason he was stuck, forced to be here against his will and away from his dogs.

Nex's suggestions surfaced. For the first time, she let herself consider them. She could do like he said and pick someone who was about to die. That wouldn't put blood on her hands. Or so she tried to tell herself.

But that voice, that awful voice she'd spent months after her parents' accident trying to get rid of, crept back in. *Isn't the blood of two people bad enough? You want to be responsible for another death?*

Kat's chest tightened so much that she had to take a quick draw of air to breathe at all. Flashes of her hands covered in her parents' blood forced her to relive the parts that made her the guiltiest.

She blinked back tears and curled on her side. No. She *couldn't* be responsible for another death. She'd figure something else out.

She had to.

Chapter 13

Affinity for Dark Things

After being dismissed from choir practice, Kat packed her binder and Bible into her messenger bag. Practice was every Wednesday, and she hadn't missed one since she was three, or so her parents told her. She couldn't remember that far back, but the building had a sense of familiarity and safeness she'd always cherish.

"Kat, will you eat these?" Bernice, one of the older women in the choir, held up a container full of cookies. Her gray hair was pulled back in her signature bun, and glasses rested on the tip of her nose.

Normally Kat would say no, but she had Nex at home, so she accepted. Things had been strange between them since the night they kissed. Nex grew distant and went back to being rude and vulgar. Maybe cookies would chill him out.

"What's new in your life?" Bernice asked, handing off the container.

At some point, it had come around to choir that there was a half-naked man in Kat's yard. The neighbors liked to gossip.

Kat sighed. "He's just a friend."

Bernice feigned innocence. "Who?"

"Funny."

"From what I heard, maybe he shouldn't be *just a friend*."

"*Bernice.*" Kat giggled, covering her face. "It's not like that. I'm dating someone else."

"Does this someone else have you blushing as much as your friend?"

Kat bit back the smile. "Yes. We've been on three dates and have a fourth planned this weekend." Kat slung her messenger bag over her shoulder and walked out of the church with Bernice.

Kat liked Jason. He was sweet and gentlemanly. Kissing him didn't have the same effect on her as kissing Nex, but she attributed that to Nex stealing her first kiss, one that was more intimate with her in his lap.

"I'm glad you're going out and making friends." Bernice smiled warmly, linking her arm through Kat's. Bernice lived directly across the street from the church in a small, cottage-like home. Kat always saw her to the door. "Oh, I almost forgot." Bernice rummaged in her purse as they crossed the street, pavement wet and reflective from the rain during choir practice. "I finished the book you lent me." She pulled out "The Canterville Ghost" by Oscar Wilde.

Kat took the short story. "What did you think?"

"I think for a cheerful young woman, you certainly have an affinity for dark things." Bernice laughed. "I enjoyed it. Humorous despite its morbidity."

"I warned you." Kat slipped the worn paperback into her messenger bag and paused in front of Bernice's house.

"You did, and I'd like to see more." Bernice eyed Kat. "I know you have more."

Kat grinned. "I'll bring something Sunday."

"That would be lovely." Bernice kissed Kat's cheek. "I'll see you Sunday, darling."

Bernice went inside, and Kat meandered home. An after-rain chill fogged the air, and she wrapped her jacket around herself tighter. Unable to stop herself, and not so anxious to get home to whatever plans Nex had, she kicked puddles as she walked.

Music boomed from her house, louder the closer she got. Kat wondered what Nex was doing now. Every day he drove her crazy, then reminded her she could get rid of him if she "cooperated".

Inside, Kat found two other people sitting beside Nex on the couch.

Nex glanced back at her with a devilish smirk. "Hey, kitten. Come meet my friends." He gestured to the two strangers. "We're having a demon party."

A new attempt on Nex's part wasn't surprising, but it was almost insulting he thought something so simple would break her.

Kat greeted the two men with a warm smile. "Hi, I'm Kat."

"Lucian," the one with silver hair said.

"Marcus," the other said. He had black hair like Nex, but unlike Nex, his hung past his shoulders and was complimented with a trimmed beard.

Both demons had an unnatural red tint to their eyes, although Marcus's were darker, and Lucian's were pale to the point they were almost pink.

Kat spent enough time around Nex to know he enjoyed sweet things. If they did too, she wanted on their good side. She held up the container. "Would you like cookies?"

"Oh hell yes." Marcus reached for it.

Nex sent Marcus a glare, but Marcus ignored it, opening the container. Kat smiled at Nex in victory and turned for the kitchen.

"We're planning to be up late," Nex called.

"That's okay." Kat lifted her shoulders in a shrug. "I've got earplugs. Unless you want to deal with the neighbors, I suggest you turn the volume down." Kat opened a kitchen cupboard and hummed to herself.

Lucian and Marcus looked at Nex in amusement, and he scowled.

Nex snatched another beer. "Shut up."

"She's good," Marcus said with a mouthful of cookies.

Nex smacked a cookie out of his hand, and they growled at each other.

"Don't be rude to our guests." Kat's scolding made Lucian and Marcus snort.

Nex flipped them off before going into the kitchen, where Kat was making tea. "I can't promise nothing will be broken by tomorrow." He crossed his arms and leaned against the counter. "We party hard. We might invite girls."

"Use protection and stay out of my parents' room. And you can't break anything. It was part of the agreement when I called off the exorcists."

"Maybe I won't keep my word."

Frowning, Kat turned to him. "That's not nice, Nex. Why don't you put your energy into finding a way home that doesn't involve murder?"

Nex sneered. "Because that's worked out oh so well for you the last three weeks."

"I could be making progress. We don't know." Kat carried her tea to the kitchen table. "Did you guys eat dinner?"

Marcus perked up. "Dinner?"

Ignoring Nex's glare, Kat addressed his friends. "Yeah, you guys want some? I'll cook."

"What?" Nex pouted. "You never cook for me."

"That's because you're rude." Kat sipped her tea. "They've been nice."

Marcus and Lucian snorted again, causing Nex to growl. "You were supposed to be here to help me."

"Oh, right." Marcus pulled a piece of paper from his jacket. "I made a list of people and their sins so awful you'll be able to kill without feeling guilty."

Kat set the tea down and took the paper. She skimmed it, crumpled it, and dropped it in the garbage. "It's not happening. If you don't bring it up again, I'll make dessert."

Marcus lifted his beer in cheers. "Done."

Nex threw his arms up. "Really?"

"You were right." Marcus lounged back, stretching his legs. "She's a tough one to crack."

"Aw, did you talk me up to your friends?" Kat cooed, pinching Nex's cheek. "That's sweet. I'll make enough for you, too."

Lucian bit back the smile, but Marcus didn't bother hiding his. Nex fumed while Kat started dinner. She never looked back, which annoyed him further.

Opening another beer, Nex plopped on the couch. "She's impossible."

"She's also pretty cute," Marcus said.

"Don't even think about it. Besides, she's dating someone."

"Is that," Lucian's gaze flitted between Kat and Nex, "jealousy I hear?"

"No." Nex scoffed. "I'm not jealous. Just annoyed."

"You better hope Lilith never catches wind of this," Lucian said.

"She won't. Assuming everyone's been careful." Nex eyed them both.

Lucian's head inclined toward Marcus. "I'm not the one you need to worry about."

"Don't look at me. I've barely tried to help. I'm here for the food and the beer and the view." Marcus leaned over the couch to where Kat busied herself making dinner.

Nex blocked his view with a shadow. "Don't ogle her."

"Why? Got a claim?"

Nex snarled. "Don't."

"Careful, Nex," Lucian warned. "Lilith is sensitive to jealousy. If she decides to look for you, she'll be able to smell it a mile away, and that won't end well. For you or her."

"It's not jealousy." Nex stood. "You two were supposed to help, but you're pissing me off."

"Kat's right." Marcus swigged his beer. "You are rude."

Nex inhaled and considered setting Marcus on fire but decided against it. Instead, he returned to the kitchen where Kat chopped vegetables. Unaware of Nex's presence, she grabbed her vibrating phone and opened the message from Jason. A giggle escaped. Nex rolled his eyes and snatched the phone.

"Hey!" Kat tried to get it back.

Nex slipped the phone into his back pocket. "You shouldn't let your phone distract you when the stove is on, but if you want it back, you're more than welcome to get it yourself."

Grumbling under her breath, Kat returned to her vegetables.

"You can't like him that much if you're going to let me stop you from talking to him."

"I do like him. I also like not fighting, and you're trying to start a fight." Kat dropped the vegetables into a skillet where chicken was already cooking. "*Again.*"

"Fighting is fun, kitten. It gets people passionate. You'll understand when you finally have sex. Don't tell me you're going to let him be the one to do it."

"What if I am?" Kat whirled around to face him. "You're the one who said I should get it over with."

A muscle in Nex's jaw ticked. "Not with someone like him."

"Then with who?"

"Someone who can make your skin feel like fire from one look," Nex brushed his fingers against her neck, "and a simple touch."

Cheeks reddening, Kat stepped away. "Don't you have friends to bother?"

"They're annoying me. Why bother saving yourself this long if you aren't going to wait for the right person?"

"Who says he's not the right person? I wasn't intentionally saving myself. I just never met anyone I wanted to be close to in that way."

"And you think he's that someone? Why?"

"He's nice to me, Nex. I know that's not a word you know the meaning of, but it means a lot to me that he's nice. He opens doors and listens to me, and he—"

"Compliments your clothes, holds your hand, talks about your interests at dinner instead of his own?"

Kat pulled on her shirt. "Yeah. He does. Why are you saying it like it's a bad thing?"

"Because, kitten," Nex threw his head back with a loud exhale, "he's playing you. If he was genuinely interested, he wouldn't be able to keep his hands off you, and he'd tell you about himself. Relationships go two ways. It's not all one person talking about their life while the other says nothing. Do you know anything about him?"

"There's nothing wrong with not being selfish. Not that you'd know."

"It's beyond that. How often does he dodge a question, turn it back to you, and make it seem like something sweet? He isn't asking about your life and taking you to fancy dinners because he cares, he's doing it to fuck you, and he's probably guessed you're a virgin and easy to scare, so he's taking it slow, playing the part of an interested suitor like the actor he is. What base have you two made it to anyway?"

Kat's fists balled. "I'm about five seconds away from calling the exorcist."

"I'm not trying to be mean. I'm telling you there's something not right about him. I feel it. I felt it that first day he said hi to you."

"You don't know him. He's a sweetheart and a gentleman."

"That sounds horribly boring."

"It's not boring." Kat turned, grabbed a spatula, and tended to the food. "Consistency is nice."

"Your life is full of consistency."

Nex planted his hands on her hips and moved closer until all of her back pressed against all of his front. He gathered her hair to the side and ran his nose down her neck, making her drop the spatula. "Consistency isn't what you want, is it? Deep down, you want passion." He slid his hand up her stomach, between her breasts to her neck, turning her head toward him. "You're clinging to him because you think he's safe, and the unknown excites you so much it scares you. It makes you feel out of control. And you do love being in control, don't you? I bet you'd like giving up control to someone else more." He rubbed his thumb over her lips. "Someone you can trust. It's much more exciting to be out of control. Especially if someone you want takes control for you. Wouldn't you like to not be in control, just once?"

Kat was already having a hard time breathing, but then his hand moved from her hip to her lower stomach, his finger playing with the hem of her shirt and brushing against her skin. She couldn't pull away. Nex nudged her nose with his, their lips nearly touching.

"Imagine it, kitten," he whispered. "Imagine letting someone else take control. For once, you'd have nothing to worry about. You'd sit back and let them have you, take care of you, dominate you." He ran his finger along the top of her jeans. "Someone who paid attention enough to know every sensitive spot you have." He nuzzled her neck, making her fists, and other parts, clench. "Knew you enough to know everything you like, how to push your buttons in the best way, how to take your breath away with the right words, bring paradise to you. Imagine that. Giving your control to someone who'd take care of it and reward you for giving it up. Doesn't that sound better than having to take care of everything yourself all the time? You're so tired, Katherine. With the right person, you could feel invigorated and empowered. You should be worshipped and tended to." He grazed his thumb over the lip she bit until she released it. "Now, doesn't that sound *heavenly?*"

While he spoke, Kat leaned back against him. His hand slid under her shirt, caressing below her belly button, sending sensations between her legs. Nex studied her reaction before leaning closer, almost touching her lips with his.

A buzz rumbled as Kat's phone rang.

Panting and overheated, Kat pushed him away. "Don't do that. I'm seeing someone." Her voice was meant to be stern, but it came out shaky.

Earlier hesitance gone, she retrieved her phone from Nex's back pocket. Jason's name lit up on the screen. Nex growled and stalked off as Kat took in a steadying breath and answered.

Chapter 14

Demon House Party

A pep talk was necessary before Kat's next date with Jason. After Nex's comments, doubt surfaced about Jason's intentions. Nex was trying to get to her, but it didn't stop her from noticing that Jason rarely answered a question about himself, and when he did, it was vague. Throughout dinner, she asked him questions, and he brought them back to her without giving much information.

Nex's words repeated in her mind. *He's playing the part like the actor he is.* Kat stared out the window of Jason's car, wringing her hands together. Nex had scared her this morning when he told her there was a centipede in her bathroom, an illusion he created himself. He also claimed to see her neighbor outside doing inappropriate things with someone much younger, which turned out not to be true. The expression on Kat's face when she looked out the window to check certainly gave him a good laugh.

That was the problem. She couldn't tell when he was being honest and when he was messing with her.

"You all right, babe?" Jason squeezed her leg as they drove back to Kat's house.

"Fine." Kat tried to push out the negative thoughts Nex put there but couldn't help herself. "Jay?" Kat twisted in her seat to look at him. The action brought his hand farther up her leg, making Kat's heart race.

He left his hand high on her thigh. "What's up?"

"What's your family like?"

"Pretty average, boring family. What about you?"

"What do average and boring mean?"

"Nothing special. Got both parents and a sibling. Hey, you wanted to see that new romance movie coming out, didn't you?"

Kat chewed the inside of her cheek. "Yeah, I did. Are you into those kinds of movies, though?"

Jason parked in front of her house, turned toward her, slid his hand behind her head, and pulled her closer. "I'm into whatever gives me another excuse to see you, gorgeous."

He kissed her, and she tried to shut out Nex's comments. *He's trying to get to me.* She kissed Jason and held her breath when he slipped a hand up her shirt onto her bare back, his other hand shifting higher on her leg.

He broke away and kissed down her neck, then paused. "Uh, do you live with someone?" He nodded behind her.

Several people exited the house, laughing and stumbling.

She held in the groan. "I have a roommate, but it's temporary."

"A roommate who likes to party, it looks like."

Oh no. He was interested, but she couldn't bring Jason into whatever crazy party Nex had. There were probably demons in there, and who knew how drunk they were? Marcus let his demon side out more after drinking—disappearing and reappearing places, playing with flames he created out of thin air. Jason couldn't know there was a demon living in her house who brought over demon friends to drive her crazy. Not only that, but Nex's response to having Jason in the house wasn't something she wanted to see.

"Yeah, I usually go in my room and stay out of it." Kat pulled away. *Maybe if I leave fast, he won't ask about it.* "I'll talk to you later."

She moved to leave, but Jason pulled her in for another kiss. "Don't you want to spend more time with me?" he asked against her lips, sliding his hand to her butt.

Kat's eyes closed, and she set her hands on his shoulders to push him back. "I do. So, we should see that movie soon. How about Sunday after I get off?"

"Yeah, Sunday's great. I'll pick you up from the bookstore. But what about the part—"

Not knowing what else to do, Kat leaned forward and kissed him. He groaned and grabbed her waist, drawing her closer. Sounds from the party gave Kat pause, concerned about someone coming out to find them. She pushed him back before getting out of the car. "Sunday it is. I'll text you later!" She shut the door and rushed away.

Kat smiled at the demons outside and entered the house. Her eyes widened at the number of people. People who could use a hotel room.

"Kat." Marcus slung an arm over her shoulder and leaned on her so much she faltered. "We're playing a drinking game. Play with us."

"Oh, I don't know." Kat stepped closer to Marcus as a much bigger demon, too big to be human, walked by.

"It'll be fun." Marcus nudged her toward the kitchen table.

Kat wasn't great at saying no to people, but when she saw who was at the table, she stopped. One girl sat in Nex's lap, another beside him, whispering in his ear. Kat couldn't be jealous. She *shouldn't* be jealous. She was with Jason.

Didn't mean she wanted to watch.

Kat looked up at Marcus. "I think I need a bit to drink to catch up."

"That's more like it!" Marcus grinned, setting his hand on her back as they walked to the kitchen.

Nex's voice boomed in Marcus's head so loud it hurt. *Hands off.*

Relax, jealous freak. Would you rather her walk through this party alone? Marcus asked.

No response. Marcus clicked his tongue and grabbed whiskey but paused when Kat drank directly from a large bottle of tequila.

Marcus arched an eyebrow. "Bad date?"

"My date was fine." Kat's gaze flicked to Nex, who was still with those two girls, whispering things to them and leaving Kat frustrated with herself for not liking it. She took another swig and winced.

"Slow down, Kitty Kat." Marcus took the bottle, following her gaze to Nex and back. "You good?"

Kat swiped the bottle and took another big drink before walking away. "I'm good."

"Fucking children, I swear." Marcus shook his head at both of them and approached Nex. "If your plan is to make her jealous, it's working. If it's not, I suggest you cut it out," he sat across from Nex, "because you're upsetting her."

"I don't care if she's jealous." Nex ran his fingers down the arm of the demon sitting in his lap. "I'm trying to get her sick of me, so she'll send me home."

"Right. Keep it up then because you're successfully pissing her off."

"Good." Nex focused on the girls next to him. The distractions didn't stop him wishing someone else sat on his lap. Participating in the card game in front of him, he focused on not looking for Kat.

That was until one of his friends and occasional fuck buddies, Arda, traipsed over and gripped the table, swaying. "Nex," she slurred. "I adore your pet human. She's so *sweet*."

Nex frowned. "What?"

Arda giggled. "She showed me how to get bloodstains out of clothes. Not like I need that information, but it was sweet of her to teach me. She's scrumptious. Tell me you've had a taste because I find her delightful, and I'd like *all* the details on what it's like to have her."

"She did what?" Nex guided the demon off his lap. Kat never interacted at parties, just locked herself in her room. "Where is she?"

"Near the kitchen with Armand, listening to his woes." Arda giggled, covering her mouth. "She's got a whole pile of demons waiting their turn for her sage wisdom."

"You've got to be fucking kidding me." Nex rose and stalked past Arda.

It wasn't hard to spot Kat. Her scent was never far from his mind, and it stuck out amongst the group of demons.

Stopping abruptly, Nex came upon Armand lying with his head in Kat's lap, Laris sitting close by as well as two other demons. All hung on her every word.

"Listen, Armand." Kat brushed hair from his eyes. "You don't deserve to be treated like that. Stop saying you're a demon and that makes it okay to be treated badly by this girl because it doesn't. Stand up for yourself." As she spoke, her hand waved around sloppily, her eyes glazed over.

"She's right, Armand," Laris said. "Vicky's no good for you, and she doesn't want the same things."

"For the love of all that's unholy," Nex muttered and strode forward, stopping in front of them. "Scram."

They scattered at his angry tone, and Kat glowered at him. "What was that for?"

"What are you doing? Are you insane? These are *demons*." He gestured around the room. "They don't understand your innocence. You're lucky Armand didn't make a move on you with his face in your fucking lap." Nex grabbed her hands, yanked her to her feet, wrapped an arm around her waist, and led her to her room. "You're going to bed."

"I don't want to go to bed." Kat stumbled away from him. "You don't get to tell me what to do. If you're throwing a party at *my* house, then I get to join if I feel like it."

She stomped to the kitchen, leaving Nex focused on breathing as his fists clenched and unclenched. When she grabbed another drink, he approached and took the bottle from her hands. "That's enough. I think you've drunk all you can handle."

Kat reached for the bottle, but he held it too high. "Can't you go away? Don't you have people to," her eyes drifted to the girls that had fawned over him, "*entertain*?"

Nex narrowed his eyes and snatched the next bottle Kat reached for.

"Jealous, kitten?"

"Of course not." A blush crept up her cheeks, and she stuck out her lower lip. "Stop taking all the alcohol."

Nex groaned because her pout had more power over him than it should. He glanced back at the girls he was with earlier and considered forcing Kat to admit she was jealous. Until a new plan formed. "I'll give you alcohol if you sit with me. Be my good luck charm for our games." He inclined his head to the table. "What do you say?"

"Don't you have other good luck charms?"

"None as lovely as you." Kat tried again to get the bottle, and he caught her hand, tugging her toward him. "You're my ticket home, and I can't have you running around here drunk. It's dangerous. I may not be able to use my abilities on you, but others can. Come sit with me, and I'll give you your favorite wine."

"I didn't see my wine."

"That's because I was keeping it for you." Nex opened a cabinet and removed her wine from the top shelf. "Come on. You know you want to."

"Fine." Kat stole a wine glass from the cabinet and walked past him.

Using his abilities, Nex appeared in front of her, startling her. She scowled, and he ignored it, shooing demons into seats, so there was only one empty. He plopped down and grabbed Kat's hands, pulling her onto his lap.

Kat squeaked and stiffened when Nex's arm wrapped around her waist, his hand resting on her hip. "What are you doing?" Kat asked, remembering the last time she was in his lap. Last time was different because she was straddling him. The memories warmed her body.

"Do you see any empty chairs?" Nex asked.

"I can—" One of the demons intended to offer their seat, but Nex's vicious stare silenced her.

Kat almost spoke at the exchange, but a door slammed. She jumped and turned to her parents' door shut and three demons backing away from it.

"I said to stay *out* of that room." Nex growled, making the windows and walls shake. "Take it somewhere else." Nex maintained his glare at the offenders until they were nowhere near the door.

His gaze returned to Kat's, and she opened her mouth to speak, but she didn't know what to say. For all his annoying quirks, he never touched on subjects she couldn't handle. There was something about him respecting the part of her that was still so tender she couldn't stand to talk about it that made her heart flutter in a way she'd never felt before. With anyone.

"What?" Nex asked, surprised to find her staring.

"Nothing." Kat reached for the wine. "Let's play the game."

Chapter 15

True Form

K at almost asked Nex to buy more wine, but she was concerned about what he'd want in return. Not because she was afraid of him, but because she didn't trust herself around him. He knew what to say and how to touch and how to reach some new part of her.

It was disarming.

Still, she had a long day thanks to rehearsals and being around Ashley for several hours. On Kat's way out the theater door, a pair of hands pulled her into a closet. The culprit spun her around, and she breathed a sigh of relief mixed with disappointment. *Jason.*

Forcing a smile, she couldn't figure out her emotions. Except she knew what she felt with Nex wasn't okay. The demon wouldn't be around forever. He was waiting to get out of her life, trying to get out of this realm, pushing her buttons so she'd send him home. Letting her affection for him grow would only lead to pain. After everything she'd lost, it'd be too much.

Heart already broken, letting him break it more wasn't an option, so she threw herself into her relationship with Jason and tried to shut out anything she felt for the demon she slept with every night.

Jason backed her to the wall. "Hey, gorgeous."

Kat wrapped her arms around his neck. "Hi."

"You did great today. You're a natural on stage." He kissed her.

Their intimacy had increased over their last few dates. Several times, they'd parked in her driveway and made out before she went inside and avoided Nex. Partly because he was often in a terrible mood when she got home from dates and partly because, unfortunately, he was a better kisser than Jason. He didn't need to know that. Things had gotten weirder with Nex when Jason asked her to officially be his girlfriend.

Nex didn't stay home that night.

Jason's hands slid into her back pockets. He pulled her against him, his tongue slipping between her lips. She met his tongue with hers, gaining a little more confidence in kissing. He groaned and trailed his lips down her neck.

One of his hands glided under her shirt, caressing her back before circling around and cupping her breast. They'd already made it that far, but it still made Kat nervous. Nervous because she wasn't sure how to proceed normally in a relationship, and it was all so new, she felt awkward.

His hand lowered to her jeans, then her thigh, getting close to a part of her that awakened when Nex showed up. Jason lifted his head, pressing his forehead against hers. "I was thinking," his hand stopped between her thighs, almost touching her, "why don't we have dinner at my place tomorrow night instead of going out? I'll make it special. Maybe you could stay the night?"

Kat's eyes widened. Staying the night meant . . .

Was she ready? They hadn't dated long, but according to Frida, most people hooked up after three dates, and they'd been on ten. She considered what Nex said and how it was close to advice Frida gave her years ago. *Get it over with. The first time is always awkward. You learn to enjoy it after you get used to it.*

Kat's heart hammered, but she took in a steadying breath. "Okay. That sounds good."

"Great. I'll make it nice. I promise."

When he kissed her again, nerves overtook her body, and she had a hard time getting into it.

Agreeing was hard, but what was harder was standing in a lingerie store with no idea what was sexy. She sent pictures to Frida, who thought it was for Nex and knew nothing about Jason. On Frida's suggestion, Kat bought a red, lacy bra and matching underwear. Picking it out was weird, but buying it was mortifying. She hid it in her messenger bag so Nex wouldn't see.

Between stressing about Nex, tomorrow night, and Ashley being Ashley, Kat was anxious. She didn't drink often, but she wanted it. Since Nex arrived, she'd been drinking more. They often had drinking-game nights with Marcus and Lucian. Just Marcus and Lucian. For reasons unbeknownst to Kat, Nex didn't throw another party like the one the night she ended up in his lap.

She made it home, unsurprised that Marcus and Lucian were there. They'd been around more, but Nex's plan backfired. She didn't mind company. She actually loved it. The house had been unbearably quiet since her parents died.

"Hey, Kat," Marcus greeted, his gaze on the TV.

"Hey." She looked around. Lucian and Marcus were there, but Nex wasn't. "Where's Nex?"

"Shower," Lucian said. "He went on a mission with me, and it got messy."

"I thought he couldn't hurt anyone unless I tell him to."

"He can't physically hurt anyone. He can only scare them. But I can, and he got too close."

"Oh." Kat wrinkled her nose at what 'messy' meant. "Did it . . . go well?" She didn't know how to ask about it. They mostly killed bad people or people that were getting too close to the truth of what they were.

Lucian chuckled. "You don't have to ask. I know it creeps you out."

"I'm allowed to care about your day even if I don't get it. I need to be in pajamas. I don't suppose you have any alcohol left?"

"We do, but you're a minor," Marcus teased.

Kat narrowed her eyes. "I dare you to keep me from the bottle today."

Marcus grinned. "I'll make you a drink."

Hoping Nex wouldn't get nosy, Kat went to her room and pushed her bag under her side of the bed. She changed into pajamas in the closet, so if Nex came out, he wouldn't catch her undressing. They'd crossed too many lines.

Kat exited the closet at the same time Nex came out of the bathroom. Only in a towel. His lean body on display, beads of water rolled down his abs and that V, dripping to . . . Kat darted her eyes away and moved around him for the bathroom.

Nex stepped aside but grabbed her arm. "What's wrong?"

"Nothing."

"Bullshit. What's wrong?"

"I had a long day. I don't want to talk about it." Kat wiggled out of his hold and continued to the bathroom.

When she returned to the living room, Nex was in the kitchen, cooking while the other two watched TV. Kat went to the kitchen and found a glass next to a bottle of her favorite wine.

She pointed to the bottle. "Where'd that come from?"

"I picked it up," Nex said.

"When?"

"Just now."

"That fast?"

"Yes, kitten, that fast." He filled the glass and took her hand, placing the glass in it. "Relax. I've got dinner."

"Thank you. How did you do it so quickly?"

"I move fast."

"Yeah, but . . . Nobody cares when a breeze moves by them that quickly?" She cocked her head to the side. Anytime he stayed invisible, his movement created a breeze. "Doesn't that raise suspicion?"

"Not if I'm flying and hiding myself." Nex took a drink from his glass of whiskey.

"You can fly?"

"That's what I said."

"Like Peter Pan?"

"Peter Pa—" Nex squared his jaw. "No, it's not like fucking Peter Pan."

"Well, I've never seen you with wings."

"That's because I haven't been in my true form around you."

"Why not?"

"It would scare the shit out of you."

"I'm not scared. Show me."

"No."

"Please?"

"No."

"Pretty please?" Kat pouted.

Nex groaned at her pout. "Cut it out. Why do you want to see anyway?"

"Because I want to see the real you."

"Trust me, kitten. You don't."

"I'll answer one of your deeply personal and intrusive questions if you show me."

"Any question?" Nex spun toward her with a mischievous smile.

Kat shuffled her feet. "Don't make it super gross, please."

"Fine, kitten. Answer my question, and I'll let you see me."

"Fine."

He smirked. "What's the dirtiest dream you've had where the participant was someone you were attracted to? A scenario you fantasized about after."

Kat huffed and dropped her arms to her sides. "You knew I wouldn't answer that."

"I did." Nex grinned and turned to the stove. "And now I've gotten you to shut up."

Kat fumed, annoyed he won so easily. He always won, and she was tired of it. She swallowed the rest of the wine in her glass and set it down.

Glancing over at the other guys, she confirmed they were preoccupied, then stepped beside Nex and took a deep breath. "I once had a dream about one of my dad's coworkers," Kat said quietly. "A dream that I went to his office and . . ." She closed her eyes to avoid witnessing his reaction and spoke fast. "And he bent me over his desk and took me from behind while holding my hands behind my back."

Nex's eyes widened, and he whirled around to face her.

Kat hid behind her hands. "Okay, your turn," she squeaked, peeking through her fingers.

"You fantasized about him taking you like that?"

"He was attractive and powerful and . . . It doesn't matter. I held up my end. Your turn."

"I didn't think you had it in you. You're not so innocent after all." He stepped forward, his gaze sweeping up and down her body. "You *do* like the idea of being dominated."

"I didn't say I'd discuss it. Your turn. It's only fair."

"Fine. I really didn't think you'd do it."

Her confession was less embarrassing since she caught him by surprise. "I know."

Nex scrunched his face, then snatched her hand and led her outside. Once they were out, he turned to her with a nervous expression. "I don't suppose I can talk you into literally *anything* else?"

"Why don't you want me to see you?"

"I don't want to scare you. My true form has scared plenty of people."

"You won't scare me."

Nex sighed and lowered his head, closing his eyes. *Cracks* and *pops* sounded. Parts of his head, shoulders, hands, and back had an ember-like glow. Black bat wings sprouted from his back, and black horns emerged from his head. His nails turned to claws, and when he looked up, his eyes were bloodred, his teeth sharper, skin paler.

Kat kept her surprise inside since he seemed so sensitive about it. Stepping forward, she touched one of his wings. Nex stiffened, and she withdrew her hand. "Sorry, did I hurt you?"

"No . . . What are you doing?"

"I'm curious." She stroked his wing again, running her hand along it before reaching for his horns. "It's pretty awesome."

"It's what?"

"Pretty awesome." Kat stepped back and regarded him. "You're so dramatic. It's not scary. Maybe if I didn't know you, rounded a corner, and you were there, but it's also scary when I round a corner and see any big dude I don't know."

Mouth agape, Nex stared at her. Kat smiled, and his confusion grew. She should be running.

"Does it hurt?" she asked, brows knitting together. "The cracking sounds painful."

Nex opened his mouth. No words came out. He'd never shown himself to another person without getting a terrified reaction unless it was another demon. But there she stood, at ease. Her eyebrows lifted at his silence, and he finally found his voice.

"Not anymore. I've gotten used to it."

Kat murmured an "Oh" and smiled. The urge to be with her strengthened. Tenderness wasn't something he got a lot of, and she was full of it. Tender and sweet and innocent. Everything he wasn't.

Each day he grew more attached, craving that sweetness he'd never been on the receiving end of. He shifted to human form and went inside, muttering about dinner as he passed by, trying to ignore how good she smelled today. Every day.

Her scent was his favorite.

Chapter 16

Nerves

W ishing she had someone to get advice from, Kat stared at her reflection blankly. She'd gone back to the mall to buy a dress, hoping something pretty would trick her into feeling confident. It didn't. Neither did the makeup she spent too much time on.

Her heart pounded, reverberating through her entire body. Setting her hands on the cool, ivory bathroom counter, she counted her breaths. Her phone caught her eye, and she picked it up, running her thumb over the screen to unlock it. The only person she'd consider asking for advice was Frida, but Frida thought she was with Nex and no longer a virgin. But Frida was all Kat had.

Looking in the mirror again, everything was off. Her hair wasn't right, the red dress wasn't right, and despite the time she spent on it, her makeup wasn't right.

Am I supposed to be this nervous to have sex? Her phone buzzed, and she glanced down.

Jason: I'll be there in ten minutes, babe. You ready?

A text had never been more difficult to answer. She wanted to call Frida and ask for advice, but part of her already knew what Frida would say—the same thing she'd told her for years since Frida first had sex at seventeen. *Virginity doesn't mean anything. Get it over with. The first time won't be great, but it'll be good after that.*

Kat's thumb hovered over the "call" button on Frida's contact. It was assumed Kat wasn't a virgin because Nex was living here, but she could claim that wasn't true without twisting the story too much. Kat hit the "call" icon.

"Hey, Kitty Kat," Frida answered. "Did Nex like the lingerie?"

Kat sat on the edge of the tub, smoothing her dress. "He hasn't seen it."

"Are you okay? You sound weird. Is something wrong?"

"Um, I . . . wanted to ask you something, but it's kind of awkward."

"Oh, give me a break. You can ask me anything."

Kat dropped her voice to a whisper. Nex was in the living room, and she didn't want him to hear. "Were you—were you nervous to have sex the first time?"

"Yeah. I think everyone's a little nervous. It's not like any education properly prepares you. Why are you asking? Haven't you and Nex?"

"No."

"Oh my God! He's living with you, and you haven't had sex? Damn girl, that's restraint. He's a fine specimen."

"Uh, yeah. How do you know if you're ready? How do you know if it's too soon?"

"I don't know." Frida sighed. "It depends. If I'm being honest, I wasn't sure I was ready my first time, but I don't regret it. They say you remember your first time, but meh. I wasn't hung up on the first time being special. I more remember my first time having *good* sex rather than my first time at all. But, as you know, we were raised *very* differently." She laughed. "I love my uncle and auntie, but our parents were opposites. Sex wasn't a hushed topic in my house like it was in yours."

"Did you love Daryl?" Kat asked. Daryl was Frida's first.

"Uh, no. I thought I did, but I didn't know what love was at that age. I cringe thinking back on me in high school. I was never that mature girl like you. I was the wild one who made poor decisions and didn't think things through. You've never been like that."

"You've always told me I need to loosen up."

"You do need to loosen up, but listen. Do you *want* to have sex tonight?"

Kat hesitated. Did she? "I think so. You said to get it over with, right?"

"Only if you want to. If it was me, I'd get it over with. But you're not me. How long have you known him?"

Grateful Frida didn't know much about her and Nex, Kat could easily answer a question like that with the truth about Jason. "Over a year, but we've been dating a little over two months."

"Do you trust him?"

"Yeah."

"Well, I can't tell you what to do. If you trust him and you want to, then do it. Nerves are normal. Hell, I still get nervous when I have sex with a new person for the first time. I can only tell you what I would do, and I'd do it, but it doesn't matter what I'd do. Do what's right for you."

Another notification came through—a message from Jason saying he was here. He was here, and Kat didn't want Nex to answer the door.

"Thanks, Fri. I gotta go," Kat said. "I'll call you later."

"Hey, if you decide to do it and want to talk after, call me, okay? Time doesn't matter."

"Thanks. Bye."

She hung up and stood, glancing in the mirror one last time. She added a touch of lip gloss, then rushed to the closet and picked some strappy black heels Frida made her buy. Once she was done, she slipped into a long jacket, hoping to escape Nex's notice. She walked out as he was entering the bedroom. His gaze darted up and down her body, making her feel naked, despite the jacket.

"You look nice," he said. "Are you wearing a different perfume?"

Kat nodded and avoided his eyes.

"What're you so nervous about?"

"I'm not nervous." Kat laughed too loud and too high.

Nex regarded her through squinted eyes. "Right. Well, when you in-evitably get home at exactly eleven o'clock, we're planning to play a drink-ing game. You want more wine?"

Kat bit her lip, then stopped, remembering she put on lip gloss. She wrung her hands together. "I'm not . . . I'm not going to be home by eleven."

"Sure you aren't. You and Mr. *I Own Nothing But Khakis And Polos* are always home by eleven. So, what, getting wild and coming home at eleven thirty instead?"

She couldn't help how quiet her voice was. "I'm not coming home tonight." She didn't want to look at him, but the silence made her. Kat looked away, but she could feel his gaze like a physical touch.

He cupped her jaw, turning her to face him. "Don't. There's something not right about him, kitten. I can tell with people, and there's something off."

Kat's expression fell. She was never sure when he was being honest. Yesterday, he'd nearly convinced her he'd seen her pastor with a woman who wasn't his wife and had a great big laugh. It wouldn't be the first time he lied to mess with her.

There were no warnings that Jason wasn't a good person. Dating was foreign to Kat, but he was always nice and said sweet things. He was the first person since her parents died who made her smile. He hadn't pushed her further than she wanted to go, which could only mean this was another one of Nex's pranks.

Kat pulled her hand away. "You're saying that because you like messing with me."

"No, I'm not." Nex stiffened. "It's the truth, and I don't want you to get hurt."

"I'm not going to get hurt, and it's not your business. It's my choice, isn't it?"

"Don't do it, Katherine," he gritted. "I'm telling you it's a bad idea.

Don't get it over with. Wait until you find the right person."

"Who do you think the right person is? You?"

"No, kitten, maybe I'm not, but even I would be a better candidate than *him*."

"I'm not doing this with you." Kat brushed past him for the front door.

"Katherine." Nex appeared in front of her and gripped her shoulders. "If you go with him, I'll have to follow to babysit you."

"Don't you dare." She pushed his hands away. "I'll never forgive you. It's none of your business."

Red tinted Nex's eyes. "You want me to let you go be stupid and get hurt?"

"I want you to stay out of it."

Nex balled his fists. He took a step toward her. The doorbell rang. He growled, glaring at the door. Kat moved around him, but he grabbed her again.

"Fine." Kat faced him. "Look me in the eyes, and tell me I mean something to you. Tell me you're not messing with me, and part of you truly cares for me because last night at dinner, you snapped at me and told me you couldn't care less about me. Did you mean that? Do I mean nothing to you? Because if that's true, it means you're messing with me *again*, and you don't actually care."

Nex couldn't answer. He did say that, but he didn't mean it. Her seeing his true form and reacting calmly affected him so much he lashed out. He wasn't used to kindness and didn't know what to do with it. Kat stared, waiting for an answer he wasn't giving. He couldn't admit the real reason he snapped.

"Tell me you're not messing with me," Kat whispered, searching his eyes for the truth. "Tell me you're being honest because you genuinely care and are worried, and I'll stay with you instead of going."

Nex had never admitted to caring for anyone, and the way he cared for her was disturbing. The doorbell rang again, and he wished he had his usual abilities so he could set Jason on fire.

Kat glanced back at the door, then over at Nex. "Say something. If you're being real with me, really real, I won't go. But you have to be honest, Nex. I can't take the back and forth. If I mean something to you, say it now, and if you have any respect for me, don't you dare lie, then laugh about it later. It's not fair."

He stared down at her. The words stuck in the back of his throat with a giant lump because he'd never cared for a human so much, to the point it scared him. He wasn't supposed to be able to feel this way about anyone. He wasn't good for her, and he knew he wasn't.

Pain flashed across Kat's face, and she tried to move past him, only to be stopped again.

"Don't," he said. "Don't go with him. Don't let him have you."

"I don't trust you, Nex." Kat yanked her hand away. "One second you're lying, and the next, you're not. You mess with me, and then you're genuine. Sometimes you're cold and other times . . ." She brought her fingers to her temples. It was too much. She couldn't figure out what was real, but if he wasn't denying he was messing with her, she had no reason to believe Jason had bad intentions. "Drop it. This is happening whether you like it or not."

Kat slammed the front door behind her. Nex took a half-step forward and considered following. Car doors closed, and an engine revved. He moved toward the front door, then growled and went out the back door.

Kat tried to calm herself, but Jason could tell something was wrong. He set his hand over hers and smiled. "Don't be nervous." He squeezed her hand. "You look beautiful."

She smiled and looked out the window to avoid his gaze. Nerves weren't the problem anymore. Nex had no boundaries and no consistency. How would they find a way to send him home? The idea of him not being around anymore caused a tug in her heart.

Arriving at Jason's, they sat down to a nice, romantic, candlelit dinner.

The dinner was lasagna, warm bread, and a salad. The food would've been amazing, but in his house, her anger toward Nex faded, and nervousness at being with Jason took over. Despite the mouthwatering smell of baked bread, cheese, and sauce, she couldn't eat.

"Is something wrong with the food?" Jason asked.

"No. It's perfect. Thank you."

Jason chuckled and stood. He took her hand and pulled her up, kissing her. "Relax, gorgeous. Come on."

In the hallway, Kat held her breath as he led her to a room at the end. He opened the door to reveal his bed. Kat swallowed. "Jay?"

Jason turned, setting his hands on her hips. "Yeah?"

"I, um, I've never done this."

"Honestly, I kind of got that." Jason held her face. "Don't be nervous. I'm prepared."

Kat smiled as much as her nerves allowed. Jason wrapped his arms around her. "Hey, if you want to sleep and nothing else, that's fine. We don't have to do anything if you don't want to. No pressure, babe."

"No." Kat peered at the bed, then up at him. *Get it over with.* "I want to."

They moved toward the bed, and Kat grew more nervous with each piece of clothing removed. *Nerves are normal.*

They didn't feel normal. She couldn't relax, and her mind raced so much she couldn't enjoy the moment. Jason hovered over her with practically nothing between them, and she considered telling him she wasn't ready, but he spoke before she could.

"Are you okay?" He raised his hand to her face. "You can tell me if you want me to stop. I don't want you to be uncomfortable, and you seem uncomfortable. I'm patient, babe. I can wait for you. You're worth it."

Some of her tension eased. He cared about her enough to notice she was nervous, to stop. He stared down at her, giving her a reassuring smile that made it easier for her to smile.

"Let's not." He pressed a kiss to her lips and reached for a blanket. "I don't want to push you."

More tension dissipated. She was afraid he wouldn't take it well if she changed her mind. The fact he did confirmed her suspicion that Nex lied. Jason was a good guy, and Frida was right. Virginity didn't mean anything.

He started to get off her, and Kat held his hips. "I don't want to stop."

"You sure?"

"I'm sure."

"Okay. Tell me if that changes." He kissed her and settled between her legs.

Kat tried to relax, but the first time hurt. Even though he had lube, there was a sting. Kat closed her eyes, and it was over a lot faster than she expected. It didn't feel terrible, but she didn't understand why people liked sex. Then again, didn't Frida tell her the first time was always like that?

Jason lifted off her and sat back. "I'll be right back, okay? I gotta dump the condom."

"Okay."

He walked away, and Kat rolled to face the opposite direction. Despite having sex with him, it weirded her out to watch his naked body. An uneven breath escaped as she pulled her legs together and winced at the sting between them. Was she supposed to feel something? Happy? Satisfied? Content? Closer to him?

She didn't. Part of her wanted to leave, but that couldn't be normal. She sat up and reached for Jason's phone to check the time, and it illuminated with a text.

Ashley: Are you done with the virgin yet? I'm outside, waiting for your promise from earlier. I hope you weren't serious about her staying over. Send her home so we can enjoy the rest of the night. You stopped and reassured her before, right? Told you it'd work. You're welcome.

Dread and unease started in Kat's chest and scattered, sinking into her stomach, spreading to her hands, which shook as she reread the text. Tears stung the backs of her eyes. Then another message came in.

Ashley: Baby, hurry up. We agreed you'd dump her after you got her v-card. Mission accomplished. She won't show her face at rehearsal anymore. Now kick her out because six hours since our last fuck is six hours too long.

Tears spilled, and Kat dropped the phone. Every muscle paralyzed until the sink sounded from the bathroom. Kat got off the bed and pulled her clothes on. The words and what they meant sunk in, the tears fell quicker, and the nausea grew more aggressive.

"Hey, what are you doing?" Jason, still naked, stared at her with furrowed brows. She grabbed his phone and launched it between his legs. He groaned and cupped himself after failing to catch the phone. "What the *fuck*?"

"Sorry, will that make it hurt for you to sleep with Ashley after I'm gone?" Kat snatched her heels, heading to the door.

"What are you . . ." Jason didn't finish his sentence, not that it mattered.

Kat was already out the door, running to the kitchen to grab her things. She stuffed her phone in her purse, shoulders shaking as more tears poured. She'd lain there with him, vulnerable and exposed, falling for his lies and reassurances. Reassurances he didn't even come up with on his own. Every moment with him was a lie to get her . . .

A sob escaped, and Kat turned for the door, stopping when Jason stood in the doorway, blocking her exit. She wiped the tears and glared. "Move."

"Geeze, I didn't know you had it in you to be so mad."

Somehow, his lack of apology and not bothering to look guilty made it hurt worse. All she could think about was how, because of tonight, he knew what she looked like naked, and his stare made her feel exposed. Vulnerable. Violated.

"Move," Kat repeated when he didn't. She didn't want to touch him to get out of the house, but she would if she had to. Her heart was cracked enough, but when he chuckled, *laughed* at her, it fully split.

"God, I started to think you weren't a virgin. You were so easy."

Coldness took over as blood drained from her face. He was mocking her, and she was done. She grabbed a glass of water on the table from dinner and splashed it in his face, then raised the glass. "Move, or I'll throw this at your head."

"You wouldn—"

The glass hurtled through the air, and Jason dodged it, though he didn't need to. Kat wasn't looking for an assault charge; she just wanted out of the house before she fell apart, threw up, or both. Glass shattered, and Kat used Jason's shock to squeeze past and run out. She ran to the sidewalk, and Ashley's car was parked in front of Jason's house.

Ashley rolled her window down and hung out of it. "You didn't think he cared about you, did you?" She laughed. "So naïve, Kat. It's pathetic."

More tears formed. It'd been bad enough Jason saw her cry. Ashley didn't need to see too. Kat raced down the street as fast as her aching heart let her.

Chapter 17

The Fear of Hell

Unable to stay in the house, where everything smelled like Kat, Nex left and didn't return. When she came back, she'd smell different. Like *him*. He'd been tempted to follow them, but after arguing with himself, he let it go and stayed away.

That fucker better take it slow with her.

He met Lucian in a park and drank until he didn't picture them together. Losing count of the number of drinks, he lay in the grass, glaring at the sky. Kat had too strong of an effect on him. He wanted to go home.

Alongside Nex, Lucian clasped his hands behind his head. "Your jealousy is out of control tonight."

"It's not jealousy." Nex dug his nails into the browned grass beneath him. "She's weaseled her way into me, and I'm annoyingly concerned for her."

"I believe that. I also know you're jealous, and if you don't watch it, Lilith's going to come find you and her."

"So you've said. Many times. Shut up, and leave me alone."

"I have a mission tomorrow. Want to go? Take your mind off things?"

"Fine." Nex sat up and took another swig from a bottle of whiskey.

"I gotta get some rest." Lucian stood. "Don't get in trouble finding your way home."

Nex stood too, swaying. "My home is unreachable."

Lucian chuckled. "You're getting annoying to be around. I suggest you work on that."

Before Nex could reply, Lucian disappeared. Nex ran his hand through his hair as he headed back to the house. He drank the rest of the bottle, not liking the idea of staying alone. He'd find somewhere else to go after he got more alcohol.

He stumbled down the street and tried not to think of green eyes, wild red hair, and freckles. Or skin so pale blushes showed easily. Or the way that pale skin would redden if he kissed her neck hard enough. The idea of leaving his mark on her excited him.

The number of times he fantasized about her was disturbing. Her too innocent reactions drew him in. Every time he touched her or got close, her responsiveness amplified his desire. He wanted nothing more than to take that innocence, strip her bare so he could see every part of her raw and real instead of cool and collected. The times he'd been close gave him a brief glimpse into what having her under him would be like. Thinking about it too hard left him in ruins.

He tried to force out the memories of last night when she saw the real him and didn't run away but reached out. He hated the way it affected him, the way it touched him deeper than she understood. He hated the way she accepted Lucian and Marcus and made an effort to know them despite what they were. He hated how much of her was everything he never knew he wanted and somehow everything he needed.

You can't have her. She was taken, and even if she wasn't, she was too pure for him. Angels didn't sleep with demons, and she was the closest thing this realm had to an angel.

At the house, Nex stopped in the doorway. Kat was there. Not only there but . . . crying.

He rushed to the bedroom, where she was curled on the bed, wrapped in blankets, a bottle of whiskey next to her. Nex crouched beside her, setting his hand on her tear-stained cheek. "What's wrong? What happened?"

She turned her face into the pillow to muffle her weeping.

Nex sat on the edge of the bed and rubbed her back. "Katherine, what's wrong? Did he hurt you?"

"He—" She cried harder. "I'm so stupid. I should've listened to you." She sobbed, curling up tighter, clutching the blankets. "I hate myself. I'm so *stupid*."

Nex almost whimpered at how upset she was. He moved closer and stroked her hair while rubbing her back. The only way he'd find out what happened was if she calmed down. "Tell me what happened, kitten. Let me be here for you."

"You're going to think I'm an idiot." She squeezed her eyes shut, not wanting him to see her like that. "You're going to say you told me, and I can't, Nex. I *can't*. I know you told me. I know I was stupid." She choked on the words, her body shaking. "I don't need it hammered in any more than it has been. Trust me. No one hates me as much as I do right now."

Nex dropped his head, leaning it against hers. "I won't do that to you, Katherine. I promise. You can tell me."

She cried so hard he backed off and waited. A couple of times, she stopped enough to gulp whiskey, and that concerned him as well. Even at the party, she didn't drink that much. His imagination ran wild with the possibilities of what could've happened, but he forced them out so he could focus on her.

Finally, she was able to tell him. The terrible sex, the laughing, the game he and Ashley played. All a trick. A guise to humiliate her and break her heart. While Nex did his best to maintain a calm exterior, he raged inside. He moved behind her and curled around her, holding her until she wasn't crying as hard.

She had so much to drink her speech slurred. "I'm so stupid," Kat whispered, tears silently falling. "I hate myself so much."

Nex held her tighter. "Don't hate yourself, Katherine. You're everything good in the world. You're not stupid. *He's* stupid. *She's* stupid."

"You were right." Kat sniffled. "I should've listened," she whispered. "I wish I would've listened."

"You couldn't have known." Nex ran his hand over her hair. "It wasn't your fault. It was a fucked-up thing they did. Incredibly fucked up."

"Do you think they'll say things about me to everyone in the play?"

"Don't worry about it, Katherine. I'll handle it."

Her lip quivered. "You can't do anything."

Wanna bet?

"I'm never doing that again," she mumbled, her eyes sliding shut. Almost the entire bottle of whiskey was gone. "I'm never letting anyone that close to me again."

Nex felt a painful tug at her statement, but he stayed silent. Guilt engulfed him. Tonight was as much his fault. He knew something wasn't right about Jason, but when she asked, he couldn't form the words. Now it was too late. She was heartbroken, and he wished he would've resolved his hesitation so none of it would've happened.

On the brink of passing out, she looked back at him, and he wanted nothing more than to be something other than what he was. Something that could comfort her. He didn't have abilities like that, like angels did. He'd never wanted them until now.

Tears welled in her eyes. "You hate me, don't you?"

"Of course I don't. Why the hell would I hate you?"

"Because I . . ." She turned away.

Nex wasn't sure what she meant, but he'd do anything to make her feel better. "I don't hate you. I don't hate what's perfect."

"I'm not perfect," she whispered. "Especially now."

"Your perfection and your worth are not based in something so trivial." Nex kissed her temple. "This single incident doesn't define you. Don't for a second think it does. You are much more than what happened tonight, and anyone who thinks differently can burn in the deepest pits of hell."

The alcohol and emotional exhaustion caught up with her, and her eyes closed. Nex stayed until her heart rate and breathing slowed. He got off the bed and crouched in front of her. Pushing her hair out of her face, he wiped away the rest of the tears. Katherine being asleep made it much easier to say what he truly felt.

"I would still have you," he murmured. "This means nothing. I'd have you as eagerly as before." He kissed her forehead. "To me, you're still perfect."

He stayed there, lips against her forehead, fingers in her hair. He was ready to rip apart the entire city to find Jason, and yet, another part of him ached at the thought of leaving her alone. "Forgive me, Katherine." He leaned his forehead against hers. "Forgive me for this, but it has to be done. I will never use my powers on you like this again. I promise."

Hands on both sides of her face, he pulled in the negative emotions from tonight. All the horrible things she felt from what happened. He pulled them in until he knew the depth of her anguish. Until it was almost unbearable.

It only made his anger grow.

"Don't worry, kitten." His lips grazed the crease in her forehead. "*No one hurts you and gets away with it.*"

Standing, he straightened his jacket. The effects of the alcohol he drank had mostly worn off. He made sure the blankets were snug around Kat before walking outside to the dumpster, where she said she put the clothes from tonight. The silky dress smelled like *him*. When she got home, Kat scrubbed herself so much there was none of his scent on her, but the dress still had it.

Nex closed his eyes and inhaled. Drawing out one claw, he cut his arm, allowing the blood and scent to mingle, finding the link that would lead to Jason. The hunter in him took over, and his eyes snapped open, no longer amber but a deep bloodred. He tossed the dress back in the dumpster and followed the link to Jason's house.

Moans and grunts from Ashley and Jason made Nex's ears twitch. Good. In one place together. That made it easier. Rage coursed through him, and he cracked his knuckles, staring at Jason's front door. The worst kinds of people who brought harm to thousands didn't fill him with as much rage as the man and woman who hurt Katherine.

"You're going to wish I could kill you." A dark smile formed on his face. "No one hurts my angel."

Jason lay back, Ashley riding him. She moaned, bouncing up and down while he held her hips and thrust into her. Both were close to climax when flames enveloped the bed. The fire couldn't hurt them, but they didn't know that.

Ashley screamed and jumped off the bed. Jason clambered to his feet, nearly falling on his face.

Ashley squealed. "What the hell happened?"

"I don't know." Jason sprinted for the fire extinguisher.

Ashley leapt up to follow, but the door slammed. She gasped and backed away. The lights shut off, the fire from the bed the sole source of illumination. Ashley tried to open the door, but it wouldn't budge. A deep growl rumbled, causing her to screech and back against the wall.

Through the flames, a silhouette appeared—a creature with horns and glowing red eyes but no other visible features. She screamed and wrenched at the stuck door.

I thought you liked to play games, Ashley. A low, grating voice sounded in her head, and she cried, scrambling against the door as the dark figure drew closer.

"Don't hurt me." Ashley slid to the floor, her body trembling. "What are you?"

Nex used shadows to force her to look up at him. "An avenger for the innocent, sent from the depths of hell to punish you for your sins. Hurt any innocent people recently?"

Ashley shook her head and tried to look away, but the shadows wrapped around her like tendrils, holding her in place. In an instant, the figure and the force holding her were gone. Whimpering, she yanked the door open and dashed down the hall.

In the kitchen, Jason was backed against a wall. Knives floated in the air, points to his throat and dick. Lights flickered. A figure materialized, towering over him with glowing red eyes that stripped his soul bare.

"There's a special place in hell for people like you." The figure growled, and clawed hands wrapped around Jason's neck. "See how funny it is now."

Jason's eyes widened. Horrible, all-consuming embarrassment, shame, heartbreak, and violation took over him. He couldn't stand it. Fear and agony burned through his body. Every limb pricked with pain and paralyzation. He whimpered and nearly sank to the floor, but cool knife blades still threatened his most vulnerable parts.

"Feeling helpless and scared?" the figure asked. "How fucking horrible that must be."

The figure vanished, but the knives remained, keeping Jason from moving. Hyperventilating, he peered over at Ashley. "Help me."

Ashley shook her head, ran to the front door, and jerked on the handle. It didn't open. Utensils, dishes, and glasses flew around the kitchen, almost hitting Jason. Silverware scattered, and ceramic shattered against the floor and walls. A loud screech filled the air as letters were carved into his cupboards.

Liar.

Everything dropped to the floor, and Jason collapsed, unable to stop shaking.

"I can't get out!" Ashley screamed, pulling on the door.

Jason rushed to the door, but he couldn't open it either. The lights flickered again, and another sound raked in their ears. Scraping, screeching, and tearing. Five deep scratches on both sides of the hallway walls moved toward them, shredding the wallpaper and damaging the wood underneath. From no visible source.

"We're going to die." Jason cowered against the door with Ashley.

I'm not going to kill you, the voice boomed in their minds. *I'm going to put the fear of hell in you.*

Chapter 18

Auditions

I ntense nausea woke Kat, and she bolted to the bathroom. Alcohol from hours earlier emptied from her stomach, burning her throat as she heaved into the toilet. The hair she pushed out of her face kept falling in front of her until Nex held it back. She reached a pausing point in the vomiting but couldn't find the strength to lift her head.

"Don't do that," she muttered, squeezing her eyes shut. "I don't want you to see me like this."

"Too late. I'm not going anywhere."

Bile rose in her throat and prevented her from speaking. She gripped the toilet and retched. Nex stayed.

Blinding pain behind her eyes caused her to curl up on the floor beside the toilet, clutching her stomach. "I'm never drinking again."

"Everyone says that, but they rarely stop." Nex brushed hair off her clammy forehead. "Are you done?"

"I think so." Kat tried to sit up.

He helped her sit against the bathtub. "You need food."

Kat made a face. "Ugh, no."

"French fries are a hangover miracle."

Fast food was a rarity, but she could this one time. Kat relented. He set his hand on her back and massaged with his thumb, helping relax the tense muscles.

"I'm going to shower," Kat muttered. Nex helped her up.

Gripping her throbbing head, Kat winced as she stumbled to the sink and grabbed mouthwash. She thoroughly cleaned out her mouth with a toothbrush, then leaned against the counter, clamping her eyes shut. Everything was too bright.

Nex grasped her shoulders and turned her to the shower. "Get in. I'll get clothes for you."

Kat didn't want to think or move much, so she nodded. He left the bathroom, and she got in the shower. Once finished, she peeked out, surprised there were clothes stacked on the counter. She hadn't heard him come in.

Concerned about what clothes he brought, she scrunched up her nose, but when she picked them up, she almost smiled. Leggings and a big, warm sweater. Exactly what she wanted today, to be covered and wrapped up.

She got dressed and wandered into the living room. Nex was seated on the couch, a fast-food bag and take-out cup sitting on the coffee table. She still couldn't believe how fast he moved.

Kat shuffled over, placing her hand on her forehead where the headache was most powerful. She plopped down on the couch and closed her eyes to ease the pain. When she opened them, Nex held out the cup and painkillers.

"The caffeine in the soda will help. You can stand to be unhealthy for one morning."

Kat took the pills with soda, sipping out of the straw slowly to test how it would hit her stomach. Better than she thought. Nex handed her the bag containing french fries, and she nibbled a bit at a time. The food settled her stomach, and she ate a little faster. Pain from the headache faded, but the horrible feelings from last night returned. Strangely, they'd gone away enough for her to sleep peacefully, but now they were back. Tears spilled down her face.

"Come here." Nex opened his arms.

Too upset to worry how he'd take it or what position it would put them in, Kat lay between his legs, placing her head on his chest. Nex pulled the blanket off the back of the couch and draped it over her before wrapping his arms around her.

They stayed like that for the rest of the day. And the next. Kat called into work at Nex's insistence, and he convinced her to eat more ice cream doused in chocolate and whipped cream than she ever had. Most of the weekend was spent watching TV and crying. Nex never left her side.

Sunday night, Kat fell asleep on the couch, so Nex carried her to bed. He lay facing her.

Her eyes fluttered open and welled with tears. "I don't want to go to class tomorrow. I have class with him and rehearsal with both of them."

"I understand why you don't want to go," Nex scooted closer and brought his hand up to her cheek, "but you should. Don't give them power. I'll come with you, but you shouldn't miss class, and you definitely shouldn't miss rehearsal. It's important to you. Don't let them take that away from you."

"They're going to talk about me to the rest of the cast."

"Kitten." Nex tucked her head under his chin. "Trust me when I say it's not an issue. I took care of it."

"You keep saying that, but I don't know what you mean." Kat rested her cheek against his chest.

"Don't worry about what it means. Trust me."

Something in his tone and presence gave her confidence to go the next day. She was tense as she walked in the door, though Nex was there with his hand on her back. She searched the room for Jason, but he wasn't there. Whether not knowing where he was made her feel better or worse, she wasn't sure.

Kat sat in her usual chair, and Nex sat beside her, leaving his hand on her back throughout class while she took notes. She thought she wouldn't be able to stand anyone touching her, but Nex had a way of touching that didn't leave her uncomfortable. Not one dirty joke left his mouth the entire weekend. Although his display of affection may have looked like more to someone else, he was careful, never going too low on her back, never doing anything inappropriate. Kat hadn't known he was capable.

Class finished, and her stomach twisted as they made their way toward the theater. Entering the building, Nex wrapped his arm around her waist.

Backstage, Kat almost turned to leave, but Nex urged her forward. Other students whispered, and she was terrified to know what they whispered about. Kat thought she might throw up when one approached her.

"Did you hear what happened?" the girl asked.

Kat swallowed. "No."

"Ashley slept with the director to get the part, so he's fired, and they're redoing auditions!"

Kat's eyes widened. That wasn't what she expected.

"That explains what's wrong with Ashley, but what's Jason's problem?" another student said.

The mention of his name made Kat stiffen. Following the other students' gazes, she spotted Ashley and Jason slumped against the wall, white as ghosts, shaking. Kat frowned, that frown deepening when Jason looked over at her and immediately dropped his head.

"Something weird's going on," Kat murmured.

"I wouldn't worry about it." Nex set both hands on her waist, drawing her attention back to him. "You have to audition for that part again."

"I'm not ready. I didn't prepare. Plus, I'm not exactly full of confidence right now."

"You should be, kitten." Nex tucked her hair back. "You have a lot of talent. You should sing this time."

"Sing?" Kat shook her head. "No way."

"Yes," he insisted. "You've got this. You want the part, don't you?"

"Yeah, I guess. I don't know. If they're redoing parts, I could get out of it and not have to be around those two." She inclined her head toward Ashley and Jason.

Nex smiled. "Something tells me that won't be a problem."

What does that mean? Kat tensed when, a few moments later, Ashley and Jason clambered to their feet and headed her way. She moved to step back, but Nex held her in place.

"Stand your ground. Let them see they mean nothing." He stepped aside but kept a hand on her. "They don't hold the power. You do."

"Kat," Jason muttered, not looking her in the eye. "I'm s-sorry for what we did. Really sorry." Hands stuffed in his pockets, he bolted from the room.

Ashley wrapped her arms around herself, eyes downcast. "Yeah, I'm sorry. R-really sorry." She rushed toward the exit.

"Ash, aren't you going to audition?" one of the students asked.

"N-no." Ashley's eyes filled with tears before she hurried outside.

Kat stared after her. "What the . . ."

"Look at that," Nex said. "No need to avoid it now. You should sing."

"Did you . . ." Kat's brows furrowed.

"Did I what?"

She chewed her lip. "Nothing."

Trying to make sense of what happened, Kat suspected Nex held the answer. He said he took care of it but didn't say how. He couldn't hurt them unless she let him, but Jason and Ashley looked like they'd seen a ghost. Kat's eyes widened.

Or a demon.

She was about to ask Nex, but someone walked in carrying a briefcase. "Everyone quiet down. I'm Professor Ladlow. Your new director." He placed a piece of paper on a nearby table. "Let's get this sign-up sheet going so we can start auditions."

"That's your cue." Nex nudged her forward. "You've got this. Don't be nervous. I'll be here the whole time."

Chapter 19

Flying

With the last bookshelf in the store dusted, Kat glanced at the clock on the back wall, counting down the seconds until closing. Gusts of strong winds and colder weather made the day pass slower. That, and it was Monday. Mondays were always slow, which was why she resorted to dusting. There wasn't much else to do.

The bell over the front door chimed, and Kat strode to the end of the bookshelf to greet the customer. "Welcome to Connie's. How can I—" She glanced around, but no one was there.

It wasn't a big store, so it wasn't as if there were a lot of places for someone to hide. Kat walked to the front, checking the empty aisles on her way. *Didn't the bell go off?* She searched the store one last time. Completely quiet.

"Excuse me," someone said from behind her.

Kat jumped and spun, knocking into a display she'd arranged earlier. Embarrassment burned her cheeks as books toppled to the floor. Kat brought her gaze to the culprit—a tall, beautiful woman with black hair and eyes so dark Kat wondered if they were black.

"Sorry, sweetness." The woman's voice was smooth, and she had a wide smile on her face. "I didn't mean to scare you."

"No apology necessary." Kat put on her friendly employee face. "I'm sorry. I didn't see you there." Crouching down, she gathered the fallen books. "How can I help you?"

"Where's your romance section?" Her eyes swept Kat's body. "Preferably the erotic titles."

Kat let hair fall in her face, hiding the blush that intensified under the woman's scrutiny. "Um, yes, we have those in the romance section." She stood and returned the books to the display. "Is there a specific author you're looking for?"

The woman's eyes fixed on Kat like she was committing every small movement to memory. "Whatever you recommend, sweetness."

Despite how uncomfortable the woman made her, Kat mustered her best smile. "Okay."

Kat led her to the romance section and pointed out the books. Intending to leave the customer alone to browse, Kat turned away, but the woman grabbed her hand. The action sent a strange, unsettling sensation through Kat, and she jerked back, but the woman didn't release her.

The customer smiled, taking her time letting go. "Thank you, sweetness."

Kat nodded and hurried away, wiping her hand against her dress in the hopes it would erase the peculiar sensation. The woman still stared, so Kat retreated behind the safety of the counter. While the stranger was odd, Kat wasn't surprised. The bookstore was downtown, and it wasn't the first time she'd encountered an unusual person. This stranger wasn't as bad as the man who claimed to be some king who required many young wives and graciously chose Kat as one. Thank God for the alarm button Connie, Kat's boss, installed.

Holding her phone below the counter, Kat read a text from Nex. After Jason, Nex decided she needed a way to contact him if they dared bother her again. He'd obtained a human phone. Kat wasn't sure why it was necessary because he'd hardly left her side.

Nex: I'm caught up with Lucian. I'll be late. Don't walk with-

out me.

Kat rolled her eyes, typing a response. He wasn't keen on her going any-where without him for the past two weeks, though she wasn't as depressed as at first. She wasn't sure how to take his sudden intense protectiveness. It would be a lie to say she didn't like the way he spent time with her and checked in when he wasn't around. But she didn't want to be a burden, especially given the fact she hadn't found him a way home.

Kat: I'm used to walking alone. Don't worry about me.

The bell chimed again. Kat's head snapped up, and she frowned. Out-side, the woman passed the window. The stranger gave her a small wave and smiled before passing out of view.

Guess we didn't have what she wanted. Kat's phone vibrated.

Nex: Do not walk without me, Katherine.

Without responding, Kat slid her phone into her pocket. Nex was de-manding, and the best way to handle it was by ignoring him. Eventually, he'd learn she wouldn't do something simply because he told her to.

The clock's hands finally moved to closing time. Kat had already cleaned everything and shut the register in preparation. She slipped on her coat, grabbed her bag, and slung it over her shoulder before setting the alarm.

Two blocks down the street, Nex materialized at her side. "Which part of do *not* walk without me did you not understand?"

"Oh my God." Kat's hand flew to her chest. "Seriously, stop just appear-ing. What if someone saw you?"

"On this incredibly busy street?" He gestured to the deserted street. "The only people out at this hour on this street, *after dark,* might I add," he narrowed his eyes, "are drug addicts, and they don't know what the fuck they see or don't see."

Kat sighed and stuffed her hands in her coat pockets, continuing into a less friendly part of downtown. Lights flickered, only some of the broken windows were boarded, and the ground was littered with trash.

Nex kept stride beside her, his gaze surveying the run-down section of the city. "Please tell me you don't do this regularly." He made a face at an alleyway full of people unconscious from their vices of the day. "This is dangerous. Do you have any sense of self-preservation?"

"I'm not going to get hurt."

"You don't know that."

"Relax. You know, people having addiction problems doesn't mean they're horrible people. Just because someone's in a rough patch and homeless doesn't mean they're a deadbeat. Some people need a little help."

"Perhaps, but it often makes them dangerous. And you're young and," *beautiful*, "look like an easy target."

"Most people down here wouldn't hurt me, and if they tried, someone else would step in." Kat stepped over a broken bottle. "A lot of them know me from volunteering at shelters. If you weren't with me, I'd have an escort."

Nex had a retort, but Kat stopped in front of a brick building and pulled open a creaky, wooden door. He peered up at a food bank sign.

Kat held the door. "You're the one who wanted to come. I didn't ask you to."

"I don't *want* to. I'm here because you insist on putting yourself in danger. What am I supposed to do if you die wandering unsavory parts of the city alone?"

Kat huffed. "Are you coming in or not?"

"I cannot believe I'm fucking doing this," he muttered, following her in.

According to Kat, plenty of people volunteered at food banks on Thanksgiving Day, but charities needed help in the weeks leading up to it, packing meal boxes and sorting food. People donated a lot more during the holidays, creating more work along with it. Volunteering was something she used to do with her parents, which was the only reason Nex backed off trying to talk her out of it.

His intention was to stay hidden and be nearby in case something happened. Then he discovered Kat was staying until she helped sort *all* the donated canned foods. If he helped, they'd get out sooner. Surrounded by a bunch of humans, organizing canned food, Nex wondered what the odds were that of all the people in the world, he got summoned by someone like Katherine.

Before, he might've let her come alone, but he fucked up. Leaving a mess like he did at Jason's could draw attention from higher-ranked demons. Hopefully, it wouldn't draw the attention of one specific demon.

Lilith could be vicious, and she outranked him. That made her dangerous, especially since Nex could only do so much while bound to Katherine.

The tedious night wore on. He thought it couldn't get worse until people came in wanting food. As if that wasn't bad enough, Kat walked right up and got them settled. She even hugged some of them. Nex wasn't fond of the way they smiled at her, the way they were too comfortable around her. He didn't sense anything bad about them, but he couldn't be too careful.

He reasoned that was why the moment she was at his side packing boxes again, he planted his hand on her waist so they'd know she wasn't alone and wouldn't walk alone either. "I must've missed the part of volunteering at a food bank where it says you're to be affectionate with the dodgy people who come in."

"They're harmless. I know which ones are dangerous, and they're not. They're cold and hungry."

Nex sighed. "If you could for *one* single fucking day not be so naïve, that would make me less on edge."

"I'm not naïve. I've known them a while." She nodded to the men at the table eating the soup she brought. "They want to be treated like everyone else, Nex. Do you always judge someone the first few seconds of seeing them? There's more to people than appearances. You don't know them."

"And you do?"

"Yes." Hands on her hips, Kat faced Nex. "They're on honorably discharged vets. They both watch out for young kids who end up on the streets. They weren't here for normal dinner hours because they were watching out for other people."

"You talk to them enough to know all this? Why?"

"Because they're people, and they're kind."

"They're homeless and could be addicts for all you know."

"It's not like I don't pay attention. The dangerous people I keep a distance from. You can't label someone as one thing. Labels are toxic, Nex." She returned to packing. "People don't fit neatly into categories. Labels create division and bias. If everyone looked at each other as people with lives and emotions as complex as their own instead of labeling and judging them for something they can't control, maybe there wouldn't be so much hate in the world. Haven't you ever been misjudged?"

Of course he'd been misjudged. Being a demon wasn't easy, even with the perks. It wasn't a discussion he wanted to have, so he worked faster. Except he kept getting distracted, his gaze drawn to Kat as she sorted cans and interacted with other humans.

She was sad. He knew because he'd been around her enough. But damn, she pulled off not seeming sad. If he didn't know what happened, that she still cried occasionally, he'd never know she wasn't happy. If he didn't sleep next to her, he wouldn't know she had nightmares about the accident with her parents almost every night. If he didn't spend each day with her, he wouldn't know how often she stopped and stared at her parents' closed bedroom door, then excused herself to the bathroom where she thought he couldn't hear her cry.

While part of her was naïve, another part wasn't. She wore a mask, played the part of the cheerful young woman like she was expected to. Though there was plenty to make her unhappy, she didn't let it show. Not even with him. That mask held up so well that no one would notice it if they weren't paying close attention.

He desperately wanted to remove that mask.

By the time they left, it was late. Nex tried to convince Kat to take the bus, but she didn't like riding it. As long as something wasn't too far, she walked. Nex hated walking. It took so long for humans to get anywhere.

Picking up on his annoyance, Kat glanced at him as they wandered down the dark, nearly empty street. "What are you huffing about?"

"This." He gestured to the path in front of them. "It's fucking slow."

"No one's stopping you from going ahead. Can't you teleport?"

"Not over any distance." He slid his hands into his jean pockets. "We'd have to teleport more than once, and I can't risk appearing in front of someone. I'd need to know our location was empty ahead of time."

When he transported somewhere, he couldn't help the gust that came with it, and after tearing apart Jason's house, he was trying to keep a low profile so no one would come looking for him.

"Wait." Kat stopped, a beaming smile on her face. "Can we fly?"

Nex shook his head and walked away. "No."

"Aw, come on." Kat followed, grabbing his hand. "Please? I want to know what it's like. God, it must be so cool."

"Not happening, kitten." Nex tore his hand from hers, picking up his pace. "And for fuck's sake, stop saying that name."

"I'll stop saying it around you if you fly with me." Kat ran to keep up with his longer legs but got in front of him and set her hands on his shoulders, looking up at him with pleading eyes. "Please, Nex?"

He stared at her, intending to refuse. Except her bright green eyes held so much excitement and hope, a spark that had been missing for two weeks. A spark that made those eyes easier to get lost in. The effect she had on him made his fists clench at his sides. Something he never thought would happen was happening, whether he liked it or not.

He was weak for her.

He was weak for her, and then she did the worst thing she could possibly do and stuck out her lip in a pout. He muttered a curse and grabbed her hand, taking her down an empty alley. "Fuck," he spat. "Fine. For fuck's sake, stop fucking looking at me like that."

"Yay! Thank you, Nex."

"Whatever." He scanned the alley, though there was nobody nearby. It'd be safe to change to his demon form, but he hesitated. He'd changed in front of her once but doing it again made him tense. Reminding her what he was when he'd grown more attached wasn't something he wanted to do.

Kat tugged on his sleeve. "What's wrong?"

"Nothing. I don't know why you need to fly. You're going to freeze."

At that, Kat reached into her messenger bag, pulled out a red scarf, and circled it around her neck. "Ready."

Nex fidgeted and said nothing. Kat watched, surprised at how nervous he was, like the night he first showed her his demon side.

She took his hand, making him look at her. "I like your demon form. I like the real you. You don't scare me."

"No one likes my demon form, kitten." Ignoring the softness of her hands against his was a feat he wasn't prepared for. "It scares everyone."

"I'm not scared."

He allowed himself a single moment to stare. Staring would lead to him doing something else to her, and he wouldn't while she healed from Jason. Taking a deep breath, he stepped back, away from her touch, and more into the shadows, where he changed forms. Bones cracked, skin stretched and split, and wings broke through the back of his shirt. He caught a glimpse of Kat, and she smiled.

She moved closer and traced her hand along the edge of one wing. "You look awesome."

Having her so close wasn't helping his decision to maintain distance. The tenderness overwhelmed him. He grabbed her wrists, placed them behind his head, and wrapped his arms around her waist. The action reminded Kat of their first kiss, and her heart stopped as she looked up into his red eyes, their lips inches apart.

"Hold on tight, kitten." He slid his hands to the backs of her thighs and lifted her, securing her legs around him. "Because I don't do slow." He moved one hand to her back, holding her snug as he took to the air.

Chapter 20

More

Four weeks passed since Nex scared those two humans shitless. He thought he was in the clear. Katherine had a real audition with a director, who hadn't slept with any students, and heard back that she got the part after singing one of the songs in the play. The bigger role meant she was at rehearsal longer, and she convinced Nex she'd be okay. He didn't have to sit in every rehearsal.

She didn't understand that part of the reason he followed her around was because he was afraid leaving that much destruction at Jason's meant someone would confront him. However, a month of quiet allowed Nex to relax. That was why he honored her wishes and stopped following her, but then he had nothing to do. To be safe, he stayed away from all demons, and that limited his options to fill time.

With nothing better to do, he decided to make a dinner from one of the cooking shows he watched more than he cared to admit. He went to the store to buy ingredients and got Kat's wine as well. Another alarm clock was on the list since he broke two more, not including the first one he smashed. He couldn't help smashing the alarm clock—an automatic response when it woke him.

Every muscle he had tensed at the sight inside when he returned home.

Sitting at the kitchen table was Lilith with a terrified Kat in her lap. Lilith was much bigger than Kat, closer to Nex's size, with black hair and eyes. Lilith smiled and dragged her sharp claw down Kat's shoulder, pushing the cardigan and strap of her tank top down her arm, leaving Kat pale and frigid.

"Lilith," Nex greeted coolly, putting down the grocery bags.

Lilith's smile grew. "Nex, look how domesticated you are."

He stepped forward. "Let her go. It's me you're pissed at. Take it out on me."

"Oh, I am taking it out on you." Lilith pushed her claw into Kat's shoulder. Blood beaded, and Kat winced. "I'm just using a catalyst."

Nex growled and crept closer. "That's enough."

"Ah, ah, ah." Lilith lifted her claw to Kat's neck. Nex froze, and Kat stiffened. "I'd keep that temper in check. You've lost your temper quite enough recently, don't you think?"

Nex balled his fists. "I'm sorry for the mess I left."

"You're sorry." Lilith laughed. "Hear that, sweetness?" she cooed at Kat, lips grazing Kat's ear and making her lean away. "He's *sorry*. That makes it better."

"Dammit, Lilith! Leave her out of this."

"I don't think I can. I'm afraid you've grown too attached to this human. So attached you've put us in danger with your behavior." Lilith narrowed her eyes. "I agree, those humans were at fault, and after seeing her and," Lilith dug her nose into Kat's hair and inhaled, "smelling her," Lilith moaned, "I do get it. If we're being honest, I'm having a hard time restraining myself. She is a sweet little thing, isn't she?"

Kat jerked as Lilith's claw brought the cardigan below her elbow. Lilith held her tighter, claws digging in and bruising Kat.

Nex's eyes flashed red. "Last warning."

"You threatening me?" Lilith laughed. "That's adorable, Nex. She's got a hold on you, doesn't she? What's your secret, sweetness?" Lilith scraped her claw up to Kat's chin and directed her to face Lilith. "It can't just be physical. There must be something else that has him so riled up he rips apart an entire house and leaves two souls traumatized, causing hunters to pop up all over the place, tracking down my soldiers. There was more than attraction and jealousy behind that. He knew it was stupid."

"What?" Kat's gaze shot to Nex.

"Oh, you didn't know? Nex went and taught a lesson to those humans who hurt you. So much so they've been muttering about demons and raising uncomfortable questions." Lilith's gaze shifted to Nex and turned murderous. "I've been cleaning that mess up for the last two weeks, and I'm not even done yet."

"I'll help with whatever needs cleaning up. Let her go."

"Hmm," Lilith hummed. "Not good enough. I think you need to be taught a proper lesson. The others think I should let you off with a warning, but why should I? Shall I kill both of you? I'd rather kill her first, but if I did that, you'd be able to go home, and then I'd have to go through the whole process of officially removing your rank, which seems rather tedious." She wrinkled her nose. "So, unfortunately, I'll have to kill you first and send you to the torture chambers, cleaning up messes. Rest assured, her death won't be painless."

"You're so concerned about me causing problems, but what do you think will happen if you kill her?" Nex challenged. "She goes to church and talked about demons. Imagine the outrage if a good woman who goes to church and has demons removed from her house is violently killed, having gone to the same university as the other two. You think that won't create more problems?"

Lilith snarled, digging her claws into Kat's arm and producing a whimper. The talons stopped shy of breaking the skin, leaving more marks. Several purple and red spots already marred Kat's skin. She'd fought until she realized how easily Lilith could snap her neck.

Lilith bared her teeth at Nex. "You're clever. It's why I've always liked you. You can find your way out of almost anything, can't you?" Lilith stood, shoved Kat to the floor, and stalked toward Nex. "But you can't talk your way out of a punishment. Maybe I can't use the girl, but I can send you home with your tail between your legs."

"If you kill him, I'll tell them about you." Kat pushed herself to sit up despite her shakiness.

"Katherine," Nex scolded.

"Did the human threaten me?" Lilith turned to Kat, raising her eyebrows. "Did you?"

Kat almost cowered when Lilith fixed her eyes on her, but she swallowed and stayed strong. "It's not a threat; it's a promise. If you hurt him, I'll go to my church. My church has a lot of influence. If you think it's hard now, just wait."

It was a lie. Her church was small. Because the pastor did things so differently, it isolated them from other churches. But Lilith didn't know that.

Kat felt like she'd break under Lilith's glare. When she thought she couldn't take anymore, Lilith grinned. Kat frowned as Lilith laughed, claws retracting.

"I see why you like her," Lilith said. "Few humans would dare stand up to me." She walked to Kat and crouched. "I like you, sweetness." She hooked a claw under Kat's chin and forced her to look up. "I like your boldness. Because I like you so much, and this was his first mistake, I'll let you off with a warning. But keep in mind, I'll be watching." Lilith vanished and reappeared in front of Nex, her face inches from his. "I'll be watching *closely,* and if there's one slip-up, I don't care what consequences I face, I will kill you both."

Lilith vanished, and Nex rushed to Kat, checking the place where Lilith's claw drew blood. He cupped her cheek, raging at the marks on her. "Are you okay?"

"I'm fine." Kat's hands trembled. "Terrified but fine."

"Come here." He lifted her and carried her into the bathroom. "Why did you do that? You shouldn't have threatened her." He sat her on the counter and flicked on the light. "She's dangerous."

"I didn't want her to hurt you. I didn't want to lose you," she mumbled, darting her eyes away.

Nex pretended he didn't hear the last part because it sent his mind racing on what she meant. Kat removed her cardigan, leaving her in the tank top. She gathered her hair behind her shoulders as Nex cleaned the injury.

"What did you do to them?" Kat asked.

"I didn't physically hurt them."

"Not what I asked."

"I scared them." He pulled his gaze from the wound to her eyes. "I scared them out of doing anything like that to you or anyone else again."

"She said you ripped the house apart."

"Part of the scare tactic. Does it matter? The point is, it's taken care of." He secured a bandage over her shoulder.

"Why did you do that if you knew you'd get in trouble?"

"Because they deserved it." Nex lowered his lips, kissing the bandage. "As long as I'm here, no one's going to hurt you."

"She was scary."

"I know." Nex's face crumpled, and he pressed his forehead against hers. "Don't be scared. I won't let her hurt you. I won't let anything happen to you, Katherine. You're safe with me."

Unsure what to say or how to feel about what he did for her, she stared. Safe with him. It seemed silly to believe she was safe with a demon. Except she did feel safe with him.

Gazing into her eyes, he let his anger fade, and he stepped back, offering a hand. "I'm sorry she hurt you. I shouldn't have left you alone."

Kat took his hand and slid off the counter. Nex followed her to the main part of the house, where she picked up the groceries he bought and took them to the kitchen. She pulled out the wine, filled a glass, and took such a long drink that she had to refill it.

Nex walked into the kitchen, crossing his arms. "Say something."

"I don't know what to say. You . . . care about me?"

"I don't know how that hasn't been obvious given my relentless presence the last month." Nex stole her glass and set it down. "Do you not want me to care about you?"

"It's not that. I guess I'm surprised. I thought you felt sorry for me. I'm your ticket home, so you have to care to some degree."

Nex brought his hand under her jaw and tilted it up. "No, Katherine. When I feel sorry for someone, I don't—" He sighed and dropped his arms to his sides. "I don't do what I've been doing. I'm not like this."

"But Lilith said if you had me killed, you could go home. You didn't know me when you first got here. Why didn't you have me killed?"

"Because it took very little time to see you're everything good in this world. I may be a demon, but I've only punished those who are evil. Not the ones who are good."

"So . . ." A smile tugged on her lips. "You're a big softie, huh?"

Nex scowled. "For fuck's sake."

"It's so sweet!"

"Shut up, kitten." Nex tried not to smile at her playful expression.

"And you care about me, too."

"I'm beginning not to as much."

Kat shrugged. "I don't believe you. But I do wonder . . ."

"What?"

Confidence fading, she turned away. "Nothing."

He spun her to face him. "What?"

She bit her lip, her breathing erratic. "I wonder about the way in which you care."

Nex ran his thumb over the lip she held hostage until it was released. "How do you want me to care?"

Kat blushed and avoided his eyes. "Should we have dinner?"

Nex grabbed her chin so she'd look at him. The firm grip elicited a tingle through her body that'd been missing for weeks.

"Answer my question, kitten." Nex stared like he could see right through her. "Do you want me to care for you the way I have been, or," he caressed her waist, "do you want more?"

"What does more entail?"

"More," Nex purred, rubbing his thumb over her lower lip. "If you don't know or don't want to tell me, you're clearly not ready." He moved away and grabbed ingredients from the grocery bags. "I'll make dinner."

Nex started cooking, but Kat couldn't move. Hadn't she decided not to let anyone close again? But Nex had been good to her for the last month, had taken care of her in ways she didn't know she needed. *He's also a demon.* It couldn't be a good idea to get involved with a demon who'd eventually go home. Yet, thinking about it made her crave to be close to him.

She didn't know what to make of it. Being with him was dangerous, but being without him sounded worse. Instead of letting her mind go crazy trying to figure out what she felt or what it meant, she poured another glass of wine and left the kitchen to put distance between them.

It didn't stop her from looking back at him. Hands braced on the counter, he stared straight ahead. His gaze darted to her. Heat rushed to her cheeks and more. She couldn't look away. He broke eye contact first. She missed it. His eyes brought more peace than she thought possible after the accident. Maybe it was silly to think she could feel safe and at peace with a demon, but Nex wasn't just a demon.

He was everything.

Chapter 21

A Church Friend

Since Lilith's visit, Nex rarely left Kat unguarded. That was why he left Arda with Kat, thinking Arda could handle anything. But Arda couldn't handle Katherine.

Nex came in view of Kat's house when Arda dashed outside, tears in her eyes. "What's wrong?" Nex listened for Kat's heartbeat inside.

"She's—She's . . ." Arda wiped her nose. "So *sweet* and genuine I can't take it. I want to keep her forever."

Nex groaned. "I thought something was wrong."

"She's pure, Nex. So pure."

Nex brushed past Arda, mumbling, "I'm aware."

An incredible scent hit him as he entered the house. Katherine stood at the kitchen island, adding raspberries to a tall, round chocolate cake.

He leaned his forearms on the counter. "What did you do to Arda?"

"Nothing. She had a lot of pent-up emotions." Kat adjusted a raspberry on the cake. "It's not good. It needs to be let out."

Nex regarded her with furrowed brows. It was the second time she'd played therapist for his demon friends. He clicked his tongue, eyeing the cake. "Another cake you're taking to church that I can't have?"

"Nope. This one's for you." Her smile had a bigger impact than he liked, but it wasn't enough for him to miss that there was something else behind this.

He straightened. "What do you want?"

Kat tucked her hands behind her back. "Nothing big. A little favor."

"A favor so little it needs bribing with a cake?"

"In the grand scheme of things, it's not a big deal, and it won't take much of your time."

"Spit it out."

"I have a friend that needs help moving furniture. It'll be fast. Getting rid of something old and putting in something new."

"What friend?"

"Bernice." She avoided his eyes. "She's very nice."

"How do you know her?"

"Uh . . ." Kat wrung her hands together and smiled sheepishly. "Church."

Nex walked past her to get a drink. "No."

"Please? She's super nice, and it'll only take a second. She's seventy-nine and lives alone."

Nex grabbed a bottle of whiskey. "Shouldn't church people help her?"

"She doesn't like asking for help or admitting her limitations, but she's comfortable with me, and you're so strong we wouldn't need to ask anyone else. You could do it yourself."

Nex snorted and grabbed a glass. "Not happening."

"Don't you want some of this cake?" Kat gestured to it like it was a big prize. "I made it from scratch."

"I'm not mingling with your church friends. It's against my religion."

Kat grabbed a knife and cut a small piece of cake. She held her hand under the slice to keep crumbs from falling. "At least try it," she tempted, holding out the slice. "I bet you change your mind. I make amazing chocolate cake."

Nex glared at the delicious-smelling cake. "If I try this, it means nothing. It does *not* mean I agree to do this for you."

"Fine." A taste could make him more lenient. Food always put him in a better mood, especially sugar.

Kat tried to hand it over, but Nex grasped her hand. Tugging her closer, he ate the cake from her palm, watching the blush spread over her face. Though he enjoyed her response, he was annoyed. She *did* make amazing chocolate cake.

Their eyes met, and the restraint he intended to have slipped. Her heart beat faster, her chest rising and falling with quick breaths. He couldn't stop himself from licking the crumbs that stuck to her fingers, making her pink cheeks bright red.

They stared at each other for a moment. Kat blinked and cleared her throat. "Well?"

"It's good." His tongue darted out and took the last crumb off her fingertip. "I'm still not going."

Kat sighed. "Fine. I'll ask someone else."

"You do that." He reached for his glass but paused.

Kat scrolled through the contacts on her phone, stopping at someone named Jeremiah. She tapped the contact, and her thumb moved over the "call" button.

"Who's Jeremiah?" He placed his hand on hers before she touched the "call" icon.

"Someone from church."

A muscle in Nex's jaw twitched. "Uh-huh. And what's he like?"

"He's nice." Kat pulled her phone away, arching an eyebrow. "He got stationed here a couple of weeks ago."

"Stationed here?"

"Mm-hmm. He's a marine. He's strong, so I won't need to ask more than one person. That'll put Bernice at ease, having fewer people. That, and she knows him, so there'll be familiarity."

Nex snatched her phone. "Fine. Your trap cake worked."

Kat beamed at him. "Really?"

"Unfortunately. When?"

"Now?"

"Fine. Let's get it over with. But I'm *not* doing small talk."

"Okay." Kat grinned. "Thank you."

Nex grumbled as she grabbed her coat. It wasn't right that she could get him to do things he wouldn't for anyone else. She wrapped her red scarf around her neck, inclining her head to the door. Disgruntled, he snatched his coat and followed her out.

On the street, Kat rubbed her hands together. Thanksgiving was close, as was winter. Fall was essentially gone, and the cold had settled in. Leaves were brown instead of colorful, fallen to the ground and crunching under every step. Kat shivered, hugging herself. Nex fought the urge to bring her close and warm her.

Nearing Bernice's house, they also drew closer to Katherine's church. The sight of it made Nex tense, but they stayed on the opposite side of the street.

"Bernice is nice, but she's a little blunt."

"Your opposite then."

"I guess. Definitely not shy."

"If she starts talking about religion, I'm out."

"I doubt she will. She's not pushy. Well . . ." Kat scrunched her face, remembering countless times Bernice had been pushy. "She's not pushy about *that*, anyway."

While Nex wondered what she meant, he didn't have time to ask. Kat skipped up to a house and knocked. An older woman with a gray bun and glasses barely holding onto the tip of her nose opened the door. She smiled warmly at Kat, then shifted her gaze to Nex.

"Hi. This is Nex." Kat gestured to him.

"Oh, *this* is Nex," Bernice said with a knowing smile. "I've heard a lot about you." She surveyed him. "Quite a lot. Come in." She opened the door wider and stepped aside.

"Quite a lot?" Nex asked.

Cheeks more red from embarrassment than cold, Kat murmured, "From the neighbors."

Nex gave her a side-eye and followed her inside.

Bernice touched his arm as he passed. "It's not from the neighbors. She talks about you all the time. All I hear about anymore is *my sweet Nex did this or that for me today.*"

A smile twitched on Nex's lips.

Kat hid her face in her hands. "*Bernice.*"

"What?" Bernice shrugged. "You're the one telling a lie. This way, dears." She shuffled down the hallway. "Do you want something warm to drink? I've put the kettle on. Should be hot soon."

Kat followed Bernice and avoided looking at Nex. "Sure. Thank you."

They entered a small kitchen with not much in it except a round table in the corner. Christmas decorations were already in place—red and white candles and garland strung off the little wall shelves holding crystal angel figurines. Kat sunk into a chair and leaned over the table, keeping a curtain of hair as protection from Nex's stare.

More than amused, Nex set his hand on the table right beside hers, bending down next to her ear. "I'm sweet, am I?"

"You can be," Kat muttered. "She's exaggerating."

"Nex, do you want some tea, dear?" Bernice asked.

"I'm afraid I only like tea if it has whiskey in it."

"Whiskey I don't have. Would brandy do?"

Nex cocked an eyebrow. "Yes, thanks. What needs moving?"

"Oh, I'll show you." Bernice turned toward the hallway. "Katherine dear, you can manage the tea, can't you?"

"Of course."

Bernice patted Nex's arm. "Right this way."

She led him toward the front entrance but took him through a door on the left into a garage. Inside was a couch that wasn't new but appeared nice.

"I'm replacing my couch before my family comes in for Thanksgiving. Someone from church was getting rid of theirs, and it's much nicer than mine." She crossed the hall to a living room. "I need you to bring in the new one and leave this old one on the curb." She waved at the couch. "The city's picking it up in the morning."

Nex nodded and strode past her to the worn couch that had seen too many years. Faded in color, the couch had threads hanging from seams that were about to burst. He expected Bernice to return to Katherine, but she didn't.

She tilted her head, staring at him. "There's something different about you." Her intense scrutiny unsettled him. She squinted in a way that implied she was figuring something out. "You're not from around here, are you?" Nex shook his head. "Your name," she continued, "is interesting. Unique."

Nex circled the couch to get in position to push it out the door. "My upbringing was unique."

"Hmm. Back when I was in school, knowing your Latin roots was required."

After placing his hands on the arms of the couch, Nex hesitated. He met her gaze. *How much Latin does she know?*

"It's strange your parents would name you after death. I wonder why they did that."

"I wouldn't know. I had no say in it." He analyzed her scent. She was too tuned into him, but she was completely human.

"I'm glad you were there when that asshole did whatever he did," Bernice said. "Katherine wouldn't tell me what, but I know her, and I know it was bad."

Nex's eyebrows shot up.

Bernice laughed. "When you get as old as me, you stop caring what people think about the way you talk. I'm happy she has you." She turned for the door. "I think you're good for her. She needs a real man. It's good you're waiting for her. Just don't forget, *ex nihilo nihil fit.*"

She left without waiting for his response, and he was relieved she did.

Out of nothing, nothing is produced. A phrase to remember that achieving anything meaningful can only happen with hard work. He stared after her, then decided he needed to move fast and get the fuck out of there. Sometimes humans had another sense, and Bernice definitely noticed he wasn't all he seemed.

Old couch outside, he returned to the garage for the new one, shaking his head. The fact Katherine had him doing all these things for her grated on his nerves. She had too much control over him.

Indents in the carpet from the last couch gave him a guide for placement of the new one. Once the furniture was in place, he dusted his hands off and headed to the hallway. He could only hope to get Katherine to leave quickly.

Kat came around the doorway with a mug in her hands and nearly ran into him. "Oh, sorry." She extended the mug. "Bernice told me to bring you this."

"Oh, look at that!" Bernice clapped and pointed up.

Kat followed her direction. Mistletoe hung in the doorway. Directly above Kat and Nex.

"Uh . . ." Kat went to step aside, but Bernice placed a hand on her back.

"Now, Katherine, don't be shy." Bernice swiped the mug from Kat. "Who wouldn't want to kiss this handsome young man? You don't want to break tradition, do you?"

Despite the woman making him a little uncomfortable, Nex liked her. "Yeah, kitten. Don't you respect tradition?"

Kat's cheeks burned. His attention shifted to her lips, his eyes darkening. He lifted his gaze to hers and stepped closer. Out of the corner of his eye, Bernice backed away, leaving them alone. She wasn't so bad after all.

"What's wrong?" Nex set one hand on Kat's waist; the other, he lifted to her face. "Did you hate kissing me so much the first time?"

"No." Kat's gaze drifted to his lips before coming back to his eyes. "I didn't hate it."

He leaned closer, his nose nuzzling hers. "Does that mean you liked it?"

"I—I don't know." *Why have my lungs forgotten how to work?* "It happened so long ago. I can barely remember."

"You know I can tell when you're lying." He inhaled her scent—vanilla and pear. "It's one of my many gifts." He curled his fingers around the back of her neck. "But very well, kitten. I'll play along. You don't remember. I think that means I need to refresh your memory." He inched closer, lips almost touching hers. "Doesn't it?"

Kat hesitated. Nex scared her. Not because he was a demon, but because she felt so much with him. Something he said before was right: He made her feel out of control. But he also made her feel whole.

"It . . ." Kat licked her lips, her tongue grazing his lips in the process. His grip on her waist and neck tightened, making her want more. "It wouldn't hurt."

"Wouldn't hurt?" Nex chuckled, dragging his nose to her jaw, then to her ear, where he whispered, "You can do better than that, kitten. Do you want me to refresh your memory or not?"

He pressed his forehead to hers. Every dark fleck in his amber eyes made them so much more beautiful and complex, a pattern she wanted to explore. Whether it was a conscious decision or not, she lifted her hands to his shoulders. Hard muscles and tendons made her fingers itch to explore more.

"Maybe." The word was quiet, most of her body's energy directed to her pounding heart.

"I'll accept a maybe, this once." His lips brushed hers. "Next time, I expect a *yes*."

He pressed his lips against hers, and she melted into him. Holding her closer, he dug his fingers into her lower back and slid a hand to the back of her head. Kat locked her hands around his neck, deepening the kiss.

Their first kiss took her breath away, but it had nothing on this one. Every emotion she'd held back poured into this kiss, making it more intimate. Nex's tongue caressed the seam of her lips, asking for entrance.

She granted him access, opening her mouth for his tongue to slide in. His tongue glided along hers, eliciting an involuntary sound from Kat. Kissing her harder, Nex pushed her against the doorframe. He cupped her face, devouring her with the starving hunger he'd contained for weeks.

His hands moved down her neck, along her shoulders, and over her waist. He dug his fingers into her hips, pulling her closer. The trail of his hands, coupled with his tight grip, left Kat's body aware of every movement, sending her nerves into a state of pleasant tension.

When his teeth grazed her lower lip, sucking it in and biting down, she let out a small whimper. He soothed the bite with a sweep of his tongue and a rougher kiss. His hand tangled in her hair and held her in place as he kissed harder, seeking more, never getting enough of her soft lips.

The kiss, his hands, the doorframe, it became so much Kat couldn't breathe. She thought she was breathless before, but this added intensity, the way he pinned her to the doorframe . . . His affection stole the air from her lungs, and she couldn't get it back. She broke the kiss, panting and leaning her forehead against his.

Some of her embarrassment faded as she gazed up at him. He was as out of breath as her. They didn't move, only stared at one another, neither wanting to look away.

Ever so slowly, Nex's lips curled into a smirk. "I never cared for tradition, but I could get used to this one." He kissed her forehead. "You have no idea what you do to me."

"I do something to you?"

He nodded, rubbing his thumb across her cheek.

Dishes clattered, and she remembered where they were. Embarrassment for kissing him like that in someone else's house cleared her clouded thoughts. "We, uh, we should go. You're done, aren't you?"

Nex nodded, watching her so closely she couldn't help the blush.

She darted her eyes away. "Let's say goodbye." Kat hurried down the hall, setting her hands on her cheeks in an attempt to cool them. For once, she was eager to go out in the cold. Maybe the icy wind would soothe her overheated body.

Bernice smiled, sipping tea at the table. "All done?"

Kat pressed her lips together. "All done. I'll see you Wednesday?"

"You will." Bernice craned her neck to see Nex, who stood behind Katherine. "Thank you, my dear. I appreciate it."

Nex gave her a small smile since she was the reason he tasted Katherine's sweet lips again.

Bernice rose from the table and kissed Kat's cheek, hugging her. "I don't know what I'd do without you, Katherine. You're a blessing to me." She pulled back with a warm smile, and Kat went down the hallway.

Bernice stepped toward Nex, and he tensed at the impending hug. She laughed and offered a hand, which he took. "Thank you, dear. Have a wonderful evening."

"You too."

Nex frowned when she pressed something into his palm. He glanced down, finding mistletoe.

Bernice winked. "Everyone should have one in the house."

Nex gripped the mistletoe. The next time this human needed something, he wouldn't mind helping her.

Chapter 22

Point of No Return

Covered in flour and splatters of the many dishes she was making, Kat rushed around the kitchen. Aromas of turkey, cranberry sauce, and cinnamon wafted through the house, mixing in a mouthwatering combination. She slid pumpkin pies into the oven and turned to finish the cranberries.

The loud music she'd been playing shut off, and Nex crossed his arms. "Kitten, this is ridiculously unnecessary."

"You and the guys have never had a real Thanksgiving dinner," Kat said. "Of course it's necessary. Thanksgiving food is the *best* food."

"You're missing Thanksgiving with your church friends. That doesn't bother you?"

"I already talked to them, and they're fine." Kat pouted. "Why don't you want my Thanksgiving dinner?"

"Don't fucking pou—" Nex groaned. "Fuck. I don't not want it. It just seems like an awful amount of trouble to feed four people."

Kat stirred orange zest into the cranberries. "I don't mind. Mom, Dad, and I used to do it for the three of us, so there's one more than I'm used to."

Nex frowned and leaned over the kitchen island. One of the things he'd learned was she avoided subjects that upset her rather than talking about them. Trying to bring them up was dangerous.

"You all right, kitten? Trying to distract yourself?"

"I'm fine." Kat's gaze stayed on the cranberries. "Holidays are hard. I miss them more at holidays, and this is my first Thanksgiving without them. I would . . . like to not think about it too hard."

"Will having us here help?"

Kat moved the pan of cranberry sauce to an unused burner, avoiding his gaze. "Maybe."

"Then I'll stop asking. How can I help?"

"You want to help?"

"Might as well. I can't watch TV with your loud music anyway."

"You've fallen right into my plans." Kat giggled. "You're so easy to trap."

A growl rumbled in his chest and made her heart flutter. "Watch it. Don't make me make you pay for that."

"What does that mean? Paying for it?"

"Test me and find out."

Kat stilled, peeking at him from under her lashes. "Seems like a dangerous idea to get into anything with you without knowing what the possibilities are."

"There are lots of possibilities. One being I bend you over where you stand. Want to know what I'd do after that?"

Kat's eyes widened. She tried to ignore the way her body responded, the slight clenching. Clearing her throat, she gestured to the veggies. "They need to be chopped and arranged on a platter."

Nex would've retorted that it didn't matter how the vegetables were arranged, but he could sense her reaction and redirected his energy into the veggie tray, so he wouldn't act on it. He'd restrain himself while she healed. Something that grew more difficult after their mistletoe kiss.

Working close to her didn't help. In the small kitchen, they continuously bumped into or brushed against each other. Each time they came into the smallest amount of contact, Kat blushed and looked away. The tension increased by the second, to the point Nex went outside to breathe.

Lucian and Marcus's arrival was a relief for Kat. Being alone with Nex hadn't been easy since their kiss, and his comment didn't help. Between the warmth from the heater and the oven, Kat changed to a dress, not bothering with leggings. She made the table nice with a fall-colored centerpiece and cloth placemats, keeping space between her and Nex lest she bump into him again and risk the friction throwing her body into a fit of neediness.

Getting them all to sit and eat together without the TV on was a victory for Kat. Lucian and Marcus didn't get why they were doing it, but they wouldn't turn down good food. They both had a soft spot for the human who fed them, gave them sugar, and was always kind to them in a way no one ever had been.

When they finished dinner, Kat cleared the table and went to the kitchen to get the pies.

Kat distracted, Lucian leaned across the table toward Nex. *Lilith isn't here anymore*, Lucian said. *She's back in the underworld.*

Are you sure? Nex caught Kat in the corner of his eye. In the kitchen, cutting the pies, she was oblivious to the exchange.

Positive. Lucian nodded. *There was a surge in souls after this last human conflict. So many at once that she was ordered to return to handle it. It's going to take up a bit of her time.*

Nex rose from the table. *Let me know anything else you hear. And if she comes back.*

Nex strode into the kitchen, where Kat placed slices of pumpkin pie on plates. She sprayed canned whipped cream on each piece, then sprayed some on her finger and licked it off. She didn't have sugar often and loved whipped cream. Distracted by spraying more on her finger, she didn't notice Nex until he grabbed her wrist and brought her finger to his mouth.

Taking his time, he sucked her finger longer than necessary. He stared at her, swirling his tongue around her finger, gently biting the tip before letting it go and watching her face turn a shade of red that rivaled her hair.

"What? You can't have all the fun." He snatched the can and sprayed his own finger.

Kat's breath hitched when he raised it to her lips. Her gaze darted between him and his finger. Decency dictated she shouldn't do what he clearly wanted and what she secretly desired.

"Open." His demanding tone, which normally drove her crazy and made her rebellious, had a vastly different effect.

Kat opened her mouth and let his finger in, cleaning it with her tongue, unable to stop herself from lightly sucking. Nex removed his finger, his darkened eyes leaving more than just her cheeks warm. Breathless, she wanted to squeeze her legs together to ease the ache that had grown all day and now spiked. She couldn't tear her eyes away from him, and his intense stare didn't let her.

"Are you guys bringing dessert or what?" Marcus called.

His voice snapped Kat out of it, and she grabbed two plates, rushing to the table with Nex behind her. They ate pie while Marcus told a story about a time he almost had Thanksgiving dinner. He was sent after someone who'd embezzled money from a charity and was funding a group of demon hunters. Unfortunately, Marcus didn't get dinner because things turned messy.

In normal circumstances, the story would've riveted Kat, but she couldn't stop looking at Nex. She was magnetized to him. Not looking at him wasn't an option. Every time her attention drifted to him, Nex felt it and met her gaze. The moment their eyes locked, Kat would look away, wishing she had something to fan herself with. She crossed her legs and took a long drink of water, offering smiles to Marcus as he told his story.

Lucian and Marcus disagreed about what really happened that day, and during their argument, Kat felt Nex's gaze on her. Her breaths were deliberate so they could stay under control. *How did the house get so hot when it's freezing outside?*

Then, contact. Nex's knuckles brushed her exposed knee. The graze may have been at her knee, but the sensation spread everywhere. His electric touch sent a bolt right up her legs. She sucked in a breath and peered at him, finding that intense stare waiting.

"Give me the word, and I'll tell them to take their ridiculous argument elsewhere." Nex's eyes flitted to her lips briefly, his hand covering her knee.

Mouth dry, Kat struggled to speak. "They're fine."

His hand on her skin wasn't helping her stay focused, so she got up to clean. When the demons finished dessert, Marcus and Lucian turned on the TV, and Nex joined Kat in cleaning.

Marcus and Lucian provided a decent buffer, but their presence ended too quickly, leaving Nex and Kat alone with the TV on. Nex sent Kat to sit down, saying he'd finish cleaning—an attempt to put distance between them. The growing tension weakened his resolve. He wanted nothing more than to slide his hands up her dress.

Kat's feet hurt from spending the whole day cooking, so she protested little before curling up on the couch, watching the show Marcus and Lucian left on. Unfamiliar with it, she was caught off guard when a sex scene began. She sat up, searching for the remote to change the station but couldn't find it.

Nex appeared beside the couch, making her squeal and jump up. "What's wrong, kitten?" He held up the remote. "Not your kind of show?"

"It's unrealistic." She huffed, snatched the remote, and switched the TV off.

"How?"

"Sex isn't . . . like that." She waved at the TV.

"Your experience with sex was bad. That doesn't make sex itself bad."

"I can't imagine it feeling good."

"That's because you haven't had the right person touching you."

Nex returned to the kitchen, and Kat sunk into the couch, hiding her face. Every interaction left her craving to be closer to him. Wanting to be physically close to someone was foreign. Her entire body ached for attention from him. She thought back to his expression when she'd cleaned the whipped cream off his finger, and it did nothing to help the arousal crawling under her skin.

Embarrassment wore off as much as it was going to, and she wanted a cup of tea before bed. Nex was almost done with the dishes, and she avoided him as she got out her cup and a tea bag. She started the kettle, and the quietness hit her. The sink wasn't running anymore. She meant to turn, but Nex came up behind her, flattening his palms against the counter on either side of her, caging her in.

He picked up the tea bag and turned it, chuckling as he read the words "stress relief". "What's wrong, kitten? Need some relief?" He dragged his fingers up her arm to her shoulder, leaving a trail of fire on her skin despite the sleeves of her dress shielding her.

"Everyone needs to relax." Kat's eyes shut as he traced his finger back down her arm. How could a simple touch make her breathless?

"I can help you relax." Nex grabbed her hips and spun her. He lifted her onto the counter and stepped between her legs. Kat's mouth fell open, but she made no move to get down. He held up the whipped cream can. "Sugar makes everything better." Coating his finger with cream, he then held it in front of her lips. "Open."

Maybe there should've been hesitation, but there wasn't. She let him in. Nex had to stop himself from moaning at the sight of her lips wrapped around his finger, at the feel of her hot, wet mouth. His eyes darkened as her tongue swirled around. Her eyes dilated, her heart rate accelerated, and he could smell the sweet scent of her building arousal.

"You like that, kitten? Sucking my finger?"

Kat nodded. His finger slipped out and rubbed against her lower lip, intensifying her blush. More whipped cream applied, he brought his finger back to her lips. She didn't need prompting this time. She opened her mouth, and his finger slid in. He waited until she stopped sucking, dragged his finger out, and returned his hands to the counter.

"You like that?" His eyes bored into hers in a way that had her needing to look away and yet, not wanting to. "Would you like it as much if I was the one licking it off your skin?"

Kat licked her lips, overwhelmed by a combination of sensations—a flutter of nervousness, a burn of excitement, an ache in her heart and body to be close to him. She gulped. "Maybe."

He grabbed her jaw so she'd look at him. "What'd I say?" His darkened eyes demanded an answer. "I said, next time, I expected a *yes*. Would you like that, Katherine?"

Kat sucked her bottom lip into her mouth, biting down. The thought of his mouth on her . . . "Yes."

Nex waited for her eyes to make their way back to his, desire evident. Another jolt of excitement ran through Kat as Nex tilted her head to the side and up. She inhaled sharply when he sprayed whipped cream on her jaw and neck, leaving a trail down to her collarbone. What had her breathing harder was when he dragged his tongue from her collarbone up her neck to her jaw, licking her skin clean, his mouth closing around parts of her neck that had her clamping her thighs together and fighting the urge to moan.

"It tastes so much fucking better coming off your skin." He groaned, placing a wet kiss against her neck before lifting his head and cupping her face.

That eye contact. That stare. It held more power than she was ready for. He leaned closer, and she couldn't stop herself from curling her hands around his forearms. Nex nipped at her lips and rested his forehead against hers, thumbs rubbing her heated cheeks. They stared at each other, panting breaths mingling.

This moment was different from the others. There was no underlying guise of lessons or mistletoe or sneaky friends pushing them together; it was just them. Alone. Alone and craving to be close. The point of no return. Every passing second they stared at one another in such close proximity left the room more suffocating, like the only source of air would come from contact. Like the only oxygen they could breathe was each other's. Neither could take the tension any longer.

Kat's arms wrapped around Nex's neck, and his encircled her waist. Their lips colliding after the day of tension elicited a physical response, and Kat moaned. Hearing it drove Nex crazy, made him bolder. He slid his hands to her lower back, pulling her against him and making her whimper. His tongue slipped into her mouth, chasing after hers. Soft hands glided up his arms to the back of his head, knotting in the hair at the base of his neck.

Kat's body told her what she wanted, and her thighs pressed against his hips, bringing him closer. Nex grasped the back of her knee and draped her leg around him. She let out another whimper in their kiss and wrapped her other leg around him.

"Fuck." Nex groaned, breaking their kiss for a moment before pulling her into a firmer one. He gripped her ass and held her tight against the hardness straining at the front of his jeans, letting her feel the power she had over him. Kat gasped, and Nex traced his lips down her jaw to her neck. Moaning, she leaned her head back as he placed hot kisses against her skin.

"Kitten," Nex purred, sliding one of his hands under the hem of her dress, "let me show you how it feels to be touched by someone who appreciates you. I promise it's not unrealistic. I can make you feel so fucking good."

Kat inhaled, that ache growing into a throb as he slid his hand up her dress.

He paused and lifted his head, nuzzling her nose with his. "Let me touch you. Let me make you feel good. I'll replace that negative association." He kissed her lips, his next words a whispered reassurance. "I'll take care of you."

Kat hesitated, nervous, yet there was no doubt her body longed to let his ascension up her leg continue. All day, she'd craved his touch, to be close to him. She couldn't take it anymore. Anticipation fluttered through her body until she was nearly buzzing. She nodded. Nex grabbed the back of her head, kissing her while his hand slid to her inner thigh and up.

He didn't touch her right away. Instead, he rubbed circles against her inner thigh, slowly moving closer and closer until Kat whimpered, her hips reaching for him. He cupped her through her underwear, causing Kat to gasp and break the kiss. She wasn't expecting to feel so much with such little contact, but her body was on edge.

"So responsive, kitten," Nex murmured, kissing her neck.

He rubbed her through her underwear. Gentle at first, then firmer. Kat panted, squeezing her eyes shut. The moisture of her excitement seeped through the fabric, and Nex groaned, moving it aside and sliding his finger along her wetness.

"Fuck, you're so wet for me, kitten. I could slide into you so fucking easily." He nipped her neck as his finger circled her clit, gaining a loud cry from Kat.

She gripped his shoulders, letting out delightful sounds that left Nex's desire for her transforming into a necessity. Slowly, gently, he pushed a finger inside her, the sensation foreign and exciting to Kat. Every movement left her wanting more. Nex slid his finger in and out, and when her nails dug into his shoulders, he added a second. She moaned, and he thrust faster until he felt it, her clamping around him. Unfamiliar pressure built in her to the point she feared she might burst, but she'd only associated that sensation with one thing.

"Wait." Kat clutched his hand, stopping the movement.

Nex frowned. "What's wrong?"

"I think I have to go to the bathroom," she whispered.

"You think? Or you don't know what an orgasm feels like, and you panicked?"

"Does it feel like I have to pee?"

"It sometimes can when you're not used to it." Nex caressed her thigh.

"Trust me, kitten. I said I'd take care of you, didn't I?"

She did trust him. His eyes darted to where her hand was locked around his wrist, and she let go. Fisting her dress, her eyes slid shut as he continued. He pumped his fingers in and out until it happened again, that clamping, that intense pressure that had Kat's toes curling and her nails digging into her dress as her whole body tensed.

"Trust me, Katherine," Nex murmured, pulling her into an embrace as he kissed beneath her ear. "I've got you." He curled his fingers inside and held her close. "Come for me, kitten."

Kat tensed as the delightful pressure burst. Pleasure crashed in waves, making her throb as it released. She moaned and dropped her head against his shoulder, whimpering while she came. Nex groaned at her repeatedly clenching around his fingers. Breath ragged, she wrapped her arms around him the second his fingers left her, needing to be close after the intense experience.

"See?" He kissed her neck and hugged her. "That's how it should be, kitten. That's a taste of what real sex is like, and trust me," he grabbed her chin so she'd look at him, "sex is *much* better."

Chapter 23

Redo

Black Friday, Kat had to work a double shift at the bookstore. She got up earlier than usual, careful to be quiet as she got dressed. She looked back at Nex's sleeping form, her heart swelling and body warming at the memory of his touch.

Last night, after Nex gave Kat her first orgasm, she understood why people liked sex. It wasn't just that he made her feel incredible physically but also how he kissed and held her afterward. Panic surfaced once she came down from the high, but he kissed her slowly, deeply, dissipating her fears. She wasn't sure what to expect, but he carried her to bed where they slept close, his arm draped over her waist and her head in his chest. She couldn't remember the last time she felt so comfortable and close to someone.

She shook her head to focus for the busy day ahead, quietly shutting the bedroom door after stepping out. He liked his sleep. She knew that based on the fact he hated the alarm clock more than anything, but that didn't stop her not wanting to leave without saying something. She was buttoning her coat when Nex appeared in front of her.

Kat squealed and fell back against the wall. "Didn't I tell you to stop doing that?"

"Yes, but I ignored your request." He braced his palms against the wall on either side of her head. "Were you leaving without saying goodbye?"

"I didn't want to bother you."

"The only thing that bothers me is that you were going to leave without saying goodbye." He skimmed his nose alongside hers. "You're not going to miss me?" He moved to her neck, dragging his nose up and down.

Kat shuddered. "Of course I am."

"I was hoping to ease more tension before you left." Open-mouth kisses on her neck melted her into him. "Would you like that, kitten? Would you like me to touch you like I did last night?"

Kat's eyes closed as he placed a hand on one side of her neck while kissing the other. His other hand dropped to her lower back and pulled her against him. Work was a priority, but she couldn't resist tilting her head back, giving him better access. Containing a moan wasn't easy. He knew how to touch, how to kiss, and where to place his lips, making her too warm to wear the coat she had on.

"Yes." Her eyes fluttered when he sucked on her neck. "But I can't right now. I have work."

"Be a rebel," Nex said, teeth scraping her skin. "Be a few minutes late."

"I can't." Kat bit back a whimper while he nipped a sensitive part of her neck. "Not on Black Friday."

"Kitten." His mouth moved over her throat, tongue darting across her skin. "Do you like what I'm doing?"

Kat set her hands on his chest with the intent to push him away, but she couldn't. "Like you can't tell."

"Well, if you like that," he kissed her, sliding his tongue into her mouth, eliciting a moan, "imagine how much you'll like it when I use my tongue instead of my fingers." He slid his hand up her dress to her thigh. "Why don't you stay home today? Then you won't have to imagine."

Kat usually only called in for work when it was an emergency. It never crossed her mind to call in because she had better things to do. Until Nex. He made a compelling argument, but it didn't change the fact it was Black Friday.

"I can't." She was convinced his dark eyes held the answers to the mysteries of the universe. If only she could stay home to uncover them all. "I'd rather be with you, but I can't leave my boss to the crowds."

"Fine." Nex removed his hand from under her skirt. "I take it my plan to show you that good sex isn't unrealistic worked."

"You've given me something to think about." Heat radiated off her skin with the same intensity she cursed her work obligations. Unable to think clearly, she scooted away. "I've gotta go. I'll be home later than usual tonight."

Nex crossed his arms and propped one shoulder against the wall, his gaze never leaving her. "Very well, kitten. I'll see you tonight."

Kat backed toward the door, waving on her way out. Outside, she released a long breath and leaned back against the door. Her eyes closed, the ache between her legs worse now she knew how good Nex could make her feel. She allowed a moment to get ahold of her mind, then rushed to work.

Black Friday was the worst day for anyone who worked in retail. Crazy, loud, rude customers were an effective bucket of cold water. Loathing consumerism took her mind off Nex enough to focus. Not thinking about him was easy when the more pressing matter was getting two people to stop fighting over a book.

The day dragged, the only bright spot when snow started falling. Kat watched glittering flakes coat the street and daydreamed about being outside instead of around entitled customers. Had Nex ever built a snowman? She laughed, picturing his expression if she asked him to make a snow angel.

God, I can't stop thinking about him. Even during the busy workday, her thoughts drifted to him. The way he touched her, kissed her, held her afterward as if he knew how much she needed reassurance.

When she'd thought about being close to someone like that, she'd never considered the other parts of it. The aftercare. Plenty of people had cared for her, but he took care of her in ways she was unaware she wanted until it was done. Sleeping close elevated both her emotional and now physical attachment.

Kat tried to stop her thoughts from going to Nex, but she couldn't. She wanted to be close to him so much that every time the door chimed, she was disappointed it wasn't him. She was surprised he didn't show up during her long day. He usually came by to drive her insane while she worked.

The day came to an end, and Kat sent Connie, the owner, home after offering to close. It took longer than she liked, but she made it out and locked the shop. White flakes still fell, but thankfully not so heavily that walking home would be awful.

She trudged through the snow, regretting not wearing boots that could handle it. Her feet grew wetter and colder with each step. Walking in clothes that weren't snow-ready, she no longer fantasized about building a snowman. Instead, she longed for a warm bath.

Passing her church, Kat smiled at how pretty it looked with snow covering the roof and steeple. Streetlamps illuminated the snow, making it sparkle and creating a picture so perfect it'd be at home on a Christmas card.

A chill different from the cold caused Kat to stiffen. An instinct warning that someone was watching.

She paused and looked around, but it was late. The sidewalks were abandoned. Occasionally, a car drove by, but no one else was on foot. Kat was the only person crazy enough to walk in this weather. She took in her surroundings one more time before moving forward, her footsteps crunching in the snow one of the few sounds in the night.

Kat tried to shake the feeling, but it wouldn't leave. Oddly, she wasn't unsettled, only aware. Being watched was something that would normally unsettle her, and by some strange twist of logic, she was unsettled by her lack of unsettledness. She paused, gaze sweeping the shadows, where the streetlights didn't reach.

This time, she saw something. In her church. Movement by the window. Then nothing. Someone inside at this hour surprised her, but Pastor

Brighton often went to the church when the weather wasn't good, in case anyone needed somewhere warm to dry off. That must've been what it was.

By the time she got home, Kat was ready for a hot drink and dry clothes. Pausing under the covered porch, she removed her wet boots and socks so she wouldn't track snow inside. She opened the door, let her shoulders slump from the stress of the day, and left her work annoyances outside.

Inside, the lights were off. Multiple candles created a warm, relaxing glow throughout the house. Nex approached and handed her a glass of wine, then helped remove her coat.

Kat's heart raced. "What's going on?"

"This," Nex hung her coat on the hook by the door, "is a redo. If you'll have it."

"A redo?"

"Yes. A redo. How your first time should've gone."

Kat's racing heart slowed to a stop. "You can't redo a first time."

"You're the one who gets to decide that, Katherine." He set his hands on her waist. "What do you say? Will you let me show you how you deserved it to go?" He cradled her face, staring into her eyes in a way that made her both calm and jittery. "Will you let me show you how good it can be?"

Kat's heart thumped. She glanced at the candles, then down at the glass of wine. She didn't know she'd ever want to have sex again, but all day she craved him, and it wasn't just physical. Her craving to be close to him was based on more than how good he could make her feel.

It was him. All of him.

Nex waited for an answer. Kat wished she would've realized with Jason the nervousness was because she wasn't ready, because he didn't ignite her like Nex did. The current nervousness was anticipation.

In a twist of fate, she had a demon standing in front of her, wanting her. There should've been a part of her that said this wasn't a good idea. He would go home eventually, and the closer she got to him, the more that would hurt. That, and he was a demon.

Except she didn't see him that way. He wasn't just a demon. He was Nex. He was everything, and if she couldn't have him forever, she wanted to spend the time she had with him as close as possible, so she could hang onto it after he was gone. They'd already passed the point of no return. There was no going back, and she didn't want to.

Kat took a long sip of wine and met his gaze, etching every millimeter of his face in her mind. In a quiet voice filled with more confidence than either expected, she answered, "Yes."

Chapter 24

Whole

Nex took the wine from Katherine and set it down. Cupping her face, he kissed her. They'd already kissed, but this was more—a promise from him to her that he would cherish her giving herself to him, emphasized by his slow but deep, firm yet tender movements. Kat leaned into him, and he glided his tongue across her lips while she wrapped her arms around his neck.

Nex carried her to the bedroom, where more candles flickered. Setting her down next to the bed, he slid his hand into her hair, pulling her deeper and kissing her more intimately than he ever had with anyone. When he broke away, Kat was breathless, blinking glazed eyes up at him as that first touch of pink reached her freckled face.

He ran his thumbs over her cheekbones and placed a gentler kiss on her lips. "Do you trust me, Katherine?" Kat nodded, and a smile tugged the corner of Nex's lips. "Good. Then let me lead."

He disappeared from her line of sight but kept his hand on her waist as he circled behind her. Gathering her hair to the side revealed her dress's zipper.

Nex placed his mouth where her shoulder met her neck, eliciting goose-bumps. "Your skin is so soft," he murmured, unzipping her dress and peppering kisses along her shoulder.

The dress fell open. Cold air breezed over Kat's spine. Nex set his hands on her shoulders, banishing the chill, so she was more than warm. Still, shivers rippled through her body at every sweep of his fingertips. Sudden self-consciousness struck her. *How many people has he been with?* She didn't know what she was doing, and he was experienced. *Don't overthink it.* Tension manifested in the lift of her shoulders and stiffened posture.

Nex rubbed her shoulders. "Relax, Katherine. I'll take care of you."

Knowing he paid enough attention to notice relieved her. Nex traced his hands down her shoulders, pushing the dress off. Her breathing lost all sense of normalcy. His hands descended her arms, and the dress pooled at her feet. He pecked her shoulder, then circled in front of her and leaned in for another long, deliberate kiss.

He wouldn't rush the night. For her, he could move slow.

Pulling back, he drank in her almost naked torso. He drew a single finger from below her belly button, up between her breasts, and around the curve of one hidden beneath her white bra. The hardened peak underneath was obvious through the almost sheer material. "You're so beautiful."

Nex sank to his knees, kissing above where her leggings rested, then lower as he brought them down, placing the final kiss on the front of her underwear. He admired her smooth skin and dragged the leggings all the way down.

While she stepped out of them, he trailed kisses up her stomach. His lips pressed to hers, vowing more with a kiss than he ever could with words. One hand on her waist, he stroked her bare skin. The other hand rested on her neck, where every movement of his fingers against a sensitive spot rewarded him with another hitch in her breathing.

Each touch was light and teasing, the effect anything but. Everywhere his hands went, they left tingles and turned Kat into a mess of anticipation. She didn't know what to expect from him, but this kind of tenderness caught her by surprise.

His lips brushed her shoulder as he moved behind her again, fingers brushing the top of her increasingly damp underwear. Goosebumps erupted, following Nex's lips. Kat's eyes fluttered as he placed a wet kiss against her neck. His hands moved up, following the cups of her bra, his fingers sneaking underneath the fabric as he made his way toward the straps. Bra straps down, he kissed the newly exposed area.

He traced the band of her bra, and his fingertips found the hooks. "Katherine?"

"Yes?"

"You have the most beautiful body I've ever seen." He unhooked her bra, and it fell away. "Perfect," he whispered, kissing her shoulder, hand grazing the side of her breast.

Kat's breath caught, and Nex came in front of her. His tongue glided along her neck, his thumb caressing the underside of her breast. Kat's eyes shut, then widened when he lifted and laid her in the middle of the bed. He kissed her so deeply it pushed her back into the mattress. His tongue slipped between her lips, and she moaned. Hands moved over her body teasingly, never touching her where she wanted it most.

Sat back between her legs, he removed his shirt in one movement. She'd seen him shirtless, but not like this. The instinct to look away out of embarrassment was still there, but she didn't. Her gaze swept over his exposed torso. Broad chest, skin tight against the hard ridges of his abs that worked almost like a funnel, directing her down to a dusting of dark hair that continued beneath his pants. She sucked in her lower lip, biting down as she imagined how he'd feel against her.

Enjoying the way she grew nervous under his scrutiny, Nex took in the sight of her almost naked beneath him. He could've stared at her longer, but instead, he lowered himself, and their skin met.

Kat sighed at his chest against her bare breasts. They'd barely done anything, and already she felt so close to him. One look in his darkened eyes and the pressure of something hard pushing on her stomach told her the desire wasn't one-sided. A new level of intensity took over with such little clothing separating them.

Nex continued his gentle caress on the side and underside of her breast, and she arched her back. He cupped her breast and squeezed, pleased at the pounding of her elevated heart rate. He moved his lips to the hollow of her neck, where he could feel her pulse. "Beautiful."

He scattered kisses down her body to her underwear. Looking up, he made sure she was watching as his fingers hooked the elastic of their last remaining barrier. An unsteady breath escaped her while he dragged the underwear down. The exposure made her press her thighs together.

He caressed her calf, his mouth grazing her knee. "Open up for me, kitten." His lips moved up her thighs, and her eyes widened.

"You're not going to . . ." He'd mentioned it earlier, but mentioning it and doing it were different.

"Taste you? Yes, I am. If you spread your legs for me. Trust me. You'll like it."

Hiding her face was her first instinct, but she flexed her hands against the sheets. She wanted his mouth on her, though she didn't know why. It seemed so intimate for someone to put their mouth there. *Intimacy is the point.* She opened her legs, less nervous when a smile formed on his full lips. He kissed up her inner thigh at a torturous pace until he made it between her legs.

Kat sucked in a breath and arched her body, tilting her head back and moaning. Last night felt good, but this consumed her whole body to the point she couldn't stop her legs quivering. "Nex." She gripped the sheets and squirmed under his ministrations. He licked and sucked at varying pressures over the most sensitive parts of her, finding the combination that had her writhing.

Writhing for him. Exactly what he wanted. He'd need to do this every day, if only for the chance to have her moaning his name like that.

Nex found his rhythm, and Kat was overwhelmed at how fast she fell apart. Every sweep of his tongue made her shudder. She wanted to clamp her legs together for release but open them more so he wouldn't stop. The sounds escaping were beyond her control, and she forced her lips closed, embarrassed at how loud she was.

"Don't." Nex stared up like he could see her soul. "Don't be quiet. I want to hear what I do to you." He kissed her clit, and her toes curled. "You want me to keep going?"

"Yes." She was desperate for him to continue.

He slung her legs over his shoulders. "Then don't be quiet."

Kat was so sensitive, she almost burst from the relief of his mouth on her again. Instinct took over, and she twisted her fingers in his hair. A hummed approval created vibrations that made her gasp. The pressure built, and she couldn't take it anymore. She clawed the sheets, hips rising to meet his mouth as the orgasm hit in throbbing waves.

It took her longer to recover than last night. "Oh. That was . . ." No words were powerful enough to describe it. "Wow."

"Told you you'd like it." Nex moved over her. "Trust me, remember?"

Kat nodded, and Nex bent, catching her in a kiss. His hand skimmed down her stomach and between her legs. Still sensitive from his mouth, she gasped. Nex smirked against her lips and circled her clit, lingering on the spots that made her cling to him.

He pushed a finger inside her. She shuddered, threading her hands in his hair as he kissed and sucked on her neck while sliding his finger in and out, eventually adding a second that elevated her neediness. That bursting pressure returned, and she moaned, raising her hips to his hand.

When he added a third finger, it was tight at first, but Nex moved gently until it felt as good as two. Right on the edge of release, Kat whimpered in protest when his hand withdrew.

"Don't worry." He traced her lips with his fingers. "It's for a reason."

Nex climbed off the bed and removed his pants and boxers. Heat flooded Kat's body. His hard shaft stood at attention, the candlelight enough for her to see every thick inch. It seemed big, but she didn't know a lot and was too shy to look at that part of him for long. He drew her eyes back to it anyway when he rolled a condom on. Anticipation turned to nervousness.

Would it hurt? Her mind spiraled, but Nex climbed over her and stroked from her cheekbone down to her neck.

"Don't," he whispered, kissing the corner of her mouth. "Don't be scared. I'll take care of you."

The tension faded under his kiss. His tongue invaded her mouth, his hands caressing the sides of her breasts to her hips. Euphoric pressure was the right amount to leave her wanting more, subconsciously raising her body to his touch.

He inserted a finger inside her again, and she fell out of the kiss. Her moans caused him to slide that finger in and out several times before adding a second that made her whimper—a sound Nex was growing addicted to.

"Are you ready?" His lips tickled the shell of her ear. "I won't hurt you. I promise."

Kat ached for him. All of him. He'd already made her explode with pleasure, so he must be good at the next part too. Nerves crawled through her body, and her muscles went rigid. She didn't want to think about the last time she tried this, but her brain betrayed her.

Nex pressed his body close to hers, holding her in a relaxing kiss. "I won't hurt you," he whispered. "I can make you feel good in other ways if you're too nervous to do this." He nuzzled her neck. "Your call, kitten. I have no problem making you moan my name with my tongue all night. Tell me what you want."

The last shred of fear dissolved, and she wrapped her arms around his neck. "I want you."

Nex hummed, smiling against her skin as he slid his fingers out of her. "I want you too. Spread your legs for me."

Kat opened her legs, and he adjusted himself. He teased her clit with his tip, then trailed it back to her entrance and pressed in enough that Kat inhaled sharply.

"Don't tense." His lips moved against her neck in patient reassurance. "You're so wet for me. I'm going to slide in easily. Don't worry."

"Will it hurt this time?"

"It might hurt to be stretched out, but it won't be anything like before. If it doesn't feel good, tell me. I want to know if it's not working for you. Sex is only as good as the communication about it. That means you tell me what you like and what you don't, all right?" Kat nodded, and Nex pressed himself against her core. "Ready?"

Kat's hands curled around his shoulders. "Yes."

He sank his tip in and kissed her. She clutched his shoulders, her body tensing. When she relaxed, he pushed in more and kept his lips on hers, never breaking their kiss. There was a small amount of uncomfortableness while Kat adjusted to his size, but he was right. It was nothing like before. He sank into her fully, stealing both their breath.

"I won't start moving unless you tell me to, kitten."

He kissed her, and she slipped her hands behind his head to pull him deeper. Closer.

A new desire surfaced to feel him moving in her. Unsure how to say she was ready and not wanting to stop kissing him, she brought her knees up and braced her feet against the bed, tentatively moving her hips.

Nex groaned and began pulling out. Kat's eyes widened. The friction of him stretching her inner walls and caressing them as he withdrew had her gasping. He drew back so slow she felt every inch of him moving within her. Incredibly, she already wanted him back in as deep as before. Almost out, he sank back in.

"Oh." She whimpered. "That feels good."

"Fuck yes, it does." Nex groaned. "You're so tight, kitten. So fucking tight." Sex had never been this good. Every part of her sucked him in. Her pussy tight around him, soaked in excitement and coating him in it. He never wanted to stop.

Despite his urge to move fast and hard, he remained gentle. He could do that with her another time. This time was for her.

The slow pace continued until Kat's hips moved faster. He matched her speed, pulling out almost entirely and sinking back in. Each movement left Kat yearning for more, the pleasure growing with every motion, like somehow, even inside her, he knew exactly where and how to hit every sensitive part. *This. This* was what people said about sex.

Except this was better.

Nex quickened his pace and wrapped an arm under her back. Curling his hand around her shoulder, he held her as he sank into her faster and harder. Kat moaned and threw back her head, her fiery hair spilling across the sheets. His other hand pinned her hip in place as he thrust into her. She clamped around him so snug he could barely take anymore.

"Nex." Kat dug her nails into his shoulders as the pleasure burst. Her body tensed, pulsating around him, waves of ecstasy and intimacy nearly drowning her in a blissful state.

The moment was beyond physical. Being together was being complete, like every broken part they had somehow fit together to make them whole. Their passion and pleasure ascended to a level neither of them, not even Nex, had experienced.

He slid in a few more times, sank deep, then groaned, holding her tight with small thrusts while he finished. He dropped his head into her neck, placing a kiss on the spot that always got a reaction. It earned a tired but pleasurable sound, and he smiled against her skin. "Not so unrealistic after all, huh?"

"No." Kat panted, unable to open her eyes. "That was . . ."

"Yes." Nex's lips brushed hers. "Yes, it was."

Chapter 25

Close

K at woke with Nex close. For the past month, he'd often slept near her, especially if she'd been crying. This time they were skin to skin, his arm around her waist possessively, their bodies so close nothing could come between them. Nex's nose was buried in the crook of her neck. Kat's back was pressed against Nex's chest, his body curled around hers. His other arm came up from under her and wrapped over her breasts, hand curved around her shoulder.

Kat woke first, warm despite the chill in the house. She shifted, and Nex's grip tightened. Her eyes fluttered open, and she glanced down at his strong arms, admiring the corded muscles and veins, the way they held her like she was precious.

A smile crept over her face, and she sank back against him, closing her eyes. When they opened again, she stared at the alarm clock's obnoxious, glowing green numbers. Soon, it would go off, demanding she get up for work. She didn't want to. She wanted to stay with Nex like this forever if she could.

Deciding she'd rather not risk another broken clock—this was her fourth—she reached to shut it off, but the tips of her fingers fell shy of the button. She tried to wiggle out of his hold, but it caused him to groan and hold her tighter. Hot breath hit her neck as he nuzzled against her. The sensation elicited a tremor of excitement, more so when his raspy morning voice rumbled in her ear.

"Where do you think you're going?" His hand at her waist pet circles on her skin.

Kat's eyes slid shut. How could a simple touch make her want him again? "I have to get ready for work."

"Not yet. That annoying box hasn't gone off." His nose roamed her neck, his lips brushing her skin. "You trying to get away from me early?"

"No." Kat drew her thighs together as his hardness pushed against her butt. "I thought I'd turn it off before it bothered you."

Nex grunted and gripped her hip, rocking himself against her. "I don't think so, kitten. You're not going anywhere."

Kat angled her head to give him better access to her neck. He licked and bit, sucking her skin into his mouth and leaving a mark. Her hands curled around his forearm as he ground against her.

"Katherine." His hand moved to her thigh. "I want you. You want me inside you again?" Kat blushed and nodded. Nex chuckled and nudged her legs open, sliding his finger down the length of her aching core. He circled her clit, earning a whimper. "So wet, kitten," he said in a half-growl. "I'm not accepting a nod. Only a yes. Do you want me inside you again?"

Fire pulsed through her when his finger slid inside. "Yes."

Nex nipped her neck and added a second finger, sliding them in and out until her nails dug into his arm. Each time, he learned where to touch to have her falling apart faster.

She moaned as she came, and her inner walls gripped his fingers, overwhelming euphoria taking over. The way her body contracted and relaxed into satisfaction made her want to stay in bed longer.

As it was ending, his shaft slid into her. She gasped and tightened her hold on his arm. Something about it was better than last night.

"So fucking wet." Nex groaned, sinking inside and grasping her hip. "How does it feel, kitten? Are you sore?"

Kat moaned when he thrust. "Not sore. It feels good."

Nex moved faster, holding her where he wanted as he sank in over and over. Kat rocked against him, and he kissed and sucked her neck, deliberately over spots that made her clench. Every movement made her addiction to him grow. An addiction to the incredible physical sensation caressing the sensitive parts inside her, to the emotional intimacy of being close to him, and the undeniable high that made her feel she could float away.

His movements were harder than last night. Kat gasped, making Nex groan and hit deeper. "You like that, kitten?"

She nodded, and Nex growled, biting down on her neck so hard she yelped and moaned all at once, the action making her clench.

"Say it."

"Yes," Kat said breathlessly, squeezing her eyes shut.

Nex's hand curled under her knee, lifting it up and sinking deeper. "Good girl." He drove into her, desperate for more gasps, desperate to sink so deep she'd never forget how satisfied he could make her.

Kat clamped around him and cried out her release, her hands constricting his arm like she was afraid he'd leave. She never wanted him to leave. He challenged her, nudged her out of her comfort zone in ways no one else had braved. She wasn't a fragile, grieving orphan, nor was she an inexperienced girl. She was herself, something she hadn't been since the accident.

Nex sunk so far in that Kat whimpered. "Fuck." He groaned, giving one last thrust as he came. "You feel so good, kitten." He soothed the bite marks on her neck with featherlight kisses. "I could spend all day inside you."

"Mm," Kat hummed, the only response manageable.

"Shit." Nex pulled out. "You finished your period like two days ago, didn't you?"

Kat's mouth fell open at his question. "Um . . . How do you know that?"

"I can smell the blood." He released her and backed up, watching the come drip out of her. "You did, right?"

"Yes."

"Good." He kissed her shoulder and turned her to face him. "I'm sorry. Waking up with you distracted me. I didn't use a condom. But nothing should happen so soon after your period."

"Well . . ." Kat averted her gaze. "Nothing should happen anyway." She sat up, clutching the blankets.

"What do you mean? Are you on birth control?"

Kat let her hair cover her face. "My mom put me on it young for . . . you know . . ." She rotated her wrist in a circular motion, causing Nex to arch a brow. "For like, not sex-related reasons. I've been on it for three years."

The alarm blared, and she switched it off before Nex could smash it. The conversation had warmed her face, and she needed a splash of cold water to ease the embarrassment. She moved to get up, but he dragged her onto his lap.

"Stop being embarrassed around me, kitten. If we're going to fuck, you need to be willing to talk about these things with me."

Communication was important, but she wasn't used to discussing anything like this. She did her best to maintain eye contact, pulling the blankets above her shoulders. "Um, is that why it felt so good? Does a condom make that big a difference?"

Nex's eyes darkened. "It definitely does. In fact, now that I've had you without, I don't think I can go back. I like having you with nothing in the way." He moved her hair aside and kissed below her ear. "I like coming inside you." He bit her skin, sucking until it reddened. "You liked it, didn't you?"

"I did."

"Good." He kissed an unblemished part of her neck. "Because my craving for you has intensified." He left another mark, enjoying her moans. "I already want you again. I'm tempted to tie you to the bed for the entire day."

Kat panted while he sucked her skin and slid the blankets off her shoulders, exposing her to him and almost making her forget her obligations. "I have work."

"Call in. Stay in bed with me." He gripped her ass and pulled her against him. "I promise I'll make it worth your while."

"I can't." Kat tangled her hands in his hair, her body and conscience at war. "Black Friday weekend is ridiculous. I can't leave my boss to that insanity."

"You're too pure for your own good." He flattened his hand, following the curve of her ass and back as it ascended. "You'll be late tonight?"

Kat nodded, tightening her arms around his neck before climbing off. She tried to grab a blanket for cover, but Nex kept a firm hold on them.

"I don't think so." Nex's gaze traveled her naked body, setting her cheeks aflame. "I like looking at you too much. In fact, I'm going to enact a *no-clothes-at-home* policy."

Kat rolled her eyes and went to her dresser. "You don't make the rules."

Nex appeared behind her, his chest pressed to her bare back. "Don't I?" His hand grazed low on her stomach, almost touching between her legs. "I think I do, kitten. That is *my* come dripping down your legs, is it not?"

When he spoke that way, it usually left her embarrassed. Now they were closer, she wanted to stay and hear more. Summoning what was left of her self-control, Kat sighed. "Please put clothes on. I can't focus."

"I don't know how you thought telling me that was going to make me do anything but stay completely naked." He turned her toward him and smirked. "Go ahead. Take a look."

Swallowing, Kat knew she'd be late for work if this continued. She kept her eyes on his. Nowhere else. "I'm going to get ready."

"Oh, of course, I'll shower with you." Nex grabbed her hand and tugged her toward the bathroom.

"No!"

"Why?"

"Because you'll distract me, and I've never been late, and I'm not going to start on a busy day." Kat ducked into the bathroom, mostly closed the door, and peeked out at him.

He chuckled. "What's wrong, Katherine? Did I turn you into a sex addict? Do you want me so bad you have to hide?"

"Shut up," Kat squeaked, closing the door. "And don't appear in here!"

His response echoed in her head. *Fine. I'll imagine your naked, wet body and how it would feel against mine. But you owe me. One way or another, I'll get wet with you today.*

A squeal escaped, muffled by her hands. She had to get out of the house fast, or she wouldn't leave.

Kat cringed at her hair in the mirror, mortified Nex saw her looking like such a mess. Only allowing herself a few seconds of wallowing in humiliation, she tied her hair back, and her eyes widened at the number of hickeys covering her neck.

"Oh my God," she whispered, hiding her face in her hands, not daring to look in the mirror another time.

Thanks to Nex, she spent longer on makeup to conceal the hickeys. A great deal of her day would be focused on keeping her hair over her neck.

After dressing, she entered the living room, thankful Nex had the decency to put on boxers. "Do you have any idea what you did to my neck? Can you maybe not make it obvious what we do in private?"

Nex scoffed. "I don't know why you're upset. It's *my* handiwork that's being hidden for no reason."

"For no reason?" She set her hand on her neck, cheeks burning at the memory of how many there were. "You know why I have to cover it. Why did you do that?"

"Why did I do that?" Nex stalked toward her, and she backed up, the wall halting her retreat. "Because, kitten." He moved her hair out of the way, lowering his lips to her neck. "I want everyone to tell from one look that you're *taken*."

Kat inhaled, fingers twitching to reach for him while he kissed her neck. "What are you doing? I have to go."

"I missed a spot." He sucked on her reddening skin, and Kat's practicality battled her desire. "There. Looks good on you. Goes with your hair."

Kat narrowed her eyes, then headed for the kitchen. "You're unbeliev-able."

"In bed? I know." He followed and leaned on the counter, getting in the way of her making tea. "Believe me, kitten, you moaning my name and writhing under me told me that already."

Kat's body tingled with the memory of the actions that elicited those responses. Talking would only bait him, and that was dangerous.

Leaving the house wasn't easy. He cornered her and kissed her until she wanted to climb back into bed with him. However, she clung to her weakening resolve and thanked herself for being smart enough to pack concealer for the new hickey.

Less hectic than the day before, the bookstore still had plenty of angry and overbearing customers, the kind of people who tempted Kat to say, "Thanks for the Christmas joy you spread." Instead, she did what she was supposed to—smiled, then complained to her boss.

The hour grew later, fewer people came in, and more snow fell. Connie left to buy dinner to thank Kat for working the busy weekend and closing on Black Friday. They had to sneak food between customers, but finally, a moment came when more people read than approached the cash register.

Despite her hunger, Kat could barely focus on eating. Her mind kept returning to last night, this morning, Nex moving inside—

"Can you believe what happened last night?" Connie asked.

"What?" Kat's fork clattered to the countertop. "What about last night?"

"The weird meteor shower. Why are you blushing?"

"I-I'm not. It's warm between the heater and all the people." She cleared her throat. "What meteor shower?"

Connie eyed Kat but didn't push. "There was a meteor shower that no one saw coming. Astronomers are confused and trying to explain it. It was beautiful. I caught the end of it on my way home."

"You saw it? There's usually too much light pollution in the city to see something like that."

"That's the other reason it was so weird. But, yeah, it was bright, and there weren't that many of them. Though, they were bigger than usual."

"Huh. Too bad I missed it. Do you think anyone got a video?"

"People tried, but none of the videos turned out well, and it ended too fast for anyone to set up."

"Weird," Kat murmured, picking up her fork.

"What's going on with you?" Connie picked at her sweet and sour pork. "You're practically glowing today."

Kat tried to hide her smile with a forkful of rice and teriyaki chicken. "Nothing."

"Really?"

"I'm . . . happy."

Connie smiled. "It shows. Did something happen between you and Nex?"

Kat choked on a mushroom. "What makes you say that?"

"He's the only one who makes you blush that much, and you two definitely have chemistry."

"You think so?"

Connie laughed. "Obviously. But tell him to stop coming here during your shifts. He's too distracting." Her teasing made Kat's gaze drop to her food. "It's slow, and you closed last night. Why don't you head home?"

"Are you sure?" Kat tried to mute her excitement.

Connie nodded to the door. "Go ahead. Thanks for your help last night."

"No problem. Thanks for letting me go early and for dinner."

"Sure thing, kiddo. Get outta here. I'll see you tomorrow."

Kat sealed her take-out container and gathered her things in her fastest store exit ever. A bounce in her step, she skipped along her route home, excitement fueling a fast pace. Until it happened again. The chill. Hair stood on the back of her neck, and her instincts screamed that she wasn't alone.

She paused and peered toward the church. *Bad weather again. Probably Pastor Brighton. Probably . . .*

Except it wasn't like him not to wave or say something. If he saw her walking alone and didn't have anyone inside, he'd walk her home. The likelihood that two nights in a row, he'd be there and not say a thing quickened her pace.

Tightening her coat, she glanced back. Either she was paranoid because of the Lilith incident, or she needed to tell Nex. If it was paranoia, she'd feel silly telling him about it. Lilith couldn't go on holy ground. Plus, while the snow was beautiful, it came with a reminder of her parents' accident. Between that and Lilith, her nerves were a mess of confusion and anxiety. That was a more likely reason for her unsettledness than someone spying on her.

"Stop being a baby," Kat muttered to herself, but she continued glancing around, her gaze lingering on the shadows.

Relief filled her when home came into view. She took her shoes off at the door, glad she'd worn better boots and didn't have wet feet the whole walk.

Inside was unusually quiet.

"Nex?" she called, heading to the kitchen. She put her take-out container away and was closing the fridge when his arms surrounded her from behind.

"You got dinner, kitten?"

Her body came alive from his touch and the kiss he placed on her shoulder. She nodded and craned her neck to see him. The moment she did, he grabbed her chin and pulled her into a kiss.

She spun in his arms, deepening their kiss. "I missed you."

"Did you?" Nex shuffled them toward the bedroom. "Good. Then you'll have no problem with my plans."

"What plans?"

"Get your mind out of the gutter, kitten. I'm not having sex with you tonight. You're not used to it, and if I do, you'll be sore. Come on." He led her to the bathroom, where a hot bath was prepared. "You can't tell me you're not a little sore after this morning."

"I guess I am a little." Tenderness didn't stop her from wanting him.

"The bath will help." He slid her coat off and lifted her dress. "I told you I'd get you wet with me one way or another."

Even though he'd seen her, she had an urge to cover up in the bright light of the bathroom.

Nex caught her wrists and shook his head. "Don't. I want to look at you. You're beautiful."

Kat fought her instincts while he undressed her and then himself. He got in first and offered her a hand into the water. He sat and drew her back against him, arms around her waist, lips against her neck and then her ear. The closeness made Kat smile and sink into him. She set her hands on his, letting her eyes shut. She didn't know there were so many ways to be intimate without having sex. His arms locked around her made her feel more relaxed and at home than she had in a long time.

Panic surfaced. *What if I'm the only one this attached?* Her grip tightened.

Nex threaded his fingers through hers, his lips grazing the shell of her ear, his words a reassurance that allowed her tension to ease. "I missed you too, kitten."

Chapter 26

Hers

K at was at church, the one place Nex couldn't follow and the only major source of tension between them. He didn't care for her going to church. Although he didn't outright say it, it was evident in the small comments and sulking when she returned. Because of that, she wasn't anxious to get home like usual.

Until her phone vibrated.

> *Nex: I want to fulfill that dream you told me about. The one with your father's coworker. I want to be the face attached to all your fantasies. What do you say, kitten? You want me to bend you over and have my way with you?*

Kat flipped the phone screen down in her lap. *Not an appropriate conversation for church.* She stared ahead, ignoring the weight of her phone, focusing on Pastor Brighton. She crossed her legs, then uncrossed and crossed them again. *Don't answer. Don't answer in church.*

She bit her lip and opened the message, fingertips flitting across the screen.

> *Kat: I'd like that.*

She sent it and shook her head to clear the lustful thoughts.

As soon as the service ended, she gathered her things into her messenger bag and darted toward the door, hoping to avoid social interactions. Then someone grabbed her arm. The touch relaxed her body in a sense of complete peace. She glanced up at the bluest eyes attached to an almost unrealistically perfect face. His face was mature but free of all blemishes and crinkles that indicated an aging body.

"Hello," the stranger greeted with a friendly smile.

Kat stepped out of his hold. "Hi."

"Forgive me. I wanted to say your voice is beautiful."

"Oh." Despite Nex not liking her attendance at church, when she was offered a solo singing position every other week, he encouraged her to accept. This week was her first time. "Thank you. I was a little nervous."

"Nervous? I find that hard to believe." He chuckled, and the sound reminded her of cozying up with a blanket at home. His black slacks had no wrinkles, nor did the crisp white shirt tucked into those slacks. The tie emphasized the vibrancy of his eyes, and he stood almost a foot taller than her. "You have a stunning voice."

"Thank you." While his touch was calming, his continued eye contact was scrutinizing. "I'm sorry, I don't think we've met. Have you been here before?"

In the small congregation, she would've noticed him. There was something different about him.

"I'm Gabriel." He gave her a pearly-white smile and offered his hand. "And no, it's my first time. I quite enjoyed it. How long have you been attending?"

Kat shook his hand and pulled back as soon as was polite. "I'm Katherine, and I've been coming since before I can remember."

"Wonderful. So, it's worth staying then? I'm visiting the area for an unknown amount of time. For work. Trying to find a place to fit in while I'm here."

"What do you do for work?"

His smile faltered for such a minimal moment, Kat wasn't sure it happened. "Counseling."

"Oh, that's great. We need more counselors. You'll fit in well. Everyone's kind and welcoming."

"I've noticed."

It was almost unsettling how white his teeth were, how musical his voice was, how perfectly aligned his clothes were—like he was Photoshopped. Nowhere near as perfect as Nex, in her opinion.

"Well." Kat shifted from one foot to the other. "Nice to meet you, but I better get go—"

"I'm new to the area. Do you have any food recommendations?"

"Oh, um, what do you like?"

He grinned. "Anything at all."

"Well, down the street, there's a place called Misty's Café." She gestured in the direction of Misty's. "They have a variety of food. Burgers, pasta, rice bowls. It's great."

"Sounds wonderful. Would you join me?"

Kat's eyebrows raised. She increased the distance between them and gave her politest smile. "Thank you, but I'm afraid I have to go."

"It wouldn't take long." That unsettlingly flawless smile returned. "I eat fast. Don't want to dine alone, you know?"

"Oh." Kat wrung her hands together and scanned the room, spotting Pastor Brighton a few feet away. "I'm sure Pastor Brighton and his family would love to go. They often take newcomers for lunch. I'm sorry, I have someone waiting on me."

"She certainly does." Bernice approached and nudged Kat's shoulder with hers. "When are you going to bring that handsome young Nex to church?"

Kat hid the amusement at Bernice's question for more than one reason. First, Nex wasn't even sort of young. Second, he couldn't set foot in here even if he wanted to.

A muscle in Gabriel's square jaw ticked. "A boyfriend?"

Boyfriend. They hadn't discussed it. They'd been intimate nearly constantly over the last couple of weeks. Trouble sleeping was no longer a problem because Nex made sure she was exhausted every night.

Kat smiled, rubbing her arms. "Sort of. We haven't labeled it."

"So, free to see other people?"

Other people weren't a consideration for Kat. *Nex wouldn't do that.* Except they hadn't made rules, and he spent a lot of time without her while she worked and rehearsed.

"Nex and Katherine don't need a label." Bernice patted Kat's arm. "It's obvious when you see them together that they only see each other."

Unhappy with where her thoughts were headed and not enjoying the awkward conversation, Kat forced a smile at Bernice. There was no reason to doubt Nex. She had to get out of there. "I've got to go, but I'll see you here next week?" Kat asked Gabriel.

"Indeed, you will."

"Great." Kat turned to Bernice. "See you Wednesday."

"Wednesday, my dear," Bernice said. "Don't forget to tell Nex to find a time the two of you can come for dinner."

Kat's smile strained. "Right." Nex liked Bernice well enough, but his displeased expression when she'd asked if he'd have dinner with her was answer enough. "Bye." She waved and rushed outside into the ever-colder weather.

Kat hurried home and walked in on Nex and Marcus talking so intensely they didn't notice she'd arrived. She slipped off her coat and wandered to the kitchen table where they sat.

"You can't feed him that." Nex dropped his fist to the table. "He has a sensitive stomach."

"You're being ridiculous." Marcus leaned back and scratched his beard. "They're fine. They're happy."

"Everything okay?" Kat dropped her messenger bag on the table with a *thud*.

Nex glanced up, annoyed that Marcus bugged him enough he didn't hear Katherine come in. "Everything's fine. Marcus is just a cunt."

"I'm taking care of your hounds. You're welcome, by the way." Marcus threw his arms up. "For fuck's sake. Kat, how do you put up with this?"

"You're going to make Sicarius sick with the shit you're feeding him," Nex snapped.

"He and Venandi are fine. Stop being a baby. You know, I don't have to take care of them. I could've left them with nowhere to go, waiting to get eaten by something bigger."

Nex grumbled and slouched in his chair. "I should've asked Lucian."

Marcus stood, patting Kat on the back. "I'm out. Good luck."

A cloud of smoke took his place before Kat responded. She turned to Nex with a frown. "You're worried about your puppies."

Nex huffed. "For the last time, they're *not* puppies. I'm sure they're fine. I don't like relying on someone else to watch them."

"Can they come here somehow?"

"No. They're hell hounds, and they're dangerous to humans. They're only allowed in this realm under special circumstances and only with their trainer. Me. Being accidentally summoned by a human isn't the kind of thing I need a hell hound for."

"I'm sorry." Guilt crept in that he couldn't go home and see his dogs. She'd be lying if she said she was searching for a way to send him back as much as before they became intimate. Being with Nex took up a lot of time, but it wasn't only that. Motivation to help him leave had dissipated.

Recognizing that was selfish, she ignored the ache in her heart at his impending absence. "I should go to the library." Unable to look at him, she fiddled with the ends of her sleeves. "Do some research to . . ." The words wouldn't come. She gazed over at him and couldn't interpret the look on his face. His expression was often unreadable.

Nex, however, read the conflict on her face. The same conflict in his heart. The last thing he wanted was to discuss it. Instead, a slow smirk spread over his face. "No, you should stay where you are." He stood. "The table will work."

Nex had certain expressions that traveled through her whole body in rippling promises of pleasure. As if the look wasn't enough, she tensed in the most delightful way when he walked behind her and swept her hair to the side.

"We had plans, did we not? Are you trying to cancel on me?" His hands trailed from her shoulders to her arms, then her wrists, his fingers curling around them. "What's wrong? It was a better idea in your head?" He pinned her wrists behind her and pressed against her backside. "You don't want me to take you like this?" He held her wrists with one hand and tangled the other in her hair, tugging, so she looked back at him. "You'll have to tell me what you want, kitten. Because you tried to leave, but your racing heart and flushed skin tell me you don't want to leave. So, what do you want? Do you want me to have you like this?"

Kat's lips could barely form words when they could only think of meeting his lips and the hardness pressed against her butt. He'd barely touched her, but it was enough to crave more. Her answer came out as an unintentional whisper. "Yes."

"Yes?" He bent her over the table, grinding against her. "That was awfully quiet, kitten. Hearing you say yes is the best part of my day. Try again."

She moaned as his hand tightened in her hair, giving him more control over her movement. "Yes."

"Good." Nex released her hair and straightened. He tugged her leggings and underwear down before thrusting his fingers into her.

Whimpering, she dropped her forehead to the table. Faster and harder than usual, his actions left her aching to feel him inside her. His fingers slid out to circle where she was so sensitive she jerked at the contact. His expert movement suggested he had the blueprint of her body that identified what she liked most. He pumped into her again, leaving her a mess of desperation, body writhing until she couldn't take it anymore, but then his fingers slid out, replaced by something much bigger.

Nex licked her sweetness off his fingers, then threaded them in her hair and tugged her up. He slammed into her, and she cried out. "Too hard, kitten?"

"No." Kat panted, her eyes sliding shut when soft kisses landed on her neck. She was about to burst, but his tenderness warmed her heart. The way he'd check in with her any time he tried something new made her attachment worse. "Not too hard." Her body clenched at the thought of him doing it again. "It . . ." Still unaccustomed to being vocal, she couldn't stop the timidity in her voice. "It feels good."

Nex growled and bent her over again, thrusting harder. Kat cried out, and he tightened his hold on her wrists and hair, his actions growing rougher. Through it all, the roughness never scared her. The edge of the table dug into her thighs with every thrust, but the added friction set her body more alight. His hands held her wrists firmly but loose enough that she was confident he'd let go if she became overwhelmed. The fingers in her hair were tight, but she didn't feel controlled. She felt desired.

Every movement sent her body into a heightened state of ecstasy she wanted to bottle and hold for eternity. Bent over, the powerful movements and the way he held her in place made her fall apart so intensely that her entire body trembled. The cool surface of the table did nothing to help the overpowering heat as its firm surface added to the excitement of being at his mercy.

"Nex." She whimpered, clenching around him. Pleasure rippled through her, starting at her core and spreading until her limbs pulsated in response to her climax. People said dreams were better than reality. As her body quivered, she took a firm stance that reality was better when Nex was involved. Much better.

Nex slammed into her, staying deep as he finished. Sucking in breaths, he pulled her up, turned her, and caught her in a feverish kiss. Kat moaned and wrapped her arms around his shoulders as he lifted her onto the table and held her against him.

"Better than the fantasy?" He trailed his lips down her jaw. Eager hands slid down, pulling her leggings and underwear off the rest of the way. He nuzzled her neck, placing light kisses on her skin. Kat nodded and leaned into the crook of his neck. She gasped when he grabbed some of her hair and tugged her head back, so their eyes met. "Words." He narrowed his eyes. "You know I want to hear you say it."

"Yes." She panted. "Yes, Nex."

"That's better," he murmured, restarting his path of kissing down her neck, wrapping her legs around him.

"Will you tell me what your fantasies are?" Kat asked. It seemed unfair he fulfilled hers, and she didn't know his.

Nex lifted his head, a dark smile forming. "Trust me, kitten. You're *not* ready for the things I want to do to you."

"How do you know? What do you want to do?"

"What do I want to do to you?" His hand moved at a tantalizingly slow speed up her stomach and between her breasts, fingers curling around her throat. "I want to dominate you. What I want is much rougher than what I just did. I want to punish you when you give me trouble. I want to make you wait to come until you feel like it's less of a want and more of a *need*." He turned her head and bit her neck hard enough a moan built in her throat. "I want to tie you up and smack that beautiful ass until it turns red while I fuck you. I want to claim and taint every inch of you until there's no doubt in your mind that you're *mine*, until I've ingrained myself so much you can't be touched by someone else without thinking of me and wishing my hands were on you."

Kat's lips parted. It wasn't foreign to her, just different to hear out loud. Although her hands fidgeted, the neediness between her legs heightened with every word.

He released her throat and traced her lips, watched her tongue dart out and touch his thumb. A half-smile escaped, and Kat took it as a victory. Moments when he stared like that made her feel she couldn't go a day in her life without him.

Sobering, she chewed her lip, the comments about their relationship eating at her nerves. "Nex?"

"What?" His expression softened. "What is it?"

"What, um . . ." She tugged on the neckline of her dress. "Uh." Unsure how he'd respond, her breaths shallowed. Was it silly to want a label given he didn't live in this realm?

"What's wrong, kitten? Was I too rough?"

"No." Kat shook her head. "No, that was," she licked her lips, heat flooding her body, "mm-hmm."

"Mm-hmm?" Nex quirked an eyebrow and tried not to laugh at how adorable she was.

"Don't." Kat planted her face in his chest.

"Don't what?" Nex wrapped his arms around her and rested his chin on her head, backing off before she retreated to another room and refused to speak to him. It'd already happened once, and while it was entertaining, he didn't want to embarrass her. "It was mm-hmm for me too. Now, what's wrong?"

"Nothing's wrong." Kat folded her hands in her lap. "Today, someone asked if you were my boyfriend." She looked at him out of the corner of her eye. "And I-I didn't know what to say."

"What do you want to say? Are you bringing it up because that's what you want?"

"I don't know. I guess I want to know . . . that there's only me."

Nex grabbed her chin. "Katherine, there's no one but you. Only you. I better be the only one for you."

"Of course you are. I don't want anyone else." Kat's gaze dropped to her dress, where she smoothed out wrinkles that weren't there. "So, you don't want to be together like that?" She looked up at him, heart pounding so hard she wasn't convinced it wouldn't leap out.

"If you want to call it that, call it that. You want to be my girlfriend? Very well, you're my girlfriend. The label doesn't matter to me because it means nothing in my realm. There aren't titles that shift depending on how serious someone is or isn't. There's no *it's complicated* or boyfriends or fiancés or spouses. That's not how it works, but if it makes you feel better, then sure, you're my girlfriend, and I'm your boyfriend. But if we're abiding by human labels, then you better submit to mine as well."

Kat tilted her head. "What's yours?"

"Mine." His hand slid between her legs. "Mine is that you are *mine*." He flattened his palm on her back to hold her in place, thrusting his fingers into her. "You belong to me. Call me whatever you like, kitten, but when I ask who you belong to," he sunk his fingers in harder, "your answer damn well better be me."

Kat whimpered. His fingers pumped in and out, building her up again. Kat set her hand on his face. "Are you mine, too?"

The gesture swelled Nex's heart. Innocence poured from her big green eyes. Her tender touch and delicate hands crumbled the walls he'd kept up for everyone else. He'd never belonged to anyone, but Kat was different. She wasn't just his. He was hers, and every part of him belonged to her.

"Of course I'm yours." He turned, kissing the palm of her hand. "I belong to you and only you, Katherine. No one will ever compare to you. Your turn." He growled, stuffing her with a third finger. "Tell me what I want to hear."

"I'm yours." Kat whimpered as he curled his fingers inside her.

"Who do you belong to?" He shoved them in harder.

She panted, eyes shut, on the brink of another release. "You."

"Look at me when you say it." He snatched her jaw and turned it toward him. He needed to hear it again, to hear it a million times, because he couldn't imagine being without her. "Who do you belong to?"

"You." She stared into his eyes, never wanting to look into any others. Her hands fisted his shirt as the pleasure washed over her, lightening her body all the way down to her toes. "I'm yours, Nex."

Nex admired her flushed face, her glazed eyes. He was unsure how he reached this point with her. The point he couldn't imagine not being with her. The first time in all the years he'd existed that he belonged to someone.

"You're mine." Nex brushed their lips together so lightly it tickled. Her hot breath, panting because of him, drove him wild and made him draw her closer. He wrapped his arms around her and buried his face in her hair. "And I belong to you."

Chapter 27

Haunted

Kat and Nex fell into a comfortable rhythm of her going to class, rehearsal, and work, then coming home to him pulling her into the bedroom and taking her body through an enrapturing expedition where she learned there were far more sensual parts of her body than she knew. Their intimacy never reached a monotonous level, with exploration of new sensations each time. Every day, she grew more attached. Every day, he brought up home less, to the point he didn't bring it up at all.

Even when he was being a pain, he left her randomly smiling more than she had in a year. But on opening day for her play, unable to find her mother's bracelet, she didn't feel much like smiling.

After helping Lucian with a mission, Nex came home to a mess. It concerned him because Kat was *very* particular about how things were organized and cleaned. The house was always tidy, and everything was in "its spot", as Kat referred to it. If he so much as put a glass in the wrong position in the cupboard, she'd be there, fixing it in a second. For there to be drawers emptied and things scattered on the counter, the table, the couch . . . It was unlike her.

Nex hurried into the bedroom, where Kat sat on the floor surrounded by tiny cardboard boxes of varying sizes and colors. Several were open, tossed aside with jewelry half hanging out. She picked up another box, opened it, then tossed it on the ground so hard it bounced.

"Katherine."

Kat jumped and mumbled a quiet, "Hi." She picked up another box only to throw it too.

"Are you all right?"

"I'm fine." She rummaged through the pile, searching for a box she hadn't checked.

Nex stepped around the mess. He stopped in front of her and bent down, catching her wrist when she reached for another box. "What is it? What's wrong?"

"I can't find the bracelet," she said, her voice wavering. He'd never seen someone upset over jewelry. "I can't find it anywhere."

"What do you need a bracelet for? I thought you would've left by now. Aren't you supposed to be there early?"

"Yes, but . . ." Kat pierced her lip with her teeth to stop tears welling in her eyes.

Nex grabbed her chin. "What's wrong, Katherine?"

"It's nothing."

She tried to look away, but his grip tightened. "Don't lie. Tell me what's wrong."

She swallowed the lump in her throat. "It's my mom's bracelet. It's my mom's, and I was supposed to wear it tonight because—" She sucked in a breath and brushed away the tears falling down her face. "Because I wanted to."

Nex frowned and pushed the boxes aside to sit on the floor. He pulled her onto his lap and caught the fresh tears with his thumbs. "What does it look like?"

"It's nothing special." She dusted his shoulder as if something were there. "A little pink butterfly charm and a simple silver chain. My costume hides it enough it doesn't mess anything up. The director said I was okay to wear it under the sleeve."

"Where have you not looked?" The entire house was chaos. Which reminded him there were two places she probably wouldn't search. Her parents' room and the car were off-limits. They were the only topics that made her snap at him.

Kat's shoulders slumped. "I've looked everywhere."

Her phone rang, and she frowned at the name on the screen—Chelsea from the play, probably wondering where she was. "I have to go."

She stood, and Nex stood with her. "I'll walk you."

She shook her head. "No, I don't want you to wait around for three hours."

"I don't mind, kitten."

"I need to be alone for a bit, okay?" She wrapped her arms around herself and left.

Nex often pushed, but she was thankful he didn't right then. She took deep breaths so she wouldn't be crying when she arrived at the theater. She'd have to do her makeup, and she couldn't do that if she didn't stop crying.

Every passing car on the way to the bus dredged up buried memories of the accident. Hugging herself tighter, she shook her head as if that would make them go away and willed herself to think of anything other than *that* night.

She crossed a grocery store parking lot, picking up her pace as the bus stop came into view. The last thing she wanted was to ride the bus, but she didn't have time to walk. She was already late.

"Katherine, what a coincidence."

Kat glanced over her shoulder at Gabriel. She faced away and wiped stray tears, putting on her best fake smile. She wasn't in the mood to talk to him, or anyone for that matter, but she wasn't rude.

"Hi," she greeted, turning toward him.

"Are you all right?"

She fingered the zipper of her coat. "I'm fine."

"It looks like you've been crying." He stepped closer. "Boyfriend upset you?"

Kat's brows furrowed. *Why would he assume Nex is the reason I'm upset?* Gabriel had been at church the last couple of weeks and continued to approach her. The way he phrased things always made it seem like he thought Nex wasn't a good person.

"Of course not. Nex is wonderful," Kat said. "I wasn't crying. It's allergies."

"Right." His smile faltered, and Kat shuffled her feet. "Where are you off to?" He gestured to a car. "Need a ride?"

"No." Kat backed away, and Gabriel frowned. "Sorry." She kicked at the asphalt. "I appreciate the offer, but I'm fine. I've gotta get to the bus."

"The bus?" A crease formed in Gabriel's forehead. "I can drive you."

"No." Kat shook her head and stepped back again. She wasn't sure if it was because she was already upset before running into him, but he was starting to bother her. "Sorry, gotta go. See you Sunday." She turned and ran before he could respond.

The second she was on the bus, she gripped the bar and tensed when the wheels rolled forward. Chest tight, she reminded herself to breathe, but her knuckles whitened around the metal. An eternity passed before she arrived at the theater.

The cast went through one last rehearsal and set check, ensuring everything was where it needed to be for scene changes and that all props were accounted for. Stage crew tested the lighting and music, and by the time the play was scheduled to start, Kat sat in the empty dressing room, trying not to cry.

She hadn't expected to be this emotional about the play. She knew it might hit a soft spot but thought she could keep it together. Instead, it snuck up on her, and now she couldn't relax, couldn't stop her mind from going to that night. Nausea rolled through her stomach. *Pull yourself together.*

None of her usual methods of control worked. She counted, breathed, tried to ground herself in what was real. Frustrated, she set her head in her hands and cried again.

"Don't cry, kitten," Nex murmured, rubbing her shoulders.

Kat jumped less than usual. Unannounced appearances were becoming normal. He crouched and gazed up at her, wishing he could banish the sadness.

"I'm fine," she whispered.

"Stop lying. Tell me what's wrong. Why is it so important to you?"

"I don't want to talk about it."

"You only have ten minutes to curtain. I think you better get over not wanting to talk about it and tell me anyway, or it's going to distract you."

Agonizing moments of silence passed before she could speak. Kat stared at her lap. "I was always too chicken to try out for theater." Her voice was so quiet, he wouldn't have heard as a human. "I don't have the confidence, but I love it. My parents were so supportive, and I got a small part in this Christmas play at church. We were on our way to the last show at my pastor's house when . . ." Her lower lip quivered. "That was the last play I was in."

Nex's eyes widened. He took her hands and kissed the backs. "I'm sorry."

"I wish they could be here. I wish they were here to see me. Christmas Eve was going to have the biggest turnout, and my mom put her bracelet on me before we left the house. She said when I got nervous to," her eyes squeezed shut and expelled more tears, "look at it and know I wasn't alone. Even if I couldn't see her, I'd know she was with me. I wanted to wear it so I could feel like they were here."

"I understand." Nex brushed the tears away with his knuckles. "It's a good thing you have it then, isn't it?"

"What?"

He dangled the bracelet in front of her. "It was in your parents' room, but I swear I didn't touch a thing except this bracelet."

Mouth agape, Kat stared at the bracelet with wide eyes. "You found it?"

"Hold out your hand. I'll put it on you." He unclasped the bracelet and opened it. "Everything's all right now."

Kat extended her unsteady hand. Nex secured the bracelet around her wrist, then pressed a kiss against it, looking up at her. Although she'd hoped a piece of her mother would be the thing to get her to stop crying, she cried harder.

Nex knew she wouldn't be ready to go on stage in ten minutes when she was this upset. He picked her up and sat on the chair with her in his lap, her legs either side of his. Holding her close, he cupped her cheek with his other hand to sweep away tears.

"I'm sorry." She hid her face in her hands. "I don't cry like this. I'm fine."

"You're not fine." Nex uncovered her face and guided her to look at him. "And you're not fine because you're trying to act like you are. Let it out. You've been holding it in too long." He traced her tear-stained freckles. "You're mine, Katherine. Talk to me."

She hated talking about it. Hated thinking about it. It hurt too much and took her back to that dark place she was in the first few months after it happened. But with Nex, she didn't want to pretend she was okay.

"I miss them." She cried and threw her arms around his shoulders. He cradled her head into the crook of his neck. "I miss them so much, and it's almost Christmas, an-and I—" Gasps and tears broke her words. "Ever since the accident, I sometimes get so anxious around cars I see things that aren't there. I watch it happen over and over." She burrowed her face against his skin. "It happened so fast, and . . ." Her body shook with the memory. "There was so much blood, and it was on me and—" She clung to him as sobs took over. "I can't stop watching them die."

Anguish had never caused Nex's throat to close. In hell, there was no mercy or empathy because the souls there earned their place. Kat's suffering was worse.

She sniffled. "I'm going to be late."

"Something tells me the play is going to run a little late." Nex focused on the shadows, guiding them. They drifted to the lights onstage, engulfing the bulbs and darkening the area.

The lighting coordinator's panic didn't matter to him. What mattered was the woman in his arms. The accident was worse than he realized. She wasn't letting herself heal from it. Resting his chin on her head, he stroked her hair. He didn't give the lighting coordinator peace until she'd stopped for a while. The sniffling ceased, and she went still in his arms, her body exhausted.

He pet soothing circles on her back. "Have you told anyone what happened that night?"

"My pastor knows most of it. He was my counselor. If it was up to him, I'd still be in counseling, but I," she sighed, "wanted to get through it myself."

"Will you tell me what happened?"

"I can't." Her arms tightened, needing to hold him, so she wouldn't fall apart again. "It's not that I don't want you to know. I-I can't relive it."

"It's all right." He kissed her head. "You don't have to tell me."

"I want to. I don't suppose one of your tricks involves going into my mind and finding out for yourself?" she joked, desperate to lighten the mood because she couldn't take the heaviness.

"No." *But I know someone who can.* "Say I could find a way. Would you want me to?"

Kat hesitated. "Only if you don't look at me the way everyone else did."

"How did everyone look at you?"

"Like . . ." Her eyes welled. "*Oh, the poor traumatized orphan.*" Her voice cracked. "Nobody could be normal with me except my pastor and Bernice. Everyone talked to me like I'd break, and I got tired of that look. The pity look." She winced when she pictured it. "Because of that, I isolated. I lost most of my friends because I couldn't stand being stared at like that all the time. Being lonely was better. It was suffocating to have people constantly wanting me to talk about it, waiting for me to break."

"Katherine, you're never going to heal if you don't admit it still haunts you. I'm here for you. You belonging to me means I take care of you in every way." He pulled her out of her hiding place against his neck. "You can cry on me. I want you to cry on me. Your pleasure isn't the only thing that belongs to me. All of you belongs to me. That includes your grief." He kissed her lips, then her forehead. "I want *all* of you."

His words almost brought on tears of a different kind. She didn't often make the first move, but she pressed her lips against his in an urgent kiss. He threaded his hand through her hair as their lips moved together in perfect sync like they were made to kiss each other.

"I have to get ready." Kat sighed into the kiss. "Everyone's going to know I was crying."

"No, they won't." Nex tilted her chin up. "Keep your head up, kitten. This is nothing makeup tricks can't hide. We'll have you fixed up in no time, but that makeup comes off as soon as we get home. I want to see you. Just you."

Kat bit back a smile. "Deal."

"Good. Let's get you stage ready."

Kat nodded and got off Nex's lap, wiping her eyes one last time. He watched her count under her breath before she gave him a small smile and unzipped her makeup bag. He'd act normal for her sake, but he was concerned. She'd gone through it alone and still was.

There was one way he could know what happened and how better to comfort her. One person could help him. He'd never encountered her, sometimes pointedly avoided her, but no longer.

He was going to pay Death a visit.

Chapter 28

Death

Nex swept Kat's curls off her forehead and replaced them with his lips. On the rare occasion clothes were worn to bed, she wore his. Currently, she was bundled up in a black shirt, the sleeves so long that only the tips of her fingers were visible.

Katherine was the only living being who could make him subconsciously smile, even when she was asleep.

He ran his fingers over her cheeks and secured the blankets around her. She stirred, curling up and clinging to the comforter. He might've smiled again if not for the slight frown on her sleeping face and the puffiness of her closed eyes.

Whether he was impressed or concerned at how easily she put on a fake smile and got through the play as if nothing was wrong, he wasn't sure. Her performance went so well, she was approached afterward by several people complimenting her. While in front of others she appeared excited, it didn't cheer her up. Flying her home didn't make it better either. It lifted her spirits, but he'd spent enough time around her to know she was trying hard to act like her cheerful self, though she wasn't.

He wanted to understand and help, which was why his gaze lingered on her for only a moment. On his way out of the bedroom, he picked up the bracelet from her dresser. He held it in a tight fist, passed through the house walls, and emerged on the back porch.

Lucian had tracked down Death, and she wasn't far. She never was.

Death was everywhere.

Nex made himself invisible to mortals, released his wings, and flew to the city. He found Death near the food bank, in an abandoned building with cracked windows and an unpleasant stench. Inside, three people lay on the ground. Overdosed. The walls were stained, torn blankets and pillows littered a corner, and needles scattered the floor. Even without winter, the room was cold.

Although he could feel Death's presence, he didn't see her right away. Not until she spoke.

"Isn't it funny that we both deal in death, yet this is the first time I'm meeting you? You always leave before I arrive. Were you avoiding me?"

Nex turned and found her standing behind him, donned in a long, black dress that flowed around her ankles. Her movements were surreal and light, airy. Despite the black heeled boots, every step across the cement tiles was soundless. She walked with a grace that couldn't be matched by anyone, human or otherwise.

No scars blemished her smooth umber skin. Her hair was short, the pale gray of storm clouds after they'd calmed. Her eyes were somewhere between white and black, a milky gray whose tone changed with her actions.

"You can't avoid me. You and I," she gestured between them, "the angels and the other demons need each other. You occasionally take care of the physical form, and I get the soul where it needs to go. Then you demons and the angels take care of those essences once they're home and wait for me to send you more. The system would collapse without our balance, Nex. It never goes well when a soul doesn't get taken care of properly." She walked toward him slowly, tilting her head to the side. "You know," she crouched next to one of the bodies, "you are the only demon that has not asked me."

Part of the reason Nex avoided her was because of this. He decided a long time ago that he didn't want to know what he'd done in his past life that led to him becoming a demon. He didn't want to know how bad he must've been to earn the title. An unpopular opinion. Most demons got curious enough to ask, and everyone assumed Nex would be the same if he gave it a while longer.

Time didn't matter. Whatever person he was in that life would remain unknown.

"Is that why you're here?" Death's hand glided over the body but never touched it. A ball of white light emerged from the chest and floated to her palm. She hummed and nodded, closing her eyes, her hands covering the glow. "Do you want to know?" She opened her fingers, the light gone.

"I'm not here for me."

Death moved to the next body, repeating the process.

"There's something else I need."

"What's that?" Death closed her hands around the next light with a melancholic frown, muttering "Poor soul" under her breath as she sent it to its resting place.

"Do you remember every soul?"

"I do. Although it is not in the way you think." She moved to the next body. "My memories are different than yours. It may not be fresh in my mind, but it is never fully gone. If it wasn't in the last few weeks, I need a reminder."

Nex's hands tightened on Katherine's mother's bracelet, and he waited for the last soul to be sent off. Death turned to him, her gaze landing on the chain dangling in his hands.

"I see." She bowed her head in respect for the grief lingering on the chain. "You want someone else's memory."

"You can do that, can't you?"

She nodded. "I can. Though I rarely do. It's not fair to other souls to have their memories repeated."

"I have a reason." Nex held out the bracelet. "She wants me to know. She just needs help."

"Show me." Death extended her hand but didn't take the bracelet. Nex stiffened, and she released a breathy laugh. "Give me your hand, Nex. I can sort out your intentions without much effort. I mean you no harm. You would know I never mean harm if you had not hidden from me. I carry an unfortunate reputation. You know what that's like, do you not?"

Nex hesitated, then set his hand in hers. He felt nothing, but her eyes shut, and a smile spread over her face.

She pulled her hand back and opened her dark eyes, a deep sadness in them. "This cannot end well. It's beautiful, what you have, but it cannot last."

"That's not necessarily true. I have reason to be here. I was summoned. They can't claim I'm here needlessly, and I haven't manipulated her."

Death's brows drew together. "Proceed with caution, young demon. I think it unwise to assume no one will intervene."

He'd thought about it, of course. But he also knew the angels let things slide in the past, and if they were to come, they'd come to him first like they had with others.

"I understand." Death nodded. "The angels have sometimes looked the other way, but you must consider that you are not like other demons. You've moved so high up the ranks in such little time. You're only a few ranks below Lilith. That status is rare. It places pressure on you, Nex. You're considered a role model. Your actions are judged harsher." Sadness laced her smile. "It is not always a blessing to have a higher rank. I would be careful if I were you."

Nex clenched his jaw and gripped the bracelet. "Will you do it?"

"I do not mean to frustrate you. I am concerned for you and the human. I only mean to advise you. I have been around a long time." Her gaze shifted, lost in old memories. "I have seen many things happen." She blinked, and her gaze returned to him. "Things that I could not change but had to let take their course. Assumptions are dangerous. Assuming you and Katherine are safe because your circumstances are different is dangerous. I would urge you to keep a close eye on her. You may find you are not the *only* one keeping an eye on her."

Nex frowned. "You know something."

"I'm afraid not." Death laughed with no joy. "The only communication I have with angels and demons is in those brief moments when I send souls home before they get lost. It is unwise to get too involved in the affairs of anyone, be it human, demon, or angel. I warn you, some of the worst things happened when people assumed their situation made them an exception. Few true exceptions exist in the world. I would not assume that you are one of those when the odds are stacked against you."

Nex's frown deepened. He wasn't sure what to say, but he wanted to get back in case nightmares haunted Katherine. He didn't want her to wake up alone. "I'll be careful. Will you show me?"

"I sense no ill intentions from you, but there is something you must understand." She approached and paused, her hand hovering below the bracelet. "There are rules I haven't made but must follow, like the rules you have. It may seem I hold much power, and perhaps I do, but no powers are unlimited. You can only request one memory. *One.*" She raised a single finger. "If you ask this and later wish to know about your mortal life, I cannot give you an answer. If you do this, you will never know. Can you accept that?"

Nex was surprised at his hesitation. *Knowing won't do any good.* It wouldn't change the fact he was a demon or fix anything. He'd hate himself more. The memory he asked for held greater importance. "I can." He offered the bracelet. "Will this be enough? She was wearing it when it happened."

"This will work fine." Death took the bracelet and closed her eyes. "I don't need something from the souls who moved on, only something from that day. Something small," she murmured. A deep frown pulled on her lips. "Oh, my." Her eyes fluttered open. "This is an unpleasant one. Are you sure you want to see? It is not easy to watch."

"I'm sure. I've seen plenty of things."

Death *tsked*. "Do not pretend you don't know this is different. The deaths you deliver are for souls who are truly evil. You've never had to spill innocent blood. That was a path you avoided."

"I can handle it. I want to see."

"The death or the aftereffects?"

"Both."

She presented her hand. "If you're sure."

Nex placed his hand in hers, and the air knocked out of him. The sensation was similar to being summoned—movement beyond his control—so fast there was no time to see the cold, brittle in between before arriving at the destination, close to a year ago . . .

Kat's mother turned up the radio and sang "Rockin' Around the Christmas Tree" by Brenda Lee, dancing in her seat. Kat grinned and stopped the car at a traffic light. Using the rearview mirror, she found her father playing air saxophone in the back seat behind her mom. Kat giggled and returned her gaze to the road.

The light turned green, and Kat eased into the intersection. Ice coated the road, and snow decreased visibility. The streets were practically empty in the questionable weather. Between focusing on the road and the lack of headlights on the truck swerving from the right, neither she nor her parents saw it coming. They almost crossed the intersection when the truck slammed into the passenger side.

Their car jerked to the side. Kat didn't register they'd been hit before the airbag deployed, smacking her in the face. The car rotated under the force until it faced the offending truck and skidded to a halt. Unable to see anything through the airbag, Kat froze. Once it deflated, her ears rang, reverberating chimes overpowering any other sound. She clutched her temples, lightheadedness overwhelming her as smoke billowed from the hood of the car.

"Mom." She blinked her eyes into focus, and the ringing faded. "Are you ok—" She turned toward the smashed passenger side. Toward her mother's

lifeless body. At first, she couldn't process that the contorted person next to her was her mother. The car had caved in, and the unrecognizable figure was so close it almost touched Kat. Blood ran down her mother's limp arm and dripped on Kat's seat.

"Dad," she whispered, her gaze drifting to the back seat. Another mangled body wore half her father's face, a single eye open, staring. Both bodies bent in unnatural positions, twisted and broken.

Kat pressed the button, but the seatbelt wouldn't release. "Come on." She jammed the button over and over, jerking at the seatbelt. Every attempt locked it up, restraining her.

Desperation had her wrenching the seatbelt so hard her mother's bloodied arm slid closer, flopping on Kat's hand. Kat screamed and withdrew. Her mother's hand slid down, resting beside Kat's leg. Then she noticed the blood wasn't only on her parents. She gaped at her hand covered in sticky red liquid. Her coat, her pants, drenched.

"Come on," she whispered, ramming the button to release her. Yanking didn't loosen anything, only held her tighter to the seat, more unable to move away from her mother's limp arm. "Come on!"

More than an hour passed before anyone made it to the scene. Snow-packed roads and a lack of other cars out on Christmas Eve meant the accident didn't get reported for over forty-five minutes.

For seventy torturous minutes, Kat sat trapped in the car with her parents' bodies, the repeated friction from her attempted escape burning and bruising her skin while her phone rested out of reach on the floor.

She started to believe no one would hear her screams. Finally, someone came in and cut the seatbelt. By then, her cries had strained her throat and left her voiceless.

Out on the curb, Kat stared ahead, not responding to the questions fired her way. She was hardly aware of anyone's presence, incapable of doing anything except stare at her father's smashed car.

Over an hour more she waited. Alone. The officers struggled to find some-

one to call with Kat unresponsive and her emergency contacts being the people in the car with her. Shock blanket around her shoulders, she remained unaware.

The officers tried a few recent numbers, but no one answered besides family who lived hours away and had to look for an available flight. Kat's phone rang, alerting police that "Myra Brighton" was calling. They informed Myra of the accident and moved Kat to the hospital.

Kat didn't notice she was moved. Wide-eyed, she faced white hospital walls, but her parents' bloodied faces were the only things she saw. She tried to comprehend what the doctor was telling her. The words "accident" and "only survivor" stuck out. She didn't acknowledge that she was hurt and needed to be checked until she was alone. Blood coated her hands.

Blood that wasn't hers.

The image of her mother's bloodied hand flashed in her mind. She scrambled off the bed and ran to the sink in her small room. She turned on the faucet and scrubbed her hands. The mirror reflected a split lip and blood spattered across her face, sticking her hair to her skin.

Kat gasped for breath, and her chest tightened. I can't breathe. She ripped paper towels from the dispenser and placed them under the water, then scrubbed her face. Needing the blood off, she didn't register pain as she put pressure on her bruised face.

Water and blood mixed together, filling the sink. The blood spread like she would never be clean of it. She scoured her skin raw.

"Katherine," a familiar voice said.

Kat scrubbed harder. It won't come off. It's all over me.

"Katherine." He set his hand on her shoulder.

"I can't get the blood off." She whimpered at her pastor, Allen, standing behind her in the mirror. "I can't get it off." She scrubbed harder, and her voice cracked. "Their blood is on me. I can't get it off."

"Katherine, try to breathe. The blood's gone. You're going to hurt yourself."

"It's not off," Kat snapped. Tears dripped, mixing with the water and blood. *"There's more. Why is there more?"*

"Because you're aggravating the cuts from the glass." He placed his hands on hers. *"That's your blood, not theirs. Take a deep breath."*

"I have to get it off!" Kat screamed.

"Do we need to put her out?" someone asked.

"I don't think so," Allen said. "Give us a minute, please." He squeezed Kat's hands. "Listen to me, sweetheart. You're hurting yourself. You need to stop."

"I can't." Kat's body trembled. "It's on me. It's still on me!"

Allen turned Kat to face him. "Look at me. It's gone. All gone."

Kat couldn't focus enough to agree or disagree. The numbness faded, replaced by increased tautness in her chest, and the urge to run, though she didn't know where. "I must be dreaming. It wasn't real. They're not gone. They're not gone, right?"

Allen's face crumpled. "It wasn't a dream. I'm sorry, sweetheart. I'm so sorry."

"They can't be gone." Kat choked. "They can't be. We were going—" She tried to suck in a breath, but her lungs wouldn't let her. "Oh, God, they . . ." She sunk to the floor, sobs wracking her body. "I was driving. It's my fault!"

"No, it isn't." Allen descended to the floor and wrapped his arms around her. "It's not your fault, sweetheart. You did nothing wrong."

"They're gone," Kat whispered, her lungs refusing to take in air, like they only existed to cause her pain. The constriction around her heart could stop it from beating entirely and in that moment, she wondered if it'd be better if it did stop.

Exiting the memory was as abrupt and unpleasant as entering it. Nex gasped and stumbled, back in the abandoned building.

"Are you all right?" Death's brows furrowed.

"I'm fine." His answer was quiet. His mind should've been racing, but it came up blank. The only thing he knew was that he had to get back to Katherine.

He opened his mouth, but Death raised her hand. "No need to explain. I understand. Go." She held out the bracelet. "Be with her, and cherish your time. We always get less than we hope for. Don't take it for granted."

Nex grabbed the bracelet and raced to the nearest window, grateful and unsettled by Death. He flew home fast. Thinking of Kat trapped in the car with her parents' corpses made him push hard, concerned the night of stress would lead to nightmares he wouldn't be there to wake her from. He *needed* to get back to her.

Instead of dwelling on the accident, his thoughts took an unexpected turn to the day Kat brought in the exorcist. The things he'd said to make her finally snap: *Your life is pitiful. You live alone, have no friends, go to church to fight off loneliness.*

He'd never hated himself more. He'd harassed her about church when it was her pastor who comforted her after the accident. He'd called her pathetic and lonely when she'd chosen to isolate rather than deal with people looking at her differently. The snap judgments he'd made were childish, and he wished he could take them back.

He'd do anything to make it up to her.

Relief filled him when he returned to the house and found her asleep in the same position. She moved a lot when she had nightmares—something that made more sense now. The blankets hadn't shifted.

Nex returned the bracelet to her dresser and stripped down to boxers like he'd been in when they fell asleep. He crawled under the blankets behind her, wrapping his arms around her and pulling her snugly against his chest. The movement made her stir, and she curled into a tighter ball.

"Did you go somewhere?" She yawned, turning toward him and resting her head under his chin, her hands on his chest.

"Not for long." He cradled her head, unable to stop picturing her trapped in that car. "Katherine?"

"Hmm?" Her voice was soft and murmured, her eyes not opening.

Nex wasn't convinced she was fully awake. "I'm sorry for what I said to you," he whispered. "For what I said that night you brought in the exorcist."

Kat blinked her eyes halfway open and frowned. "Why are you apologizing for that now?"

"Because I was wrong, and I'm sorry. I don't think you're pathetic. I think you're incredible." He held her tighter and wished for a way to sink under her skin and let their souls wrap around each other. "I'm sorry for acting otherwise."

"You already apologized. It's forgiven." Kat kissed his cheek and buried into his chest. "I think you're incredible, too."

Nex let her fall back asleep while he pet circles on her back. He didn't deserve her forgiveness, and he certainly didn't feel incredible. The fact she said it proved he wasn't good enough for her.

He wasn't good enough for her, but he'd do everything in his power to get there.

Chapter 29

Vows

Demons lined the theater row on either side of Nex and filled the row behind him too. They may have been on good behavior, all in human form and appearing relatively normal, but he was still annoyed by their presence and unending questions.

Nex glared at Marcus. "Why did you say anything?"

"Hey, you're not the only one who cares." Marcus flipped through a program. "They wanted to be here for Kat like she was for them. We're not used to being treated nicely."

"I'm aware," Nex grumbled and leaned back in his seat. "I just think they're ridiculous."

Lucian smirked. "Says the man sitting through the same play for the fifth time."

Nex scowled. "Shut the fuck up."

"Usually, outside of hell, we escape the whips, but I guess that's not the case for you." Marcus made a whipping motion.

"I will set your seat on fire," Nex said.

"Nex!"

He recognized the voice but wasn't expecting to hear it and second-guessed himself. Frida trotted down the auditorium stairs with a bright smile, waving at him.

"Who's that?" Lucian asked.

"Katherine's cousin." Nex frowned. Unless he was mistaken, Kat told him Frida was on the other side of the continent when Kat read her blog post last night.

Frida stopped at his row and opened her arms. "Aw, come on. We're at the hugging stage, aren't we?"

"Sorry." Nex stood and accepted the hug. "I wasn't expecting you. Katherine said you were somewhere far south."

"This play's important to her, so the parents and I flew over to surprise her. We couldn't miss it, especially since we can't make it back for Christmas."

"Parents . . ." The blood drained from Nex's face. *You've got to be fucking kidding me.*

"Yeah, right, sorry. This is my mom and dad, Alice and David." She stepped back and gestured to a couple behind her. The woman had dark hair in a short bob and wore a long burgundy dress. The man was half dressed up in jeans with a blue dress shirt tucked in. "Mom and Dad, this is Kitty Kat's boyfriend, Nex."

Nex remained stiff and unresponsive. Marcus elbowed him.

Alice stepped forward and pulled Nex into a hug. "Nice to meet you."

"Heard a lot about you." David offered his hand. "Good to finally meet you."

Nex reluctantly shook his hand and tried to smile. He'd rather be in hell cleaning up blood than doing this. "You as well." He scrambled for something to talk about. He'd never been in a position like this, but there was one thing he could say. "Katherine will be thrilled you're here."

"We're excited too." Frida bounced, peering around Nex. "Lucky there are three seats in front of you, so we can all be close."

"Lucky, huh?" Marcus sniggered and nudged Nex while Frida and her parents moved to the row in front of the demons. "This is as close as you're getting to meeting the parents. Don't fuck it up."

"Your chair." Nex growled. "On fire. Shut the fuck up."

"Are these your friends?" Frida leaned over the back of her chair, surveying the group of demons occupying the entire row.

Nex kept the groan internal and nodded. "That's Marcus, Lucian, Arda, Armand . . . It keeps going. I wouldn't worry about it."

Frida's eyebrows shot up. "Wow. It's so nice they all came to support Kat." Her gaze slid to Lucian, and she bit her lip. "Hi."

Lucian blinked, also needing a prod from Marcus. "Hello."

Fucking hell, is Lucian blushing? Marcus asked Nex.

I think he is. Nex smirked.

Despite finding Frida pretty, Lucian avoided her gaze. He was on the shy side and not used to getting attention when with Marcus and Nex.

The second Lucian began talking to someone else, Frida leaned over the seat farther. "Hey," she whispered to Nex. "Is your friend single?"

Don't you fucking dare, Lucian warned. *Tell her I'm taken.*

That would be a lie, Lucian. "He's absolutely single." Nex's smile wasn't forced anymore. "He's shy, but don't let that stop you. You're exactly his type."

What is wrong with you? Lucian snapped.

Frida smiled and glanced at Lucian one more time before the lights dimmed. The director came out, and she sunk back in her seat. Nex stifled a laugh and ignored Lucian's piercing glare.

Normally, Nex got bored easily. He didn't get bored watching Katherine perform. She conquered her shyness and glowed on stage. As much as he was tense about the probability he'd have to spend the rest of the night with her family, he couldn't help but smile at the thought of how excited she'd be. He mentally rolled his eyes at himself. Marcus wasn't completely wrong with his earlier comment.

Given he'd have to interact with more humans afterward, he wished the play was longer. Time went by faster than he liked and left him standing in the parking lot with a horde of demons and Katherine's family, shifting his weight. It couldn't have been planned more poorly if it was intentional.

"She knows to meet you here?" Alice asked Nex.

Nex nodded. "It's where we've been meeting since it started. Easier than meeting in the crowded lobby."

"It's so cute you come to all her shows," Frida gushed. "She made you stop bringing flowers, huh?"

Nex cleared his throat and adjusted the collar of his jacket. "She said getting them every performance was excessive."

"I think it's freaking adorable." Frida turned to Lucian. "What'd you think of the play, Lu?"

Lucian frowned, his gaze darting to Nex, who was thankful to have the awkwardness directed at someone other than him.

"Are you speaking to me?" Lucian asked. She couldn't be. She was too pretty.

"Yeah. What," Frida cocked her head, "no one's ever given you a nickname?"

"I . . ." Lucian swallowed, unable to keep eye contact with the lovely woman in front of him. "No."

"I guess that's fair." She shrugged. "Lucian is a pretty sexy name. Better to sound it all out."

"*Frida.*" David covered his ears. "Filter, darling, filter. At least around me."

Frida sent Lucian a wink that made his brain malfunction.

"Here comes Katherine." Lucian's voice cracked at the end, and he moved back, disappearing into the crowd of demons.

Kat's focus landed on Nex immediately, and a smile spread over her face as she walked faster, then slower when she noticed who he was standing beside. She hadn't expected to see them at all this year, especially not at her play. Tears filled her eyes, and she ran toward David with open arms.

"There's our star." David grinned and caught Kat in a hug.

"No way. I can't believe you're here!" Kat squealed, throwing her arms around him. "What are you doing here?"

"We wanted to surprise you. You did amazing, sweetheart. I can't believe how beautifully you sing."

"Thank you." Kat breathed in his familiar cologne. "Feels like forever since I've seen you. I'm so glad you're here!"

David chuckled and rested his head on hers. The last time he saw her was during the month they'd stayed after his brother and sister-in-law died. He was afraid he'd never see his niece smile again, and, although he was nervous about her having a boyfriend living in the house, he hadn't missed the smile she gave Nex.

Nex happily stood aside. There were too many hugs for his liking. After Kat got over the shock of her family being there, she thanked all the demons individually, which took a lot of time. Nex sped it up because she hadn't eaten before the play, and thankfully, the rest of her family was hungry too. He suggested a bar and grill where the bartender poured generously. If he was going to sit through his first family dinner, he needed a drink.

At the bar and grill, they sat at a table, and Nex avoided engaging in conversation. He didn't know the first thing about speaking to humans in an appropriate manner. Unfortunately, when Kat got caught up talking to Frida and Alice, it left him open for attack.

"So, Nex." David leaned over the table and sipped his beer. "What is it you do for a living?"

Nex froze. *Fuck, what are normal human jobs?*

"Dad, don't do the interrogation thing." Frida rolled her eyes. "He's a sweetie. Besides, Kat told you Nex is a model. You're not senile yet, are you?" She bumped David's shoulder.

Nex stiffened and turned toward Kat, who had a guilty expression. Frida and David teased and bickered amongst each other until they were distracted. Between that and the volume in the crowded bar, Nex was confident they couldn't hear him.

He dropped his head next to Kat's. "A model? Are you fucking kidding me?"

Kat smiled meekly and rubbed her hands over her legs. "I panicked. I was on FaceTime with them, and I didn't know what to say." She wrung her hands together under his narrowing eyes. "Then Frida told them you were hot enough to be a model, so I said you were."

"For fuck's sake." Nex scrunched his face up. "Of all the fucking human jobs."

"I'm sorry." Kat rested her chin on his shoulder and gazed up at him. "Are you mad at me?"

"Like that's fucking possible." He scowled and set his hand on her lower back. "But rest assured, you're going to make it up to me later."

"Yeah?" Kat's eyes drifted to his lips. "How?"

Nex leaned over and kissed her. "However I want you to."

"Hey, Nex," Frida said. "My dude, I don't care what your religious affiliation is or isn't. You need to go to church with Kat to get that guy to stop bothering her every Sunday. Pretty sure he wants her or something. Best mark your territory, boy."

"Frida," Alice scolded.

"What?" Frida shrugged. "It's true."

"What guy?" Nex's head snapped toward Kat.

Kat pursed her lips at Frida, who mouthed *Sorry* and pretended to be interested in the menu. The intensity of Nex's stare made Kat shrink.

"What guy?"

Kat avoided his gaze. "It's nothing."

Every week Gabriel talked to her, and she grew more uncomfortable. He asked too many personal questions and engaged her in theological discussions about right versus wrong, what was sin and what wasn't. He also brought Nex up in a subtly negative way. She didn't tell Nex because his protective side could be a little out of control, and while Gabriel bothered her, she didn't want Nex taking things too far and bringing Lilith back.

"Katherine." Nex growled low in her ear. "Who is bothering you?"

"He's not bothering me." Kat let her hair fall past her shoulders to give them a little more privacy. "He's lonely and wants a friend because he's new to town. He's not socially adept. He knows I'm with you, and I talk about you all the time. Don't worry about it." She smoothed her hand over his chest. "I'm with you, Nex."

"If that's all it is, why are you venting to Frida while hiding it from me?"

Kat pulled her hand back. "You want me to vent every single annoyance in my day to you?"

"Maybe I do." He leaned closer and slid his hand under the table, resting it high on her leg. "You are mine, after all." He rubbed circles in her thigh, and she sucked in a breath. "Who is it?"

"The possibility of you overreacting is the exact reason I didn't tell you."

"Tell me." Nex brushed his lips against hers and gripped her thigh. "Now, kitten. Or you're going to have a lot to make up to me."

"Ugh, with the PDA," Frida said, making Kat hide her face and slouch in her chair. "We have something important to discuss."

"This is *not* over," Nex warned.

Kat peeked through her fingers. "What?"

Nex frowned as all humor vanished from Frida's expression, her eyes darting to her dad. David smiled stiffly. "We're only in town for tonight. Given the holiday season, I can't stay away from work too long. I wondered if—" His face fell, and Kat sat up straighter, brows furrowed. "I wondered if you'd like to visit your parents' grave with us tonight. I'd like to go. I thought you might too. Especially since we won't be here Christmas Eve."

"Oh." Kat reached under the table and grabbed Nex's hand. "Sure. We can do that."

"Nex, you're welcome to come," David said. "But there's no pressure if you'd rather not."

While Nex didn't care for the idea of being around four emotional humans, he also wouldn't leave Katherine alone. He squeezed her hand, intending to accept the offer, but Kat spoke first.

"Nex can't."

Nex frowned.

"He, um . . ." Her eyes darted around before she spoke again. "He has to make an appearance at this party for work."

Nex tried not to let it show that it bothered him she didn't want him to come. It shouldn't. It was her business. Not his. It still did.

"Oh, that's all right," David said. "I didn't want to leave him out."

Kat's smile was anything but relaxed. "We appreciate it." Her shoulders dropped when the server showed up with food, distracting the table and taking the focus off the unpleasant topic.

"You don't want me there?" Nex asked.

"Of course I want you there." Kat scooted closer and tightened her hand on his. "I always want you around." She lowered her voice to a whisper. "They're buried in the cemetery at my church. Doesn't that count as holy ground?"

Nex's eyebrows raised. It most likely did count as holy ground. He couldn't go with her. He couldn't comfort her if she cried. He couldn't go with her on Christmas Eve if she wanted to visit them. Worse, he couldn't do a damn thing to change it.

The reason he couldn't go to such an important place being because he was a demon was worse than her not wanting him to go. Appetite gone, he scooted the plate of pasta away. "I'm sorry."

"Why are you sorry? It's okay." She murmured "Thank you" to the server as food was set in front of her. She squeezed Nex's hand one last time before letting go to pick up her silverware. "Don't worry. It's not a big deal."

Except it was a big deal. How could it not be? She picked up the conversation with her family, and Nex's food remained untouched. Someone who wasn't a demon would be able to go and hold her when she cried. He'd never be able to do that for her.

"You okay?" Kat asked.

He studied her freckles, her beautiful green eyes, and her red hair she tried but failed to tame most of the time. He hated himself for what he was—someone who couldn't be there for her in the ways she needed. "I'm fine."

"You sure?"

"I'm sure, kitten." He poked at his food to avoid her.

Kat's hand landed on his leg, and she kissed his cheek. "Thanks for coming and being with my family tonight. I know it's not your thing, but," she leaned her head on his shoulder, "I'm glad you're here."

Nex rested his head on hers, some of the self-loathing easing. Doing this for her was better than nothing.

After dinner, Nex went his own way, and Kat walked with her family to the church. Every step toward the cemetery got heavier. She hadn't visited since the funeral.

"I was thinking of flying you to California for Christmas," David said. "So you don't spend the anniversary alone. What do you think?"

"Oh." Kat kicked at the snow as she walked and kept her head down. "I appreciate the offer, but I won't be alone. I have Nex and church."

"I think it might be a good idea for you to be with family," Frida tried.

"I'll be fine," Kat said. "Really."

Alice looped her arm through Kat's. "It's an open invitation if you want to come, honey. We'll gladly fly you over. We'd be happy to have you and Nex if he can."

They stopped in front of the cemetery, and Kat's throat tightened. Uncle David draped an arm around her shoulders. The metal gate creaked in protest when they opened it, as if it shared the pain embedded deep within Kat's heart. Even though Kat had only been there once for her parents, she knew where to find their grave. David gave her a reassuring squeeze on the shoulder as they paused in front of the shared headstone.

Engraved across the top was "Milton", and directly under was "Jeremiah 29:11. 'For I know the plans I have for you'." Her parents' favorite verse, and the one they often told Kat whenever life got especially hard. *There's a reason for everything, Kat,* her mother always said. Kat tried to live by that motto, but it wasn't easy after they died.

Under the verse were their names: "Joshua Elijah and Helen Katherine". Following were their birth dates, as well as the date Kat would never forget, no matter how much she wished she could. That day stuck out more than the day of the funeral, though she'd never forget their caskets lowering into the ground. Her chest constricted, and she swallowed against the sting in her eyes.

"They would've been proud of you." Alice patted Kat's shoulder next to David's hand.

"They would've been in the front row," Frida grasped Kat's hand, "watching and cheering you on."

"They were watching." Kat's words came out in a broken whisper. She hated crying in front of people, so although the tears were about to overflow, she held them back. Her legs were ready to give out, and she was tempted to let them. "They were watching from somewhere else."

The walk home was almost impossible. One visit to that cemetery drained the energy from her body. Telling stories about her parents should've been a positive thing, but it didn't help. Kat needed a minute alone because tears were about to fall.

At the house, Kat excused herself to the main bathroom. She rested her hands on the counter and dropped her head as the tears spilled. If her parents were alive, they would've been in the front row. If they were alive, the house would be full of Christmas decorations, not completely void. If they were alive, Kat would come home to the smell of baking treats and cinnamon candles. They would watch Christmas movies, tour light displays, and listen to carols.

Every *if* scenario brought more tears until she was shaking. The door opened, and she wiped her eyes. "It's occupied." Through the mirror, she saw Nex standing behind her.

"I know." Nex brushed his fingers along her back, shoulders, then arm, all the way down to her trembling hand.

They stared at each other. Kat hated crying in front of anyone, but at that moment, she needed his arms around her. The second she turned into him, he hugged her.

He could see her barely holding herself together at the cemetery. He'd watched from a distance, hoping that maybe it didn't count as holy ground. Hope was lost when he walked into a wall only he could feel. So, he was held at bay as Kat broke down. He wasn't done asking about the man bothering her, but the last thing she needed right now was anything other than what he was giving her.

As he stood with his arms around her, rubbing her back in what he hoped was a soothing motion, he realized how far gone he was. Marcus was right. It wasn't like him to go to plays, to sit at family dinners, to socialize with people he didn't know, or to stick around when someone cried. But this was Katherine.

He would do anything for her.

He would do anything for her, and watching from a distance at the cemetery left him helpless, distracting him so much that he didn't notice the person in the window of the church. The same person who now stared out into the snow with a frown. In all his years as an angel, he'd never seen a demon behave like this.

"What's taking so long?"

Gabriel turned, finding his brother Uriel behind him. "I'm working on it."

"It's simple," Uriel said. "Separate them."

"I'm trying. She's attached to him."

"It doesn't matter if she's attached. Are you forgetting your vows?"

"Of course I'm not," Gabriel snapped. "I told you I'm working on it. I can only push her so far, or she'll get suspicious. If the demon knows we're here, he'll never let her out of his sight. This is the safest place to approach her. It's the only place he cannot follow. That only gives me twice a week to speak with her."

Uriel's lips pressed into a thin line. "Push harder. Unless you want me to intervene. We swore oaths, Gabriel. Do not forgo your duty, or I will take over."

Gabriel didn't want that. Uriel could be as ruthless as a demon. "Your presence isn't necessary. Aren't you supposed to be in London?"

"I am." Uriel nodded. "And if this isn't finished by the time I resolve that problem, then expect to be disciplined by *them*. We have vows to honor, Gabriel."

"I'm aware." Gabriel leaned on the windowsill. "I will handle it."

Chapter 30

Perfect

K at wiped spilled punch from the church floor. As Bernice got older, a past injury in her hand gave her trouble, making it hard to hold things. She was embarrassed, but Kat cleaned it up and dropped the paper towels in the trash before returning to the table.

"It's all right." Kat crouched beside Bernice, patting her hand. "Accidents happen. Don't be embarrassed. Look. I have something for you." Kat reached into her messenger bag and pulled out a velvet pouch. "They're Chinese Baoding balls." Kat opened the pouch and let the chiming balls fall into her hand. "You roll them in your hand like this." She demonstrated circling them in her palm. "It's supposed to help arthritis and build hand strength."

"Oh." Bernice smiled and set her hand on Kat's face. "Thank you, Katherine. You're so sweet."

"Well, I learned from a wonderful woman." Kat smiled and placed the Baoding balls in Bernice's hand. "Why don't you try? I'll get you some of my frog eye salad you like so much."

"That would be lovely, dear. Thank you."

Kat made her way to the long table of food. Her church had a fellowship meal today, and, despite Nex's passive-aggressive comments, she stayed. He could get over it. She wasn't about to compromise the things that mattered to her because he didn't like them. He tended to bounce back quickly, even if she made him mad, but he did seem angrier than usual. Today was more of a fight—their first big argument since they'd grown closer.

It sat unhappily as a heavy weight in her stomach and tension in her shoulders. She didn't want to fight, but she wasn't going to give up this part of herself.

"That was kind of you." Gabriel came alongside Kat and nodded to Bernice. Every week, he'd talk to her. He even attended choir rehearsals.

Kat's smile was disingenuous. His presence was calming, yet she felt off around him, and that confusing combination left her tense. "It was nothing. She's a lovely woman." Kat spooned frog eye salad onto a paper plate.

"It's not nothing to her." Gabriel gestured to the salad. "Did you make this?"

"Yeah, I did. It was my mom's recipe."

Gabriel flashed a bright smile. "It's delicious. Interesting sermon today, don't you think?"

Kat let her hair fall, forming a shield. The sermon about demons and how they tempt and prey made her uncomfortable, given the fact Nex was an actual demon. Though she didn't think what she did with him was wrong.

He was nothing like the demons she'd heard about. He tempted her, definitely, but he was also more tender and caring than she knew a person could be. Calling him a demon was too simple a label for such a complex man.

Kat gave a stiff nod to Gabriel. "It was."

"Sometimes a sermon speaks to you," Gabriel said. "Almost as if it was made to be heard by you specifically. Sometimes as a warning, I think." Kat's gaze snapped to him. "Or sometimes as a reminder to get ourselves back on track. Sometimes it makes you want to pray and find yourself again as the conviction takes over your heart. It certainly had that effect on me. Would you want to pray with me, Katherine?"

Kat's brows furrowed. He couldn't know. "I normally pray privately,

Gabriel. If you want someone to pray with you and help you find yourself, I'm sure our pastor would be happy to."

She stepped away to return to Bernice, but Gabriel moved in front of her. "And you wouldn't? You seem like the type of person who wants to help people, who wants to be good."

"I am." Kat peered up at him with a slight narrowing of her eyes. "I do help people, and I do my best to be a good person, but forgive me, Gabriel. It almost sounds like you're implying I have something I need to repent about. Have I done something to offend you?"

"I'm implying no such thing." He showed off another too-bright smile. "But if you're feeling attacked, that's often because you're holding guilt in your heart. Do you have something you should feel guilty over?"

Kat's eyebrows lifted. "Excuse me? Are you suggesting I'm doing something wrong?"

His smile faltered. "*Are* you doing something wrong? Are you letting yourself be tempted by demons and carried down a dark path? People are not always what they seem. Your boyfriend won't accompany you to church. What does that say about him? Perhaps he isn't the best person for someone who seems otherwise honorable."

"I don't appreciate your forwardness." Kat's tone was clipped. "Nex being my boyfriend doesn't mean he has to believe what I believe or attend church with me. Him not wanting to come doesn't make him a bad person. There isn't anything I've done that I should feel guilty for, and you know why? Because my morals are ironclad, and if I had something I *should* feel guilty over, then I would. But I don't. I know the difference between right and wrong. Based on your behavior, I'd wager you don't. Take your convictions to Pastor Brighton if that makes you feel better. As for me, what I do and what I believe is right are between me and who I choose, be it another person or God. My convictions are my own. They're not something I have to explain to you."

Kat stalked away, but Gabriel caught her arm. "Katherine—"

"I'll thank you not to bother me again, Gabriel." Kat yanked her arm free and returned to Bernice with the salad, trying to keep the smile on her face despite the shake in her hands.

Don't look at him. Don't give him the benefit. Hair on the back of her neck rose, and she looked over, finding him talking to someone else. The moment her eyes landed on him, his gaze darted to her. That peacefulness he usually exuded wasn't so calming. Something about him was off, and she squirmed at the prospect of walking home alone, so she broke the tense silence with Nex.

Kat: Wanna have dinner with me at that bar you like?

It didn't matter that Kat was underage. If anyone considered asking for ID, one look from Nex changed their mind.

Kat chewed her lip and waited for his response. Usually, they came fast, but he wasn't happy when she left. He often walked her to church, but today he was so mad he didn't. Her phone vibrated, and she swiped open the text.

Nex: Trying to make up for spending all day in a place you know I can't be? They don't have any of your healthy food at that bar.

Kat sighed and typed a response, then deleted it, typed another, and deleted that. Thumbs hovering over the screen and heart aching, she frowned. She hoped he would've cooled off by now. Another message came in, and her shoulders relaxed.

Nex: You don't have anything to make up to me. It's not your fault I can't go on holy ground. I'm sorry for fighting with you this morning. The truth is, now I'm only upset with you because you ruined a surprise. I made dinner for you. As part of my apology for losing my temper and being an ass. So no, I don't want to go to a restaurant with other people. You're the only one I want to see. I miss you, my kitten. Do you miss me?

A warm smile spread over her face. Part of her wondered if she should bring up Gabriel instead of misleading Nex, but he got overprotective too easily, and as annoyed as she was with Gabriel, she didn't want Nex doing anything rash. Lilith scared her. Nex's short temper would definitely come out if he knew what happened with Gabriel today, and that could attract Lilith's attention.

Kat: Of course I miss you. I always miss you. Will you come walk home with me so I don't lose any more time with you today?

The hair on the back of her neck rose. She glanced back, then snapped her head forward when she saw Gabriel still staring.

Nex: For fuck's sake, stop ruining every surprise I have. Look outside.

Heart hammering, she walked to the window. Outside the church boundary stood Nex. She had planned to stay a little longer, but now she wanted to be in his arms. She gave him a small wave then said quick goodbyes to her congregation.

On the snowy path, she ran and threw her arms around Nex. "I'm sorry." She buried her face in his neck. "I'm not trying to hurt you by coming here."

"Don't be sorry." Nex stroked her hair. "I'm sorry for being an asshole. I know it's important to you. I'll stop pestering you about it if you agree that however long you spend where I can't reach you, I get equal time with you completely naked."

"Oh, good grief." Kat rolled her eyes and grabbed his hand. "As if you don't get that already."

"You misunderstand, kitten." Nex squeezed her hand, then released it and wrapped his arm around her waist as they walked. "I want you naked, not just in the bedroom. I want you naked all the time. Fighting with your hair, making your tea. I think it's time to enact that *no-clothes-at-home policy*."

Kat leaned into his side. "Not happening."

Nex shrugged. "Challenge accepted. I'll make it so you can't get to any of your clothes. Then you'll have to be naked for me."

"I thought you were trying to make up this morning to me?"

"I was, but you ruined the surprises I planned, so now you have something to make up to me." His fingers pressed into her waist, and he kissed her temple. "I'll decide how you do that. It's not an easy decision because I do very much like watching your face twist in pleasure while I fuck you, but I also thoroughly enjoy bending you over. Perhaps I'll do both."

Kat smacked his chest and glanced around to make sure nobody was nearby. "What did I say about talking about these things in public?"

"I don't know. I stop listening when you tell me what I'm allowed to say to the woman who belongs to me."

Kat turned her face into his coat to hide her embarrassment as they crossed her snow-covered yard. "You're ridiculous."

Nex scoffed. "You like how I am. Don't bother denying it. So . . . How was it?"

"You don't have to ask. It's not for you. That's okay." She unlocked and opened the front door. "We don't have to agree on everything, Nex. We can respect each other without agreeing."

"Katherine." Nex lifted her the second they were inside, making her squeal. He kicked the door shut and carried her to the bed, dropping her on it and picking up her foot to remove her boot. "You make an effort to ask me about things you don't care for. Answer my question, so I can pretend I'm good enough for you by listening to your answer without giving a sarcastic comment."

"You're good enough for me." Kat sat up, setting her hands on his face. "Do you think you're not?"

"What kind of question is that?" Nex removed her other boot and sat on the edge of the bed, facing away from her. "I'm a demon, kitten. I'm clearly not good enough for you. I can't even walk into a fucking building with you. I can't go to a place that's important to you."

Important was an understatement when describing the place her closest friends were. A place she associated with her parents. Where they were buried. A place she felt safe and loved. A place dear to her.

A place Nex would never be able to step foot in.

"It doesn't bother me that you can't come with me. That doesn't matter. You're not just a demon." Kat crawled to the edge of the bed and hugged him from behind, resting her chin on his shoulder. "You're so many things. And you're more than good enough for me. You . . ." She licked her lips, her face heating. "You make me feel whole. I haven't felt that way since I lost my parents. I felt empty, but I don't with you. You fill up voids I thought would always stay empty."

Kat's words swelled Nex's heart. He turned to face her, questioning how someone so perfect could want him. He wanted to tell her how much she meant to him but couldn't. The way he felt for her wasn't something he'd experienced before. His own personal angel.

There was one way to convey his feelings.

"I can fill you in other ways." He smirked and slid her coat off. "I can fill you over and over."

Kat covered her eyes and red cheeks.

"Still shy with me, kitten?" Nex stroked her cheek. "Even though I've fucked you in practically every room of this house, you're still going to be shy?"

Kat peeked at him over her fingers. "It's not that."

"What then?"

"I . . ." Kat swallowed and dropped her hands, wringing them together. Nex frowned. She was innocent and shy, but this was something else. Kat crawled off the bed and stood in front of him.

He pulled her toward him. "Is something wrong?"

"No." Kat blew out a puff of air and fiddled with the collar of his shirt. "I want to do something. For you. But I-I don't know how."

"Spit it out."

"Every morning you . . ."

Nex smirked. "Have you as an appetizer to breakfast?"

"Um, yes," Kat whispered.

Although it was true, he meant it as a joke. Even if they didn't have sex, she never left the bed without him going down on her.

"The thing is, I want to, you know," she darted her eyes away, her next word almost inaudible, "reciprocate."

Adjusting himself, Nex cleared his throat. "You want to suck my cock, kitten?"

Kat's face burned, and she covered it. "Geeze, don't say it like that."

Nex chuckled and pulled her hands down so he could see her. "You should know by now I don't censor things. Look at me." She brought her eyes to his. "I don't want you to do this because you think you owe me. That's bullshit. Don't ever do something because you think you owe me."

Kat chewed her lip. "You don't want me to?"

"Of course I want you to." Nex's voice was huskier as he dragged his fingers across her lips. "I've thought about your lips around my cock more times than you know, but I won't have you doing it because you think you owe me."

"That's not why I want to." Kat shifted her weight from one foot to the other. "I want to because—" She set her palms on her face again, hoping the coldness would chill the burn. "I want to make you feel good like you do for me. I just don't know how."

Nex's eyes darkened. "You want to?" Kat nodded. He stood, gripping her waist. "You sure?"

He stared with such intensity her body ached to lean into his touch. All he had to do was look at her like that, and she wanted him.

She shivered as his hands ascended her body, grazing her breasts. "Yes."

"Very well, kitten." He gripped her shoulders and guided her down. "On your knees."

Kat caught her lip between her teeth and gazed up for guidance. She was still embarrassed by her lack of experience, but she maintained eye contact.

"Fuck." He shrugged off his coat and tossed it away. "You have no idea what seeing you on your knees in front of me does. It brings out that urge to dominate you." He cupped her face and ran his thumb over her cheekbone. Then, he undid his pants and pushed them down. "What are you doing to me?" He slid his boxers down, freeing his cock. "Give me your hand."

Kat placed her hand in his, and he guided it around him. His cock twitched. Kat looked up at him, and he groaned, threading his hands in her hair. "You're too fucking perfect for me, Katherine." Pain flashed over his face. "I'm going to ruin you."

She shook her head and curled her fingers around him. "You won't. I want you. All of you. I don't see anyone else, Nex."

"Fuck." He bent and kissed her head, breathing in her scent. "Open your mouth." He grabbed her jaw. "Open, and suck me in."

Kat obeyed. She licked her lips before tentatively wrapping them around his tip. Nex's hands tightened in her hair, and an unsteady breath escaped him. Her mouth was warm and enticing. He rubbed soothing circles against her jaw. "Bigger, kitten."

Kat dropped her jaw and took more of him in. He groaned and held her head as he sank into the back of her throat. Kat made a surprised sound, her eyes watering.

Nex moved both hands behind her head. "Look at me." Kat gazed up, and he sank farther down her throat, making her choke. Her eyes closed briefly as she gagged. Somehow, not in an unpleasant way. "Are you mine, Katherine?" Kat nodded, and Nex reminded himself to move slow. "Fuck yes, you are." He growled, sliding out of her mouth and letting her catch her breath before he slid back in. Kat's eyes shut, and she tentatively skimmed her tongue along him, sucking lightly. "*Fuck,*" Nex whispered. He pulled out, and she looked between him and his hardness.

Breathless, she wiped her mouth. "Am I doing it wrong?"

Nex's expression softened. He was so goddamn turned on having her like this, he didn't want to cut the heavenly moment short by coming too soon. "Definitely not. You're perfect. Open up, and take it at your speed. I'll let you have control. Next time, I'm going to fuck that pretty mouth." He rubbed his thumb over her lips, making them part. His cock tensed, and he leaned forward, pressing his tip to her parted lips. "But this time, take your time."

Kat opened, and he pushed back in. He panted and guided her down his whole length before pulling her back, repeating the motion until she didn't need guidance. He stared down at her and moaned, watching her bob back and forth. He prided himself on stamina, but the sight of her sucking him off, the humility that the woman in front of him wanted him like this . . . He was ready to burst.

"If you don't want to swallow, you better stop."

Kat sped up, and Nex groaned, gripping her hair. She moved faster, sucking him deeper so she could hear him enjoy it. The sounds coming out of him made her wet and desperate to do it again.

He held her in place, sinking into her throat as he came. Panting, he stayed in her mouth for a moment. After he pulled out, Kat took a deep breath, wiping her mouth and looking up at him with big green eyes he adored. How someone could still look innocent after that, he didn't know.

"Did I do okay?" Her brows knitted as if she was worried.

"Did you—" Nex shook his head, not believing what he was hearing. He needed to teach her to have confidence. He picked her up, tossed her on the bed, and pushed her dress up her legs, his lips following the fabric. "Yes, kitten. You did more than okay. That was the best fucking blow job I've ever had." He yanked down her underwear and leggings, a growl rumbling in his chest at the sight of her wet slit. "You want me to show you how much I liked it? You want me to put my mouth on you? Make you come?"

Kat's heart raced, and she preemptively gripped the blankets. "Yes."

Nex didn't move right away. He stared up at her. How was it possible one person could be so perfect? He stared so long she looked away, face flushing.

"What?"

Nex swallowed. "Nothing. You're just so fucking beautiful." He dropped his head between her legs, his last words too quiet for her to hear. "My angel." He dragged his tongue over her, reveling in the reward of her moan.

Chapter 31

The Strongest Force in the World

Even on a stepstool, Kat had to stand on her tiptoes to reach the shelf at the front of the chapel. She straightened the candle until it matched the one on the opposite side of the communion table. Stepping down, she glanced back and forth between the pair of shelves to ensure both candles were centered.

"I'm surprised you didn't bring a measuring tape this time," Bernice said from where she sat in the front pew, untangling Christmas lights.

"I was going to, but I forgot."

It was Nex's fault. She had it sitting by the door, but he nearly convinced her to stay home rather than decorate the church. His attempt left her too distracted to remember everything.

Bernice smiled. "It looks lovely, dear. Did you hear..."

Gaze drifting across the church, Kat missed what Bernice said. Other volunteers decorated garlands over the pews and lights around the windows. Her eyes landed on Gabriel. Uneasiness crept through her stomach and twisted into a knot. It grew when Gabriel's eyes locked with hers. She snapped her gaze to Bernice who raised an eyebrow.

"Sorry." Kat clasped her hands together. "What did you say?"

Bernice frowned between Kat and Gabriel before settling on Kat. "He's been bothering you, hasn't he?"

Kat shrugged and picked up another strand of tangled lights.

"Katherine, say something to Allen."

Kat loved Pastor Brighton dearly but didn't want to make a big deal of it. Settling next to Bernice, she focused on untangling lights. "It's fine. I set boundaries last time we spoke."

Bernice peered at Kat over her glasses but stayed silent. Kat was thankful she didn't bring it up again, instead finding more lighthearted conversation. As much as Kat usually enjoyed Bernice's company, she couldn't sit still with Gabriel watching her.

Ready to get out of there and home to Nex, Kat worked fast. When the last lights were untangled, someone else walked Bernice across the street. By the time Kat finished the decorations, she was on her own. She buttoned her coat and secured her red scarf around her neck on her way to the door.

A figure stepped in front of the exit. Kat tensed. Gabriel blocked her path. She tried to move around him, but he stepped in front of her again.

"I need to talk to you."

Kat lifted her chin. "I think it's better we keep our distance, Gabriel. We clearly have clashing personalities. Excuse me."

She reached for the door, but he grabbed her arm and pulled her to the side. "Katherine, I need to talk to you. I'm trying to help you."

Yanking her arm out of his hold, she held her hand up. "I don't need help. What do you want from me?"

"I want you to be safe, and I don't think you're safe at home. Not with your boyfriend there."

Kat balled her fists. "You don't even know him. It's also none of your business. In case you've forgotten, I asked you not to bother me."

His hand closed around her arm. "Katherine, *please*. Please hear me out. I'm not doing this to hurt yo—"

A hand gripped Gabriel's arm. "Let her go."

Kat's shoulders relaxed at the sight of Pastor Brighton.

Gabriel stepped back, holding his hands up. "It's not how it looks. We were simply having a discussion."

"A discussion doesn't require you to put your hands on her." Allen narrowed his eyes. "Another member informed me that this isn't the first time you've bothered her despite her asking you to stay away. If you can't respect her wishes, then there's clearly a problem."

"There's no problem," Gabriel said. "I was reconciling a misunderstanding."

"Is that what happened?" Allen asked Kat.

Kat shuffled her feet. "No, that's not what he was doing."

"Gabriel, if you want to continue attending this church, then it will require you to keep your distance from Katherine and meet with me to discuss what kind of behavior is appropriate." Allen stepped next to Katherine and crossed his arms.

"Pastor Brighton, with all due respect, you've only heard one side of the story," Gabriel said.

"If you're implying that Katherine's being dishonest, then we have an even bigger problem." Allen squeezed Kat's shoulder, and she moved closer to him. "Because I've known her since she was a baby, and she doesn't have a lying bone in her body. I don't appreciate you twisting the story. If you want to attend church next week, give me a call to meet before Sunday. Because I won't tolerate this behavior." Allen directed Kat around Gabriel toward the door. "I'll walk you home?"

"Please." She didn't want to walk alone after that.

"Just a minute." Allen approached his wife, Myra. "I'm going to walk Katherine home, love. If I'm not back by the time you're ready to leave, will you pick me up? I asked Derek to lock up for the night."

"I can do that." Myra kissed his cheek, then looked to Kat. "Goodnight, sweetheart." She waved. "Thanks for helping."

Kat waved and tried to smile. "Goodnight."

Allen opened the church doors and motioned Kat ahead. They walked out into the snow, and Kat rubbed her arms as a chill that had little to do with the cold crept up her spine. Something was off about Gabriel.

Allen's gaze drifted to Kat as they strolled down the sidewalk. "Why didn't you tell me something was wrong?"

Kat tugged on the fringe at the ends of her scarf. "I didn't want to make it into a big thing."

"Katherine." Allen sighed. "I know you're private, but if something like that's happening, I need to be informed. I can't have people making the young women in our church feel uncomfortable in a place that should be safe."

Kat chewed her lip. "You're right. I'll tell you if it happens again."

Allen smiled, but Kat didn't feel much like smiling. The way Gabriel looked at her made the hair on her neck stand up. The same way it did every time she passed the church recently.

She side-stepped a telephone pole. "Have you been at the church a lot the last couple of weeks at night?"

"No. Grace has had several photoshoots at night, and she wanted me with her, so I've been tied up with that. Unfortunately, all our elders have been busy too. I've had to lock the church. I did post a sign with phone numbers and directions to shelters in case anyone came by."

Kat frowned. It wasn't Pastor Brighton. Someone else had been in the church. Someone who shouldn't have been because the door was locked. Kat shivered, and her gaze dropped to the snowy ground dirtied with muddy shoe prints.

Am I reading too much into it, or do I need to be worried? Since the accident, she didn't trust herself not to be paranoid. The first few months after it happened, she struggled, saw things that weren't there, and got jumpy and anxious for no reason. For all she knew, she'd imagined the movement. She didn't *actually* see anyone.

Not wanting to think about the accident or talk about Gabriel, she went for the least obvious subject change. "How's Grace doing?"

Allen's oldest daughter was an aspiring model. She was stunning inside and out. Although Kat wasn't close friends with her, they were the same age, and Kat knew her well from growing up in church together.

A smile spread across Allen's face. "She's doing well. Her last agent wasn't a great fit, but this new one is wonderful. She's secured all kinds of contracts that Gracie's excited about. Sometimes Gracie gets nervous about shooting at night, so I go with her and work on my sermons. I don't mind. She amazes me with her poise under pressure. Must be something she learned from her mother because she certainly didn't learn it from me." He chuckled. "I'm proud of her."

"That's great." They paused in front of Kat's house.

Allen stared with a sad expression at the home noticeably dark compared to the rest of the street full of Christmas lights. "No Christmas decorations this year?"

Kat fiddled with the buttons on her coat. "No. I," she kicked at the snow, "um, couldn't." She took a deep breath and stuck her hands into her pockets. "It's stupid and silly, but I couldn't."

"You don't have to explain." He inclined his head to the bench on Kat's covered porch. "Do you have a minute?"

Kat waved him ahead, and they sat. Nex was out with Lucian. He'd started turning on the lights inside when he was home so he wouldn't startle Kat. The lights were off, so she had time to talk.

Allen leaned forward and rested his elbows on his knees. "You know, sometimes it's terrifying to be a parent to girls. This world we live in, it's scary. Gracie asks me to attend photoshoots because she's often in a studio alone with two male photographers. That, and she has to park downtown and walk alone after dark to get there. I wish we didn't live in a world where my daughter was scared to go to work and walk down a street, but we do, and I don't blame her for being scared. I'm scared." He clasped his hands together. "I'm glad she asks me to go. I wish things were different, but it's how it is, and at least I can say I'm glad my daughter knows she can come to me when she's scared. Sometimes," he glanced at Kat, "we need help when someone makes us uncomfortable, and that's okay."

Kat's lips pulled down. Even if she wasn't sure how much of it was paranoia, it was better to be safe. Pastor Brighton knowing Gabriel bothered her was good, but maybe she needed to tell Nex.

"You know the other thing that's hard about having girls?" Allen continued. "I try to bring them up right. I encourage them to be themselves, to know their value, to feel comfortable in their skin, and be anything they want to be. But society tells them something else." He dragged his shoe across the porch to scrape off the snow. "Society tells them to be, look, and act a certain way. That there's only one way to be beautiful and successful. Hope's on this kick of wanting to be a firefighter. She talked me into buying her an outfit and everything. She walks around the house with this pretend hose, putting out *fires*." He made air quotes with his fingers. "Saves her stuffed animals from burning buildings." He laughed. "It's adorable, and I encourage it. If my daughter wants to be a firefighter, she can be a firefighter."

Despite the uneasiness from Gabriel, Kat smiled. Hope was Allen's youngest—six years old and an absolute delight. All his daughters were. His whole family was warm and welcoming.

"One day, Hope went to school wearing her outfit, and a boy told her she couldn't be a firefighter. Only boys are firefighters. When she cried, he said that's exactly why only boys can be firefighters, because girls are too emotional." Allen rolled his eyes. "Something his parents taught him, I'm sure. So, Myra and I had to explain sexism to our six-year-old. She's *six*. My girl shouldn't have to worry about things like that, but it starts young and doesn't stop. It's a constant battle. You know one of the more important things I wish I could get through to them?"

Kat twisted on the bench to face him. "What?"

He turned toward her as well. "To have compassion for themselves. Life can be difficult. People can be cruel, sometimes consciously and sometimes not. Things go wrong. Accidents happen. Biases exist though they shouldn't, and it affects us more than we'd like to admit. Then there's outside pressure telling us there's an appropriate way to react. Gracie had a fellow model mock her for bringing me with her." He pressed his lips into a thin line. "She told her she was a bad role model for needing a man with her, and that was something Gracie already felt self-conscious about."

"She shouldn't feel that way." Kat breathed on her hands to warm them. "Everyone has their own levels of comfort."

"I agree." Allen rested his palms on his knees. "And Gracie does too, but it doesn't mean those words don't affect her. Hope knows she can be what she wants. It doesn't mean that boy's words didn't hurt. Then there's Faith." He ran his hand through his salt-and-pepper hair. "Faith struggles with self-esteem. Myra and I tell her she's beautiful, but thirteen's a difficult age. Half of her friends dress up and wear makeup. The other half say that conforms to society, making her feel guilty if she puts in extra effort. All three of my girls have these struggles." His downcast eyes and sad expression made Kat's heart ache. "Gracie feels like being scared makes her weak. Faith feels like she's not pretty enough but doesn't want to try *too* hard. Hope feels bad that she cried and gave that boy more firepower. My girls come home, and they're so hard on themselves because there's outside pressure pulling them in different directions, telling them that to be a *proper* female, they must be soft but not too soft, strong but not too strong, pretty but not too pretty. Crying makes you emotional, but if you don't, you're cold and heartless. That's an awful amount of pressure to put on girls so young."

Kat made a face. "It's unfair." She had no idea the girls were going through so much. It had been a long time since she had dinner at their house.

"It is unfair. People think there's one right way to go through something, and that's not true. If Gracie's scared, she should be able to ask me to be there. If Faith wants to dress a certain way to feel good about herself, she should. And Hope should be able to be what she wants and cry if she needs to. There's no one right way of handling these scenarios. We all have struggles we have no control over that make life difficult. Knowing that everyone struggles in their own unique ways should make us compassionate to one another and to ourselves, don't you think?"

Kat stared at her lap. He had a lesson coming.

He set his hand on her shoulder. "It's not stupid or silly that you don't have decorations out."

Kat was only able to give a small nod. The whole thing was confusing and painful. Skipping Christmas seemed silly, but she couldn't imagine a Christmas without them or go into the garage where the decorations and her mother's car were.

"You know what I tell my girls when they're being too hard on themselves?"

"What?"

"I ask them, if a friend had the same problem, would they tell their friend they were overreacting and not responding right? Or would they have compassion and encourage their friend?" He squeezed her shoulder, his expression softening. "So, Katherine, let me ask you. If a friend lost their parents, would you tell them the way they handled their grief was silly and stupid, or show them love and tell them however they got through it, that was the right way to get through it?"

A lump formed in Kat's throat. He had a point. If only her heart was as empathetic inwardly as it was outwardly.

"Do you remember how we worked through your guilt over the accident?"

She didn't remember all her counseling sessions, but she did remember the ones about her guilt because it was all-consuming. So was her anger. She spent several months so angry she couldn't stand to be around anyone. Luckily, Allen had patience enough to help her through it. She barely recognized herself during that time.

"We worked through it by saying you needed compassion for yourself because what happened wasn't your fault or within your control. While I know part of you still feels guilty, you've made a lot of progress, haven't you?" Kat nodded, afraid her voice would crack if she spoke. "Good, because I want you to channel that compassion again. If you need to skip Christmas, or at least the decorations because it's too much, then do that and don't feel guilty or silly. As long as you're not hurting yourself or someone else, there's no wrong way to grieve. You know that, right?"

"I guess." Kat pulled on a loose thread on her coat. "I wish . . ." She sucked in a breath, her gaze fixed on the snow while tears stung her eyes. "I wish it was easier. It's almost been a year, and I still have bad days."

"A year isn't so long. Grief doesn't have an expiration date, Katherine. Grief takes as long as it takes. I don't think it ever goes away, just hurts less. But you'll still experience it. Years from now, you'll still grieve when a memory comes up. And that will be a bittersweet moment because you'll hurt from what you lost, but you'll be thankful for the memories you have. It's okay to miss them. It's okay to grieve in your own way, to be angry or confused or sad. No one can tell you the right way to miss the ones you love. Just try not to be hard on yourself, all right? Compassion, Kat. We have to have compassion for ourselves as much as we do for others. There's a reason we have that verse: 'Love your neighbor as yourself'. Loving yourself means having compassion for yourself."

Kat's lower lip trembled, and she nodded, the tears ready to fall. She did feel silly for avoiding Christmas, but he was right. She wouldn't think it was silly if someone else was going through the same thing.

"Myra and I are here. We want to help, but we can't if you don't let us. I'm available for counseling any time you want. I wish I could take your pain away, but the only thing that's going to make it better is time." He rose from the bench, and Kat stood with him. "When you're having a rough day, remember that love can get you through anything. Love always wins in the end. There's nothing stronger. But you have to let the love in."

Kat hugged him. He always knew what to say. He and Nex were the only people she wasn't embarrassed crying in front of, so she let the tears out.

He rested his chin on her head. "I know you haven't come over because you don't want to go on that street again, but that doesn't mean we can't see you. We can meet you somewhere for dinner."

"Okay." Kat pulled back and wiped her tears. "That would be nice."

Allen smiled, gaze drifting past Kat to someone approaching the house. "Oh, you must be Nex."

Nex stared between Kat and the person he recognized from her memory. The one who showed up at the hospital. That meant he was . . .

"I'm Allen. Katherine's pastor. Nice to meet you." Allen offered his hand. "I've heard a lot about you."

Nex froze, unable to believe he was about to shake hands with a pastor. "I've heard about you as well." Nex made the handshake quick. His gaze moved to Katherine's red eyes.

Allen offered Kat a reassuring smile. "Remember what I said, okay?"

"Okay." Kat gave him another quick hug before he waved and headed back to church.

Kat turned to Nex, wringing her hands together. "Sorry. I hope you weren't uncomfortable." She unlocked the door, and they walked inside. "He walked me home."

"He was fine." Although Nex did feel strange being in the presence of a pastor, he also knew that pastor was important to her. As soon as Kat was done hanging her coat, Nex turned her to face him. "What's wrong?"

She twiddled her fingers. "We were talking about Christmas and my parents."

Nex frowned. Christmas. The day grew closer, and Kat stopped sleeping well. She had nightmares almost every night that he couldn't chase away. "Is there something you want to do on Christmas?"

Kat moved toward the kitchen, tears spilling. "I don't know."

She didn't make it far. Nex pulled her against him, cupping her face. "Don't walk away from me when you're crying. Do you want to talk about it?"

Kat blinked away tears. "No. I've been thinking about it so much. It's exhausting me. I want to not think about it for a while."

Nex wrapped his arms around her waist. "You want a distraction?" She nodded. He grabbed her hand and turned for the door. "I won't give you any more trouble about volunteering."

Kat stayed where she was, lacing her fingers with his. Nex turned, and Kat draped her arms around his neck, pulling him into a kiss. He groaned in surprise and slid his hand behind her head. "I thought you were making me be around a bunch of humans at the food bank tonight."

"We can do that tomorrow. I'm on break from school, so I have more time." She fisted his shirt. "I don't want to be around humans either. I just want to be with you."

The corner of Nex's mouth quirked up, and his hands glided to the back of her thighs, lifting her. "Lucky for you, I'm not human." A groan passed through him when she circled her legs around him. "And I'm *very* good at distractions."

Chapter 32

Misfits

"Explain one more time why we're doing this," Lucian said, giving Nex a side-glance.

On Christmas Eve, Kat and her parents would walk downtown to look at Christmas displays. This was the first year she didn't have them with her for the tradition. Nex made the mistake of saying demons stayed away from the holiday. Then, when Kat told him to invite his friends, he made the mistake of making up that none of them had scarves or hats to keep them warm.

That backfired. She spent the next several days knitting scarves and hats for every single demon and now approached each of them, handing out those items along with candy canes.

Nex sneered at Lucian. "Because it's what she wants. Drop it and play along."

"Do you do everything she wants?" Marcus asked.

"Fuck you." Nex glared at Marcus. "Go ahead. Say no to her. I dare you. When she comes over and looks at you with those big green eyes and that sweet face, if you can say no, by all means, give me shit. If you can't, let it go."

Kat stopped in front of Marcus with a big smile and held out a candy cane. "Candy cane?"

Marcus opened his mouth to refuse. Instead, he accepted the candy cane.

Kat's smile turned to a frown when she saw the scarf in his hand, not around his neck. "Do you not like it?"

Marcus tried not to care, but she looked at him with the very green eyes Nex complained about. "It's good, Kat. I . . . I've never worn a scarf." Demons could generate heat and had no need for warm clothes, but no one had the heart to tell her.

"Oh, I'll show you how to put it on." Kat took the scarf and tossed it around Marcus's neck.

He stayed in place as Kat bundled him up, muttering a curse when she went off to give out a second round of candy canes.

Nex raised an eyebrow. "See?"

Marcus rubbed the back of his neck and scrunched his face. "Yeah, yeah."

Kat skipped to Nex and draped her arms around his neck, lifting on her toes to kiss him. "Ready?"

"Ready, kitten."

She led him and the other demons down the street. There were vendors, music, lights, and a lot of people. Although he didn't care for the crowds, Nex did his best to be enthused. Any other day, he'd fight her on this, but not today.

Today was the anniversary of her parents' deaths, and she'd spent the morning crying and trying not to cry in between her family calling repeatedly to check in, as well as the pastor and Bernice both stopping by. A hellish day. He'd do anything to keep her from being miserable all night, even if it meant making his friends cooperate and walk with them to see silly displays.

Nex knew little about Christmas and had seen few Christmas movies. He struggled with things to say as they walked by decorations. Kat stopped at most of them but passed by a popular one.

"Do you not like—"Nex peered over the crowd to read the display's title. "Rudolph?"

"I like Rudolph." Kat stopped in front of a collection of illuminated penguins going down slides. "I don't care for that adaptation of Rudolph."

"Why not?" Lots of people took pictures of the reindeer she hadn't stopped at. "It seems popular."

Kat wrinkled her nose. "It's sexist."

"Sexist?"

"Yeah! It's a classic, sure. I'm not going to lie and say I don't love the misfit song, but it's sexist. Rudolph goes missing, and the mom wants to help look for him, but the dad is like," Kat changed her voice to a deeper tone, mimicking the dad in an over-the-top way, "*no, this is man's work!*"

Nex snorted and shook his head.

"So, I don't care for it, but I like the misfit song." Kat sang the chorus.

Nex chuckled. "For fuck's sake."

"What?"

"Nothing." He pulled her closer and kissed her temple. "You're fucking adorable, that's all."

Turning away to hide the smile, Kat spotted a hot chocolate stand. "Do you want some cocoa?"

"Do you?" Nex asked. Kat nodded, and Nex stepped toward the stand. "I'll get it for you. You don't have to stop looking."

Kat clung to his hand. "No, I'll come with you."

"I don't think so, kitten." He smirked down at her. "This is *man's* work."

Kat smacked his chest, but he caught her hand and tucked her close to his side. They stood in line, and Kat glanced back at Lucian and Marcus standing close by.

"Do you want some?" Kat inclined her head to the stand.

Their answers were lost in the start of a song. Memories flashed in Kat's mind. The same song she used to dance around the Christmas tree to with her parents. The same song that played when the truck slammed into the car. Images of their smashed bodies and blood that had to be too much for two people flooded her mind like she was reliving it.

"Katherine." Nex's voice was distant but firm.

Kat blinked. Nex had her against a wall away from the crowd. He brushed the tears she didn't notice were falling. She shook under his hands as he rubbed her arms.

"What happened?"

"I don't know." Kat squeezed her eyes shut and tried to stop the tears.

"Come here." Nex pulled her into his chest, one hand cradling her head, the other around her back.

"I'm sor—"

"Don't apologize." He kissed her head. "It's all right."

Kat sunk into his arms and took deliberate breaths until the shaking stopped. Nex stroked her hair, and her body relaxed against him.

"What happened?" he asked. There weren't any cars on the street since the whole thing was blocked for the display. *What set her off?*

"It's stupid," Kat mumbled, hiding in his chest.

"For fuck's sake, Katherine. Stop saying that." Nex guided her back so he could look at her. "Don't minimize it. What happened?"

"A song." Her lip trembled. "That was playing when . . ."

Nex pulled her back in and held her tighter. "I understand why you want to be here." He glanced at the crowd. He actually didn't understand why anyone wanted to be here, but he did understand she associated it with her parents. "But perhaps it's a little much." He tilted her chin up. "Is it too much?"

Kat pressed her lips together to contain the sob. She didn't want to admit it was. She should be doing it to honor their memory. One glimpse at the displays had her body trembling and tears building faster. She nodded and avoided Nex's gaze.

He kissed her forehead. "Then we won't stay."

"What about everyone else?"

"They'll understand." He laced his fingers with hers. "Let's go watch that sexist movie and make fun of it."

"That sounds fun." Kat giggled, wiping her tears. He gave her a small smile, and her heart filled. She rubbed her thumb over his cheek. "Thank you." She kissed the opposite cheek. "I don't know what I'd do without you. I . . . I'm glad I accidentally summoned you."

Words weren't Nex's strong point, so he kissed her and led her away from the crowds and bright lights. Passing her church on the way home, she was distracted, and Nex put all his energy into cheering her up. Neither of them noticed Gabriel in the window.

Another man approached, clad in robes so bright they glowed against the dark church and his umber skin. He paused beside Gabriel, staring out into the snow at the couple. "That's them?"

Gabriel nodded.

Kat and Nex started a snowball fight, and the man frowned while they chased each other and fell in the snow, laughing like two perfectly innocent people. "Are we sure?" He recognized Nex, but it couldn't be.

"I'm sure." Gabriel nodded. "You know the rules. We have to make an example of him, or more will do the same, thinking if he can get away with it, anyone can. He needs to be taught a lesson before he's sent back to the underworld."

The man's eyebrows furrowed more each second he watched them. It didn't seem right to tear them apart, to make them suffer when the aura they emitted was so bright it was easily recognizable.

Love.

"Is there no other—"

"I don't make the rules, Melchizedek." Gabriel smoothed the front of his white shirt. "I enforce them. I tried to pull her away from him so she wouldn't be part of it, but she's too attached. This is the only way. I don't know why you're even here. I'm handling it."

Gabriel strode toward the front of the chapel to pray, but Melchizedek stayed by the window, his frown deepening.

"Don't you know why I'm here?" Melchizedek asked. Gabriel stopped. "I'm here because a high-ranked demon is breaking the rules, and it was your turn to handle this kind of problem, and yet," he glanced over his shoulder, "you haven't. You usually work quickly, but you've spent more time on this incident than any other. Why is that, Gabriel? Why is it taking so long?"

"She's stubborn." Gabriel's jaw clenched. "I was trying to be discreet, but it's not working."

"Is that really why?" Melchizedek turned to Gabriel. "Or is it because you doubt that what you were sent to do is right? You approach humans delicately, and yet from the beginning, you did not give this human the calmness you know how to give. It almost seems you intentionally drove her away. Why is that?"

Gabriel's gaze fell to the cross on the pulpit, a physical representation of his duties and why he couldn't let this go. Angels weren't allowed to lie, and Gabriel was unwilling to admit he had doubts from the moment he first saw them together.

"Are you stalling?" Melchizedek asked. "You've given her more than enough reason to shy away from you. Is it because you think separating them is wrong? Because I'm beginning to think we need to handle this differently."

"It doesn't matter. If we don't handle it, Uriel will. We both know that will be much more brutal. Our way won't hurt as much," he whispered, watching Kat and Nex play in the snow outside the church grounds. He'd never seen a human soften a demon like she'd softened Nex.

Normally, Kat would look back at the church because she loved the way the snow coated the steeple in white flakes, making the entire thing glimmer, but dodging Nex's snowballs took priority. Nex was too focused on her to notice anything else. Kat slipped and almost fell, but Nex caught her before she hit the ground, making her giggle.

"Let me down," she said.

"In the snow? Weren't you complaining it's too cold?"

She gave him a playful glare and loosened ice chunks from her hair.

"You've covered me in snow anyway. It doesn't matter."

"Fine." Nex lowered her into the snow, and she spread her arms and legs to make a snow angel.

She beamed up at the sky, breathing in the scent of crisp coldness only falling snow could create. Nex wasn't one for wasting time staring at anything, but he could watch her lying in the snow like that forever. The white snow shimmered like it was covered in glitter.

Pure, like she was pure.

"Why don't you make one with me?" Kat grinned as she made the snow angel.

"Very funny."

"Aw, come on. It would be cute!" Kat spread her arms to make the wings bigger.

"I don't need to make one, Katherine. I've got you."

Kat smiled, flutters erupting in her stomach. "Okay, now I'm really cold." She hopped up and rubbed her hands along her arms. "Let's go home."

"Home." Nex nodded and wrapped his arm around her waist. Back in the underworld was supposed to be home, and while he missed his hounds, that place wasn't home. His home was with Kat.

She shivered as they stepped inside the house. "I need to warm up before I can do anything."

Nex smirked, shrugging off his coat. "I can help with that."

Biting her lip, Kat backed away. He raised an eyebrow and followed with predatory steps. "Are you trying to get me to chase you?"

"No." Kat tucked her hands behind her and quickened her retreat, failing to keep the smile at bay.

They stared each other down for a moment before Kat turned and bolted into the bedroom. Nex caught her easily and pulled her into a kiss that made her warm right up.

Kat's favorite moments with Nex were the ones where he was intense with her and followed it with tenderness. And that's what he did. In the shower, he had her against the wall, thrusting into her so hard she cried out, clinging to his shoulders, weak in the wake of her orgasm. After, he held her close, washing her body like her skin would break if he rubbed too hard. He washed her hair and massaged her scalp. Gestures she believed small before didn't seem small. Everything felt intimate with Nex.

Once they were dry, Kat bundled herself in a robe and was applying lotion when Nex came out in a towel, his magnificent body exposed. He never got cold like she did. She followed his every move as he gathered clothes from the dresser, admiring the flexes in his strong body.

She thought about the things he said he wanted from her. Wanted to do to her. With her. At the time, the idea had excited her but also made her nervous. That was before. He'd shown he could be tender when she needed it.

She wanted more. Every part. She wanted to see that side of him, and the idea of being with him in that way now excited her more than made her nervous.

"Nex?"

"What is it, kitten?" He turned. The robe she'd been wearing was gone, leaving her bare to him. His eyes darted up and down her naked body, and he felt himself grow, ready to have her all over again. In her hands was the soft strap that had held her robe closed. Her lips parted, her tongue darting out to wet them.

She held out the strap. "Tie me up."

Chapter 33

Villanelle

Nex secured Kat's wrists to the bars of the metal headboard with her robe strap. He slipped a couple of fingers between, so it wasn't too tight. Moving down, he hovered over her, staring with hungry eyes.

"What's your safe word?" he asked, running his hand gently down her face.

It took everything in him not to pounce on her the moment she told him to tie her up. Normally that would get him going, but she meant too much. He told her to choose a word she could say that would tell him to stop if she didn't like something.

"Villanelle." She stared at him, her gaze drifting down his hard chest, his abs . . .

"A strange choice, kitten."

"You said anything."

"I did." He ran his fingers across her red lips. "Fuck, I've been wanting this for so long." He kissed her.

Kat's instincts were to wrap her arms around his neck, but the ties held her back, and a jolt of excitement passed through her. He had control.

"Before I do anything, I want you to know something."

"What?"

"I'm yours." He kissed her forehead. "I belong to you, and that means I only want what you want. If you don't want something I'm doing, you tell me, and I'll stop, all right?"

Heart swelling, Kat nodded. "Okay."

"This means, right now, you're submitting to me." He dragged a finger up and down her side, and her breath quickened. "That means, right now, I get to fuck you and touch you how I want. Means I can slide my fingers in you when I want, how roughly I want. Are you sure you want that?"

Kat's face warmed. "I'm sure. I trust you."

He peppered kisses along her jaw and down her neck. "What do you think of the blindfold?"

He sucked on her skin, and Kat panted, trying to focus on his question. "I'll try it."

Nex hummed in approval and stroked her body until he reached between her legs. "You sure, Katherine?"

Kat's eyes fluttered at his finger dragging up and down her wet entrance. "I'm sure."

He thrust a finger into her, making Kat cry out. He curled his finger against her G-spot. "Who do you belong to?"

Kat whimpered and raised her hips to his hand. "You."

"Are you mine, Katherine?" He slid his finger out and shoved two in.

"Yes." Kat clenched, squeezing her eyes shut. "I'm yours, Nex." She looked up at him, lips parted as she panted while he repeatedly curled his fingers in her.

"Good girl," he murmured, placing a long kiss on her lips before getting off her.

He returned with one of her silk scarves, folded it, then placed it over her eyes. Nex kissed her while he secured it and left her more breathless when he moved away. There was something thrilling about not being able to see or know what he was going to do next.

Full of anticipation, she jumped when his finger landed on her neck. He dragged it over the curve of her breast, along her stomach to her hip, then to her inner thigh, where it disappeared. It was strange, the way a touch left her needy. He did it again on her other side, this time running over the hardened peak of her breast. Kat bit her lip harder the closer his finger got to her wetness. She tensed in anticipation, but he lifted his finger off again, and she was left raising her hips to nothing.

Hot breath fanned one side of her neck, his palm on the other. His hand descended, circled around and over her breast but not where she longed for his touch. She pulled at her restraints when his hand moved off her, his lips grazing down her neck, over her collarbone to her breast. His tongue darted out, circling like his finger had until the contact was gone. The next sensation came on her thigh, where he dragged a finger up, almost touching but not quite. Kat whimpered as he inched closer to where she ached when suddenly, his intoxicating touch was gone again.

Breathless and desperate for more, she whined. "Nex."

"Who do you belong to?" Nex wrapped his hand around her throat, and his breath hit her ear.

She licked her lips. "You."

"That's right, kitten." Nex growled, nipping her ear. "I'll touch you how I want. You'll come when I let you. You're mine." He bit and sucked on her skin, pleased it left a mark. "Mine," he repeated, pressing a kiss to the mark. "Understood?" Kat nodded, and Nex's chest rumbled. He bit her skin and cupped her breast, pinching her nipple hard enough she whimpered and moaned all at once. "Words."

Pleasure mixed with a small amount of pain. Heat pooled between her legs. "Yes, Nex."

"What's your safe word?" His words turned softer, softer like the way he kissed the nipple he'd pinched.

Kat panted. "Villanelle."

"Do you need to use it?"

"No. I don't want you to stop."

"So fucking perfect, my Katherine." He placed a long kiss on her lips, and she leaned up for more as he drifted away.

Silence. No contact left her cold and squirming. Her heart raced, and her breath grew out of control as she moved her head side to side, though she couldn't see.

Her legs jerked open, and his hands moved from her ankles, up her calves to her thighs. She stilled when he breathed against where she ached for attention.

A kiss landed high on her thigh, right below where she wanted it. She raised her hips toward him, but he held her down, teasing her, dragging his tongue along her skin but not where she needed it most.

"Nex." Kat's toes curled. "Please."

"What's that, kitten?" He ran a single finger up her moistened slit, making her hiss and clench.

"Please."

"Please, what? Lick you, touch you, fuck you?"

Kat nodded fervently. "Yes. All of that."

Nex chuckled and kissed her clit, eliciting a moan. "You're on my time, kitten. I'll do those things when I damn well please." He thrust a finger into her, and her back arched. The sounds escaping her drove Nex forward. "I like making you ache for me." He withdrew his fingers and smiled at her body rising to chase after them. "I'm going to make you come so hard, kitten." He kissed her clit, then moved away and left her frowning and clamping her thighs together. "Don't do that." Nex growled, pulling her legs apart. "Unless you want me to tie your legs too."

Kat swallowed, and her inner walls clenched. *I don't hate the sound of that.* Her body grew cold at his absence, and she bit back the sob. She thought she wanted him before, but this state of waiting her body was in was much more intense. Waiting to be touched, held, kissed . . .

His tongue dragged over her clit, and she gasped. She tilted her hips to meet him, but he set his hands on her hipbones, holding her down as he flicked his tongue, enough to make her throb but not to send her over the edge. Kat threw her head back as he sucked on her clit, pleasure pulsating through her body. His tongue swirled around her most sensitive spots and stopped when she got close.

She felt him at her wrists and frowned. Her hands stayed bound, but he untied her from the headboard. "What are you doing?"

He wrapped his hand around her throat. "Whatever I want, kitten. Who do you belong to?"

Eager to have him touch her more, Kat was quick to answer, "You."

"Good girl." He kissed her, then guided her to sit on the edge of the bed.

"Come here." He pulled her to her feet, and her heart pounded at her complete dependence on him. He was in control, and it made her body stand at attention, ready to take any touch he gave. He pushed her shoulders until she was on her knees. Her bound hands lifted above her head, and his hardness touched her lips. "Open."

Obeying, Kat opened her mouth, and he slid inside. A surprised squeak left her throat, and he reached the back of it, making her gag slightly. Last time, they took it slow for her to adjust, but this time he came in fast and hard. Another pulse of excitement ran through her when he pushed in deeper. Kat's eyes watered, the blindfold came off, and he pulled out of her mouth. The blindfold dropped around her neck, and she blinked away tears, staring up at Nex.

"I'm going to fuck your mouth, kitten." He caressed her cheek. "I'm not planning to be gentle. You can't use a safe word if your mouth is stuffed with my cock, so if something isn't working for you," he tugged the strap around her wrists and held them in such a way her fingers reached his hand, "tap three times, and I'll stop. All right?"

Kat nodded, and Nex grabbed her throat, squeezing until she gasped. She didn't need to be reminded this time. His actions and eyes said enough. "Yes, Nex."

A smile tugged on his lips at her eagerness. "Good girl. Keep your eyes on me. It's so fucking sexy when you look up at me with my cock in your mouth. Open."

Kat opened and let him slide in, doing her best to keep her gaze on him.

He threaded his fingers through her hair and held her in place as he thrust in and out of her mouth. Kat moaned, the sensation vibrating Nex. He cursed at how good it felt.

His thrusts continued until Kat's sounds became too much to handle on top of the way her warm mouth caressed him. He lodged himself deep, going down her throat. Kat's eyes watered, and he stayed there, come emptying into her mouth. He slid out and stared at her. Those green eyes could suck him in and make him forget anything.

"Up." He pulled her by her wrists. "Good girl."

His lips slammed down on hers, and she moaned, draping her arms over his shoulders. He lifted her onto the bed, ducked out of her embrace, returned the blindfold over her eyes, and retied her hands to the headboard.

Kat lifted her head as if she could see. "Are you going to touch me?"

"You were a good girl." His rough hands moved down her smooth body. "Good girls get rewarded."

His hands moved away, and she held her breath, body tingling in aware-ness, waiting for his return. Then his mouth was on her, and she moaned, tugging on her restraints and writhing under him. Everything he'd done made her so sensitive she exploded, coming faster than she ever had. The orgasm hit in intense, repeated rushes of pleasure made more powerful by his tongue continuing to drag across her until her release tapered.

Kat's body relaxed, and she sank into the bed, panting. Nothing had ever felt so good or left her so exhausted. Nex flipped her over, and she yelped, landing on her stomach. A second later, her ass was lifted up, her knees beneath her hips.

"I'm not done." He ran his hand over the curve of her ass. "I'm not even close to being done, kitten. I'm going to claim every inch of you."

"What are you going to do?"

A gasp-inducing smack to the ass answered her. A sting spread at the same time her core clenched, and a moan slipped out.

"You don't get to ask questions when you're submitting to me, kitten."

He caressed her ass, the sting from his smack fading. "Do you need to use your safe word?" He bent and kissed the red spot he'd created.

"No." Kat swallowed, her cheeks burning at the truth. "I . . . I liked it."

"You liked it?" Nex smacked her ass again, earning another yelp followed by a moan.

"Yes, Nex."

He groaned and spread her legs. "Fuck, you're going to be the death of me." He plunged his face between her legs.

Kat moaned at the angle change and relentless attention from his lips and tongue. When she was close, he stopped. She whimpered in protest, and he smacked her ass, silencing her.

He pushed two fingers into her and did the same thing, pumping them in and out, then stopping when she neared the edge. Complaining would earn another spank, but part of her craved that again. His hand came down hard on her ass, and she moaned, lifting it for more.

Again and again, he brought her close, alternating between his mouth and his fingers, never letting her quite reach her peak. Kat let out desperate cries at the growing intensity. Every touch was heightened the more times he edged her. Things she didn't expect to become sensitive did. Even the friction of the sheet rubbing against her breasts affected her. If he stopped again, she'd go crazy.

"Nex," Kat pleaded when his fingers slid out of her. She lost count of how many times he'd done it. She squirmed under him, desperate for any kind of friction. "Please."

Her response came with his hand around her throat, his hardness pressed against her ass. "What did I say?" His hand tightened on her throat. "I said you're on *my* time." He smacked her ass. "I'll let you come when I want you to. Do you need to use your safe word?"

Kat shook her head. "No." Despite the fact she ached for him something horrible, she wanted to keep going. She craved him in this unfamiliar, intimate way.

"Good girl." He kissed down her spine, smacking her ass again as he sat back. He set his hands on her hips and stared at where she dripped for him. He brought his finger up, teasing the outside of her, enjoying the way she grumbled and dropped her head on the bed. "What's wrong, kitten?" He slid a finger into her, and her whole body trembled. "Feeling like you *need* me inside you?"

She couldn't remember needing anything else. "Yes, Nex."

"Do you want me or need me?" He slid his fingers out and pulled away, not touching her at all.

Kat whimpered, her body cold without his touch. "I *need* you."

"You need me to fuck you, kitten?" He pressed his tip against her, and she tensed, adjusting her knees to be more open for him.

"Yes. I need you."

His hand collided with her ass in a loud *smack*. "Say it again."

Kat panted and craved another. "I need you."

He caressed her, then brought his hand down. *Slap.* "Again."

Kat pushed herself back against him. "I need you, Nex."

Nex groaned and gripped her hips, holding her in place as he thrust into her hard. She cried out and clenched around him, pleasure exploding shudders through her body.

"Who do you belong to?" Nex growled, smacking her ass before caressing it, easing the sting.

A guttural moan escaped when he sank deeper. "You."

"Good girl."

No longer holding back, Nex moved in and out of her. His hand glided up her spine, and grabbed the back of her neck, pinning her to the bed. Raising her hips with his other hand, he sank in harder.

Kat cried out, clenching around Nex and making him groan. It wasn't just the intensity of the action; it was the trust she had with him and only him. The way he cared for her. The way she saw another side of him, a side she very much liked. She wanted to see all his sides as he wanted to see hers.

Much more than physical, every motion brought them closer together until they were one. Nex moved wildly, restraining her and sinking deep and hard when he came. He groaned when she tightened around him, finding her own release and trembling as she screamed. Her whole body tensed and relaxed over and over before she slumped on the bed.

Breathless, Nex kissed her back and caressed her ass while he slid out. He turned her over, untied her wrists, removed the blindfold, and caught her in a soft kiss. Kat moaned and hugged him, enjoying the comfort of his arms holding her close after that intensity.

"You didn't use the safe word." He kissed her cheeks, forehead, lips, jaw. All soft and light. "You promised me you would if it was too much."

"I didn't need to use it." Kat struggled to catch her breath. "It wasn't too much."

"Fuck, Katherine, you're so perfect," Nex murmured against her lips. "So fucking perfect, my kitten. My angel, I . . ." He stopped at the words that almost escaped. Words he'd never said to anyone. Words he didn't think he was capable of saying. There was no denying what she meant to him, but he couldn't say it, so he opted for something less terrifying. "I'm glad you summoned me too." He rolled to his back and drew her to his chest, thinking the words he couldn't bring himself to say, keeping them locked in his mind as the realization of what he felt sank in.

He wasn't supposed to be able to feel anything like this, but he couldn't deny it. Kat was everything to him. He'd never been more himself, more at peace, than with her. He'd never craved something as simple as a hug with anyone but her.

He'd never been able to stop the self-loathing over being a demon until she made him think he could be something better.

There was no denying it, but he couldn't bring himself to say it, only allowing himself to admit it within his own mind.

I love you.

Chapter 34

Not Crazy

K at leaned over the bookstore counter with *The Picture of Dorian Gray* by Oscar Wilde in her hands. Reading was her intention. Instead, she daydreamed about going home to Nex and reread the same paragraph she'd been stuck on for several minutes.

The bell dinged, announcing the door opening. Her gaze shot up, hoping for Nex but finding a customer. He passed in front of a display, concealing his face. It didn't matter. She said the same thing to every customer.

"Welcome to Connie's. How can I help you?"

The man rounded the corner, and Kat's eyes widened. He was so beautiful he hardly seemed real—brown hair, brown eyes, rich umber skin, the picture of a model. He had nothing on Nex, but then again, no one did. Still, she couldn't deny he was beautiful, and the flawless, white-toothed smile he gave was almost blinding.

"I'm just browsing." He approached the counter and drummed his fingers against the top. "I arrived in town yesterday, so I'm exploring."

"Okay." Kat forced a smile. Something about him reminded her of Gabriel. Not the exact aura, but similar. It made her uneasy after their confrontation. "Feel free to look around. If you have any questions, don't hesitate to ask."

"I won't." He flashed another grin, and his gaze dropped to her nametag. "Thank you, Katherine."

Kat's polite smile faded as he disappeared down an aisle, and she picked her book up again. Her phone buzzed, and she made sure the customer wasn't looking

Nex: Mondays are slow. Close early, and come home to me.

Kat: I can't. I have a customer.

Nex: Send them away, then come home. I miss you. I want to spend the night together. Just us.

Kat couldn't contain the smile. Him missing her always made her heart flutter.

Kat: I miss you too, but be patient. I thought the boys were coming over for dinner.

Nex: I forgot about that. I'll tell them to fuck off. I want you to myself. Fuck everyone else. You're the only one I want to be around.

Kat bit her lip against a growing smile. She glanced up at the customer approaching and put her phone away. She nodded to the books in his hands. "You found something."

"Indeed, I did." He set them on the counter.

The one on top was a Bible, and Kat smiled up at him. "Is this a gift? I still have wrapping paper from Christmas."

"Oh, no. It's for me."

"Are you a new believer?"

"No, no. I have been for a long time," he said. "And you?"

"My whole life." Kat patted the Bible resting on the counter from earlier

when she was working through the Bible study questionnaire Allen handed out.

The man's eyes darted to the leather Bible she had a hand on. Her name
was engraved on the cover. He frowned and returned his gaze to her. It
didn't add up that this was the girl he was supposed to mark.

"Oh, how funny." Kat pointed to the Oscar Wilde novel under the Bible.
"I'm reading that."

"Have you read it before?"

Kat beamed as she checked out his books. "A million times, but I don't
get tired of it. I'm a big Oscar Wilde fan." She slid his books into a paper
bag. "That'll be twenty-five dollars and fifty-nine cents."

He handed her cash. "You like the classics then?"

"Definitely." Kat accepted the money and counted his change. Feeling
him staring, she peered up to see not a smile on his face but a concentrated
frown and intense stare. She shifted her weight, and his frown was replaced
with a smile.

She passed him the change, and he took it with one hand but grabbed
her wrist with the other. He turned her palm upward and examined it.
Brows knitting, he ran his fingers over her skin. Kat opened her mouth,
but nothing came out.

He turned her hand over and placed a kiss on her knuckles. "Thank you,
Katherine."

Kat jerked her hand back and slid the bag across the counter so she
wouldn't risk them touching again. She was working alone. "Have a good
day."

"You as well." He made his way to the door but paused and glanced back
at her. "Stay safe, Katherine."

The door closed behind him. Kat swallowed and fiddled with the ends
of her sleeves, then grabbed her phone.

Kat: Will you please walk me home? My last customer gave me the creeps, and he was a lot bigger than me.

Nex: I'll be right there. Is he hanging around? Lock the door.

Kat crept to the window. She looked both ways but didn't see him anywhere. A strange tingling remained where he'd touched her, neither pleasant nor unpleasant, just noticeable. She wiped her hand on her jeans to erase the sensation.

After surveying the sidewalk for several minutes, she decided he must be gone. She opened her phone and started a message, but hands landed on her shoulders, and she screamed.

"It's me." Nex rubbed her back and pressed his lips against her ear. "What's wrong, Katherine?" He turned her to face him. "What did he do?"

"He . . . I don't know." In Nex's arms, she was able to relax her shoulders. "He said something weird about being safe. It was a feeling, and how he looked at me and . . ." Wanting to tell Nex about the strange way he examined her palm, she worried she'd sound crazy. "He kissed my hand. I don't think that was appropriate."

"It most certainly wasn't." Nex growled, tightening his arms around her. "You shouldn't walk home alone anymore. Especially at night."

"Okay." Kat chewed her lip. "I'm sorry. It was probably nothing. Maybe he was trying to be flirty. Guys are like that sometimes."

"Don't apologize. You shouldn't ignore your instincts. Humans do that too often, and most often, their instincts are right. Never ignore yours." He kissed her softly. "You're much too beautiful, and the world is full of shitty people. If someone makes you uncomfortable, you call me right away."

"Thank you." She stretched on her toes to peck his lips. "Thank you for being nice."

"I'm always nice."

Kat rolled her eyes and pulled away. "That's a load of baloney."

"Baloney?" Nex followed as she started her loop around the store to ensure everything was back where it was supposed to be before closing. "For fuck's sake, Katherine. Being with you is so back and forth."

Kat frowned and grabbed a book someone left in the wrong place. "What do you mean?"

"You're so innocent and proper, but then I take you home, and the moment I get my hands on you, it gets about as far from proper and innocent as it could." He slipped his hand up the back of her shirt.

Kat pushed him away so he wouldn't distract her and returned the book to its rightful place, then picked up another in the wrong place. "You're ridiculous."

"Come on, then." He followed while she put the last book away. "Say one curse word."

"No." Kat scrunched her face, returned to the counter, and straightened the displays. "I don't like talking like that."

"Oh, but you like when I talk like that." He wrapped his arms around her from behind. "You like it a lot, don't you? You like when I talk dirty. I bet you're wet thinking about me sliding into you over and over until you scream." Nex placed a hot kiss under her ear.

Kat's breath hitched. There were cameras in the store, and he was too tempting. "You're not supposed to put the moves on me at work."

"Put the moves on you?" Nex laughed. "For the love of all that's unholy, you are too pure for me, Katherine." He released her and leaned against the counter. "I love that about you."

The instant the words left his mouth, Kat's eyebrows shot up. They stared at each other for a moment, and Nex cleared his throat, averting his gaze. "One curse word. You've done it before. You called me an asshole, remember?"

"Well, that's because you—" Kat sighed, sending him a dirty look. "You got me all riled up."

"Is that all I have to do?" He cocked his head. "In that case, prepare to get riled up."

"Or you could, I don't know, be nice?"

"Be nice? You said I'm not nice most of the time. I have a reputation to uphold."

Kat gave him a scolding glare and checked the clock. Closing time. She turned off the open sign and shut the blinds before going to the alarm system. Nex came alongside her and held out his hand. She dropped the keys in his palm, and he strode to the front door. He'd been enough times he was used to closing with her.

Alarm activated, Kat stepped out the door Nex held open. He shut and locked it while Kat bundled her coat around herself, shivering against the frigid breeze. She dug in her pockets for her gloves, thinking about the man and the strange feeling she got from him.

Tugging on one of her curls, she twisted her finger around her hair as Nex locked the store. "Nex?"

"What is it?"

"Um . . ." Her gaze went to the snow-covered sidewalk. "The man who came by today reminded me a lot of—" Kat's heartbeat spiked.

A child across the street ran straight into oncoming traffic. The cars didn't slow. Kat's eyes bulged, and she rushed into the busy street. She pushed the child out of the way and almost got hit by a speeding sedan. The car's side-view mirror smacked into her hand. She hissed, a bite of pain passing through her hand before numbness took over.

Nex was at her side in a moment, taking her injured hand. "Katherine, what the hell were you doing?"

"The little boy was about to be hit." She searched for him, but he was gone.

"What little boy?"

"I—" Kat spun around. "He was here a second ago. He was right here."

"Katherine." Nex's brows furrowed. "There was no child."

"There was. I saw him. I felt him when I pushed him out of the way."

Nex surveyed her, then glanced around. There was no one nearby, not even an adult, let alone a child. No one was out walking in this cold with the snow piled up.

Sometimes Kat hallucinated around cars, a problem since the accident, but the boy was solid against her hands when she pushed him to safety. "I'm not crazy."

Nex's expression softened. "I don't think you are. Give me your hand."

He took her hand, but there was no mark or redness.

Kat sucked in a breath. "The car hit my hand." She turned her palm up, but there was nothing. The pain was gone.

"It did." Nex examined her again, fingers tracing her palm.

The action reminded her of the strange man. She drew in her lower lip. "Nex?"

"What?"

"The man who came in."

His eyes snapped to hers. "Yes?"

"Before he kissed my hand, he picked it up," she took Nex's hand and turned it over, "and stared at my palm for a while, touching me like this." She ran her fingers over Nex the same way the customer had to her.

Nex narrowed his eyes. "He did what?"

"He stared and ran his fingers over it." The intense glint in Nex's eyes made her chest clench. "What's wrong? Does that mean something?"

Nex pressed a kiss to her palm. "It means nothing, Katherine. Just sounds creepy. Like you said." He wrapped his arm around her waist and tugged her with him down the sidewalk. "Let's get home."

"Are you okay?"

"I'm fine." Nex swallowed. "I want to get you home." He kissed the side of her head and glanced around, keeping her tucked in at his side.

Closer than usual.

Chapter 35

Exception

N ex paced in front of the couch where Lucian and Marcus sat, frowns on all their faces. Marcus opened his mouth a couple of times but closed it again and stroked his beard.

Lucian leaned forward, elbows on his knees, fingers steepled against his lips. "It was probably nothing. There are plenty of strange people in the world. Maybe he took a liking to her and wanted her to remember him. Maybe he's planning on going back to ask her out."

"What about the child?" Nex asked. "And her hand?"

"She told us she sometimes sees things since her parents' accident, remember?" Marcus said. "Especially around cars. You know she freaks out around cars."

Nex sighed. "I know, but her hand."

"It was probably more the shock of it." Lucian tapped his fingers against his chin. "You said it barely touched her, didn't you? The pain might have been in her head. Again, we're dealing with the car issue."

All that was true, but something didn't sit well with Nex. Most palm readers were full of shit, but the art wasn't a complete lie. Hands were special. A lot could be learned from a person's hands. Nex didn't know exactly how to read palms, only the basics. He couldn't read into the soul like others could. *Too coincidental.* "If you hear anything or notice any unnatural people enter this realm, tell me right away."

Lucian nodded. "We will. Relax, Nex. I'm sure you're on edge because of what happened with Lilith. Who's still occupied in the underworld, by the way."

"Right." He wasn't convinced, but he had no evidence of anything else.

The front door opened, and Kat walked in, brushing snow off her hair. Nex strode over to her. "What are you doing here? It's early."

"Choir got canceled because of this blizzard." Kat shrugged off her coat and rubbed her arms. "Man, it's cold out there."

"Katherine." Nex's stern tone made her eyebrows raise. "You're supposed to let me walk you home, so you're not alone. Why didn't you call me?"

"I didn't walk home alone. I walked with Annabelle." She gestured toward her neighbor's house. "I don't want to put you out every time I need to get somewhere."

"You aren't putting me out. Next time, do *not* walk alone."

"I wasn't alone. What's gotten into you?" Kat huffed. "You're hungry, aren't you? You're always crabby when you're hungry."

Marcus grinned. "She has a point."

"Oh, hi guys." She waved and smiled. "I'm freezing. I'm going to take a hot shower to warm up. Are you staying for dinner?"

"No." Lucian rose from the couch. "Just stopping by."

"Are you sure?" Kat asked. "The weather's crazy. I can set you up to stay the night."

Lucian smiled but shook his head. "No, thank you. We move fast, and besides, we have a common mission tonight."

"Oh, okay." Kat rubbed her hands together to warm them. "Stay safe."

Nex rolled his eyes, but her comment made Lucian and Marcus grin. They'd never been treated well by humans until her. They said goodbye, and as soon as they were out the door, Nex pulled Kat into a kiss and lifted her.

She squeaked in surprise and wrapped her legs around his waist. "What are you doing?" She breathed against his lips.

"I thought you wanted to warm up." He sucked her lower lip into his mouth and bit down. "You didn't think I'd let you do that alone, did you?"

Kat dropped her head in his neck to hide the smile. Nex chuckled and held her with one hand, tugging on her shirt with the other. "Clothes off, Katherine. I'm anxious to be inside you."

"Why are you so persistent about me not walking alone?" She lifted her head to peek at him. "Is something wrong?"

Nex paused. As a demon, lying came easy. Not around her. He couldn't bring himself to tell her what Death said, the rules they were breaking, the concerns he had. *She's already going through so much.* He didn't want his time with her to end, and she had enough on her mind with Christmas passing. "I want you to be safe. I *need* you to be safe, Katherine. For me. I need you to not walk alone. Is that too much to ask?"

Kat tilted her head. "I guess not."

"Good. Then don't walk alone."

"I wasn't alone."

"Keep it that way." He grabbed the back of her head and kissed her as he walked them to the bathroom.

Their shower went so long that the hot water ran out. Between the shower and Nex pressing her into the wall and thrusting into her, Kat more than warmed up. Still, she bundled up afterward and dropped a blanket over them as they lay on the couch. Nex ran his fingers through her damp hair, *Dead Poets Society* playing on the television.

"This movie is depressing." Nex made a face. "Why do you like it?"

"It's sad but good." Kat snuggled against his chest. "I just like it."

"Can't we watch a romance for once? You have the strangest taste in movies."

Kat set her chin on his chest and gazed up at him. "Do you like romances?"

"Depends on the movie, but no, I mostly like them because they tend to lead to more interesting activities when you're, say, with a beautiful woman." Nex smirked, and Kat nudged him in the side. "What about a horror movie?"

"Ew, no." Kat shuddered. "They're too scary. I watched one with Frida in high school, and I am *never* watching one again."

"What did you watch with Frida?"

"I don't remember the name. A little boy sees dead people."

"A little boy sees dea— Are you fucking kidding me? *That* movie scared you? You've never watched any other horror movies except that one?"

"No." Kat wrinkled her nose. "I don't like being scared. I don't understand why people enjoy scary movies. Being scared isn't fun."

"That movie isn't even—" He gave up, considering it unlikely she'd agree the movie wasn't scary. "It's no wonder you didn't realize you were summoning a demon. That's really the only horror movie you've ever watched?"

"I mean, I saw bits and pieces of other movies, and sometimes I saw previews but never fully watched another one."

"I can't believe of all the movies, that one scared you."

Kat shrugged. "I scare easy."

Nex raised an eyebrow. "You scare easy?"

"Mm-hmm."

"That's bullshit."

Kat lifted her head and frowned. "How would you know?"

"Maybe because I'm a *demon,* and the first thing you did was hit me on the head with an umbrella."

"Oh, I was definitely scared. You can be scared and still defend yourself. Also, it hadn't registered that you were a demon. I thought you were a crazy person."

"Well, now you know." He twirled one of her curls around his finger. "You're brave enough to defy a demon, fuck and sleep with him every night, and stand up to someone like Lilith, but somehow you're not brave enough to watch a scary movie?"

"First of all," Kat held up a finger, "part of the reason scary movies are so scary is because you can't control what happens, and everyone in scary movies is stupid and lacks basic common sense. I mean, why is there always a girl running around completely naked when she *knows* there's a killer on the loose? I haven't seen much, but I know that happens a lot." She shook her head. "And second, you're not scary."

"Obviously those scenes exist for the boobs, and—" He scowled. "What did you say?"

Kat folded her arms over his chest and rested her chin on her hands. "Which part?"

He clenched his jaw. "About me not being scary."

She shrugged. "You're not."

"I'm terrifying." Nex growled.

Under Nex's increasingly unhappy glare, Kat stifled a laugh and dropped her head in her arms to control it. "Um, okay." She pressed her lips together to hold back the smile. "You're terrifying."

"You don't think I'm scary?"

"I think you're adorable."

"I am *not* adorable," Nex snapped, his eyes turning red.

"Are you insulted that I don't find you scary?"

"Of course I am! I'm a demon, for fuck's sake. If I'm not scary, then what the hell am I?"

Kat grinned. "Adorable."

Nex inhaled deeply. "Not funny."

"Okay, okay." She moved up and kissed his cheek. "How about this? You were terrifying when I first met you, and had I not gotten to know you, I'd still be scared of you. Is that better?"

"I suppose," Nex grumbled.

"Don't be mad." Kat pouted and laid her head on his chest, looking up at him through her eyelashes. "You're the scariest demon to ever have lived."

"Now you're coddling me."

"Nex?"

He sighed. "What?"

She set her hand on his face and smiled in the way that always melted away any annoyance. "You're my favorite demon."

He wanted to still be annoyed. He didn't want to smile. He couldn't help it, so he looked away. "I'm going to get you to watch a scary movie."

"How about you watch the movie that's on right now? It's a good movie."

"I'm not denying it's interesting." Nex dragged his hand up and down her back. "I just don't know why humans enjoy movies that make them sad."

Kat rested her head on his chest again, focusing on the screen. They were quiet for a while before she spoke, softer. "It was my dad's favorite."

Nex paused stroking her back. Christmas Eve may have been a great night for them intimately, but the entire holiday the next day left her less able to deny how much it hurt to be without her parents. Her cheerful self was not quite as cheerful. She'd put a lot more effort into it than she usually did.

"What did he like about it?" Nex asked, flattening his palm on her back and holding her tighter.

Kat chewed her lip for a moment. "It's real. It doesn't dance around hard topics and shows that time and people are precious." She traced the collar of his shirt. "Sometimes things we think are important don't mean anything because we won't remember every time something didn't go how we wanted. We remember moments. Moments where time stands still, and everything is perfect. And those moments are infinitely more precious because you know it can't stay that way forever. Art is important because it captures those moments." She looked at the TV again. "That's why it's so good. Because it shows special, unforgettable moments in the midst of tragedy and loss and injustices, and that's how real life is. Things don't always go like you hope. The people you love don't always get to stick around. People you should be able to trust hurt you. It tells us to cling to what's important and not let the other stuff bother us so much we forget to live in the moment."

"What's important to you, Katherine?"

Kat blushed and peeked up at him. "Right now?" He nodded. "You. You're everything to me."

"And will our perfect moment not last?"

"I don't know. Are you going to stay with me or . . ." Her heart sank at the thought. "Or are you still trying to get home?"

"Katherine." Nex pulled her closer and held her face. "I am home. My home is where you are." He kissed her.

The air left her lungs, her heart leaped from her chest, and every inch of her filled with contentment. True intimacy, true openness, true . . . Worry lines creased her forehead. "You're not going to leave me?"

The words he couldn't say floated in his mind but failed to find an escape. At least not before. But as Nex stared down at her big eyes full of fear, his hesitance washed away. She needed to hear it more than he was scared to say it. "I . . ." His heart pounded. "I'm not going to leave you." He leaned closer and ran his thumb over her cheek. "I can't."

"Because I won't pick a name, I know." Kat's voice grew quieter. "I'm sorry."

"That's not why." Nex caressed her jaw. "I can't leave because I can't be away from you. Because I . . ." He swallowed and stared at her. He wasn't supposed to be able to feel this way. He thought he was losing his mind, but her eyes told him there was no denying it. "I love you, Katherine. I'm not going anywhere."

Kat's eyes widened, and she set her hand on his face. "You love me?"

"I do." He brushed his lips against hers. "Very much."

"I love you too." Kat wrapped her arms around his neck and kissed him. "So much," she whispered against his lips. "I love you so much."

Melchizedek leaned over the pew and opened his eyes, leaving them to their privacy. He was supposed to mark her as the target. That was it. But he couldn't help himself. He had to know why they were different.

Settling matters like this—separating humans from demons—was no problem for him. However, this situation wasn't like any other, so he left a kiss on her hand that allowed him to see them together. When he examined her palm, he discovered nothing tainted. When he searched her eyes, there was purity. She passed the test he set up with the child. None of his observations added up, so he wanted to watch her with Nex in private to discover what made them unique. The purpose wasn't to invade their privacy but to understand, and what he heard shocked him.

In all the centuries Melchizedek had been alive, a demon had never said they loved anyone and meant it. He tried to deny the aura that surrounded them in the snow, but there was no denying what he witnessed.

Nex loved the human, and she loved him.

Gabriel stepped into the church. "Did you send for it?"

Melchizedek shook his head. "I'm not convinced it is the right thing to do."

"We have an obligation under the law. That's how we know it's right."

"We're working under old laws that existed as a blanket statement for a blanket issue. When demons were manipulating the minds of humans to get what they wanted." Melchizedek stood. "He has not manipulated her mind. I looked into her soul, Gabriel. She is the same person, just one who loves someone who returns that love."

"Love?" Gabriel frowned. It couldn't be. "Demons are not capable of love."

"Are they not? Are they not brothers and sisters in a different form, from another realm?"

Gabriel gritted his teeth. "It's not the same. They are *demons*."

"Descendants of a fallen angel," Melchizedek corrected. "Technically speaking, they are *all* angels, just fallen ones. They are not so different from us. You say their titles with disgust, yet you call on them, so you don't get your hands dirty."

"The ones who are there want to be there. We don't force anyone to become a demon. They find that path on their own."

Melchizedek nodded. "That was true once upon a time. It's not that simple anymore. Some demons do not wish to be demons. They have no other choice since humans learned they could summon and make deals. Do you know why Nex is a demon? Have you looked into his past?"

Gabriel pursed his lips. "I don't need to know. This is our duty. It's unfortunate, it is, but I made vows, and I intend to honor them before I get disciplined or Uriel arrives and makes the situation worse. Nex's past is—"

"Something you don't want to know because you're afraid. Admit it. You don't want to know because this has already been difficult for you, and knowing his past would make it worse."

"Or easier."

Melchizedek let out a breathy laugh. "You don't think that. He's too good to be all evil. I know you see that. If you didn't, you wouldn't have spent so much time stalling and hoping other angels wouldn't notice so you could look the other way. You should know better. His status is too high to be ignored."

"Exactly why it doesn't matter what his past is. We must handle it."

"His sister was sick with yellow fever," Melchizedek revealed. "She was about to die. He offered his soul in exchange for her to be well, so she could live a full life. Then he caught the disease himself and died taking care of her before he got to see her well. Does knowing that make this easier?"

Gabriel hesitated, torn between duty and personal ethics. "That is still a choice. He chose to do that. He *chose* this life."

"He was desperate." Melchizedek rested his hands on a pew. "Desperate people sometimes take drastic measures. He'd already lost his parents and younger brother to the same disease. I don't think it felt like a choice to him. It was an act of love, Gabriel."

"He's killed and tortured people. If we don't settle this, Uriel will. Do you want Uriel being part of this?"

"Of course I don't." Melchizedek crossed his arms. "Nex has killed and tortured under the same authority we follow. I've seen nothing in his past of him hurting innocents. He's rarely acted outside of his duty. Of all the demons we encounter, despite his rudeness, he's the easiest to work with. He manages several lower-level demons, and the ones under his command are the best behaved. I think we should take this problem to *them* instead of abiding by old laws that do not apply."

"I will not bring this issue to *them* and have our ability called into question, then have Uriel step in and make a bigger mess," Gabriel snapped. "If you cannot follow through, I will. Even stalling is breaking our vows. Every second we waste makes it more likely Uriel will come, and he will not handle it as tenderly as we would."

"You already stalled, and I'm going to ask you to continue because I will not take part in tearing them apart." Melchizedek squared his jaw. "I will not. I will take this to *them* and ask you refrain from any action until I return."

Gabriel clenched and unclenched his fists, then dropped his gaze to the floor.

Melchizedek headed to the doors of the church but paused and looked back at Gabriel. "You won't act until I speak with them."

Gabriel's shoulders slumped. "I will wait."

Chapter 36

Red Scarf

Outside the bookstore window, snow in small flakes, coating the street and sidewalk. The journey home would be cold, making today one of the few times Kat wished she wasn't terrified of driving. Nex had offered to help her overcome her fear a little at a time. They'd sat in her mother's car for an hour before work without it turned on. Though it was hard, she couldn't help but smile thinking about it.

"Don't be tense, Katherine." Nex set his hand on her back. "It's not on, and we're in a garage."

Kat gripped the steering wheel and counted her breaths. "I know."

Nex rubbed circles in her back. "It's all right. Let's pretend we're going somewhere. Where would you go if you could go anywhere by car?"

Kat smiled sheepishly. "Vegas."

"Vegas?" He chuckled. "Still, huh?" Kat nodded, and he kissed her cheek. "Very well. Pretend we're driving to Vegas." He covered her hand with his, and the view outside the car shifted to a street with endless bright buildings and flashing lights.

Kat gasped and swiveled her head, spotting several casinos and hotels. "Is this . . ."

"What it looks like. Three years ago, at least. We're not actually there, kitten. Why don't you pretend you're driving and see how you feel?"

The scene changed, and they were on an empty highway overlooking the Vegas Strip. Kat took a few deep breaths and pressed the gas pedal. In reality,

they didn't move, but with his abilities, Nex made it seem like they were
driving toward the lights as the sun set and shot out beautiful reds and
oranges.

"Kat." Connie's voice brought Kat back to the present.

Kat smiled, hoping Connie didn't notice she was daydreaming again.

"Honey, a storm's coming in. Worse than this one." She gestured to the
window. "There's no reason for us to stay open. No one's going to come
out in this."

"Okay. Why don't you get going, and I'll close?"

Connie dusted the countertop and straightened the bookmark display.
"I can't do that. You have to walk home. You should leave before it gets
worse."

"You have a much farther drive, and I won't walk home alone. Nex will
come. My house isn't far." Kat knotted her fingers together. "I don't want
you to wait any longer while the roads get worse. It'll get more dangerous."

Connie tapped her foot. She knew it was a sensitive topic, so as much as
she didn't care for the idea of Kat walking home in the storm, she let it go.
"Are you sure?"

"I'm sure." Kat waved her hand. "Don't worry about it."

"Thanks. Come into work a little early on Wednesday, please. I have
something to talk to you about."

Kat tensed. "Should I be worried?"

"Of course not, Kat." Connie laughed. "You're the best employee I could
ask for. I want to thank you for being the best employee I have, all right?"

"Oh." Kat's shoulders relaxed. "Thank you, Connie."

"Thank *you*, kiddo." Connie buttoned her worn wool coat. "Do me a
favor and call me when you're home, so I know you made it there safe."

Connie waved and hurried out the door, and Kat started closing. There
wasn't much to do. With the weather so bad, not many people had come
in and messed up her displays except the bookmarks Connie had already
fixed. All that was left was to get the blinds shut, lights off, and alarm set.

Kat stopped to text Nex before she got too far in the process.

> *Kat: Getting off in about ten minutes. Would you please come early?*

She set her phone down and took care of the cash register, then lowered the blinds and killed the lights. She returned to her phone. No response. He usually responded quickly. She opened the message and discovered hers didn't send. Shrugging, she dialed his number and held the phone between her ear and shoulder as she tidied the counter.

The ring didn't start. Kat brought the phone down. The screen displayed "Connecting . . ." but never got anywhere. *Strange, I always have service at work.* She reached for the work phone but found no dial tone.

A burst of wind knocked over a sign outside, causing a loud clatter. Kat jumped. The storm must've messed with the phone lines. Snow pelted down harder, the flakes whirling in the wind. Nex had been adamant about her not walking alone, especially after dark, but she didn't have many options. She locked up and tried her phone again outside.

Her messages continued not to send, and when she tried to call, she got the same "Connecting . . ." display that never went through. A powerful gust whipped around her and knocked her scarf off, blowing it down the street.

"Dang it." Kat raced after it.

She bent to pick up the scarf but paused. Down an adjacent street was a bridge with a steep ledge on one side. The snow eased enough to reveal a person standing on the ledge. Her eyes widened, and she ran, leaving her scarf behind.

At home, Nex drifted about the kitchen, following a recipe of Kat's mom's that Kat had been craving. Pasta from scratch was a first. He analyzed the instructions and groaned, then checked his phone again. No messages from Katherine. She usually texted him at least occasionally, and the snow was falling heavier.

He was dialing her number when Lucian appeared in front of him. "Nex, angels came into the realm. I don't know how we missed them, but one had contact with Kat. And a couple of hours ago, they released a demon. They were trying to keep it quiet, but it's here, and I've heard she's been marked. Marcus is headed to the bookstore."

"How the fuck did we miss that?" Nex growled, dialed Kat's number, and raised the phone to his ear. He paled. Straight to voicemail. Trying her work number was equally useless. "Fuck." He rushed out the door and shifted to his demon form, wings breaking through his skin when his foot hit the pavement.

He landed at the bookstore in seconds, not bothering to hide. No humans were out in this weather. The darkened bookstore accelerated his fear.

"Shit," Lucian spat, pacing back and forth.

Marcus ran up to them. "Did you find her?"

"Does it look like I fucking found her?" Nex snapped his gaze around. A red scarf caught his eye. Snagged on a bench and whipping in the wind.

He sped down the street, picked it up, and inhaled Kat's scent. Intending to use his tracking abilities, he picked up a fresh scent when the wind shifted. Kat's and another's. Another demon. His head snapped to the side toward a bridge, fiery curls catching his eye. Kat approached the demon, who looked like a regular human about to go off the edge.

"No." Nex sprinted down the street, too far away to push his voice into her head. "Katherine!"

Kat thought she heard someone calling through the wind, but she couldn't lose focus on this person about to jump. Approaching slowly, she hoped she'd say the right thing. "Hey," she said softly.

The person stiffened but didn't turn.

"It's okay. I just want to talk. My name's Katherine. What's yours?"

The person's voice was dry and uneven. "Doesn't matter."

"It does matter." Kat stepped closer. "You matter. Has someone made you feel like you don't?"

The person said nothing, but it sounded like they were crying.

Kat inched forward, clutching her coat. "I know this time of year is hard. Christmas passing. . . . It's not easy to get through holidays when you're hurting. I get it. Sometimes that pain feels unbearable."

They almost looked back.

Kat moved closer. She set a hand on their back, and they stiffened again. "Please come down. Please. Why don't you come home with me? I'll get you warmed up, and we can talk."

"Talk?"

"Yes, talk. About anything. Doesn't have to be about this. Here." Kat held out her hand. "Let me help you down. It's okay." Kat held her breath through the silence.

Then, slowly, they placed their hand in hers. Her breath released, and she smiled, helping them off the ledge. That's when the voice she'd recognize anywhere reached her. It echoed in her head and in the world for other people to hear.

"Katherine, don't!" Nex yelled. "Get away from it!"

Kat spun and found Nex speeding toward her. Humans weren't supposed to see him move that fast. She turned back to the person, but what stood beside her wasn't quite a person. It seemed human, but something was off. A smile grew until most its features were overtaken by a wide mouth.

"How good of you." It snatched her wrists. "Perhaps it'll be enough to keep you out of hell," the demon said before it threw her off the edge.

Chapter 37

An Angel to Visit

Katherine's scream echoed through Nex's mind until it became a permanent part of it. The sound burrowed inside him, tearing at the soul he didn't know he had until he met Katherine.

Do not let that fucker get away. I'll deal with him later. Nex's voice boomed in Lucian's and Marcus's minds. He raced forward and jumped off the bridge, released his wings, and dove after Kat.

Frigid air pricked at Kat's face like thousands of tiny needles. The distance between her and the rocky terrain closed fast, and she squeezed her eyes shut, unable to do anything but flail and scream. She landed in Nex's arms with a *thump* moments before she hit the ground. Holding her close, Nex flew away from the demon. Kat shook in his hold, but with the wind and how fast he moved, he couldn't comfort her until they got home. In a way, he was thankful the demon threw her. He'd been certain it would kill her instantly. Throwing her over the edge gave him time to get to her.

Nex landed in Kat's backyard and passed through the walls with Kat in his arms. The second they were inside, he set her on the kitchen counter and slipped her coat off, checking for injuries.

"Nex." Her voice trembled in time with her body. "That . . . I-it—"

"I know." Nex pulled her into an embrace. "I've got you. You're okay." He cradled her to his chest and kissed her head. "Did he hurt you? Did he touch you other than throwing you over?"

"N-no, but what was that?" She wrapped her arms around his neck.

"What happened?"

"That," Nex closed his eyes and squeezed her, trying to keep his rage inside so he didn't scare her, "was my fucking fault," he whispered, burying his face in her curls. "I'm so sorry, my angel. I should've been watching you more carefully."

Kat didn't understand but was too shaken to ask. She wrapped her legs around him, needing closeness. He held her tight until the trembling stopped, and her heart wasn't racing as fast.

"Katherine," Nex murmured, stroking her back. "Have you met any new people recently? Anyone who gave off a strange feeling? Maybe even a peaceful feeling?"

Kat frowned and lifted her head, wiping away tears that trickled out. "Why are you asking?"

"Because it's important. Have you?"

"Just Gabriel from church and that weird customer." Kat sunk her head against his chest. "I thought Gabriel was nice at first, but then he started being a jerk."

"Gabriel." Nex growled. "What did he say to you?"

"Do you know him?"

Nex's jaw clenched. "You could say that."

"He's a demon?" A look of puzzlement crossed her face. "He can't be. I met him at church."

Nex narrowed his eyes. "How long ago? Was he the one bothering you?"

"I don't know, a few weeks ago, and yeah, he was." Kat's brows furrowed. "What's going on? How do you know Gabriel?"

Nex pressed his lips to her forehead, allowing his eyes to shut. The image of her plummeting off that bridge wasn't going away anytime soon, but he had to make sure she was okay before he dealt with the people responsible. "You could say Gabriel and I work together."

Kat pulled away and raised an eyebrow. "Work together?"

Nex sighed and drew her into a tight hug. "He's an angel. And they're not particularly keen on demons interacting with humans the way I am with you. Don't know how he thinks killing you is the right fucking way to handle it." He rested his head on hers and tried not to think about it too hard. He could've lost her today. "He should've fucking come to me first."

Nex expected questions, but he got none. Kat's slender arms locked tighter around him, and she stayed unusually silent. He was about to question her when Lucian and Marcus entered the house.

Marcus's boots thudded across the floorboards. "You all right, Kat?"

Kat nodded but continued clinging to Nex. Nex ran his hands helplessly up and down her back, wishing he knew better how to comfort. *Where is he?* Nex asked, glancing over at his friends.

We have people holding him, Lucian answered. *We're not the only ones upset about this. She's grown on a lot of demons. They're pissed and ready to fight over it.*

Good. I could use a fight. Nex's eyes flashed red. *Keep watch outside until I get her settled in bed. Then we'll deal with this bullshit.*

Lucian and Marcus nodded and hurried out the back door. Nex slid his hands under Kat's legs and carried her toward the bedroom.

"What are you doing?" Kat didn't move from her place in his chest. Still shaken, his arms were the only thing holding her together.

"You've had a shock, Katherine. We need to warm you up and get you into bed."

"What's going to happen?"

Nex didn't know what to say. He knew it might become a problem at some point but assumed as long as he wasn't hurting anyone, they'd let it slide, and if they didn't, they'd come for him, not her. *Why did they go after Kat?* There was no reason she should be punished for him breaking the rules. Historically, angels let other things slide. Nex considered it complete bullshit their reaction to this was so extreme.

"Nothing's going to happen. They can't keep us apart. I won't let them. More importantly," he set her on the bathroom counter and cupped her face, "I won't let them hurt you. I promise. I won't leave you vulnerable again. I'm sorry." He rested his forehead on hers and closed his eyes against the sting. "I'm so sorry, my angel. I won't let anything like that happen again."

"It wasn't your fault." Kat stroked his face. Nex opened his eyes to look into hers, giving her a pained expression. "It wasn't." Kat kissed him, then hugged him.

Silence in the atmosphere was a stark contrast to the endless stream of thoughts and fears bouncing around both their minds. Nex wasn't ready to stop hugging her, but he had angels to deal with. That and Kat shivered, reminding him she needed to warm up. He turned on the shower, making it hot like she enjoyed, before gripping the hem of her shirt.

"What's so wrong about us being together?" she asked.

"Demons aren't meant to be with humans." He tugged her shirt off. "We're meant to stay in our realm and not bother humans unless we're ordered to. They don't like us meddling with people and *tainting* their souls."

"You aren't tainting me. I want you here. Doesn't that count for anything?"

"Apparently not." Nex pulled off his shirt, then gave her a gentle kiss. "I'm going to fix this. If they think they can take you from me, they have another thing coming."

"I don't want you to get hurt."

"Don't worry about me, Katherine." He nuzzled her neck and breathed in her scent—vanilla and pear. "I have a few tricks up my sleeve."

Nex undressed them and stepped into the shower with Kat, holding her close as hot water cascaded over them. He drifted his hand up and down her back. Often, washing her led to something fun, but that was far from his mind. He wanted her warm and relaxed enough to sleep.

When the water ran cold, they dried off. Kat slipped on leggings and opted for one of Nex's long-sleeve shirts, which almost reached her knees.

They climbed onto the bed, and Nex held her against him, running his hand through her hair, gaze fixed over her shoulder out the window where his fellow demons were arriving.

Kat's hands fisted in his shirt, her eyes wide open.

His chest clenched, and he tilted her chin up. "Sleep, my angel." He brushed his lips along hers. "I'm here. No one can touch you."

"How are you planning to fix it?"

"Let me worry about that."

"Last time I let you worry about taking care of something, Lilith showed up." Kat blanched and cuddled closer. "What are you going to do?"

"Have a chat with Gabriel. Explain the situation and make an appeal. Don't worry yourself over it. You've been through enough for one night."

"Would it help if I talked to him too?"

"I'm afraid this needs to come from me. I'm the one breaking the rules you didn't know existed. I created the problem, and I'll fix it."

"Don't get hurt," Kat whispered, tightening her hands in his shirt. "Please don't do anything where you could get hurt."

"I'll be fine." Nex rested his head on hers. "Sleep with me for now."

He nestled the blankets snugly around her. It took longer than usual for her to fall asleep, but once she did, he carefully untangled himself from her, then stared down at her sleeping form. Red hair spread over the sheets, her eyelashes fanned her cheeks, and her hands reached for the place he'd occupied. She found a pillow and tugged it to her chest.

Nex bent and kissed her forehead, brushing his fingers over her freckle-covered cheek. He only allowed himself a moment to admire her, then stalked outside.

The wind whipped around him and his fellow demons in Kat's backyard, but the snow melted before it reached him. Anger blazed through his veins, and each step melted more snow.

"I need several guards to stay with her," Nex said. "The rest of you, come with me." He changed into his demon form, eyes glowing brighter red than usual. "We have an angel to visit."

Chapter 38

Unforgivable

Melchizedek returned to the church and found Gabriel lying across a pew, tossing and catching a ball of light. He smacked the light from Gabriel's hand. It bounced down the aisle and faded.

"You weren't supposed to act until I returned," Melchizedek gritted out. "Yet, I hear a demon was released."

"What?" Gabriel sat up. "I did not release a demon. I told you I would wait, and I did."

"Then what happened? The mark I placed on her was tracked." Melchizedek crossed his arms. "I felt it happen."

"I don't know, but I did not send a demon. If I were going to send anyone, it would have been an angel to hold her until we figured this out."

"*I* released the demon."

Gabriel and Melchizedek turned to the low, clipped voice.

"Uriel." Melchizedek struggled to keep his tone even at the sight of his brother by the pulpit. "Why did you send a demon of all things after Katherine? We only resort to that if we don't successfully separate them. Did you send an angel first?"

"I won't forgo my duties because the two of you did." Uriel strode between the pews. "We have a responsibility, a duty to fulfill, under *their* command. *They* aren't going to change the laws for one demon."

"*Old* laws." Melchizedek pinched the bridge of his nose. "You had no right to act on this."

Uriel seethed. "I have every right. I'm the only one acting under the law."

"This wasn't your situation to handle." Gabriel sprung to his feet.

"The laws do not specifically address a situation like this," Melchizedek said. "Their situation is unique and requires us to approach it as such."

"The laws do address it," Uriel said. "They say demons cannot mingle with humans."

"You know as well as I do that was made for demons who possessed and manipulated." Melchizedek's eyes emitted a low glow. "He has not done that. He loves her, Uriel. He loves her, and she loves him. Who are we to say they cannot love each other?"

"We are not the ones who say." Uriel glowered as he stepped up to Melchizedek. "We made vows, in case you've forgotten, to uphold the laws. It is our duty whether we like it or not."

Melchizedek squared his jaw and clasped his hands as they itched to smack Uriel on the back of the head. "Our duty is not to approach—"

"Gabriel!" A thunderous growl shook the building.

Melchizedek approached a window that vibrated in its frame. His eyes widened. Beyond the boundary, Lucian and Marcus flanked Nex, several pairs of red eyes behind them, hidden in the storm. Snow melted around them, the fury in Nex's eyes a promise of the hellish fire he was ready to release.

"What did you do?" Melchizedek glared over his shoulder at Uriel. "I know you summoned the demon, but what did you do? Is she dead? Please, tell me you did *not* kill her."

"She's not dead. Yet." Uriel crossed his arms. "I underestimated how quickly he would get to her. It won't happen again."

"That was not the way to handle this," Gabriel said. "Death is the last resort. Where is your wisdom?"

"Do not question my wisdom." Uriel turned his aggressive stance on Gabriel. "You were not fulfilling your duties."

"You should have spoken with the demon before going after the girl like that!" Gabriel held his ground despite Uriel getting in his face. "We hadn't separated them yet."

"Gabriel, I know you're hiding in there. Get your ass out here now." Nex's growl shook the floorboards and rattled the doors. "Or so help me, I'll have every single fucking human who makes their way down this street slaughtered, and you can listen to their screams."

"That's who you're defending." Uriel gestured toward the window. "Did you hear what he said?"

"You tried to kill the woman he loves," Melchizedek said. "You activated that anger. You better be ready to face it." He threw open the doors and strode out into the snow.

"Melchizedek," Nex snarled, balling his fists. "I should've known. When one is here, the other isn't far behind. I'm not certain you two aren't fucking each other. Do you ever go on missions alone?"

"Nex." Melchizedek held his hands up. "I had no part in hurting Katherine. Let's take a breath, shall we?"

"No part?" Nex paced the property line. "Wasn't it you who marked her? You who sent her into fucking traffic? Or do I have someone else to hunt down?"

"The mark was meant to have someone pull her away from you, not kill her. I did not let her get hurt. The traffic incident was a test. That's all. I wouldn't let her come to harm."

"A test?" Nex's eyes flamed. "I'm sick of you and your realm's fucking tests. Stop being cowards. Come out here."

"You don't want to start a fight. You don't have your leader's support. Let's work something out without violence."

"I don't need my leader's support." Nex's wings flapped, creating a gust that drove snow against the church and the angels. "You're the ones who started the violence. Not me. You fucking started it. I swear on everything that's unholy, if you two don't come over here, I will raise hell. I will rip this city apart, and that will be on you."

"I see your point." Uriel emerged from the doors and descended the stairs, sending Melchizedek a side-glance. "He's perfectly reasonable. I don't know why I didn't approach him first."

"Uriel." Nex's mouth fell open. "What the fuck are you doing here?"

"Uriel was the one who sent the demon." Gabriel stood alongside Melchizedek. "I would not send someone to kill her, Nex. If anything, I would've separated the two of you."

"You sent the demon after Katherine." Nex fumed at Uriel. "When I get my hands on you—"

"You'll do what?" Uriel smirked. "What powers do you possess while you're trapped in this blood bond?"

Nex inclined his head to the demons behind him. "I have help."

"No blood needs to be shed." Melchizedek glanced between Uriel and Nex. "Nex, you know the rules with humans. Surely you knew discipline would be coming. Let's agree that both parties could have handled this better and resolve it without a fight."

"Is that what you call trying to kill an innocent woman? *Discipline?*" Nex scoffed. "Call me what you like, maybe I am a demon, but I've never spilled innocent blood. Can you say the same?"

"That wasn't the way it should have been handled. Uriel was not supposed to be part of it," Melchizedek said. "I apologize for his actions. I don't blame you for being angry, but she's fine, and we need to work something out."

"She's *fine*? You think she's fine? She was thrown off a fucking bridge! She's had enough trauma in her life, and you made it worse. She's not fucking fine."

"Thrown off a bridge?" Gabriel rubbed his forehead.

Uriel shrugged. "I didn't specify how the demon was to get rid of her. The method doesn't matter. They need to be made an example of, or there will be more instances like this." He gestured to the demons whose glowing eyes were all that were visible through the snow. "Look at them. Already they're threatening us."

"It's only still a threat because you're too much of a coward to get off that fucking holy ground." Nex growled. "I will force your hand, Uriel. If you have no problem spilling innocent blood, why should we?"

"Let's not spill any blood," Melchizedek said. "We won't come after Katherine again. There's no reason to continue the violence."

"You won't come after Katherine again?" Nex cocked his head to the side. "I thought you couldn't lie, Melchizedek."

Melchizedek spun toward Uriel, who only gave him the briefest glance before continuing his staredown with Nex. "What did you do now?" Melchizedek asked.

"Our duty. I'm fulfilling the vows I made. The girl is not innocent. She's been knowingly sleeping with a demon. It ends now. It wasn't smart of you to leave her alone." Uriel narrowed his eyes at Nex. "If you truly loved her, you would have stayed with her instead of coming after me. That action proves it's not love. It's infatuation and lust. If you loved her, your love would've controlled your temper."

"What did you do?" Melchizedek repeated.

"He sent an angel to do the job," Nex said. "Isn't that right, Uriel? One of your angels finally decided to get their hands dirty. Did you think I'd leave her unguarded after what you did? Did you think I wouldn't do *everything* to protect her? Don't fucking tell me what I have with her isn't real. She's everything to me. There's nothing I wouldn't do for her."

Gabriel and Uriel stilled.

Melchizedek closed his eyes, shook his head, and took a deep breath. "Nex, what did you do?"

"What did *I* do?" Nex laughed. "I made sure my innocent Katherine was protected." He stepped aside, and the head of an angel rolled from the crowd, stopping in front of Uriel. "Send as many angels as you like. They're weak from centuries of having us do the work they couldn't handle. Send all your angels for all I care." He crossed his arms as several hundred demons emerged from the snow, surrounding the church. "You won't win, and you will *not* lay a hand on her again."

"*Nex,*" Melchizedek scolded. "I was trying to get a pardon for you. Do you have any idea how unlikely that is to happen now that you've had an angel killed? That's practically unforgivable."

"It's not *practically* unforgivable. It *is* unforgivable." Uriel stalked toward Nex. "This ends now." Demons moved in front of Nex as Uriel approached, a sword appearing in his hands. "You think your fellow demons can help you?" A flash in Uriel's eyes forced all the demons to sink to their knees. "Tell me again how weak we are." The sword slashed through the air as he swung it down at Nex's head.

Another blade caught Uriel's with a *clank* and knocked it off course, sparing Nex's skull.

"Enough." Gabriel shoved Uriel back onto holy ground, away from the demons. "Enough blood has been spilled and attempted to be spilled. This is not how we handle things."

Uriel turned on Gabriel. "You dare step in when you failed to fulfill your duties?"

"I dare to do a lot of things when you take things too far." Light flashed in Gabriel's eyes, paralyzing Uriel. "We are angels. We do not spill innocent blood. We do not act relentlessly."

"As angels, we—" Uriel started.

"I think you've lost the right to call yourself an angel." Nex glowered. "Go ahead, hide on holy ground. I've got time. I intend to stay with her until our last breaths, and I will keep her safe no matter who I have to fight."

"Nex, I understand you're angry, but you need to breathe. You don't want to start a war with us," Melchizedek said. "You know you won't win. *They* will be on our side, and you will still lose her. The only way I can fix this is with cooperation on your part."

"Or we'll send for Lilith," Uriel said. "She wants to handle this problem, and she could handle it quickly."

"*Uriel,*" Melchizedek hissed.

"How dare you call yourself an angel," Nex snapped at Uriel. "How the fuck can you look Katherine in the eyes and give her a death sentence for something she didn't know was against the rules? What kind of fucking justice is that?" Nex turned to Melchizedek. "You looked into her soul. She told me how you touched her hand." His eyes glowed brighter. "I may not be able to look into her soul as deeply as you, but I don't need to. I know purity when I see it, and Katherine is the embodiment of it. There isn't a soul in the world purer than her, and you're going to kill her because of me?"

"No." Melchizedek raised his hands. "We are not calling Lilith, and we won't send someone to kill Katherine. I'm doing what I can, Nex, but you cannot leave it all on me. I need you to calm down." His expression softened, and he took a step forward. "For her sake, calm down. You know fighting us won't help. You're smart. You know this," he gestured between Uriel and Nex, "will make things worse. I cannot help if you're so angry you cannot think straight."

"He's a demon. He is not going to control his temper," Uriel said. "It's not in his nature."

Nex's eyes whipped to Uriel, his nostrils flaring, fists clenching. He briefly wondered what the odds were he could get Katherine to give him Uriel's name to kill. He could find a way back to her after. He *would* find a way back to her after. Nothing would keep him from her.

Melchizedek's voice was soft and calm. "For Katherine, he can."

Nex's gaze drifted back to Melchizedek, his nails digging into his palms, drawing blood. He closed his eyes and breathed. When he opened them again, they were slightly less full of unbridled rage. "I don't trust you." Nex scowled at Melchizedek. "I don't trust any of you."

"I understand why you don't trust Uriel, but when have I been unfair to you?" Melchizedek asked. "We've worked together for over two hundred years, Nex. When have I betrayed your trust?"

"When you marked my Katherine. When you let your brother send someone to go after that mark."

"Nex, I'm sorry for what happened. Trust me when I say I will handle it." He shot an annoyed glance at Uriel before refocusing on Nex. "I will make an appeal for you, and I will take Uriel with me to keep you at ease. I felt confident I would succeed until this." Melchizedek waved over the severed angel's head discarded in the snow. They'd be reborn, but the action was reprehensible. "*They* are not going to let that slide without discipline, Nex. You must give me time and patience. If you let me close to her, I will remove the mark an—"

"Remove the mark?" Gabriel interjected. "You cannot do that. I'm sorry things happened this way," he said, looking at Nex. "I'm sorry Uriel acted ruthlessly, but it does not change the fact we have to do something. We at least have to separate them. It's the law, and if we don't uphold it, we will be disciplined ourselves."

"Go ahead and fucking try to take her from me." Nex's claws emerged. "I fucking dare you."

"Gabriel and Uriel, go inside." Melchizedek waved his hand. "You're not helping."

"You cannot remove the mark from the girl," Gabriel said.

"If you think I'd let you anywhere near her after tonight, you're really fucking stupid," Nex said.

Melchizedek turned up his palms. "Nex, I wouldn't hurt her."

"You already did. You marked her. You knew what that meant. Even if you didn't intend to have her killed, you intended to have someone take her from me. That would've scared the shit out of her."

"And now I want to make it right and remove that mark as a peace offering."

"No." Nex clenched his jaw. "Neither you nor any of your pets are coming anywhere near her."

"It's for her safet—"

"I don't fucking trust you!" Nex's voice boomed, shaking snow loose from the trees. "Stay away from her."

Melchizedek sighed. "I will make an appeal for you. I suggest you and your friends be on your best behavior because *they* aren't going to be happy about you killing an angel. Keep your head down while I try to smooth this over, all right? No attacks on Gabriel or Uriel."

Nex's gaze slid to Uriel, and while every part of him wished for his normal abilities so he could rip Uriel apart, he wanted to stay with Katherine more. Nex and Uriel stared each other down for a long moment before Nex's gaze returned to Melchizedek.

"I'm not leaving her. I don't care what happens. I don't care what verdict is reached. If you try to separate us, I will not go down without a fight. Keep that pathetic excuse of an angel away from Katherine." He spat at Uriel's feet. "If any angel comes within a mile of her, they die. Consequences be damned. I will *not* let them live."

Chapter 39

Vulnerable

Kat woke to Nex holding her tighter than he ever had. So snug, she was a little uncomfortable. She opened her eyes to his sleeping face. Her heart ached at his pulled-down lips. Even asleep, his exhaustion was obvious.

She didn't want to wake him, but she could barely breathe. She tried to stretch and loosen his arms, but that only increased his hold, making it more impossible to move.

"Nex," she said softly, pushing dark strands off his forehead.

The moment her fingers touched his skin, his eyes snapped open, and his arms constricted the remaining air from her lungs. "What's wrong?"

Kat wheezed. "I can't breathe."

"Fuck." He loosened his arms and kissed her forehead. "Sorry. How'd you sleep?"

When he returned home, his fellow demons let him know she'd been restless, though that changed when he climbed into bed with her. She was still restless but less so once he held her. Shaken from what happened, he'd inadvertently gripped her tighter and tighter all night.

"Fine." Kat assessed the dark circles beneath his eyes. "Did you sleep?"

"Some." He nuzzled her nose and rested his cheek against hers. "Don't worry about me. You never ate last night. Are you hungry?"

"I have other things on my mind." Kat sat up. "When are you going to talk to Gabriel?"

Nex laid his head in her lap and cuddled her waist. "I already did."

"Last night?" Kat frowned, and Nex nodded. "I didn't know you left."

"I didn't want to, my angel." He reached up and skimmed his fingers along her jaw. "I had to deal with it."

"Why didn't you tell me?"

"You almost died. I didn't want to put anything else on you."

Kat combed her fingers through his hair. "I'm tougher than you think. What happened?"

"Gabriel wasn't the one responsible. It was Uriel, and he's a fucking cunt." Nex growled. "I still don't trust Gabriel. Melchizedek is the one who'll hopefully help us. *If* he can be trusted."

"Melchizedek?" Kat's frown deepened. "Uriel?"

"Uriel's the one who sent someone after you. Melchizedek was the weird customer at the bookstore. They're here together."

Kat nodded, then shook her head. "I don't understand. I've read about these angels, but why would they all need to be here?"

"Because of me." Nex burrowed against her stomach. "Because I'm a bigger problem since I'm a higher rank."

"So, a higher rank means what?"

"That my actions are judged more harshly." Nex remembered Death's words. "Because I'm a role model."

"Oh."

"Let's get you something to eat." Nex sat up and kissed her. A long, deep, intimate kiss that had her chasing after him when he pulled away. He rested his hand against her cheek and stared at her while her screams from the night before echoed in his mind. "Fuck, Katherine, can you ever forgive me?"

"Forgive you for what?"

"For letting that happen." He closed his eyes, unable to look at her. "For not being more careful."

"That wasn't your fault." Kat guided him to face her. He reluctantly opened his eyes, exposing the pain and guilt swirling within them. "It wasn't your fault."

"I knew it could become a problem, and I didn't watch over you like I should have. I never should've let you out of my sight." He slid out of bed and shuffled toward the kitchen. "I don't know how you can stand to look at me."

"Because you didn't do anything." Kat climbed off the bed and followed him. "I don't blame you. I only wish you would've told me something was going on, but I should've told you about Gabriel. I don't blame you for any of it."

In the kitchen, Nex shook his head and reached for the kettle. "You should."

Kat wrapped her arms around him from behind, pressing her cheek against his warm back. "I love you," she whispered. "Don't hate yourself, please. Just let me love you. Let me love you enough it takes the place of everything negative."

Nex's arms dropped to his sides, and he stared down at her delicate hands clasped over his stomach. *I could've lost her. I could've never seen her again.* The memory of her scream pierced his soul, and he couldn't take it. He needed to be close to her. Turning in her arms, he dragged her into a hard kiss. She squealed in surprise—something he loved to get out of her. *That* was the sound he wanted to hear. Not her terrified scream.

He couldn't say enough how sorry he was. The sincerity of his regrets poured into his kiss, and he sought out her tongue, kissing her hard enough her lips would be swollen. Seeing them swollen from his attention drove him crazy. Moaning into the kiss, Kat slid her hands into his hair. Nex groaned and slipped his hands under the shirt of his she had on.

"Fuck, I need you." He hooked his fingers in her leggings. "I *need* you." He tugged her leggings and underwear down in one swift motion, lifted her onto the counter, spread her legs, and dove under her shirt, craving her taste. Kat gasped when his tongue swept over the ache he'd created. Her fingers curled in his hair, tightening in it as she threw her head back and moaned.

He moved his lips and tongue over her clit in a rhythmic pattern until she came, shuddering around his face. While she trembled from the remnants of her orgasm, he stood and traced the outline of her jaw. "I need to have you."

"Then have me." She pressed her hands against his chest and gazed up at him. "I'm yours."

Nex groaned and tugged his pants down enough to let himself out. He moved between her legs and positioned himself at her hot, waiting core. They both released a moan as he slid into her and stayed deep inside. Kat held his face and pulled him into another kiss.

"I'll give you points for passion. I wasn't expecting the show, but I'll gladly take it."

Ice replaced the raging fire inside, freezing them in place. Nex peeked over his shoulder at Lilith near the back door. He pulled out of Kat and yanked his pants up as Kat tugged the shirt she was wearing further down her legs. Kat might've been embarrassed if her hands weren't shaking so bad.

"Don't stop on my account." Lilith gestured for them to continue. "You may as well fuck her. You might not get another opportunity after I'm done with you."

Nex helped Kat off the counter and ushered her behind him. "The angels called you, I suppose. I thought you didn't answer to them."

"I'm not here because of the angels. Uriel may have come to me, but I knew what happened. You know I don't fucking answer to them. I'm here because of *you*." She growled, stalking toward them.

Nex reached out for the demons who'd been there since the bridge incident, but he was blocked. He scowled. *Lilith.*

"Don't bother. They're on their knees. They made me force them to stand down. I was already pissed, Nex." She bared her teeth. "Now I'm *really* fucking pissed. I had to use my powers to make my own soldiers submit."

"If you're not here because of the angels, then why are you here?" Nex asked, backing him and Katherine away.

"Why am I here?" Lilith seethed. "Because one of my high-ranked soldiers had a fucking angel killed. An *angel*. What the fuck were you thinking? Do you know how bad that makes me look?" Her claws grew longer, her voice disembodied. "It makes it look like I have no control over my damn demons. You were on the brink of causing inflation in this stupid fucking human realm, but you've made a bigger mess that makes me look like a shitty leader. It makes the angels think we need better regulation, need more of their involvement. I'm done giving you chances." Her eyes turned solid black. "Now, you pay for it."

The moment she said the words, shadows snatched Kat and dragged her to Lilith. Nex lunged for her, but Lilith shoved him, and he fell to the floor.

"Don't hurt her." Nex jumped up and darted forward. "Don't you dare hurt her!"

"What are you going to do about it?" Lilith tilted her head and flicked her wrist. Kat was jerked to the demon's side, suspended in the air. "Long time no see, sweetness. Nex has certainly been fucking you good, hasn't he?"

Nex charged at Lilith. She rolled her eyes, and the second he reached her, his eyes widened. Time slowed, but only for him. Lilith clutched him by his hair, an invisible force drove him to his knees, and Lilith wrenched his head back to make him look up at her.

"Don't be naïve. You think I'm going to stroll in here, kill you both, and leave it at that?" She cackled, the sound grating on Kat and Nex's ears like a physical invasion. "No, you no longer get the luxury of a quick death. I'm going to make you *suffer*. I'm going to break your spirit and shatter your soul. I'm going to separate you in a way that crushes you both so you don't *ever* think about putting me in this position again."

"Nex!" Kat screamed as Lilith released his hair, and his head slumped to the ground.

"Since you've abused your powers, you no longer get to have them unless they're for the purpose you came here to serve." Black tendrils coiled around Nex's throat, cutting off his oxygen. "Your powers are gone. Your demon guards are gone. I am forcing them all back to the underworld until this shit is over. You're as vulnerable as a mortal and just as easy to kill. The only time your powers will return is if your beloved human gives you a name, and you'll only be able to use them on that target. Then, when you return to the underworld," Lilith's teeth grew to sharp points, "mark my words, Nex, you will *never* leave that realm. And you will never see your precious human again. Good luck protecting her when you have nothing to protect her with."

Chapter 40

Love Always Perseveres

Nex peered out the window as if that would help when someone came for them. He was more vulnerable than he'd ever been. Basic senses were missing. He couldn't hear as well, couldn't move as fast, wasn't as strong, couldn't smell as well. He didn't realize how terrible human senses were compared to what he was used to.

Regardless, every sound put him on edge. He'd done nothing but keep watch since Lilith's threat. The combination of sleep deprivation and the stress of what might happen made him short-tempered, which was why Kat opted to sit in another room while he moved between the windows.

A small creak in the floorboard—not enough to mean anything but enough to make Nex anxious—sounded from their bedroom, and he rushed in. Kat knelt on the floor in front of the bed with her hands together, eyes closed, murmuring so quietly he couldn't make out what she said.

Nex's eyes narrowed. "Don't tell me you're doing what I think you're doing."

"I'm not asking you to do it with me," Kat said calmly and continued murmuring.

"You think any higher power is going to help us?"

Kat took a deep breath, opened her eyes, and stared at the Bible on the bed. "I've never pushed my faith on you. I'd appreciate it if you respect that I have faith, even if you don't." She stood and faced him. "You need sleep.

It's been days, Nex."

"You think I can sleep right now? Someone needs to do something more than pray to a being who *isn't listening*."

"You don't know that." Kat's hands fell to her sides. "You're angry, and I understand why, but—"

"The being you're praying to would've let you die! It's their angels that are here."

"The God I believe in is a God of love." Kat clasped her hands. "Maybe I didn't die because you were there. The timing worked out a little perfectly, don't you think? If the demon killed me instead of throwing me off the bridge, you wouldn't have gotten to me. If you'd come a few seconds later, I would've died. What was it that made Lucian suddenly aware of the angels' presence so you could get to me in time?"

"How can you still be so fucking naïve?"

"Nex." Kat covered her face with her hands. "I'm sorry everything's a mess, and I'm sorry you're scared, but how is getting upset with me going to help? Do you want me to sit by the windows and doors like you do, waiting for something bad to happen? How does that help?"

"How does *praying* help?"

"I don't know. Except that I have faith."

"*Faith*." Nex's laugh held no humor. "That's certainly helped in your life so far."

Kat's face crumpled. "Don't do this. Don't fight with me and say mean things because you don't know what else to do. Don't push me away because you're scared. Do you think pushing me away is going to make it hurt less if something happens?"

Nex ground his teeth. "It's not an *if*. It's a *when*. Something *is* going to happen. Lilith doesn't make empty threats."

"Okay, something *is* going to happen." Kat's shoulders slumped under the weight of exhaustion. She didn't know what to do, but she did know that she didn't want her possibly last moments with Nex to be like this.

"You can't do anything. And neither can I. It's out of our hands and getting upset—"

The doorbell chimed. Nex tensed and pulled her against him. A few seconds later, there was a knock. Kat tried to move, but Nex held her back. "No one comes in."

"Nex." Kat wiggled out of his hold. "If it was an angel or demon or someone here to hurt us, do you think they'd *ring the doorbell*?"

"It could be a trap."

"Can't demons walk through walls? Uriel was strong enough to force the other demons to take a knee. Do you think us not answering the door is going to stop a supernatural being from getting in here?"

Nex opened his mouth to argue, but she was right. Though, it didn't stop his suspicions of what was on the other side of the door. A knock echoed through the house, and Kat walked into the living room with Nex following close behind. She peeked out the peephole, and Nex set his hands on her hips in case he needed to pull her away.

"It's a friend." Kat glanced back at him. "Give me a minute, okay?"

"What? No." His grip tightened. "Demons can take different forms in case you've forgotten the one who almost killed you."

"My previous point stands. If it's a demon, me not answering the door won't stop anything from happening."

Nex whimpered. "Katherine . . ."

Kat turned toward him. "We've been locked in this house for *eleven* days. I've called into work, missed church, haven't spoken to anyone, and everyone is worried about us. And for what? If I'm a target, I'm a target." She dropped her arms in defeat, not because she didn't take it seriously, but because her reaction wouldn't change the outcome. It would only make her miserable until it happened. "There's nothing I can do about that. But I will not spend my last moments alive fighting and bickering with the man I love, isolating from the people I care about, and waiting to die."

She slipped out the door, closing it behind her. Nex tensed and pressed his ear against the door. Muffled talking. No screams. Peeking through the peephole, he bristled. Kat was with a man as tall as Nex but admittedly more muscular. To make matters worse, they hugged. A long hug with no end. Jealousy bubbled in his chest. *Who the fuck does he think he is?* Nex twisted the doorknob at the same time Kat turned it to come inside.

She stepped in and gave him a small smile. "See? It was nothing."

Bloodred irises replaced Nex's usual amber. "Nothing?"

"What's wrong?" She rubbed his bicep.

"Who was the man?"

"Outside?" She earned a curt nod from Nex. "Jeremiah."

"*That's* Jeremiah? The one you mentioned about helping Bernice move the couch. The marine."

"Yes." Kat tilted her head to the side. "Are you mad at me?"

"Shouldn't I be?" Nex stepped back. "Why did he not only have his hands on you, but you *allowed* it? Why was he here?"

"It was just a hug." Kat pulled her hand back. "And he was here because I've been missing and not responding to him. He was worried."

"Not responding? He's been texting you?"

"Yeah." Kat's brows furrowed. "He's a friend, and I've been helping hi—"

"I don't want you to text him. I don't want anyone touching you except me." He grabbed her waist and pulled her toward him. "Are you forgetting who you belong to?" He lowered his lips toward hers. "Should I remind you?"

Kat turned her head before their lips met and set her hands on his chest, pushing him back. "No." She folded her arms. "Why are you mad? I didn't do anything wrong. Jeremiah's a friend, and he's going through some personal stuff. He doesn't have a lot of friends. He's shy like me."

"You're mine. Just mine. Other men can't touch you. I don't give a fuck if it's a hug."

"What do you think me belonging to you means? I thought it meant that in terms of intimacy, you're mine, and I'm yours, and there's no one else involved. But you're treating me like property, which is not how you treat someone you love. Why are you so jealous?"

"How would you like it if I brought Arda here and hugged her in front of you?"

"I wouldn't mind." Kat lifted her chin, then walked to the kitchen and grabbed the kettle. "You don't see her like that anymore, and sometimes Arda needs a hug, and you two are friends, so there's nothing wrong with that." She filled the kettle, needing some tea to soothe her, and hopefully Nex's, nerves. "I wouldn't have a problem, and you shouldn't have a problem with me having a friend that happens to be a guy."

"I do have a problem, Katherine." He stomped after her. "You can't see him again. I don't want him texting you, and I certainly don't want him touching you."

"Are you serious?" Kat set the kettle down and turned toward him, clenching her fists. "You're trying to tell me I can't see a friend?"

"I'm not *trying* to tell you, Katherine. I'm *telling* you. It's not fucking happening."

"That's ridiculous." Kat threw her arms up. "You can't tell me what to do and who to see. Don't you trust me?"

"It's not you I don't trust. It's everyone else. You're mine. All of you is mine. You belonging to me—"

"Doesn't mean you control me." Kat rested her hands on the counter and fixed him with a glare that made him step back. "When I say I belong to you, I mean my romantic intimacy belongs to you. My heart belongs to you. You're the only person I want to be close to in the way we're close. You're the only one I want to fall asleep with and," she blushed, darting her gaze away, "be intimate with. But it does *not* mean you control who I see, tell me who I'm allowed to be friends with or hug. That's not respectful." She slammed her hand on the counter, and he hated the heartbroken expression on her face. "You think I'd hurt you like that? Let someone else in and leave you? That hurts, Nex." She shook her head. "It hurts that you think so lowly of me. I'm not yours because I'm property to control. I'm yours because my heart is yours." She turned the stove on and placed the kettle on the burner. "I'm a person, Nex, not an object."

Blinking, Nex stayed in place. Anytime Katherine wasn't calm and reasonable was because he'd crossed a line. He couldn't help it. His fear of losing her was amplified by the new threat and his inability to protect her. The thought of losing her dropped a weight in his heart so heavy it suffocated his lungs and sank to his stomach in a tight knot. Regardless, it was unfair to put that insecurity on her.

Guilt crept in for hurting her, for snapping at her since the incident with Lilith, for doing exactly what she said—pushing her away. As if that would make it easier to lose her. He deserved a whipping. Pain and fear surrounded them, and instead of consoling her, he made it worse. His stomach churned, and his gaze dropped to the wooden floor.

He didn't deserve her, but he promised himself he'd do everything he could to get there. His outburst wasn't a move in the right direction but admitting fault was. He stood behind her, turned the burner off, and pulled her against him. "I'm sorry." He rested his forehead on the back of her head. "I'm sorry, my angel. Truly. You're right. I was wrong." He nuzzled her curls and breathed in her scent. "Can you forgive me?"

Kat twisted to face him. "Are you going to throw a tantrum if you see me with Jeremiah again?"

Nex shook his head. That wasn't fair. "It won't happen again." He raised her hand to his face, hating that he hurt her, vowing to never repeat the action. "I . . ."

"What?"

"I don't want to lose you." Nex covered her hand with his. "The thought is unbearable."

"You're not going to lose me because of another guy. I only want to be with you." She rested her head in his chest. "I'm yours, Nex. I can be yours and be my own person."

"I know." Nex hugged her, relieved to have her in his arms again. He never wanted to give her another reason to want to be anywhere else. "I know I'm not good enough for you, and I'm waiting for you to see it too. I'm waiting for you to do what the angels want and walk away from me."

The moment the words left his mouth, he realized what needed to happen. He had to let her go. Let her go, or let her get hurt. He stepped away from their embrace. *Idiot. How could you not think of this sooner?*

"What does that mean?" Kat sighed, looking up at him. "How do you measure if someone is good enough for something? Why do you think about yourself like that?" She brushed her thumb over his cheek. "Stop trying to measure up to some ambiguous standard you've set. If I say you're good for me, can't that be enough?"

"No." Nex shook his head and pushed her hand away. His soul fractured, then fully cracked when he spoke the words he didn't want to, but her safety was his highest priority. "Don't you see? This is how we make sure you don't get hurt. We must be apart. If I leave, it might be enough to keep you out of it."

"Leave?" Kat's chin trembled. "No. No, you're not leaving. How can you say that?"

"I *have* to. It might be the only way to keep you from getting hurt."

"That's ridiculous. Don't do this to me." Tears welled in her eyes. "You can't leave without me giving you a name. You can't."

"I can't leave this realm, but I can be away from you, and that may be enough. The last thing I want to do is leave you." He cradled her face in his hands and kissed her forehead. "The only thing I want less than that is you getting hurt." He backed away. "It's the only way I can ensure your safety."

"It doesn't ensure my safety. You're doing it again. You're pushing me away for nothing!" Hot tears spilled down Kat's cheeks. "You can't do anything. I can't do anything. You leaving would be a shot in the dark, and I don't know what's going to happen." She threw her arms up and wiped her tears with her sleeve. "It doesn't look good, but I'm tired of waiting for them to tear us apart and not having my last moments with you be good." She flung her arms around his neck and kissed him.

He groaned and held her in the kiss, clutching her close.

"If we're going to lose each other, it's going to be because of someone else," Kat spoke against his lips. "Not because you left me, hoping for the best. That's ridiculous, and you know it. Don't find more ways to be afraid. Can't you just be with me and make it good as long as it lasts?"

"I don't want you to get hurt." His body ached to wrap around her, and his soul yearned to be good enough to stay with hers. "I'm so sorry I put you in danger."

"I'm not sorry. I'd do it again if it meant getting to love you all over." She stood on her toes and pressed her forehead to his. "I spent months grieving the fact my dad and I had a stupid fight before we left the house the day of the accident. It was tiny and meant nothing, and we made up, but I still hurt because I spent twenty minutes being mad over something that didn't matter, and that was twenty minutes less I got to have with my dad before I couldn't see him again." She swallowed the lump in her throat. "So, I don't want my last twenty minutes, or last twenty days, or last whatever amount of time to be spent away from you, hurting. I want to spend it *with* you. Not checking the window every five seconds. Not jumping at every sound. I just want to be with you and love you."

Nex pulled her into a hard kiss, paying close attention to the curve of her lips so they'd become a permanent memory. "Why are you so fucking perfect?" he murmured against her mouth. "I'm sorry, Katherine. I don't know what to do. I've never been this vulnerable."

"It's a first for both of us, so how about instead of picking fights, we take it on together? Maybe it won't work out in our favor, but at least we won't give up on each other." She kissed his cheek and left her lips there, memorizing the feeling.

"I'm sorry for hurting you." Nex reveled in the soft touch of her lips, cursing himself from ten minutes ago. "Seeing you with someone else while I'm terrified of losing you," his face crumpled, "wasn't easy, but I don't want to hurt you."

"Trusting me would be a good way to avoid that." Kat slid her hands behind his head. "Because Jeremiah's probably going to spend more time here, and if you love me like you say you do, that shouldn't be a problem. Should it?"

Nex stiffened, closed his eyes, and took a deep breath. "Of course not. Why might he be around more?"

"Because he's my friend and . . ."

"And what?"

"I'm setting him up with a guy from theater, but it has to be discreet because Jeremiah isn't out yet." Nex's shoulders slumped in relief. "I volunteered to let them have a date here so they wouldn't be stressed about someone seeing them together." Kat gave Nex one of her smiles he cursed because they made him weak. "So, remember how I was supposed to help hand out supplies and lunches at that school tomorrow?" Nex opened his mouth to argue, and Kat silenced him with a finger against his lips. "Don't tell me we have to stay home. Can a demon or angel come in here no matter what? Is there any way that staying in this house means we're safer against people who can walk through walls?"

Instinct compelled him to argue, to say yes, they were safer at the house. Except they weren't. Locked doors and windows wouldn't slow down anything that came for them. They weren't safe anywhere.

He sighed. "I guess not."

"Okay, then I'm going tomorrow."

Nex clicked his tongue. "*We're* going tomorrow."

"And Jeremiah and Remy will be in the house while we're gone." She grinned. "I'm hoping it works out because I already came up with their couple name."

"You what?"

"Yeah. It's *Jeremy*." Her smile grew. "Isn't it cute?"

"Cute." Nex scrunched his face. "You couldn't have mentioned he was gay before I got upset?"

"No." Kat propped her hands on her hips. "Because it shouldn't matter. I can have guy friends that are interested in women, right?"

Nex shuffled his feet. "Right."

"Good. We'll leave at eleven tomorrow."

Nex tensed, and Kat draped her arms over his shoulders, looking up at him in a way that made him melt. The amount of power she held over him was disarming.

"I'm nervous," he admitted.

"I won't make us go, but what's the point in living if we stay in this house and don't live? You're the one who told me I don't enjoy life. Sitting here waiting for something to happen isn't enjoying the time we have left."

"I know." Nex nudged her nose with his. "Please, don't leave my side tomorrow. For any reason."

"I won't. Promise." Kat curled her fingers in his hair. "Now, we should stop fighting and enjoy each other while we can."

She kissed him, and Nex groaned in surprise when she guided them to the couch. The back of his knees hit the edge, and he sat in the very spot where he'd kissed her for the first time. "Katherine." Her name on his lips was a breathless whisper, plea, and worship all at once.

She hooked her fingers in her leggings and underwear and tugged them off, leaving her in nothing except his shirt.

"Look at you, my angel, seducing me instead of the other way around." He leaned forward and snatched her wrists. "Get over here."

She straddled his lap, and he pulled her into a kiss. "Nex," she murmured when his hand slid under her shirt and between her legs.

"This what you want, my Katherine?" His lips brushed her neck while his fingers danced along her inner thighs. "You want me to touch you? Enjoy you?"

Kat shut her eyes and focused on the sensations of his lips and hands. "Yes."

His fingers moved over her in a way that had her whimpering. She craved to be close to him for every moment she could, and that craving intensified when his fingers slipped inside her. She moaned and rolled her hips against his hand until she was right on the edge of a release, but he stopped. Kat whimpered in protest, and he dragged her lips to his.

"I want you to finish with me." He reached between them and pulled himself out of his pants.

Kat stared down at his hardness and bit her lip. "I don't know how to do it."

"Let your instincts take over. Do what feels good."

Kat closed her eyes and shifted her hips down, gasping as he sank into her. Nex groaned and gripped her hips, pulling her down harder, pushing himself deeper.

"Nex." Lips parted, Kat clutched his shoulders. She lifted her hips until he was almost out, then sank back down and moaned at the new sensations in this position. "That feels good." She squeezed her eyes shut as he thrust up into her and pulled her hips down. "Does it feel good for you?"

"Katherine, my love, I'm *inside* you." Breathless, he stared into the green eyes that would always be home to him, no matter where they ended up. "There are few things you could do to make this anything less than fucking amazing. Do what feels good. Trust me; it feels more than good for me."

Kat moved up and down, rolling her hips and crying out when she found a rhythm. Nex's fingers dug into her hips, letting her lead and moving with her, thrusting deep each time she made a new sound of ecstasy.

They moved together like souls who'd always known each other. All the stress from the past several days poured into that moment, which, for all they knew, could be their last time together. Each movement, touch, and kiss was an attempt to etch every detail of one another into their memory—the sound of their voice, the touch of their skin, the brush of their lips. It was more intimate than any other time because this was more. It was a promise to never forget what it felt like to love each other, even if they were apart.

They grew closer to bursting, and Kat's head dropped against Nex's shoulder, but he tugged it back and kissed her. He held her in that kiss as the muffled moans from them finishing broke their mouths apart. They reconnected during and after, every touch a treasured moment.

"I love you," Nex whispered. He opened his eyes to look into hers, scanning every inch of their beautiful shape and color.

"I love you too." Kat stared back for a moment before she hugged him. Not caring how strange the timing might be, she sent another prayer as she clung to Nex, remembering the verse in her Bible about love:

"It always protects, always trusts, always hopes, always perseveres."

Chapter 41

Find a Way

Nex stood on the porch of Katherine's house and checked the street for the fifth time while she welcomed Jeremiah inside. Logically, he understood they weren't in more danger outside the house. It didn't stop his hands flexing or his stomach knotting.

Kat stepped outside, putting on her gloves. "Ready?"

He focused on her lovely smile to conjure one of his own. Wrapping an arm around her waist, he kept her close on the walk to the garage. Kat would never get to the point where driving a car was possible if she couldn't stand to ride in anything other than the bus, so Nex offered to drive. The elementary school they were donating supplies and lunches to was in a poorer part of the city and too far to walk.

Nex was certain something terrible would happen in the car on the drive. Lilith had a dark sense of humor; she would tamper with the engine and kill Katherine in a car accident after she'd already survived one. Nex gripped Kat's hand and monitored the road, examining each car and stop. A sigh escaped when he had the car parked safely in the school lot. It might've been the first time he was more tense in a vehicle than Kat was. They got out, and he was at her side in an instant.

She stood on her tiptoes to kiss his cheek. "It's okay."

"I should be the one saying that to you."

He dropped the car keys into her hand, and she stowed them in her purse. The lot overflowed with vans loaded with supplies, and church people who Kat greeted.

"Kat, I wasn't sure you'd make it with how sick you've been," a woman with curly, black hair said.

"I'm doing better," Kat said, embracing the woman. Kat hated lying, but she couldn't say she'd been hiding from angels and demons. "This is Nex. Nex, this is Myra. She's married to Allen."

"Oh, it's nice to meet you." Myra smiled and hugged Nex. Only used to Katherine's hugs, he stiffened. "I hear about you all the time." Myra pulled back, and her eyes widened at something behind him.

He tensed and glanced back, finding a child getting into the food sacks.

"Hope, don't do that," Myra scolded. She dashed past Kat and Nex with an apologetic smile. "Sorry, I'll catch up with you in a little bit."

"I wasn't sure you two would be here." Bernice was next in line to hug Kat. "How are you feeling?"

"Much better."

"Uh-huh." Bernice dropped her voice to a whisper. "It's not a *stomach bug*, is it?"

Nex spluttered, and Kat blushed, hiding behind her hands. "No, Bernice. Oh my God."

"Just checking." Bernice pinched Kat's cheek and hugged Nex. "You better marry her before you get her pregnant, or we'll have a problem," Bernice whispered, patting his back.

Nex choked on nothing, and Bernice smiled, then wandered away.

"What did she say to you?" Kat asked Nex.

"Nothing." Nex grabbed her hand. "Let's get this over with. What are we supposed to do?"

Kat pouted but let it go and led them to where Allen was assigning tasks. Nex did his best to remain polite as he stayed by Kat's side. He carried the bags Katherine told him to and headed into the school, sticking close to her at each classroom they dropped the bags in. The school asked the volunteers to come during an assembly, so the classrooms were empty.

Some teachers hung back to let them in, locking the rooms after they were done. They got most classrooms stocked before it was time to take the lunches into the cafeteria, which connected to the gym where the assembly was happening.

Nex and Kat took the last set of lunches into the cafeteria, then moved to the gymnasium during the end of the assembly. They waited near the doors leading to the cafeteria as the teachers finished their announcements. Kat couldn't help but grin at the kids who fidgeted in their seats with wide smiles and endless chattering.

The heaters were running, and with all the extra people, the air turned stuffy. Kat removed her scarf and tossed it around Nex's neck. "Will you hold this for me?" She rested her chin against his chest and looked up at him with a smile they both knew full well he couldn't resist.

Nex narrowed his eyes. "Don't pretend like you don't know the answer to that."

Kat beamed, wrapped her arms around him, and watched the assembly. The principal announced the special lunch in the cafeteria, and the kids cheered and jumped from their seats, smiles plastering their faces. They bounced up and down while teachers reminded them to wait their turn.

Lines were formed, and the teachers led the kids past the volunteers so they could thank them as they made their way into the cafeteria. There were only a couple of classrooms' worth of kids left when a gunshot rang through the hallway opposite where people were headed. Everyone screamed and ducked. The gym was still for a moment, then another shot went off.

"Get those doors locked." Allen rushed past the kids for the hallway where the shots came from. "Get the kids out of here. Get them in the cafeteria and lock the doors. Someone call the police!" He sprinted toward the doors with the principal and several others on his heels. They barricaded the entry while everyone else ran to the cafeteria and barricaded those doors and windows with plastic chairs and folding tables.

Kat moved to help get the kids inside, but Nex hauled her back against the wall. "I told you we weren't safe outside the house. We have to get out of here."

"I'm not leaving without helping." Kat broke away and ran to the back of the line of kids. An alarm blared and more shots cracked through the air. Nex muttered a curse and raced toward Allen. He was better off helping with barricading than calming down children.

He moved as fast as he could and watched Katherine usher out the last of the children. She hurried in his direction after almost everyone made it to the cafeteria. Nex abandoned the barricade and strode toward her.

"Is there any other way into this building that we haven't secured?" Allen asked the principal.

The principal's face paled as he stared at the barricaded door. "No, we should have it covered as long as the cafeteria doors are locked."

"Wait, there's the side entrance they recently added after we got the playground set up." The janitor pointed at the door, hand shaking. Before he could move, the door opened.

The *creak* of the door contrasted with the deafening shots that followed.

"Get inside, and keep those doors locked!" Allen yelled to the janitor, who stood closest to the cafeteria.

He nodded and ran, closing the doors as quietly as he could.

Soft footsteps crept across the floor, and a figure carrying a bag and an automatic rifle entered the gymnasium.

Nex pulled Kat behind the bleachers. He switched the lights off and crushed her against him. "Don't make a sound." Crouching, he pulled her down with him.

Volunteers and teachers darted behind bleachers on the opposite side of the gym. The shooter's footsteps echoed in the silent space. Only a hooded silhouette could be made out in the dark room. He glanced around, then fired blindly. Kat jumped, and Nex wrapped himself around her. If any bullets made it their way, they'd hit him, not her.

Quiet descended after the shots, making Kat hopeful no one was hit. The lack of screams and cries had to be a good sign. Kat peered through the bleachers and muffled a gasp as the shooter turned his attention to the cafeteria.

In the darkness, another figure emerged from behind the opposite bleachers and crept up behind the gunman. A squeak of shoes alerted the gunman, and he spun, firing another round of bullets. The person scurried back to the bleachers, thankfully unscathed.

Kat wasn't sure if anyone had called the police or if help was on the way. Someone had to do something. The doors would only hold for so long, and the kids inside were easy targets. Someone had to . . .

Dread, cold like Kat hadn't experienced since she lost her parents, filled her until she couldn't move. Her stomach twisted. Paralysis took over, a nausea building inside her as the shooter lifted the gun and fired at the door, earning screams from the people on the other side.

Kat closed her eyes, releasing tears. *You know what you need to do.* There was no other choice.

When she opened her eyes, she found Nex staring at her and knew he had the same thought.

He stared at her for a long time, his face crumpling as he cupped her jaw and kissed her. "I will find a way back to you."

"You won't." Kat choked, clinging to him, knotting her fingers in his shirt. "She won't let you."

"I will find a way back to you no matter what, Katherine." He pressed his lips to her forehead. "I know you, my angel. You could never live with yourself if we did nothing, could you?"

More tears spilled. "I'm sorry." She hugged him and breathed him in, holding onto as much of him as she could. "I'm so sorry. I love you so much."

"I love you." Nex cradled her head in his chest, and his own eyes stung. "I'll find a way back to you. I will."

Kat sniffled, then tensed when another shot fired at the door. She couldn't put it off any longer, or someone would get hurt. She looked into Nex's eyes and memorized his features as she ran her fingertips over his face.

Another round of shots. Tears stained her face and dripped down her neck. She took in a shaky breath before whispering, "Kill the shooter."

Nex's heart split open, bare to Kat and raw to every part of his life that wouldn't have her. He kissed her temple, one hand in her hair, the other on her cheek. He wiped her tears and held back his own. His ability to walk through objects returned, and he passed through the bleachers, stalking toward the shooter, who was oblivious to Nex's invisible approach.

Kat tucked her knees to her chest, unable to watch. Another round of shots started, but it was shorter. Then, silence. Something thumped to the ground followed by the clatter of metal. Kat held her breath, hoping maybe she'd see Nex one last time. Maybe . . .

"What happened?" someone whispered.

"I don't know. The shooter collapsed. I think he's . . . I think he's dead," someone else said.

Another few moments of silence passed, and a light flickered on.

Allen stood in front of Kat, staring past her. He gazed down at her, shoulders slumping. "It's okay. It's over," he said. "Are you okay? Where's Nex? Did you get separated?"

Kat released a shaky breath and turned toward where the shooter lay sprawled across the floor. Alone. No evidence Nex had been there.

Except her red scarf lying beside the body.

Chapter 42

The Praeteritus

Traveling between realms was never pleasant, but unpleasant was an understatement on this occasion. Nex kept his eyes shut as he was dragged into the familiar, unbearable speed he had no control over. The movement would nauseate him if he looked before his feet hit solid ground.

He landed and opened his eyes exactly where he'd been when he was summoned, in the empty wilderness where his hounds could hunt for food. Sulfur invaded his nostrils, and an endless desert of dark sand and rocks stretched in front of him. Part of him had missed the underworld, but now it was the last place he wanted to be.

There was no way around Lilith sensing his return, but Marcus's lair was on the way out of hell. Nex sprinted in that direction, racing past pinnacled rock formations and red-eyed beasts that darted into holes in the ground as he passed. As long as he was breaking rules, he was bringing his hounds with him back to Katherine.

Marcus wasn't in his cave, but Venandi and Sicarius were. They rushed to Nex, their coats a smooth coal black. The only difference in them was they didn't seem to be getting as much exercise as they had with Nex. Relieved, he sighed that they were healthy. Venandi was larger, but both were so big that their eyes were nearly level with Nex's.

He wrapped his arms around Venandi, who reached him first. "I know, girl, I know." He scratched her ears, then patted Sicarius. "We have to be fast."

Nex took off with the hounds close behind, leaving the cool air of Marcus's cave and stepping back into the scorching heat. They made their way to The Lacus, a place that appeared to be nothing more than a cave but acted as the way in and out of the underworld when traveling without a summoning.

A few feet from the entrance, Nex lost control of his legs. They stayed in place as if they'd become one with the ground. Nex let out a low growl, his nails growing to claws as he prepared to make a move, but the thing about Lilith was he'd never be as strong as her.

"Nice try." Lilith kicked the back of his legs, and his knees hit rock, merging with the stone he knelt on. Venandi and Sicarius lunged, and Lilith extended her hand. "Stop." They cowered and whined, sinking to the ground. "You didn't think you'd get out of here, did you?" Lilith crouched and grabbed a fistful of Nex's hair, yanking it back so she could see him. Just like that, his powers were gone. "I always thought you were smart, but you suddenly seem stupid. Did being around humans dumb you down?"

"I'm sorry I made you look bad." Nex met her gaze and clenched his jaw. He wanted to scream at her, but he wanted Katherine back more. "I swear, it won't happen again. Punish me however you like, but then let me go back to the mortal realm."

"Oh, I will." Lilith smiled. "I *will*." She stood and rested a hand on her hip. "Maybe in about three hundred years or so, after I'm confident you've learned your lesson. Long after your precious human is gone. Maybe you can visit her grave. Unless, of course, she's buried on holy ground. Then I suppose you can look from a distance."

"Don't do this," Nex pleaded. "I'm sorry for the position I put you in. Aside from this, I've been good to you. You know I have. Give me your worst punishment, then let me have my freedom of travel back."

"Oh, I don't think you'll get that back." Lilith picked at her nails. "You broke my trust. It's worse because I did trust you, Nex. I trusted you to keep a level head, to be a good leader despite having less experience. I thought you'd do things right, but now that you've shown your loyalty can switch so quickly over a single human," her eyes flashed, and she grew bigger for a moment—back to her regular size, leaner but taller than Nex, "and completely fuck me over, you're not getting that trust back. You'll be lucky if you move up from torturing after pulling this shit."

"Lilith, I'm begging you. Please."

"Did you say *please*?" Lilith laughed. "That's adorable. This human really did change you, didn't she? At least you'll always have that to remember while you rot in a dungeon." She snapped her fingers. Four demons appeared and stalked toward Nex. "Take him away. His hounds too." She nodded to Venandi and Sicarius. "If you really want to get to him, hurt the things he loves. *All* the things he loves."

"No," Nex hissed as the demons wrapped chains around Venandi and Sicarius's necks. "Don't hurt them, and Lilith, don't you dare hurt her!" Nex roared, jerking against the force holding him down. "You have me. Don't hurt Katherine!"

"My, my, someone's forgotten who makes the rules around here." Lilith glanced back, barely making eye contact with him before focusing on the other demons. "Make sure he doesn't forget again."

"Lilith, don't you fucking touch her!" Nex struggled as they dragged him away. Breaking free of the lower-ranked demons should've been easy, but he was one of them again. He felt it. The power he'd held was gone, his strength drained. He couldn't teleport out of their grip. Adding to the hopelessness, the demons who took him and his hounds to the dungeon weren't strangers, and they were no friends of his. None of them would help him.

They dragged him down into a series of tunnels that led to darkened caves, where screams echoed through the corridors. The stench of blood overpowered his other senses, and the light was so dim a human couldn't navigate their way through. Incline after steep incline, the boiling temperature plummeted. A bitter cold Nex wasn't used to with his usual ability to keep himself warm, soaked through his clothes and pricked his bones.

Hope dwindled further as they entered the last of the tunnels. He was familiar with it. Not a place people came out of quickly, if they came out at all. Every descent was another level of torture to be endured.

Nex and his hounds were at the bottom.

The demons threw him into one of the caves, where it wasn't screams that were unsettling but the unfathomable silence and freezing temperature. Not even footsteps could be heard as the demons stripped Nex down and left him with his hounds. Venandi and Sicarius whined and surrounded Nex to keep him warm. Pointless against the icy stone floor. All three shivered.

He dragged his hand across Sicarius's head, then Venandi's. "It's going to be fine."

"You don't really think that," a shrill voice said.

Nex sighed, torn between annoyance and fear. Annoyed because he knew this trick, and the fact she'd use it on him as a scare tactic was insulting. Fear because she'd take pleasure in his torture.

"Aren't you too old for this shit, Poena?" Nex didn't bother to look around. He wouldn't see her.

"Don't take all the fun out of it." She emerged from the shadows. Her horns curled back, almost touching her neck, her claws longer than her fingers, and her eyes a dark green that seemed much too happy to see him here. "It's more fun when they don't know what's coming. That's all right, though." She held out her hand, and a chain appeared, starting in her palm, spreading to the ground. "It's a challenge. Now I can get creative."

Nex tried to usher the hounds behind him, but for once, they didn't obey. Both stepped in front of him and growled at Poena, pounding their paws against the ground and baring their teeth.

"Aw. Look at them. So ready to protect you. Stupid mutts." A whip formed in her other hand, and her smile broadened. She snapped the whip toward Sicarius.

Sicarius dodged and caught the whip in his teeth, growling at Poena. Venandi charged, and Poena laughed.

"Goodness, I underestimated them." Poena's eyes flashed, and Venandi and Sicarius stilled as if they were statues.

Nex lunged forward, but chains appeared from nowhere, locking around his ankles and wrists, jerking him back against the wall.

"Oh, come on." Poena rolled her eyes. "You're acting like you don't know how it works down here. You know you can't touch me." She flicked her wrist and sent the whip across Venandi's ribs, making her whimper as a deep cut formed while she remained frozen.

"Bitch," Nex hissed. "Leave them out of it."

"See, that's what'll make this worse for you." She lashed Sicarius's back, earning a yelp. "You're acting so foolishly. You know there's no hope. But, by all means, keep thinking there is." She grabbed his jaw and grinned, showing off her razor-like teeth. "Because it's *so* much fun to watch hope leave a person's eyes. We're not quite there yet, are we? No, we have something else to settle first."

She stepped aside and inclined her head to the metal bars locking them in. The door opened, and Lucian was shoved through, his body covered in cuts and bruises, one eye swollen shut. Nex tried to move, but the chains restrained him. Lilith strode in, grabbed Lucian's shoulder, and rammed him to his knees.

"Look what you made me do." Lilith massaged her temples. "I have to kill one of my own and send him to The Praeteritus because of you. And I *liked* him, Nex. I really did."

The Praeteritus was a place of lost and forgotten souls. A place some argued was worse than torture, where there was no escape. Souls were locked in with no way out, wandering for eternity in anguish, no memory of who they were or what they'd done, so if someone came looking, they couldn't be found.

"You don't have to kill Lucian," Nex said. "For fuck's sake, Lilith, don't punish Lucian because of me!"

"Thanks to you, I have no choice." She withdrew a knife from the sheath on her hip. "He killed an angel for you and that human. You both knew that was unforgivable. You both knew there would be consequences. You're lucky you didn't have the power to do it yourself. Otherwise, this would be you." She grabbed Lucian's long, white hair and jerked his head back, exposing his neck. "I hope you're happy. I hope fucking her was worth the pain you'll endure. I hope it was worth getting your friend killed."

"Lilith, don't!" Nex threw his weight against the chains, but the cold metal cut into his skin and held him too far away. "Kill me instea—"

She drew the blade across Lucian's throat. Blood poured after the knife. Gurgling and choking, Lucian spluttered blood from his mouth. His one eye blinked slowly before staying open, and he fell face-first to the ground. His body turned to stone, similar to the others in the cave, then crumbled to dust. His soul—a dim ball of white light—bounded around the cavern before it disappeared into the ground.

Chapter 43

Faith

K atherine had to stay at the school too long. Thankfully, only one person was shot, and it wasn't critical. So many people—police, church volunteers, school staff—asked what happened, what she saw, where Nex was. She couldn't think of anything that made sense and repeated Allen's comment, saying they got separated. Which was why they were now under the impression they had to search for him.

The shooter had a heart attack, the police told everyone. A lethal heart attack. Unusual given his age and overall health. No one had an explanation, but when the security tapes were played, all they showed was the shooter going rigid. He clutched his chest, sunk to the ground, and died with his eyes open.

Hours dragged by before Kat could leave. As soon as she was released, she ran to the parking lot. She dove into the car and dug her keys out, hands shaking too much to get the key in the ignition.

"You can do this." She tried to get control of the shaking, tried not to let her mind take her back to the accident. "You can do this." She raised the key to the ignition again and mentally repeated the same phrase in Nex's voice, reminding herself how he sat beside her and told her she didn't have to let fear control her.

She inserted the key and took a deep breath. Starting the car, she set her trembling hands on the steering wheel. "You can do this." Tears fell down her face as she adjusted the seat and mirror. She pulled the seatbelt across her chest and focused on Nex instead of the memory of the last time she drove. *It's not too tight. It's not too tight. It's not too tight.*

Kat allowed herself a few seconds to calm before putting the car in gear. She pulled out of the parking lot and remained stiff as she drove to church. She kept reminding herself to breathe, to not panic when a car passed her, to not feel like the seatbelt was going to lock. Rather than letting fear take over, she imagined Nex's face and soothing voice, and that got her through the streets and traffic lights until she parked the car.

Snow kicked up behind her as she rushed across the street and ascended the church's steps. Grateful the door was unlocked, she shoved it open and stepped inside. The heavy wooden door closed behind her with a *thud*, and she jumped. Her gaze darted around the seemingly empty building. Except, if she'd learned anything through all of this, things weren't always how they appeared.

If her attempts would matter, if they would change anything, she didn't know, but she had to try. The only thing giving her confidence that she could be convincing was that she had the Bible on her side. Years in Sunday school classes, Bible studies, youth groups, and sitting through sermons where she memorized countless verses were what she armed herself with.

"Melchizedek?" she called. A long shot—the likelihood he hung around after Nex left was small, but she wasn't giving up. Light filtered through the windows illuminating the center aisle in front of her feet. "Melchizedek?"

Silence answered. Tears filled her eyes, and she flexed her hands as she glanced around. *Don't lose faith,* she chanted in her head. She closed her eyes, attempting to control the crying. The red scarf barely had a hint of Nex's scent on it, but she clutched it, her knuckles whitening. "Please, someone talk to me."

"We're not here to answer anyone's call."

Kat spun toward the door, where a man she didn't recognize stood. Gray eyes surveyed her, and steady hands clasped in front of his white robes. He emitted a similar feeling to Gabriel, yet not as calm or peaceful. While he looked approachable, she didn't sense he was. There was only one angel Nex mentioned who she hadn't met.

"Uriel?" She stepped forward.

His response was a curt nod.

Kat narrowed her eyes, snatched a Bible off a pew, marched over to him, and shoved it in his chest. "I think it's time you brush up your knowledge on this." She tapped the cover. "Having me thrown off a bridge wasn't very angelic behavior. When's the last time you read the Bible? Are you senile or something?"

Uriel blinked, then glared at her. He took a step forward but froze in place. Knowing there was only one angel who could immobilize him, he huffed.

"You deserved that."

Kat's head snapped to the side.

Gabriel leaned against the wall with his arms crossed. His eyes softened when she looked at him. "I'm sorry about today."

"Did you do that?" Kat gripped the scarf tighter. "Did a demon do that? How could you let that happen? Someone got *hurt*."

Gabriel shook his head. "We didn't cause that, Katherine. Nor did Lilith or any other demon. Some people are evil by nature."

"I want to talk to Melchizedek." Kat approached Gabriel. "Please. I need to talk to him."

"We cannot change what happened. We cannot turn back time."

"But you can bring Nex back."

"No, we can—"

"Don't tell me you can't." Kat stomped her foot. "You're angels. You're telling me you can't bring back one demon after *he*," she pointed at Uriel, "brought them all to their knees? You can't do something as simple as bring one back?"

Gabriel straightened. "Katherine, it's not that simple. We don't have unlimited power. We can't do whatever we wish. This was an inevitable outcome."

Kat lifted her chin. "I refuse to believe that. There has to be something you can do."

"It's not in our hands anymore. He's under Lilith an—"

"And she's going to hurt him." Kat's vision blurred beneath more tears. "People would've died today if not for him. How can that not mean anything? How can that not be enough? What did he do that was so bad he can't redeem himself?"

Gabriel shuffled his feet and shifted his gaze to a window so he wouldn't have to maintain eye contact.

"You know, don't you? You know why he became a demon." Gabriel only gave her a small nod. "What did he do?"

Gabriel sighed. "Katherine—"

"Tell me what he did!" Kat slammed her hand on a pew. "What was so bad nothing he does can make up for it? Because Psalm 86:5 says that God is 'forgiving and good, abounding in love to all who call.' So, what did Nex do that was so bad my loving God can't forgive him?"

Gabriel's face crumpled. "Katherine, I—"

"'Above all, love each other deeply, because love covers over a multitude of sins,'" Kat quoted 1 Peter 4:8. "I love him. And I love because God first loved me," she said, referring to 1 John 4:19. "So, tell me what he did, and let me love him anyway." She swiped tears with her sleeve. "If you're not going to help me, the least you can do is tell me why the man I love, who *saved* lives today, can't be redeemed."

"He traded his soul for his sister's life," a deeper voice said. The strange customer from the bookstore—Melchizedek—strolled up the aisle.

Kat's hands shook. "What?"

"He made a deal," Melchizedek said. "His sister was sick and about to die. He made a deal that hell would gain his soul if his sister's life was spared."

Kat frowned, opening and closing her mouth. "*That's* what he did?

That's ridiculous! Would he have gone to heaven if he hadn't done that?"

"It doesn't matter." Uriel scowled. "He's a demon."

"Gabriel, please escort Uriel anywhere that isn't here." Melchizedek flicked his wrist.

Gabriel nodded, and while Uriel was less than pleased, he had no option. Gabriel set his hand on Uriel's shoulder, and they vanished in a flash of light.

Kat stared at the empty space they'd occupied, shook her head, then focused on Melchizedek. "Would he have gone to heaven?"

Melchizedek nodded. "He would have."

"So, bring him back." Kat's voice cracked. "Lilith will hurt him. Please, bring him back to me, or at least, don't let her hurt him." She moved closer and gazed up at him. "*Please*, Melchizedek. I love him. I need him to be okay."

"You asked for *them* to have mercy and protect you both," Melchizedek said. "You haven't lost your faith. Even after all this, you haven't lost your faith?"

"How do you know what I asked for?"

"Because I was with them when you asked."

Kat frowned. "Them?"

Melchizedek's lips quirked into a smile. "God has no gender, Katherine. God isn't bound to human delegation. I was with them when you prayed and asked for help because I was also there, asking for guidance."

Kat twisted the scarf around her hands. "They were listening?" Melchizedek nodded. "What did they say? Will they help?"

"Do you still have faith, Katherine?"

Kat bit her lip, her gaze shifting to a Bible resting on a pew before she met Melchizedek's gaze. Too many things had happened that could've been worse but weren't. That had to mean someone was watching. "Yes."

"Good." Melchizedek smiled, setting his hands on her shaking ones, where her fingers numbed from holding the scarf so tight. "Because they know the plans they have for you. And they know the plans they have for Nex."

"What does that mean?"

"It means," Melchizedek squeezed her hands, "don't lose faith. Love perseveres."

Chapter 44

Love Always Hopes

If not for the chains suspending his body, Nex would've been on the ground. With no energy left, he hung, ignoring the metal around his wrists cutting into his skin from the weight of hunching over. Venandi and Sicarius tried to keep him upright, but they too had little strength.

Venandi lifted her head and struggled to stand. She licked Nex's face and whined.

"I know." His voice was hoarse. "I'm sorry."

"Aw." Poena's taunt filled the cave. Nex and his hounds stiffened. "How sweet it all is. Did you miss me?"

Nex didn't bother to lift his head because he knew what was coming. He'd hoped for a longer break before the torture continued, but hope was a silly thing to have in a place so dark.

"Don't tell me I broke you already." Poena pouted and nudged Nex's leg with her foot. "Where's that fighting spirit?"

He had it still. Plenty of it. But the highest priority was getting his hounds out of there and returning to Katherine. That meant he had to be smart. If he fought back, Poena would enjoy it too much. The punishment would last longer the more fun she had. If he bored her, she'd want to move on.

"Nex." Poena whined, unsheathed a knife strapped to her thigh, and raised it to his neck. She grabbed the back of his head and jerked it up, so he had to look at her. "Come on. You can do better than that. I want to see what impressed Lilith so much she made you a high rank. Don't tell me my torture was too much after I was passed up for promotion because of *you*."

Nex didn't answer. One of the reasons Lilith let Poena take the lead on his punishment was because there was no chance Poena would take pity on him. She hadn't liked Nex since the day Lilith chose him over her to advance up the ranks when Nex had far less experience. Poena remained bitter, convinced the only reason Nex moved up was because Lilith wanted something else from him.

"Nothing to say?" She twirled the knife. "After all these years of you supposedly being the stronger, smarter one, I have you speechless? *You?*" She laughed. "I don't think anyone thought you were capable of being silenced. Your pet human made you weak."

Nex wanted to respond, but her impatience and boredom wouldn't outlast his determination. She might lash out at him, but she'd get sick of no one playing her game. Using all his self-restraint, he thought of Katherine and bit his tongue. No matter what he had to do, he'd find a way back to her.

"Hmm." Poena dragged the blade across his skin, leaving pink marks but not drawing blood. "I think I know what will get a reaction. I wonder what your pet human is up to right now. Should I find out?"

Nex narrowed his eyes. The action made Poena's smile grow wider.

"Oh, there it is." She flicked the knife to the corner of his eye. "A reaction. I bet it would be better with her here." She released Nex and stepped toward the exit. "Perhaps I ought to find her and bring her here. Let her see all the *fun* we've had."

"You can't go near her," Nex said, trying to breathe through his racing heart. "Lilith finally chose you over me. You want to risk pissing her off, get her in deeper shit by bringing a pure soul down here?"

Poena laughed. "Nice try. Lilith gave me freedom to handle this how I like. The human isn't off-limits. In fact, Lilith said this human may be the only way we truly make you understand what happens when you don't play by our rules."

"She has a church full of people who love her." He wanted to rip through the chains, but he wasn't strong enough, and it would only fuel Poena's desire to follow through with her threat. "They'll talk. They'll ask questions. You'll create more problems, and Lilith will resent you for not handling it as discreetly as I would've. She'll compare your ability to mine. You know she will. I set a standard you'll never reach if you involve humans."

Poena's smile faltered. "You're awfully full of yourself for someone who's responsible for a fellow demon's death." She gestured to the pile of dust-like stone that used to be Lucian. "For someone responsible for the pain of his hounds." She spat at his bleeding hounds. "For someone who's going to be responsible for the death of a woman he supposedly loved. I was going to save her for the finale, but you've moved up my timeline with your pathetic attempt at getting in my head." She crouched and grabbed his chin, a wicked smile on her lips. "Excuse me while I fetch her. It may take some time. I can't bring a human down here and *not* give her a tour. I can't *not* introduce her to our many demons who haven't earned the freedom of travel and who would love to know what it feels like to have a human body warm them."

Calm shattered, he snapped his head forward into Poena's nose with a satisfying *crack*. "You fucking touch her, I'll spend the rest of eternity making your life unbearable. Lilith will forgive me eventually. I'll steal your rank *again*, then I'll fucking tear you apart until you beg to go to The Praeteritus. And I'll have centuries of pent-up anger leading to that moment, so don't you fucking *think* about touching her."

Poena growled and reset her nose before grabbing her dagger. "Because of that outburst, I'm going to bring all those unforgiving demons into this dungeon, so you have to watch her suffer. Until I return, let this serve as a reminder that I have no problem taking this to a cruel level, even by demon standards." She lifted her blade and stabbed it down on Venandi's head.

A shrill ring sounded like metal on metal. Despite the force, the blade didn't touch Venandi.

Poena frowned and brought the knife down again, but it never touched her. Poena growled and tried Sicarius, but the same thing happened. Last, she tried Nex, shoving the blade toward his chest, but it collided with an invisible force.

"What the fuck?" Poena spat. "In the name of all that's unholy—"

"It's not what's *un*holy, Poena."

Nex and Poena turned to the source of the voice.

He stood in stark white robes. Despite the underworld being an unclean place, the dim lighting did nothing to diminish the faint glow around Melchizedek as he stepped into the cell with his hands tucked behind his back. He inclined his head to the door. "You may go, Poena."

"None of this is angel business." Poena stalked toward him. "Get the fuck out of my dungeon!"

"I said," Melchizedek tilted his head, and Poena stiffened, the hold on her dagger loosening without permission and slipping from her hand, clattering to the ground, "you may go."

"You have no authority here! He's mine to deal with."

"My authority is not limited to one realm." Melchizedek stepped aside so Poena could leave. "This is no longer your concern. You may go."

"I'm not leav—" Poena's vocal cords failed.

Melchizedek shook his head. "Poena, I'm afraid you misunderstand. When I say you may go, I mean that Nex is no longer your concern, and I need you to leave. I'm giving you the option to do it without force." He clasped his hands together and smiled. "Please, don't make me call Lilith to set you straight about whose authority you're required to submit to. I don't want to do that. I prefer to let you leave peacefully."

Poena tried to growl, but no sound came out. She bared her teeth and lunged at Melchizedek, but her knife stopped centimeters from where she tried to jam the blade between his eyes.

"That was quite unwise." Melchizedek pushed the dagger and Poena's hand aside. "Didn't Nex get punished for killing an angel? You think coming after me is a good idea?" He gestured to her frozen state. "See, you have made this more complicated. I didn't want to have to do this, but you aren't giving me many options." A bright light sparked from his eyes, and Poena stepped back before her whole body was paralyzed. "Poena, *leave*. Go to Lilith."

Poena's body moved despite the protest of her mind, her legs walking her out, leaving Melchizedek alone with Nex and the hounds. Nex eyed Melchizedek's approach.

"What are you doing here?" Nex asked. "Isn't it your duty to protect humans from demons? They're threatening to go after Katherine. If you want to abide by your precious duties, you should be watching her."

"Katherine is safe." Melchizedek paused in front of Nex. "I made her untouchable. The highest-ranked demon couldn't hurt her if they wanted to."

Untouchable. They rarely made humans untouchable by demons. The last time was over a century ago. Nex opened his mouth but gritted his teeth when Melchizedek crouched and set his hand on Venandi's head. The deep cuts and scrapes, the bruises that were undoubtedly hidden under her fur, all disappeared. Venandi perked up, lifting her head toward Melchizedek, who patted her affectionately before doing the same for Sicarius.

"What are you doing here?" Nex repeated, gaze fixed on every movement Melchizedek made toward the hounds.

"I'm not allowed to lie." White threads formed in Melchizedek's hand—separate strands that wove together and became longer until he had a full sheet. "Nor would I want to."

The chains holding Nex vanished. He nearly collapsed, but Melchizedek caught him, gently pushing him to sit up as he draped the sheet around Nex's cold, naked body.

"I said you could trust me, and you can." Melchizedek set his hand on

Nex's shoulder. All the pain, the bruises and gashes, the lashes from the whip, the cuts around his wrists, faded to nothing.

"Why are you doing this?" Nex huddled under the sheet. Despite it being thin, it banished the chill. "Why are you here?"

"I'm here to right a wrong that happened years ago. Tell me, what would you do to get back to her? Anything?"

"I'm not in the mood for your fucking tests." Nex glared. "Lucian died while you were doing whatever the fuck it was you were doing."

"I heard." Melchizedek squeezed Nex's shoulder. "I am sorry about that. I'll see what I can do for him, but I need you to let go of that anger because I want to help you, but I can't if you won't tone down the animosity."

"Help me how?"

"Katherine came to me. She drove to—"

"She drove?" Nex's eyes bugged, and he almost dropped his sheet. His Katherine *drove*?

Melchizedek smiled. "It wasn't easy for her, but she thought of you. She thought of you and drove to the church, looking for me. She wanted to talk. To ask me to bring you back, or at the very least to keep you from getting hurt."

"I thought that was against your rules."

"Perhaps, but things are phrased certain ways, are they not? And humans have done quite an awful job interpreting the Bible. They've twisted it, turned it into something it was never meant to be, used it out of context to justify bias and treating each other poorly." His face contorted. "The ridiculous thing is they think they know everything, enough to justify terrible behavior, to justify killing and harming under the name of religion while conveniently forgetting that love is at the center of it. Love perseveres. Isn't that right? I don't think there's much you wouldn't do for love."

Nex eyed Melchizedek, weighing whether he trusted him. Venandi and Sicarius scooted closer and laid their heads in Nex's lap.

"Put aside the anger you feel toward God as a demon, and think about the question I'm about to ask," Melchizedek said. "Do you think if there was a soul meant to come to *them*, but instead it got lost because of an outside force, they would never find a way to bring it back? Do you think they wouldn't go after that soul to bring it home?"

"I suppose *they* would always make sure they retrieved the souls they wanted." Nex exhaled. Angels never got to the damn point and had to make everything poetic to a confounding degree.

"I suppose they would too. You know what's interesting? It's against our vows of protecting humans to allow a demon to be with a human." He gave Nex a pointed look. "So, let me ask again, what would you do to return to Katherine? Is there anything you wouldn't be willing to give up to be with her again?"

Nex needed no time to consider. "There's nothing I wouldn't do for her."

"Then trust me like you did before all this happened." Melchizedek stood and offered a hand. "Come with me."

"Where?"

"To ask *them* to do something for you I cannot do myself."

"You think they'll let me go back to her?" Hope had never worked out well for him, but Katherine changed that. Normally he'd have no expectation of a positive outcome, but she'd taught him differently. He couldn't contain the shred of hope that formed deep in his soul from a place that seemed familiar yet distant.

"I think your soul is more precious than you realize." Melchizedek extended his hand farther. "Trust me. Have a little faith."

Nex hesitated but accepted Melchizedek's hand. Although he didn't care to have help up, he was weak from what Poena put him through. He stood on shaky legs and clutched Melchizedek's arm. "Wait."

Melchizedek glanced down. "What?"

"If I go," Nex set his hands on Venandi and Sicarius's heads as they stood next to him, "my hounds come with me."

Chapter 45

Grow Old

Patience was a virtue Katherine, for the first time in her life, ran out of. Melchizedek said time moved differently in other realms, and she would have to be patient. Patience wasn't usually difficult for her, but as days passed, her patience dwindled.

Praying, reading, she tried to do anything but dwell on the situation. Instead, her mind drifted back to Nex. Was he okay? What was happening? Was Lilith hurting him?

Tears filled her eyes and blurred the words of her eighth distraction book. She wiped her eyes and stared into the empty, soundless house. In a sense, it was like when her parents died, and she came home for the first time without her uncle, aunt, or cousin. The agonizing quiet almost drove her mad.

Silence had a way of being unbearably loud.

Once again, the hollowness of the house grated on her sanity. No Nex with his chatter and sarcastic humor. No Marcus purposely annoying Nex and instigating endless banter. No Lucian quietly sitting beside her, amused at Nex and Marcus's incessant arguments. She was alone. Alone like she was for months before accidentally summoning a demon who filled her heart with the most love it'd held since her parents' deaths.

Kat's eyes widened. *Of course. How did I not think of it sooner?* She rushed to the kitchen and checked the calendar, dragging her finger down the paper until she found it. The next full moon. Two days. She remembered what Nex said to her the day she summoned him.

You need fire, blood, and the light of a full moon. You also have to repeat the phrase three times.

Melchizedek told her to be patient, but it'd been days. *I can't do nothing.* If she didn't try everything she could think of, she'd never forgive herself. Forgoing patience, she rushed to her bedroom and dug through her desk, searching for the script. The words were ingrained in her brain after the number of times she'd said them, but now was not the time to take chances.

Two days crawled by like two decades. Time dragged slower still when the day came, and Kat sat by the window, waiting for the sun to set. She got out the same candles she'd used before, arranged them in a circle, turned off every light, and unplugged all the electronics to mimic the power going out. Whether each event that night mattered, she didn't know. She only hoped it gave her a better chance.

Candles lit, she scoured her mind for every detail of that day. Sitting back in the middle of the circle, she glanced to the window. Clouds blanketed the sky, but there was a break in those clouds, and moonlight shone in. She hesitated for a moment. *What if I don't summon Nex but someone else?*

She didn't care. She'd exhaust every possibility.

Scrunching her face, she lifted the paper and refused to look as she purposely gave herself a paper cut. She winced and let blood fall on the candles.

Between rehearsals and the play, she'd read the words a million times but still took care to make the pronunciation perfect. "*Fasciculus hic nugarum vage et male translatus est, sed scire non debes. Fasciculus hic nugarum vage et male translatus est, sed scire non debes.*" She said it louder each time, just like the night she summoned Nex. "*Fasciculus hic nugarum vage et—*"

The room darkened, and she strained to see the script. Kat grimaced when clouds covered the moon. Thunder shook the house, and flashes of light illuminated the dark clouds.

Kat ran to the window, and her shoulders slumped at the storm clouds.

"No, no, no. It *has* to clear at some point."

She sprinted out the front door and past the end of her covered porch. Wind blew from every direction, causing the clouds to circle in a strange pattern. Kat waited for them to dissipate, for *something* to happen that would give her another opening.

Raindrops hit the ground.

Kat stared up at where the moon hid, and she tried. She tried so hard not to cry. She'd tried to keep her hopes up since her talk with Melchizedek, but each day that passed with no news chipped away at her optimism until her heartbreak over losing Nex fractured the little hope she had left of getting him back.

Rain spattered on the ground, dampened her face, soaked her sweater, and landed on the earth beneath her until everything was darker. She stared up at where the moon should be, but unforgiving clouds concealed it. How would she survive another heartbreak?

First her parents. Now Nex. She couldn't take it. Covering her face with her hands, she sobbed into her palms. Her shoulders shook, and her legs threatened to give out. She grew wetter and colder by the second, but the discomfort was nothing compared to the icy emptiness in her heart.

She dropped her hands, tugging her sleeves down and letting her tears fall. They mixed with raindrops, lost in the myriad of precipitation that washed away the last of her hope. Her eyes slid shut in defeat.

Something touched her hand. A dog. Sniffing and licking at her clenched fist.

Kat sniffled and blinked. A dog with coal-black fur, much bigger than most dogs, licked her hand and gazed up at her. Then a second approached and did the same, gazing up, wagging its tail. Kat frowned. She didn't recognize them.

A light *pop-swish* sounded above her, and she tilted her head back. A polka-dot umbrella shielded her from the rain.

A hand rested on her shoulder, followed by a voice she associated with the warmth of home. "Don't cry, my angel."

Unblinking, Kat stared at the umbrella for a moment before focusing ahead. His presence sunk in slower than she meant it to, but she couldn't move. Her heart fluttered, and she was almost afraid to look back, terrified she was imagining the entire thing. Except she turned, and there he was.

Instead of improving, her crying worsened at the sight of Nex standing behind her. Not quite believing he was real, she said, "You're here."

Whether it was a question or statement, neither could tell.

"I'm here." He stepped closer and wiped tears from her face.

Kat threw her arms around him and sobbed. He led her under the porch and tossed the umbrella aside. Wrapping his arms around her, he buried his face in her hair and relished the feel of holding her, the smell of her vanilla and pear leave-in conditioner, and the comfort he'd only experienced when she was close.

"I thought I lost you." Kat squeezed him tight, afraid if she loosened, he'd be gone. "How are you here?"

"Melchizedek helped us." Nex brushed her wet hair back and kissed her forehead. "I'm here to stay, Katherine." He cupped her face and leaned in, so their lips touched. "Nothing will come between us again."

Kat's heart raced, and her lungs struggled to keep up. "To stay? You don't have to go back? Lilith won't come for you?"

"Lilith can't come for something that isn't hers. I've been given a second chance at mortal life."

Kat frowned. "You mean . . . You're human?"

"Yes. Human, and here to grow old with you."

He kissed her, and Kat whimpered. Not just because she wanted him or because she'd missed him, but because the ache that had been in her heart since he disappeared didn't feel so heavy, and emotion overwhelmed her. *Grow old with me.* He wouldn't vanish. He was there to stay. She couldn't believe her ears. She wanted to ensure nothing could hurt him again.

"Wait." She broke their kiss. "You're here to stay? For sure? Nobody will come for you?"

"No one can interfere. Melchizedek made sure of that. I'm here to live my mortal life with you and follow you into the eternal life as well."

"But what about—" She gasped, remembering the dogs that approached her. "Were those . . ." She glanced to the side. Two giant dogs sat on her porch, gazing up at Kat and Nex. Both their tails wagged when her eyes shifted toward them. "Are those your hounds?"

Nex smiled and nodded, holding Kat close to him as he set his hand on Venandi's head. "This is Venandi." He moved his hand to Sicarius. "And this is Sicarius."

"Oh my goodness." Kat smiled when he crouched and scratched behind their ears. "They're precious. How could you tell me I can't call them puppies?" Kat petted both, and they melted under her touch, tails hitting the ground with repeated *thuds*. "Look at them!"

Nex held back the sigh and stood. "You'll have plenty of time to fuss over them because they're staying too." He grabbed her wrists and pulled her in front of him. He cupped her jaw and stared into her eyes, the same eyes that it felt like centuries ago he thought he was staring into for the last time. "How is it possible you're more beautiful than when I left?"

Kat wrapped her arms around his neck. "I tried to summon you again."

"Let's refrain from things like that and not push our luck." He rested his forehead on hers. "I can't lose you again, my love. I missed you more than I can begin to explain."

"I missed you so much." Kat's words were whispered through the growing lump in her throat. "I thought I'd never see you again."

"I told you I'd find a way back to you, but you saved us, didn't you?" A smile pulled on his lips. "You *drove* for help."

"I was terrified, but I was more afraid of losing you."

"You're not going to lose me." He ran his thumb over her freckled cheek. "I'm never going to be away from you again."

"You hated being human." The eleven days he was upset when his powers were gone had been awful. "Are you sure you can handle it?"

"I could handle the worst pain imaginable. It'd still come second to losing you."

"So, you're staying?" Kat's eyes overflowed. This time, it wasn't hopelessness escaping; it was relief. Relief to have the man she loved back in her arms. "For good?"

"I told you." He cupped her face. "I love you. I'm not going anywhere."

He pressed a kiss to her lips that had them sinking into each other, holding on like they would never let go.

And they never did.

Epilogue: Personal Heaven

Nex stood in front of the mirror. Not used to dressing up, he tugged at his clothes. When he'd been on Earth before, he'd stuck to jeans and T-shirts. Today, he wore a button-up shirt and black pants. He pulled at the tie Katherine put on him and sighed, walking into the kitchen where Katherine crouched, rubbing Venandi's belly.

"You're such a good girl, Nandi," Katherine cooed. Venandi barked playfully, sat up, and licked Kat's face.

"Really?" Nex crossed his arms. "With the nicknames?"

"Says the man who gave me a nickname shortly after meeting me." She ignored Nex's scowl and scratched behind Sicarius's ears. "You're a good puppy, too, Cari. You're going to take good care of the house while we're gone, aren't you? You're going to be so good for Jeremiah."

"Cari?" Nex huffed. "Absolutely not. We're *not* calling Sicarius, *Cari.*"

"You can call him whatever you want," Kat kissed Sicarius's head and stood, "but I'm calling him Cari."

"You're asking for it."

"You think I'm always asking for it." Kat pecked Nex's cheek. "I think it's wishful thinking on your part."

"Don't pretend you don't like the idea too." He wrapped his arms around her and pulled her lips to his.

Kat melted against him and circled her arms around his neck. "It's time to go."

"Or, we could stay home." Nex slid his hands under her lavender and white sundress, gliding them up her legs and lifting her. "And be alone."

Kat moaned when he kissed her harder. Using all her inner strength, she pulled out of the kiss, panting. "You're welcome to stay home, but I'm going. We can be alone as much as you want later."

"But I want to be alone and not go anywhere *now*." Nex dropped his head into her neck and kissed where she was sensitive.

"Stop trying to distract me. It's not fair. You know I can hardly ever say no to you." Throbbing for him already, she squirmed and pushed until he set her down. "You don't have to come. I didn't ask you to."

"I know you didn't." Nex made a face and kept his arms loosely around her waist. "How long does it last?"

"About an hour." Kat gave him a light kiss. "I'll hold your hand the whole time." She walked over and opened the back door, then crouched and gave both dogs a hug. "We'll be back, puppies."

Nex grimaced and stayed inside while Kat went out to fill the hounds' water dishes. He shifted his weight from one foot to the other, his eyes landing on the photograph Katherine made them take on Christmas Eve. At the time, he wasn't happy about having his picture taken. Now, he was glad he had the reminder of his friend.

The photo was taken before they left for their walk to look at lights. The two of them with Marcus and Lucian. Demons didn't take pictures, so this was the only one they had of Lucian. Kat had it printed and framed, devastated when she learned what had happened to him.

Every day, she'd pick flowers from the backyard and set them by the picture on the windowsill. Nex wasn't surprised when she came back inside with two bunches of flowers and arranged one bunch in front of the picture, keeping the other in her hand for their next stop. She smiled sadly at the photo, ran her fingers along the edge, then reached for Nex's hand.

"Are you okay?" She gazed up with a small frown.

"I'm fine." Nex tore his eyes away from Lucian's face. "Let's get this over with."

"I want to say once again that no one is forcing you." Kat squeezed his hand. "I don't want you to go if you're going to be miserable and uncomfortable."

"I'll be fine." He kissed her forehead. "Stop worrying."

They walked outside, not bothering with jackets in the spring sunshine. While Nex never had a preference for seasons on Earth as a demon, he now preferred spring over winter. Spring meant Katherine's legs were bare under her dresses, and sometimes she wore shorts and a tank top, showing off her skin.

Yes, spring was his favorite so far.

They strolled down the street, fingers laced together and Kat resting her head on his arm.

"Are you ready to fly for the first time?" Kat giggled. She found the fact he was going to be on a plane later that day incredibly amusing, considering he was accustomed to flying, just not inside anything.

Nex rolled his eyes. "I don't know that ready is the right word as much as *resigned*."

"You're the one who bought the tickets."

He did buy the tickets. With money from his job. His *human* job.

After he settled into being human, he hated not being able to buy anything he wanted, not being able to buy Katherine things like he could before. As much as he loathed the idea, he knew he had to get used to it. The last thing he expected was for Allen to set him up as a sous-chef in a restaurant Allen's friend owned. He didn't hate it as much as he was afraid he would. Katherine suggested he think about going to culinary school since cooking seemed to be the human thing he enjoyed most.

Nex was undecided, still learning human ways, and worried he'd grow bored after what he was used to. The only thing he knew for certain he'd never get bored of was the woman beside him.

"I don't understand why, if the flight is at six, we have to be there two hours prior." Nex gave Kat a side-glance. "Seems like an awful lot of unnecessary human interaction."

"It's the way airports work." Kat shrugged. "Nobody likes going to the airport. They do because it gets them to fun places faster. Places like Las Vegas." A huge smile spread over her face, and she held his hand tighter.

The smile was worth going on a stupid human plane.

"I suppose you have it all planned out for when we arrive," Nex said.

Kat nodded. "We're going to order in. The hotel we're staying at has a buffet in the casino you can order food from."

"Order in?" Nex's brows knit together. "I thought you had so many different shows and places you wanted to see, restaurants you wanted to eat at."

"We'll be able to see the lights from our window."

Nex paused and spun her into him. "Are you doing this because you know I'm on edge being around all these humans? Because I'll be fine. I'm taking you for *you*. I survived hell for over two hundred years. I can survive an evening of crowds."

"And I am going with the man I love, and I don't want him to be uncomfortable." Kat draped her arms over his shoulders. "Besides, the room you booked has a hot tub. No matter what we do while we're there, I'm ending every single day in that hot tub, and we'll be getting there late anyway, so," a touch of pink reached her cheeks, "we might as well relax inside. Alone."

"Now you've caught my attention." A smile pulled on the corner of his mouth. "Fine, but tomorrow we work through that ridiculously long list you have."

"Deal." Kat pressed a quick kiss to his lips, turned, and tried to walk ahead, but there was a tug on her hand that told her Nex wasn't moving. She glanced back and gave him an encouraging smile. "It's okay. You can leave at any point. Or, you don't have to come in."

Nex swallowed as he stared at the church. "I'm coming."

Crossing onto ground he'd never been able to set foot on felt strange. He tentatively stepped forward, where time and time again he'd been blocked from entering. For a moment, he was paranoid he'd hit that same invisible wall, but his foot landed on the ground. Onto the church's official property. No barrier.

Kat waited until he edged across the boundary. She squeezed his hand reassuringly and smiled up at him. "I'm right here."

Instead of walking up to the church, they wandered around to the cemetery. It was the first time Nex was able to go with her, and her parents' wedding anniversary was during the time they'd be in Vegas.

They paused in front of the tombstone, and Kat crouched, placing the flowers on the ground. When she stood, Nex wrapped his arms around her from behind. He'd never had to do anything like this, so he was uncertain how to behave. Silence and holding her was the best option he could think of.

Kat placed a kiss on her fingertips, then pressed her fingertips to the epitaph. "Happy anniversary," she murmured, running her fingers along the edge. She turned in Nex's arms to return the hug.

He wasn't sure what to expect, but she seemed more okay than any other time she'd visited. Glancing at the epitaph one more time, she clutched Nex's hand, then led them to the front of the church.

At the top of the steps, Nex paused at the big wooden doors, worried someone would recognize he couldn't be there and stop him. Or maybe the invisible barrier would make an appearance. An inch at a time, he shifted forward. Nothing happened. He was inside a church for the first time.

Kat kept him close and tried to keep people from flocking over. They were excited to meet the person she'd talked about for so long, but she gently directed them away with the shortest introductions possible. The end of an empty pew was the perfect place for her to settle Nex, so no one could sit next to him but her.

Kat snuggled into his side. "Okay?" She lifted his hand and kissed his knuckles.

Nex nodded and couldn't stop the smile because he apparently had no ability not to melt under any type of affection from her.

Bernice turned from the pew in front of them. "Excited for the trip?"

"Very." Kat bounced in her seat. "We'll be back Friday."

Bernice grinned. "Take lots of pictures. And please don't elope while you're there. I want to be at your wedding. Did you decide on a date yet? And a place?"

"Not yet." A slow smile formed as Kat glanced down at her finger where her mother's engagement ring rested. "We've barely started talking about it. You'll be the first to know, I promise."

"I better be." Bernice gave a playful glare and faced forward.

"You want to get married in the church, Katherine," Nex whispered, placing his hand under her chin and turning her toward him. "Let's do it here. It's where your parents got married. The others will understand."

"I want Marcus and Arda and everyone to be there," Kat said. "It's just a building. Outdoor weddings are nice too."

"Katherine." Nex's serious tone and expression told her it was unlikely she'd change his mind. "We can have a party with the others afterward. Don't change your plans for a handful of people. You only get to do this once. For once in your life, be selfish, for fuck's sake."

"*Nex*," Kat scolded.

"Right." He cleared his throat. He promised he wouldn't curse in church, but some habits were hard to break. "Sorry, but I'm serious. They'll understand. They can hear very well. They can stand outside and listen to the whole thing."

Kat fiddled with her ring. "It's not the same. Who will be your best man if not Marcus?"

"I couldn't care less. I just want to be with you, Katherine. Pick my best man for me for all I care. It's a human thing I'm not familiar with."

Kat straightened his tie. "It's *our* wedding, not mine."

"I gave you feedback on the single thing that matters to me."

"My—" Kat glanced around to make sure no one was listening. "My lingerie for the wedding night and honeymoon doesn't count as a wedding plan."

"*Highly* debatable."

Kat opened her mouth, but the service began, so she leaned against Nex's shoulder.

Allen stepped up to the podium. "All right, we've been working through the New Testament, and we've come to a set of verses many are familiar with, and that brings us to today's topic. Love." Allen opened his Bible. "Reading from 1 Corinthians 13:4-7." He cleared his throat, a smile reaching his face while his eyes darted to his wife. "'Love is patient, love is kind.'"

Kat cuddled closer to Nex, setting her free hand on their clasped ones.

"'It does not envy, it does not boast, it is not proud.'"

Nex glanced down at Kat, bringing their hands up and kissing the back of hers.

"'It does not dishonor others, it is not self-seeking, it is not easily angered, it keeps no record of wrongs.'"

Kat rested her chin on Nex's shoulder, mouthing *I love you*.

"'Love does not delight in evil but rejoices with the truth.'"

Nex mouthed it back and kissed her temple, holding her hand tighter.

"'It always protects, always trusts, always hopes, always perseveres.'"

Allen went on, but Nex was distracted, staring down at Katherine. After considering the words Allen read, he realized something. Katherine was the embodiment of love. When she looked up at him and gave him another one of the smiles he loved so much, he considered it worth it to spend two hundred years in hell if the result was this, living in this time period with his own personal heaven sitting next to him.

Thank you for reading!

Enjoyed this book? Please consider taking a moment to leave a review! They are highly important for indie authors to get recognition and visibility. Thirsty for more? Access an additional steamy scene when you join Jaide's newsletter: https://www.jaideharley.com/email-newsletter-subscription/

About the Author

Jaide is an indie author who loves to write various forms of romance. She's been writing since she was a child and has a Bachelor's degree in creative writing. Most of her inspiration stems from her love of music, books, and nature. When not writing, Jaide is also a landscape and nature photographer, an artist, reader, lover of animals, and never without her headphones.

patreon.com/jaideharley

instagram.com/jaide.harley

pinterest.com/jaideharley

facebook.com/jaideharley

tiktok.com/@jaideharley

Acknowledgments

To my honey, who made me tea and kept me fed through my late nights and long hours of writing, you are my ultimate MVP. You put up with book inspiration songs on repeat for weeks, random bouts of imposter syndrome, endless stacks of books and notebooks, and several trips to the bookstore for more. Despite multiple instances of uncertainty during my publishing process, you gave me nothing but encouragement. You held me any time I came to you crying about the sufferings of my characters. You celebrated every milestone I accomplished, and the ones I had yet to reach. Thank you for believing in me, especially when I couldn't.

To my best friend, who I am incomplete without in every way, thank you for always being my person. When I almost gave up on writing, you were the one who pushed me to continue. Whether I needed tough love or a shoulder to cry on, you were and always have been, exactly what I need. Thank you for building me up and celebrating every small accomplishment along the way. I never would've made it far without you.

To my editor, Liss, and my proofreader, Makenna, this book could not have come together for publishing without you. Thank you for being patient through my innumerable questions and perfectionism.

To my patrons, I wish for a limitless expression of gratitude at least as long as this book because I know one paragraph isn't enough. As the shy and introverted person I am, the chances that I'd never have gone after publishing is high. However, any time doubt crept in, I'd read the comments on my posts, or reread messages of encouragement, and remind myself I have a community of readers who believed in me so much, they were willing to support an author who didn't even have a published book yet. Your support humbles me. Your encouragement drives me. Thank you for sticking with me even when life happened and my publishing plans got delayed. Thank you for never giving up on me, and always believing in me.

To all my readers, patrons or otherwise, you are unendingly magnificent. Without your heartfelt messages and support, I wouldn't have finished any of my books, and I wouldn't have gone after publishing. Don't underestimate your value to me, I will forever be grateful for every person who had a part in my dreams becoming reality.